About the Authors

USA Today bestselling, *RITA*®-nominated, and critically acclaimed author **Caitlin Crews** has written more than 100 books and counting. She has a Masters and Ph.D. in English Literature, thinks everyone should read more category romance, and is always available to discuss her beloved alpha heroes. Just ask. She lives in the Pacific Northwest with her comic book artist husband, is always planning her next trip, and will never, ever, read all the books in her to-be-read pile. Thank goodness.

Jennie Lucas's parents owned a bookstore and she grew up surrounded by books, dreaming about faraway lands. At twenty-two she met her future husband and after their marriage, she graduated from university with a degree in English. She started writing books a year later. Jennie won the Romance Writers of America's Golden Heart contest in 2005 and hasn't looked back since. Visit Jennie's website at: www.jennielucas.com

Dani Wade astonished her local librarians as a teenager when she carried home ten books every week – and actually read them all. Now she writes her own characters who clamour for attention in the midst of the chaos that is her life. Residing in the southern U.S. with a husband, two kids, two dogs, and one grumpy cat, she stays busy until she can closet herself away with her characters once more.

Passionate Encounters

Passionate Encounters
Consequences
of One Night

CAITLIN CREWS

JENNIE LUCAS

DANI WADE

MILLS & BOON

All rights reserved including the right of reproduction in whole or in part in any form. This edition is published by arrangement with Harlequin Enterprises ULC.

This is a work of fiction. Names, characters, places, locations and incidents are purely fictional and bear no relationship to any real life individuals, living or dead, or to any actual places, business establishments, locations, events or incidents. Any resemblance is entirely coincidental.

This book is sold subject to the condition that it shall not, by way of trade or otherwise, be lent, resold, hired out or otherwise circulated without the prior consent of the publisher in any form of binding or cover other than that in which it is published and without a similar condition including this condition being imposed on the subsequent purchaser.

® and ™ are trademarks owned and used by the trademark owner and/ or its licensee. Trademarks marked with ® are registered with the United Kingdom Patent Office and/or the Office for Harmonisation in the Internal Market and in other countries.

First Published in Great Britain 2022
by Mills & Boon, an imprint of HarperCollins*Publishers* Ltd,
1 London Bridge Street, London, SE1 9GF

www.harpercollins.co.uk

HarperCollins*Publishers*
1st Floor, Watermarque Building,
Ringsend Road, Dublin 4, Ireland

PASSIONATE ENCOUNTERS: CONSEQUENCES OF ONE NIGHT © 2022 Harlequin Enterprises ULC.

A Baby to Bind His Bride © 2017 Caitlin Crews
Sensible Housekeeper, Scandalously Pregnant © 2010 Jennie Lucas

DUDLEY
LIBRARIES

000003127123	
Askews & Holts	23-May-2022
AF ROM	£7.99
2GL	

A BABY TO BIND
HIS BRIDE

CAITLIN CREWS

CHAPTER ONE

"THEY CALL HIM the Count," the gruff man told her as he led her deeper and deeper into the wild, wearing more flannel and plaid than Susannah Betancur had ever seen on a single person. "Never a name, always *the Count*. But they treat him like a god."

"An actual god or a pretend god?" Susannah asked, as if that would make any difference. If the Count was the man she sought, it certainly wouldn't.

Her guide shot her a look. "Not sure it really matters this far up the side of a hill, ma'am."

The hill they were trudging up was more properly a mountain, to Susannah's way of thinking, but then, everything in the American Rockies appeared to be built on a grand scale. Her impression of the Wild, Wild West was that it was an endless sprawl of jaw-dropping mountains bedecked with evergreens and quaint place names, as if the towering splendor in every direction could be contained by calling the highest peak around something like Little Summit.

"How droll," Susannah muttered beneath her breath as she dug in and tried her best not to topple down the way she'd come. Or give in to what she thought was the high elevation, making her feel a little bit light-headed.

That she was also breathless went without saying.

Her friend in flannel had driven as far as he could on what passed for a road out in the remote Idaho wilderness. It was more properly a rutted, muddy dirt track that had wound deeper and deeper into the thick woods even as the sharp incline clearly indicated that they were going higher and higher at the same time. Then he'd stopped, long after Susannah had resigned herself to that lurching and bouncing lasting forever, or at least until it jostled her into a thousand tiny little jet-lagged pieces. Her driver had then indicated they needed to walk the rest of the way to what he called *the compound*, and little as Susannah had wanted to do anything of the kind after flying all the way here from the far more settled and civilized hills of her home on the other side of the world in Rome, she'd followed along.

Because Susannah might not be a particularly avid hiker. But she was the Widow Betancur, whether she liked it or not. She had no choice but to see this through.

She concentrated on putting one booted foot in front of the other now, well aware that her clothes were not exactly suited to an adventure in the great outdoors. It hadn't occurred to her that she'd actually be *in* the wilderness instead of merely adjacent to it. Unlike every person she'd seen since the Betancur private jet had landed on an airfield in the middle of nowhere, Susannah wore head-to-toe black to announce her state of permanent mourning at a glance. It was her custom. Today it was a sleek cashmere coat over a winter dress in merino wool and deceptively sturdy knee-high boots, because she'd expected the cold, just not the forced march to go along with it.

"Are you sure you don't want to change?" her guide had asked her. They'd stared each other down in his ramshackle little cabin standing at lopsided attention in an overgrown field strewn with various auto parts. It had made her security detail twitchy. It had been his office, presumably. "Something less…?"

"Less?" Susannah had echoed as if she failed to catch his meaning, lifting a brow in an approximation of the ruthless husband she'd lost.

"There's no real road in," her guide had replied, eyeing her as if he expected her to wilt before him at that news. As if a mountain man or even the Rocky Mountains themselves, however challenging, could compare to the intrigues of her own complicated life and the multinational Betancur Corporation that had been in her control, at least nominally, these last few years, because she'd refused to let the rest of them win—her family and her late husband's family and the entire board that had been so sure they could steamroll right over her. "It's off the grid in the sense it's, you know. Rough. You might want to dress for the elements."

Susannah had politely demurred. She wore only black in public and had done so ever since the funeral, because she held the dubious distinction of being the very young widow of one of the richest men in the world. She found that relentless black broadcast the right message about her intention to remain in mourning indefinitely, no matter what designs her conspiring parents and in-laws, or anyone else, had on her at any given time.

She intended to remain the Widow Betancur for a very long while. No new husbands to take the reins and take control, no matter how hard she was pushed from all sides to remarry.

If it was up to her she'd wear black forever, because her widowhood kept her free.

Unless, that was, Leonidas Cristiano Betancur hadn't actually died four years ago in that plane crash, which was exactly what Susannah had hauled herself across the planet to find out.

Leonidas had been headed out to a remote ranch in this same wilderness for a meeting with some potential investors into one of his pet projects when his small plane had gone down in these acres and acres of near-impenetrable national forest. No bodies had ever been found, but the authorities had been convinced that the explosion had burned so hot that all evidence had been incinerated.

Susannah was less convinced. Or maybe it was more accurate to say that she'd been increasingly more convinced over time that what had happened to her husband—on their wedding night, no less—had not been any accident.

That had led to years of deploying private investigators and poring over grainy photographs of dark, grim men who were never Leonidas. Years of playing Penelope games with her conniving parents and her equally scheming in-laws like she was something straight out of *The Odyssey*, pretending to be so distraught by Leonidas's death that she couldn't possibly bear so much as a conversation about whom she might marry next.

When the truth was she was not distraught. She'd hardly known the older son of old family friends whom her parents had groomed her to marry so young. She'd harbored girlish fantasies, as anyone would have at that age, but Leonidas had dashed all of those when he'd patted her on the head at their wedding like she was a puppy and had then disappeared in the middle of their reception because business called.

"Don't be so self-indulgent, Susannah," her mother had said coldly that night while Susannah stood there, abandoned in her big white dress, trying not to cry. "Fantasies of fairy tales are for little girls. You are now the wife of the heir to the Betancur fortune. I suggest you take the opportunity to decide what kind of wife you will be. A pampered princess locked away on one of the Betancur estates or a force to be reckoned with?"

Before morning, word had come that Leonidas was lost. And Susannah had chosen to be a force indeed these past four years, during which time she'd grown from a sheltered, naive nineteen-year-old into a woman who was many things, but was always—*always*—someone to be reckoned with. She'd decided she was more than just a trophy wife, and she'd proved it.

And it had led here, to the side of a mountain in an American state Susannah had heard of only in the vaguest terms, trekking up to some "off the grid" compound where a man meeting Leonidas's description was rumored to be heading up a local cult.

"It's not exactly a doomsday cult," her investigator had told her in the grand penthouse in Rome, where Susannah lived because it was the closest of her husband's properties to the Betancur Corporation's European headquarters, where she liked to make her presence known. It kept things running more smoothly, she'd found.

"Do such distinctions matter?" she'd asked, trying so hard to sound distant and unaffected with those photographs in her hands. Shots of a man in flowing white, hair longer than Leonidas had ever worn it, and still, that same ruthlessness in his dark gaze. That same lean, athletic frame, rangy and dangerous, with new scars that would make sense on someone who'd been in a plane crash.

Leonidas Betancur in the flesh. She would have sworn on it.

And her reaction to that swept over her from the inside, one earthquake after another, while she tried to smile blandly at her investigator.

"The distinction only matters in the sense that if you actually go there, *signora*, it is unlikely that you'll be held or killed," the man told her.

"Something to look forward to, then," Susannah had replied, with another cool smile as punctuation.

While inside, everything had continued that low, shattering roll, because her husband was alive. *Alive.*

She couldn't help thinking that if Leonidas really had repaired to the wilderness and assembled a following, he'd been trained for the vagaries of cult leadership in the best possible classroom: the shark-infested waters of the Betancur Corporation, the sprawling family business that had made him and all his relatives so filthy rich they thought they could do things like bring down the planes of disobedient, uncontrollable heirs when it suited them.

Susannah had learned a lot in her four years of treading that same water. Mainly, that when the assorted Betancurs wanted something—like, say, Leonidas out of the way of a deal that would make the company a lot of money but which Leonidas had thought was shady—they usually found a way to get it.

Being the Widow Betancur kept her free from all that conniving. Above it. But there was one thing better than being Leonidas Betancur's widow, Susannah had thought, and it was bringing him back from the dead.

He could run his damned business himself. And Susannah could get back the life she hadn't known she wanted when she was nineteen. She could be happily divorced, footloose and fancy free by her twenty-fourth birthday, free of all Betancurs and much better at standing up for herself against her own parents.

Free, full stop.

Flying across the planet and into the Idaho wilderness was a small price to pay for her own freedom.

"What kind of leader is the Count?" Susannah asked crisply now, focusing on the rough terrain as she followed her surprisingly hardy guide. "Benevolent? Or something more dire?"

"I can't say as I know the difference," her guide replied out of the side of his mouth. "One cult seems like another to me."

As if they were a dime a dozen in these parts. Perhaps they were.

And then it didn't matter anyway, because they'd reached the compound.

One moment there was nothing but forest and then the next, great gates reared up on the other side of a small clearing, swaddled in unfriendly barbed wire, festooned with gruff signs warning intruders to Keep Out while listing the grisly consequences of trespassing, and mounted with aggressively swiveling video cameras.

"This is as far as I go," her guide said then, keeping to the last of the trees.

Susannah didn't even know his name. And she wished he could come with her, since he'd gotten her this far already. But that wasn't the deal. "I understand."

"I'll wait down by the truck until you need to go down the hill," the man continued. "I'd take you inside…"

"I understand that you can't," Susannah said, because this had all been explained to her down in that ramshackle cabin. "I have to do the rest of this alone."

That was the part that had given her security detail fits. But everyone had agreed. There was no way that Susannah could descend upon some faraway compound with an entire complement of Betancur security guards in tow when it was likely her husband was hiding from the world. She couldn't turn up with her own small army, in other words. Even a few hardy locals would be too much, her guide had told her, because the sort of people who holed up in nearly inaccessible compounds in the Rocky Mountains were usually also the sort who didn't much care for visitors. Particularly not if said visitors were armed.

But a young woman who called herself a widow and was dressed to look as out of place on this mountain as Susannah felt was something else entirely.

Something wholly nonthreatening, she hoped.

Susannah didn't let herself think too much about what she was doing. She'd read too many thrillers while locked away in the Swiss boarding school where her parents had insisted she remain throughout her adolescence, and every last one of them was running through her head on a loop this afternoon.

Not helpful, she snapped at herself. She didn't want to think about the risks. All she wanted—all she'd ever wanted—was to find out what had happened to Leonidas.

Because the sad truth was, she might be the only one who cared.

And she told herself that the only reason *why* she cared was because finding him would set her free.

Susannah strode toward the gates, her skin crawling with every step she took. She knew the video cameras were trained on her, but she was worried about something worse than surveillance. Like snipers. She rather doubted anyone built a great fortress in the woods like the one she saw before her, sprawling this way and that, if they didn't intend to defend it.

"Stop right there!"

She couldn't see where the voice came from, exactly. But Susannah stopped anyway. And raised her hands up, though not entirely over her head. There was no point coming over completely submissive.

"I'm here to see the Count," she called into the silent, chilly forest all around her.

Nothing happened.

For a moment Susannah thought nothing would. But then, slowly, a door at the side of one of the great gates before her swung open.

She held her breath. Would this be Leonidas after all this time?

A man came out through the door, but it wasn't Leonidas. This man was much shorter than the husband she'd lost, with an alarming semiautomatic rifle slung over his shoulder and a distinctly unfriendly expression on his round face.

"You need to get off our mountain," he told her, waving the rifle as punctuation.

But he was frowning at her as he spoke. At her clothes, Susannah realized after a moment. Because she certainly wasn't dressed for an assault on a compound. Or even a walk in the woods, for that matter.

"I have no particular desire to be on this mountain," she replied crisply. "I only want to see the Count."

"The Count sees who he wants to see, and never on demand." The man's voice throbbed with fervor. And more than that, fury. As if he couldn't believe Susannah's temerity in suggesting she should have access to a being of such greatness.

It was possible she was imagining that part. What did she know about cult members?

She inclined her head at the man. "He'll want to see me."

"The count is a busy man," the man scoffed. "He doesn't have time for strange women who appear out of nowhere like they're begging to get shot."

That would be a direct threat where she came from,

Susannah reflected, while her heart beat out a desperate tattoo in her chest. She reminded herself that here, in the middle of this vast and dangerous wilderness, the people who held these places had a different relationship to their weapons. And to threats, for that matter.

The man before her was perhaps being nothing but matter-of-fact.

"I'm not looking to get shot," she told him as calmly as possible. "But the Count will want to see me, I'm sure of it." She wasn't sure of any such thing. The fact that Leonidas had locked himself away in this place and started calling himself something so ridiculous suggested that he had no desire to be located. Ever. But she wasn't going to get into that with one of his wild-eyed true believers. She aimed a cool smile the guard's way instead. "Why don't you take me to him and he can tell you so himself?"

"Lady, I'm not going to tell you again. You should turn around. You need to get off this hill and never come back here again."

"I'm not going to do that," Susannah said, with that iron matter-of-factness she'd developed over the past few years. As if she expected her orders to be obeyed simply because she'd issued them. As if she was Leonidas himself instead of the young widow everyone knew he'd never meant to leave in charge of anything, much less the whole of his fortune. But Susannah had done exactly what her mother had told her to do. She'd taken Leonidas's name and gained his authority at the same time. She'd been confounding people in the corporate world he'd left behind with this exact same attitude for years now. "I have to see the Count. That's nonnegotiable. Whatever needs to happen so that I can do that is up to you. I don't care."

"Listen, lady—"

"Or you can shoot me," Susannah suggested coolly. "But those are the only two possible outcomes here."

The man blinked at her as if he didn't know what to do. Susannah didn't entirely blame him. She didn't cower. She didn't shift her weight from side to side or give any indication that she was anything but perfectly calm. She simply stood there as if it was completely natural that she should be thousands of feet high on the side of a mountain in the Idaho wilderness. She gazed back at the strange man before her as if she marched up to the doors of cults and demanded entry every day of the week.

She stared at him until it became clear that he was the one who was ill at ease, not her.

"Who the hell are you?" he finally demanded.

"I'm so glad you asked," Susannah said then, and this time, her smile was something less than cool. Something more like a weapon and she'd had four years to learn how to shoot it. "I'm the Count's wife."

CHAPTER TWO

THE COUNT DIDN'T have a wife.

Or he hadn't had one in as long as he could remember—but that was the trouble with everything, wasn't it? It was eating at him more and more these days that there were so many things he couldn't remember.

There were more things he couldn't remember than things he could. And all of them had happened in the last four years.

His followers told the stories of how they'd found this place. How they'd come here, each finding his or her own way up the mountain and proving themselves worthy of entry. They spoke of what they'd left behind. The people, the places. The things. The dreams and expectations.

But the Count knew only the compound.

His first memory was of waking up in the expansive set of rooms he still occupied. He been battered, broken. It had taken him a long time to return to anything approaching health. To sit, then stand. Then slowly, painfully, walk. And even when he'd been walking around of his own volition at last, he hadn't felt that his body was back to his standard.

Though he couldn't have said what his standard was.

It had taken him almost eighteen months to feel something like normal.

And another eighteen months to realize that no matter what he pretended because it seemed to make his people so nervous when he did not, he didn't really know what *normal* was.

Because he still couldn't remember anything but this. Here. Now.

His people assured him it was preordained. They told him that it was all a part of the same glorious plan. They had gathered, they had prayed, and so to them a leader had appeared in this same forest where they lived. The end.

The Count had agreed because there was no reason not to agree.

He certainly felt like a leader. He had since the first moment he'd opened his eyes. When he issued an order and people leaped to fill it, it didn't feel new. It felt deeply familiar. Right and good.

He rarely shared with anyone how much he liked the things that felt familiar. It seemed to shy too close to some kind of admission he didn't want to make.

His every need was attended to here, of course. His people gathered to hear him speak. They fretted over his health. They fed him and they clothed him and they followed him. What more could a man want?

And yet there was a woman in the compound, claiming she was his wife, and the Count felt as if something in him he'd never known was there had cracked wide open.

"She's quite insistent," his closest adviser, Robert, said. Again—and this time with more obvious disapproval. "She says she's been looking for you for some time."

"And yet I do not have a wife," the Count replied. "Have you not told me this from the start?"

Robert was the only follower with him then, watching

the woman in question on the bank of monitors before them. The Count waited to feel some kind of familiarity or recognition. He waited to know her one way or another, but like everything in his life, there was no knowing. There was no memory.

Sometimes he told his people that he was grateful for this blank canvas.

But then there were other times, like this, when the things he didn't feel, the things he didn't know, seemed to batter at him like a winter storm.

"Of course you do not have a wife," Robert was saying, sounding something like scandalized. "That is not your path. That is for lesser men."

This was a place of purity. That was one of the few things that had always been clear to the Count, and it was handy that he'd never been tempted to stray from that path. The men and women here practiced a version of the same radical purity that he did—with a special dispensation for those who were married—or they left.

But in all this time, the Count had never gazed upon a female and felt something other than that same purity, drowning out anything else.

Until now.

It took him a moment to recognize what was happening to him, and he supposed that he should have been horrified. But he wasn't. Lust rolled through him like an old friend, and he couldn't have said why that failed to set off any alarms within him. He told himself temptation was good, as it would make him even more powerful to conquer it. He told himself that this was nothing more than a test.

The woman who filled his screens looked impatient. That was the first thing that separated her from the handful of women who lived here. More than that, she looked... Fragile. Not weathered and hardy the way his people were. Not prepared for any eventuality. She looked soft.

The Count had no idea why he wanted to touch her to see if she could possibly be as soft as she looked.

She was dressed in clothes that didn't make any sense to him, here on top of the mountain. He could never remember being off the mountain, of course, but he knew that there was a whole world out there. He'd been told. And all that black, sleek and slick over her trim little figure, made him think of cities.

It had never occurred to him before, but he didn't really think about cities. And now that he had, it was as if they all ran through his head like a travelogue. *New York. London. Shanghai. New Delhi. Berlin. Cairo. Auckland.*

As if he'd been to each and every one of them.

He shoved that oddity aside and studied the woman. They'd brought her inside the compound walls and placed her in a sealed-off room that no one ever called a cell. But that's what it was. It was outfitted with nothing more than an old sofa, a toilet behind a screen in the corner and cameras in the walls.

If she was as uncomfortable as the last three law enforcement officials had been when they'd visited, she didn't show it. She sat on the sofa as if she could do it forever. Her face was perfectly calm, her blue eyes clear. She looked almost serene, he might have said, which only drew attention to the fact that she was almost incomprehensibly pretty.

Not that he had many other women to compare her with. But somehow the Count knew that if he lined up every woman out there in the world he couldn't remember, he would still find this one stunning.

Her legs were long and shapely, even in the boots she

wore, and she crossed them neatly as if she hadn't noticed they were splattered with mud. She wore only one rather large ring on her left hand that kept catching the light when she moved, and she crossed her fingers in her lap before her as if she knew it and was trying to divert attention away from all that excessive sparkle. Her mouth caught at him in ways he didn't entirely understand, greed and hunger like a ball inside him, and the Count wasn't sure he liked it. He concentrated on her remarkably glossy blond hair instead, swept back from her face into something complicated at her nape.

A chignon, he thought.

It was a word the Count didn't know. But it was also the proper term to describe how she had styled her hair. He knew that in the way he knew all the things he shouldn't have, so he shoved it aside and kept on.

"Bring her to me," he said before he thought better of it.

Then he thought better of it and still said nothing to contradict himself.

"She's not your wife," Robert said, scowling. "You have no wife. You are the Count, the leader of the glorious path, and the answer to every question of the faithful!"

"Yes, yes," the Count said with a wave of his hand. What he thought was that Robert didn't actually know if this woman was his wife. Neither did he. Because he couldn't simply have appeared from nowhere in a shower of flame, the way everyone claimed. He'd understood that from the start. At the very least, he'd thought, if he'd simply appeared one day in a burst of glory, he wouldn't have needed all that time to recover, would he?

But these mysteries of faith, he'd learned, were not something he could explore in public.

What he knew was that if he'd come from somewhere

else, that meant he'd had a life there. Wherever it was. And if this woman thought she knew him, it was possible she could prove to be a font of information.

The Count wanted information more than anything.

He didn't wait to see if Robert would obey him. He knew the other man would, because everyone did. The Count left the surveillance room behind and walked back through his compound. He knew it so well, every room and every wall built of logs. The fireplaces of stone and the thick rugs on the common floors. He had never thought beyond this place. Because everything he wanted and needed was right here. The mountain gave and the followers received, that was the way.

Sydney. Saint Petersburg. Vancouver. Reykjavik. Oslo. Rome.

What did it mean that he could suddenly *see* so many more places? Places not hewn from wood and tucked away in these mountains, with nothing to see in all directions but trees and weather? He wasn't sure he wanted to know.

The Count made his way to his own private rooms, set apart from the dormitories where the rest of his people slept. He kept his expression blank as he moved, as if he was communing with the Spirit the way he was supposed to do, the better to discourage anyone from approaching him.

The good news was that no one would dare. They watched him as he walked and the more attention-seeking among them pitched their prayers even louder, but no one tried to catch his eye.

When he got to his rooms, he waited in the outer chamber. When he'd first started to come into awareness, to become himself, he'd recoiled from the starkness of these rooms. It had felt like a prison, though he knew, somehow, he'd never been in one. But now he'd come to prefer it to the relatively cozier rooms on the other side of his doors. Stark-white walls. Minimal furnishings. Nothing to distract a man from his purpose.

It was between him and his conscience that he'd never quite managed to feel that purpose the way everyone assumed he did.

He didn't have to wait long for them to bring her in. And when they did, the starkness of the walls seemed to make the shock of her black clothes that much bolder in comparison. Everything was white. The clothes he wore, loose and flowing. His walls, the hardwood floor, even the chair he sat in, like an ivory throne.

And then this woman in the middle of it all, black clothes, blue eyes and unbent knees. This woman who stared at him, her lips slightly parted and a sheen in her eyes he couldn't quite read.

This woman who called herself his wife.

"I do not have a wife," he told her when his followers had left them alone at last. He told himself there was no reason his anticipation should make him so...restless. "The leader has no wife. His path is pure."

He stayed where he was, sitting on the only chair in the room. But if standing there before him like one of his supplicants bothered her—though, of course, his followers would all be prostrate before his magnificence rather than stand and risk his displeasure—she didn't let it show.

In fact, the look on her face was something that edged more toward astonishment. With an undertone he was fairly sure was temper—not that he'd seen such a thing with his own eyes. Not directed at him.

"You've got to be kidding."

That was all she said. It was a harsh little whisper, nothing more.

And the Count found himself fascinated by her eyes. They were so tremendously blue it made him think of the breathless summers here, and they were filled with a brilliant, diamond-cut emotion he couldn't begin to understand.

"I do not kid," he said. Or he didn't think he did. He was certain he never had, anyway. Not here.

The woman before him blew out a breath as if something was hard. As if she was performing some kind of physical labor.

"How long do you intend to hide out here?" She threw the words at him in a tight sort of voice that suggested she was upset.

The Count could not think of any reason at all that she should be.

"Where else would I be?" He tilted his head slightly to one side as he regarded her, trying to make sense of all the emotion he could see swirling around her, written into every line of her black-clad body. Trying to puzzle out its cause. "And I'm not hiding. This is my home."

She let out a sharp little laugh, but not as if she thought anything was funny. The Count found himself frowning, which never happened.

"You have many homes," she said in a voice that sounded almost…gritty. "I enjoy the penthouse in Rome, certainly, but there's something to be said for the New Zealand vineyard. The island in the South Pacific. The town house in London or the Greek villa. Or all those acres of land your family owns in Brazil. You have multiple homes on every possible continent, is my point, and not one of them is a sanitarium in a mountain tree house in Idaho."

"A sanitarium?" he echoed. It was another word he didn't know—and yet did, as soon as she said it.

But she wasn't paying attention to what he did or didn't comprehend. She was pivoting to take in the stark-white chamber, her arms crossed over her chest.

"Is this supposed to be some kind of hospital room?" she demanded. "Has this been a four-year mental health retreat from all your responsibilities?" Her blue gaze was even sharper when it landed on him again. "If you knew you were going to run away like this, why bother marrying me? Why not pull your disappearing act before the wedding? You must know exactly what I've had to deal with all this time. What did I ever do to you to deserve being left in the middle of that mess?"

"You're speaking to me as if you know me," the Count said in a low, dangerous voice that she did not seem to heed.

"I don't know you at all. That's what makes this so vicious. If you wanted to punish someone with the company and your horrible family, why choose me? I was *nineteen*. It shouldn't surprise you to learn that they tried to eat me alive."

There was something sharp inside him, like broken glass, and it was shredding him with every word she spoke. He found himself standing when he hadn't meant to move.

"I did not choose you. I did not marry you. I have no idea who you are, but I am the Count."

His hand had ended up over his chest and he dropped it, ill at ease with his own fervency.

"You are not a count," snapped the woman he was realizing, too late, was far more dangerous to him than he'd imagined anyone could be. And he couldn't tell if that was a kind of apprehension that worked in him then or, worse, something far closer to exhilaration. And she clearly wasn't finished. "Your family has certainly flirted with this or that aristocracy over the years, but you are not titled. Your mother likes to claim that she is a direct descendent of the Medicis, but I'm not sure anyone takes that seriously no matter how many times she threatens to commit a murder over a meal."

The Count's head was reeling. There was a faint, dull pain at his temples and at the base of his skull, and he knew it was her fault. He should have had her removed. Tossed back in that cell, or dropkicked down the side of his mountain.

There was no reason he should cross the room, his bare feet slapping against the bare floor, to tower there above her.

There was no reason—but she should have been concerned. If she'd been one of his followers she would have thrown up her hands in surrender and then tossed herself at his feet. She would have sobbed and begged for his forgiveness.

This woman did none of those things.

She tipped her chin up and met his gaze as if she didn't notice that he was significantly taller than she was. More, as if she didn't care.

"I would be very careful how you speak to me," he told her, managing to get the words out through the seething thing that had its claws in him and that broken glass inside.

"What is the purpose of this charade?" she demanded. "You know I'm not going to be fooled by it. You know I know exactly who you are. No threat is going to change that."

"That was not a threat. It was a warning." He realized he wanted to reach over and put his hands on her, and that threw him. But not enough to back away. Not enough to put a safe distance between them the way he should have. "There's a certain disrespect that I confess, I find almost refreshing, since it is so rare. And suicidal. But you should know my people will not accept it."

"Your people?" She shook her head as if he wasn't making sense. Worse, as if he was hurting her, somehow. "If you mean the cult on the other side of these doors, you can't really think they're anything but accessories to a crime."

"I've committed no crimes."

But he threw that out as if he was defending himself, and the Count had no idea why he would do such a thing. Nothing in his memory had prepared him for this. People did not argue with him. They did not stand before him and hurl accusations at him.

Everyone in this compound adored him. The Count had never been in the presence of someone who didn't worship him before. He found it…energizing, in a strange way. He recognized lust, but the form it took surprised him. He wanted to drag his hands through her neat, careful hair. He wanted to taste the mouth that dared say such things to him.

He wanted to drag out the broken glass inside him and let her handle it, since he might not know how or why she was doing it, but he knew it was her fault.

"You swanned away from the scene of an accident, apparently," she was saying, with the same fearlessness he couldn't quite believe, even as it was happening. And she was carrying on as if he was about as intimidating as a tiny, fragile female should have been. "Your entire family thinks you're dead. *I* thought you were dead. And yet here you are. Hale and healthy and draped in bridal white. And hidden away on the top of the mountain, while the mess you left behind gets more and more complicated by the day."

The Count laughed at her. "Who is it that you imagine I am?"

"I am not imagining anything," the woman said, and she seemed to bristle as she said it. Maybe that was why the Count found his hands on her upper arms, holding her there before him. Then dragging her closer. "I knew it was you when I saw the pictures. I don't understand how you've managed to hide it for so long. You're one of the most recognizable men alive."

"I am the Count," he repeated, but even he could taste the faintly metallic tang of what he was very much afraid was desperation. "The path—"

"I am Susannah Forrester Betancur," she interrupted him. Far from pulling away from his grip, she angled herself toward him, surging up on her toes to put her face that much closer to his. "*Your wife.* You married me four years ago and left me on our wedding night, charmer that you are."

"Impossible. The Count has no wife. That would make him less than pure."

She let out a scoffing sound, and her blue eyes burned.

"You are not the Count of anything. You are Leonidas Cristiano Betancur, and you are the heir to the Betancur Corporation. That means that you are so wealthy you could buy every mountain in this range, and then some, from your pocket change alone. It means that you are so powerful that someone—very likely a member of your own family—had to scheme up a plane crash to get around you."

The pain in his temples was sharpening. The pressure at the base of his skull was intensifying.

"I am not who you think I am," he managed to say.

"You are exactly who I think you are," she retorted. "And Leonidas, it is far past time for you to come home."

There was the pain and then a roaring, loud and rough, but he understood somehow it was inside him.

Maybe that was the demon that took him then. Maybe that was what made him haul her closer to him as if he was someone else and she was married to him the way she claimed.

Maybe that was why he crushed her mouth with his, tasting her at last. Tasting all her lies—

But that was the trouble.

One kiss, and he remembered.

He remembered everything.

Everything.

Who he was. How he'd come here. His last moments on that doomed flight and his lovely young bride, too, whom he'd left behind without a second thought because that was the man he'd been then, formidable and focused all the way through.

He was Leonidas Betancur, not a bloody count. And he had spent four years in a log cabin surrounded by acolytes obsessed with purity, which was very nearly hilarious, because there was not a damned thing about him that was or ever had been pure.

So he kissed little Susannah, who should have known better. Little Susannah who had been thrown to him like bait all those years ago, a power move by her loathsome parents and a boon to his own devious family, because he'd always avoided innocence. He'd lost his own so early.

His own, brutal father had seen to that.

He angled his head and he pulled her closer, tasting her and taking her, plundering her mouth like a man possessed.

She tasted sweet and lush, and she went straight to his head. He told himself it was only that it had been so long. The part of him that had honestly believed he was who these crazy people thought he was—the part that had developed the conscience Leonidas had never bothered with—thought he should stop.

But he didn't.

He kissed her again and again. He kissed her until the rest of her was as soft and pliable as her mouth. He kissed her until she looped her arms around his neck and slid against him as if she couldn't stand on her own feet. He kissed her until she was making tiny noises in the back of her throat.

He remembered her in a confection of a white dress and all the people their families had invited to the ceremony on the Betancur family estate in France. He remembered how wide her blue eyes had been and how young she'd seemed, the virgin sacrifice his brute of a father had bought for him before he'd died. A gift tied up in an alliance that benefited the family.

One more bit of evidence of the insupportable rot that was the Betancur blood—

But Leonidas didn't care about that.

"Leonidas," she whispered, tearing her mouth from his. "Leonidas, I—"

He didn't want to talk. He wanted her mouth, so he took it.

Susannah had found him here. Susannah had brought him back his life.

So he swept her up into his arms, never moving his mouth from hers for an instant, and Leonidas carried her into the bedroom he couldn't wait to leave at last.

But first, Susannah owed him that wedding night.

And four years later, Leonidas was ready to collect.

CHAPTER THREE

LEONIDAS'S MOUTH WAS on hers, and she couldn't seem to recover from the sweet shock of it. He kissed her again and again and again, and the only thing she could manage to do was surrender herself to the slick, epic feel of his mouth against hers.

As if she'd spent all these years stumbling around in the dark, and the taste of this man was the light at last.

She should stop him. Susannah knew that. She should step back and draw some boundaries. Make some rules. Demand that he stop pretending he didn't remember her, for a start. She didn't believe in amnesia. She didn't believe that someone like Leonidas, so bold and relentless and *bright*, could ever disappear.

But then, he'd always been larger than life to her. She'd known who he was since she was a child and had been thrilled when her parents had informed her she was to marry him. He'd been like a starry sky as far as she'd been concerned on her wedding day, and some part of her had refused to believe that a man that powerful could be snuffed out so easily, so quickly.

And before she'd had a chance to touch him like this, the way she'd imagined so fervently before their wedding—

She needed to stop him. She needed to assert herself. She needed to let him know that the girl he'd married had died the day he had and she was far more sure and powerful now than she'd been then.

But she didn't do any of the things she imagined she should.

When Leonidas kissed her, she kissed him back, inexpert and desperate. She didn't pause to tell him how little she knew of men or their ways or the things that lips and teeth and that delirious angle of his hard jaw could do. She met his mouth as best she could. She tasted him in turn.

And she surrendered.

When he lifted her up in his arms, she thought that was an excellent opportunity to do…something. Anything. But his mouth was on hers as he moved, and Susannah realized that she'd been lying to herself for a very long time.

She could hardly remember the silly teenager she'd been on the day of her wedding after all that had happened since. She'd known she was sheltered back then, in the same way she'd known that her father was a very high-level banker and that her Dutch mother loathed living in England. But knowing she was sheltered and then dealing with the ramifications of her own naïveté were two very different things, it turned out. And Susannah had been dealing with the consequences of the way she'd been raised—not to mention her parents' aspirations for their only child—for so long now, and in such a pressure cooker, that it was easy to forget the truth of things.

Such as the fact that when her parents had told her—a dreamy sixteen-year-old girl who'd spent most of her life in a very remote and strict Swiss boarding school with other heiresses to various kingdoms and fortunes—that she was destined to marry the scion of the Betancur family, Susannah hadn't been upset. She hadn't cried into her pillow every night the way her roommate did at the prospect of her own marriage, scared of the life spooling out in front of her without her permission or input.

On the contrary, she'd been delighted.

Leonidas was gorgeous, all her school friends had agreed. He was older than them, but much younger than some of her friends' betrothed, and with all his hair and teeth as far as anyone could tell. And she'd met him, so she knew firsthand that he was merciless and forbidding in ways that had made her feel tingly all over. Moreover, every time they'd interacted—as few and far between as those times might have been over the years, because he was an important man and she was just a girl, as her mother chastised her—he'd always treated her with a great patience even she'd been able to see was at complete odds with the ferocity of his dark gaze.

She forgotten that. He'd disappointed her on her wedding night, then he'd died, and she'd forgotten. She'd lost herself in the scandal and intrigue of the Betancur Corporation and all its attendant family drama, and she'd completely failed to remember that when it came to Leonidas she had always been a very, very silly girl.

Back when she was one, and again now. Clearly.

Say something, she ordered herself.

But then he was laying her down on the bed in the next room, and following her down to the mattress, and Susannah didn't have it in her to care if she was silly.

She'd been promised a wedding night. Four years ago, she'd expected to hand over her innocence to the man who'd become her husband and instead, she'd been left to years of widow's weeds and seas of enemies—not all of whom had come at her as opponents.

Susannah couldn't count the number of men who'd

tried to seduce her over the years, many related to Leonidas, but she'd always held firm. She was the Widow Betancur and she mourned. She grieved. That little bit of fiction had protected her when nothing else could.

But Leonidas wasn't dead. And more than that, as he sprawled out above her on that firm mattress and pressed her into it, all his lean, solid strength making her breathless with a dizzy sort of joy, it made her forget that he had ever disappeared in the first place.

As if this was their wedding night after all.

"This has been four years overdue," he said, his voice a low growl against her neck, and she could *feel* him just as she could hear him. There was something in his tone she didn't like—a certain skepticism, perhaps, that pricked at her—but it was swept away when his mouth fixed to hers again.

And Susannah did nothing to dig her feet into whatever ground she could find. She let Leonidas take her with a fervent joy that might have concerned her if she'd been able to think critically.

She didn't think. She kissed him instead.

His hands dug into her hair, tugging slightly until he pulled it out of the knot she'd worn the heavy mass of it in. He muttered something she couldn't quite hear, but she didn't care because he was kissing her again and again.

When he moved his mouth from hers to trace a trail down the length of her neck, she moaned, and he laughed, just a little bit. When he tugged on her cashmere coat, she lifted herself up so he could pull it from her body. He did the same with her shift dress, tugging it up and over her head. She had the vague impression that he tossed both items aside, but she didn't care where they landed.

Because she was lying beneath him with nothing on

but a bra and panties and her knee-high boots, and the look in his dark eyes was...savage.

It made Susannah shake a little. It made her feel beautiful.

Raw. Aching and alive.

As if, after all this time, she really was more than the shroud she'd been wearing like armor for all these years. As if she wasn't the little girl he'd married, but the woman she'd longed to be in her head.

"You are the perfect gift," he said, as if he really couldn't remember who she was. As if his amnesia game was real and he really believed himself some or other local god, tucked away here in the woods.

But Susannah couldn't bring herself to worry about that. Because Leonidas was touching her.

He used his mouth and his hands. He found her breasts and cupped them with his palms, then bent his head to tease first one nipple, then the next. Through the soft fabric of her bra, his mouth was so hot, so shocking, that she arched off the bed. To get away from him—or get closer to him—she couldn't quite tell.

He stripped the bra from her, then repeated himself, but this time there was no fabric between the suction of his mouth and her tender skin. Susannah had never felt anything like it in her life. She felt...open and exposed, and so bright red with too much sensation she might as well have been a beacon.

Her head thrashed against the mattress beneath her. She gripped him wherever she could touch him, grabbing fistfuls of the flowing white garments he wore at his sides, his hips, and not caring at all when her own gasps and moans filled her ears.

Then he moved lower. His tongue teased her navel, and then his big hands wrapped around her hips.

And he didn't ask. He didn't even move her panties out of his way. Leonidas merely bent his head and fastened his mouth to the place where she ached the most.

Susannah thought she exploded.

She was surprised to find, between one breath and the next, that she was still in one piece. That every bit of suction he applied between her legs made her feel like she was breaking and fusing back together again—over and over again.

She felt a tug at her hip, heard a faint tearing sound that she only dimly understood was him tearing her panties from her body, and when he bent his head to her once again, everything changed.

It had already been madness. And now it was magic.

Leonidas licked his way into her, teasing her and tasting her. It took her long moments to realize that he was humming, a low sound of intense male approval that she could feel like shock waves crashing through her body. It was like a separate thrill.

She felt his fingers tracing through her heat, and then they were inside her. Long and hard and decidedly male.

"My God…" she managed to say, her head tipped back and her eyes shut tight.

"That's what they call me," he agreed, laughter and need in his voice and his words like separate caresses against her soft heat.

He scraped the neediest part of her with his teeth, then sucked at her, hard—and that was it.

Susannah thought she died, but there was too much sensation. *Too much.* It broke her into pieces, but it didn't stop. It didn't ever stop. It went on and on and on, and she couldn't breathe.

She didn't want to breathe.

And she was still spinning around and around when

he pulled away from her. She managed to open her eyes and fix them on him, watching in a dizzy haze as Leonidas stripped himself of that flowing white shirt at last.

Susannah couldn't help the gasp she let out when she finally saw all of him.

His muscles were smooth and tight, packed hard everywhere in a manner that suggested hard labor instead of a gym. She might not have seen him naked four years ago, but she'd certainly spent time researching him online. She thought he was bigger now than he'd been when that plane went down. Tougher, somehow.

Maybe she thought that because he was covered in scars. They wound all over his chest and dipped below his waistband.

"So many scars…" she whispered.

Leonidas froze. And Susannah couldn't bear it.

She wasn't sure she'd thought much at all since the moment she'd walked through the doors to this chamber and had seen Leonidas sitting there as if he belonged on this godforsaken mountaintop. As if he wasn't a Betancur. Or her husband. Her mind had gone blank while her mouth had opened, and she saw no reason to reverse the not-thinking trend now.

Susannah reached up and traced the scars that she could touch. Over the flat plane of his chest. Across the ridged wonder of his abdomen. On the one hand, he was a perfect specimen of a male, lean and strong and enough to make her mouth water. On the other, he wore the evidence of the plane crash that everyone had said was too deadly for anyone to survive. It was as if two pictures tried to collide in her head, and neither one of them made sense. Not the Leonidas he'd been, who had left her so abruptly. Not the man who called himself the Count and hid away in this compound.

But her fingers didn't need pictures. They didn't care which version of him he was today. His skin was so hot and his body was so hard, and every time she found a new scar and ran her fingers over it as if she was trying to memorize it, he pulled in his breath with a sharp sound that she knew, somehow, had nothing to do with pain.

"Do they make me a monster?" he asked, his voice a quiet rumble.

Susannah opened her mouth to refute that—but then saw the way his dark eyes gleamed. And she remembered. This was a man who had considered himself something of a god even before he'd crash-landed in the middle of the Rocky Mountain wilderness and found some followers to agree with him.

He didn't think he was a monster. She doubted Leonidas Betancourt ever thought ill of himself at all, no matter what he was calling himself today.

She wrinkled her nose at him. "Do you care if they do? Or do you fancy yourself as much a monster as a man?"

And he laughed. Leonidas threw back his head, and he laughed and laughed.

Something speared through her then, part fear, part recognition. And something else she couldn't quite identify.

It was because he was so beautiful, she thought. There was no denying it. That thick, rich dark hair, shot through with a hint of gold and much longer than his austere cut back in the day. Those dark, tawny eyes that burned and melted in turn. His height and his whipcord strength, evident in everything he did, even sit on a makeshift throne in a white room in a guarded compound. All of that would have been enough to make him noticeable no matter what. To make him attractive no matter where he went.

He had turned her head when she'd been little more than a girl.

But he was so much more than that. It was something about the sheer, sensual perfection of his face. The way his features were sculpted so intensely and precisely, put together like an amalgam of everything that was beautiful in him. His Greek mother. His Spanish father. His Brazilian grandparents on one side, his French and Persian grandparents on the other.

He was glorious. There was no other word for it.

And when he laughed, Susannah was tempted to believe that he really was a god, after all.

"You are quite right," Leonidas said after a long while. Long after she'd been captivated by the way his laughter transformed him, right there where he sat astride her. Long after she'd lost another part of herself she couldn't quite name. "I don't care at all. Monster, god, man. It is all the same to me."

And this time when he came down over her, she was already shaking. A deep, internal trembling, as if a terrible joy was tearing her apart from inside out. Some part of Susannah wanted it no matter how she feared it, and because she couldn't tell if it was suicide or something sweeter, she threw herself into his hands.

Leonidas shifted. He kicked off his trousers, and then settled himself between her legs. He pulled her thighs up on either side of his hips while Susannah tried to make her whirling head settled down enough to accommodate him.

Then it didn't matter, because he kissed her. Again and again, he took her mouth until she felt branded. Possessed.

Taken. At last.

It made her wonder how she'd ever survived all this time without him. Without *this*.

In some distant part of her brain she knew she should tell him.

I'm a virgin, she could say. *Word of warning, our wedding really was a white one.* Maybe he would even laugh again, at the absurdity of a woman her age still so untouched. Whatever he did, whether he believed her or not, it would be said. He would know.

But Susannah couldn't seem to force the words out.

And she forgot about it anyway as his hands gripped her hips again, and he shifted her body beneath his in an even more pointed manner, as if he intended to take charge of this and do it his way.

Maybe that would be enough.

It would have to be enough, because she could feel him then. Huge and hard, flush there against the part of her that no other person had ever touched.

A different sort of shiver ran over her then. Foreboding, perhaps. Or a wild need she'd never encountered before, drawing tight all around her as if she was caught in a great fist. Again she opened her mouth to say the thing she didn't want to say, just to make sure he didn't—

But he thrust into her then, deep and sure.

Susannah couldn't control her response. She couldn't pretend. It was a deep ache, a burning kind of tear, and her body took over and bucked up against him as if her hips were trying to throw him off of their own volition. She couldn't control the little yelp that she let out, filled with the pain and shock she couldn't hide.

Though the instant it escaped her, she wished she'd bitten it back.

Above her, Leonidas went still. Forbidding.

His eyes were like flint.

And still, she could feel him there, deep inside her, stretching her and filling her, making her feel things in places she'd never realized were part of her own body. The fact she couldn't seem to catch her breath didn't help.

"It has been a while, I grant you," Leonidas said and he sounded almost…strained. Tight and something like furious at once. "But it's not supposed to hurt."

"It doesn't hurt," Susannah lied.

He studied her for a long moment. Then, not changing the intensity of his gaze at all, he lifted a hand and wiped away a bit of moisture she hadn't realized had escaped from her eye and pooled beneath it.

Leonidas repeated it on her other eye, still watching her intently.

"Try that again."

"Really." Susannah didn't want to move, possibly ever again, but there was something working in her she didn't understand. Something spurring her on, pulsing out from the ache between her legs that she knew was him, fusing with that breathlessness she couldn't control. A kind of dangerous restlessness, reckless and needy. She tested her hips against his, biting down on her lower lip as she rocked yourself against him. "It feels fantastic."

"I can see that. The tears alone suggest it, of course. And the fact that you're frowning at me proves it beyond a doubt."

Susannah was indeed frowning at him, she realized then, though she hadn't known it. She knew it now, and she let it deepen.

"Here's a newsflash," she managed to say. "Just because people worship the ground you walk on—literally—doesn't mean you can read minds. Particularly not mine."

"Tell yourself anything you need to, little one," he murmured, and that should have enraged her. But it didn't. If anything, it made her feel…warm. Too warm. Leonidas ran his hands down her sides. Once, then again.

He brushed her hair back from her face. She could still feel him inside her, so big and so hard, and yet all he did was smooth those caresses all over her. "I don't have to read your mind. Your body tells me everything I need to know. What I don't understand is how you've managed to remain innocent all this time."

She opened her mouth to answer him, but she was distracted by the way he touched her. Those big hands of his moved all over her, spreading heat and sensation everywhere he touched. He didn't move inside her. He didn't slam himself into her or any of the other things she half expected him to do. He only touched her. Caressed her. Settled there above her as if he could wait forever.

It made a little knot deep in her belly pull tight. Then glow as it began to swell into something far bigger and more unwieldy.

"I don't know what you mean," Susannah said at last, blinking more unwelcome heat from her eyes. "I am your widow. Of course I'm innocent. You died before you could change that."

If she had any doubt that he was pretending not to remember her before, it disappeared. Because the look he turned on her then was 100 percent Leonidas Betancur. The hard, ruthless man she remembered vividly, all ruthless power sharply contained.

The one who hadn't been in evidence when she'd walked into this place.

Had he truly forgotten who he was?

And if he had—when had he remembered?

"I find that hard to believe, knowing my cousins," he was saying, offering more proof. He tilted his head to one side, and his dark eyes glittered. "I would have thought they'd be on my widow like carrion crows."

"They were, of course."

"But it was your depth of feeling for me that prevented you from taking a better offer when it was presented to you?" Leonidas's voice was sardonic. The expression in his tawny dark eyes was cynical.

And that knotted thing inside her seemed harder. Edgier.

"It might surprise you to learn that I don't like your cousins very much," she told him, bracing her hands on his shoulders as if she'd half a mind to push him off her. But she didn't. Her fingers curled into him of their own accord. "I asked them to respect my mourning process. Repeatedly."

This time, when Leonidas laughed, it wasn't anything like sunshine. But Susannah still felt it deep inside her, where they were connected, and then everywhere else in a rolling wave of sensation.

"What exactly have you been mourning, little one?" he asked, that sardonic cast to his beautiful face. "Me? You hardly know me. Let me be the first to assure you I'm no better than my cousins."

"Maybe you are and maybe you're not," she retorted. "But I'm married to you, not them."

And something changed in him then, she could feel it. A deep kind of earthquake, shaking through him and then all over her.

But as if he didn't want her to notice, as if he wanted to pretend instead that it hadn't happened, that was when he chose to move.

Everything changed all over again. Because she was so slick and he was so hard, so deep. And Susannah had never felt anything like it. The thrust, the drag. The pressure, the heat. The pure, wild delight that seemed to pound through her veins, turning to a bright, hot liquid everywhere it went.

Tentatively, with growing confidence, she learned to

match his slow, steady rhythm. He was being something like careful she would have said with all her total lack of experience, but there was something in the slowness that tore her wide open with every intense stroke.

She felt it building in her all over again, that impossible fire she'd never felt before today, and she could tell from the deepening intensity on his face above her that he knew it. That he was doing this. Deliberately.

That this had been the point all along.

And something about that set her free. She didn't fight it. She didn't try to keep her body's wild responses in check. Maybe she would regret her abandon later, but here, now, it felt natural. Right. Necessary.

She simply hung on to him and let him take her wherever he wanted them to go.

This was her husband, back from the dead. This was overdue.

This was the very thing she'd wanted more than anything else in all the world, that she'd missed all these years, and Susannah hadn't known it until now. Until Leonidas had touched her and changed everything.

Until they were so deeply connected that she doubted she would ever be the same again.

He reached between them and found her center with his deliciously hard fingers, and then he made everything worse.

Better.

"Now," he ordered her, every inch of him in control of this. Of her.

And she obeyed.

Susannah shattered. She shattered and she flew, like a sweeping, sparkling thing, pouring up and out and over the side of the world.

And she thought she heard him call out her name as he followed.

CHAPTER FOUR

ALL THE CULTS Leonidas had ever heard of in his former life discouraged the departure of their members under any circumstances—sometimes rather violently.

But he had every intention of walking out of his.

He rolled out of the bed, leaving her there in this chamber of his that had somehow become most of his world, despite how tempted he was to taste her all over again. All her flushed and sweet flesh, his for the taking, as she'd curled up there and breathed unevenly into his pillows.

God, how he wanted more.

But he'd remembered who he was. And that meant he couldn't stay in these mountains—much less in this prison of a compound—another day.

He braced himself against the sink in his bathroom and didn't allow himself to gaze in the mirror that hung there above it. He wasn't sure he wanted to see what he'd become, now that he knew the difference. Now that he could remember what he had been like unscarred, unscathed.

When he'd been a different sort of god altogether.

He took a quick shower, trying to reconcile the different strands of memory—before and after the accident. Leonidas Betancur and the Count. But what he kept dwelling on instead was Susannah, spread out there in his bed with her blond hair like a bright pop against the cheerless browns and grays he'd never noticed were so grim before. She'd looked delicate lying there, the way he remembered her from their wedding, but his body knew the truth. He could still feel the way she'd gripped him, her thighs tight around him and the sweet, hot clutch of her innocence almost too perfect to bear.

Leonidas shook it off. He toweled dry, expecting he'd have to cajole her out of his bed. Or dry her tears. Or offer some other form of comfort for which he was entirely unprepared and constitutionally ill-suited. Leonidas had no experience with virgins, but conventional wisdom suggested they required more care. More…softness. That wasn't something he was familiar with, no matter who he thought he was, but he assumed he could muster up a little compassion for the young, sweet wife who had tracked him down out here in the middle of nowhere and returned him to himself. Or he could try, anyway.

But when he returned to the bedroom, Susannah wasn't still curled up in a replete, satisfied ball, like a purring cat. Nor was she sobbing into his sheets. She was on her feet and putting herself back together as if nothing had happened between them.

Nothing of significance, anyway.

That pricked at Leonidas. He opted to ignore it.

"We have to think about the optics of this, of course," his immensely surprising wife told him as she pulled her shift back on and then smoothed it over her belly and thighs with quick, efficient jerks that reminded him how she'd tasted when she'd come apart beneath him. "We can't have the lost, presumed-dead president and CEO of the Betancur Corporation shuffling out of a mountain hideaway like some kind of victim. And we can't allow anyone to suggest there was a mental break of any kind."

"I beg your pardon. A mental break?"

Susannah only looked at him over her shoulder, her blue gaze somehow mild and confronting at once.

Leonidas didn't know why he had that sour taste in his mouth. Much less why his body appeared not to mind at all, if his enthusiastic hardness at the sight of her was any guide.

His voice was stiff to his own ears when he spoke. "I have no intention of telling another soul that I lost my memory, if that's what concerns you."

"What concerns me is that we have to construct a decent narrative to explain where you've been for the past four years," she said evenly, turning around to face him as she spoke. "If we don't, someone else will. And surely you remember that you are a man with a great many enemies who will not exactly greet your return by dancing in the streets of Europe."

He didn't know who this *we* was. He hadn't known who *he* was for four years, and he certainly didn't know who Susannah was. His memories of her were so vague, after all, especially in comparison with the vibrant creature who stood before him in this room that had never held anything but his thoughts. He had a faint flash of their wedding, or the pageantry of it, and a flash of her blond hair above that theatrical dress she'd worn. He could hear the distant echo of the lectures he'd received from his mother on the topic of why it was necessary he marry a woman he had not chosen himself and what he owed the family as the acting head of it after his brutal, controlling father's death. His mother, selfish and deceitful and lavish in turn, who'd never sacrificed a thing for any reason—who had given her violent husband the son he'd demanded and then done nothing to protect Leonidas from the old man's rages. His mother, whom he'd loved despite all the evidence across the years that he shouldn't, and whom he'd obeyed because he hadn't had it in him to break her heart.

Or whatever passed for her heart, that was.

The actual woman he'd agreed to wed had been an afterthought. A placeholder. The truth was, he'd thought more about Susannah today than he ever had during the whole of their engagement or even the ceremony and reception where they'd united their two wealthy and self-satisfied families and thereby made everyone involved a great deal wealthier.

And he was thinking more about her right now than he should have been when there was a cult yet to escape and a whole life to resume. Almost as if he was the one who required cajoling and care, a notion that appalled him. So deeply it nearly made him shake.

Susannah twisted her hair back and secured it by simply knotting it there, and she frowned slightly at him when she was done. Her eyes moved from the towel knotted around his waist to the scars that tracked across his chest, and only after that did she meet his gaze.

"You're not planning to stay here, are you?" she asked, and though Leonidas looked, he couldn't see the note of doubt he heard in her voice on her face. "Not now that I've found you, surely."

And Leonidas didn't spare a glance for this room he'd spent entirely too much time in over the past few years. This room where he'd recovered from a plane crash and failed completely to recover his own mind. This room where winter after winter had howled at the walls and barricaded him inside. This room he'd once called a perfect place to clear his mind of everything but what mattered most. He'd thought he knew what that was, too. If he let it, the knowledge of how lost he'd been might bring him to his knees.

He didn't let it.

"I think not," he said.

He took his time dressing in what his followers—though it made Leonidas uneasy to call them that now that he remembered everything and found it all more than a little distasteful—would call his "out there" clothes. Meaning, something other than all that flowing white. Boots and jeans and a sweatshirt as if he was an interchangeable mountain person like the rest of them.

When he was Leonidas Betancur and always had been, no matter what the people here had told him about prophets falling from the sky.

But he remembered who he was now. And the fact that his wife—*his wife*, after all these years of chastity—stood opposite him in clothing far more suitable to their station than his…gnawed at him. The fact she'd put herself back together with such ruthless efficiency after what had happened between them, almost as if she was attempting to erase it, on the other hand, bit deep.

Leonidas didn't want her in tears, necessarily. But the fact Susannah seemed utterly unaffected by handing over her virginity to him in a cult's compound rankled. If he hadn't been watching her closely he might have missed the faintest tremor in her fingers. The hint of vulnerability in that mouth of hers he already wanted to taste again.

But he couldn't focus on that. He couldn't focus on her the way he wanted to do. Not in a place like this, where she could never be safe.

They needed to walk out of this compound before anyone in it discovered that the Count had remembered his true identity. And Leonidas needed to keep himself from burning it down on the way out. Somehow.

"Follow me," he told her when he was ready. "Do as you're told and we might just make it out without incident."

She looked startled. "Do you think there could be a problem?"

"Not if you do exactly what I tell you to do."

Leonidas cast an eye around the room, but everything in it belonged to the Count, not him. He wanted nothing that had been here.

His long, agonizing recovery. His acceptance of his role in this place. His acquiescence to the followers here, allowing them to make him into the god of their choosing. His cooperation. He wanted none of those things.

Leonidas wanted to be *himself* again.

And once he left the bedchamber, everything went as seamlessly as he could have wished. The people here had no idea that everything had changed. That their Count had woken up from the spell he'd been laboring under at last.

Leonidas told his followers that Susannah was chastened and humiliated after making such absurd claims against him, something she made believable by walking several steps behind him, her head demurely lowered, as if she really was. So chastened and humiliated, in fact, that the Count was taking her down off his mountain himself in one of his rare excursions from his sanctuary.

"In the future," he told Robert as the other man walked beside him, "we should not allow women making false claims behind our walls."

"She seemed so certain," the other man said, with that little gleam in his dark eyes. "And you seemed so intrigued, Count."

Leonidas smiled at him the way he always did, but this time, he saw what the Count never had. That Robert thought he was the leader here, for all his noisy, public piety. That perhaps he was, as he was the one who had found Leonidas and doctored him back to health. That Robert needed a prophet—because a prophet could so easily become a martyr.

Information he imagined American law enforcement might find useful when he got out of here.

"You should be more certain," he told Robert, enjoying the way the man's gaze turned defiant, though he kept his mouth shut tight in the presence of the Count. "Or perhaps you do not belong here."

And then Leonidas walked right out of this life he'd never chosen and didn't want, back out into the world he'd never meant to leave.

"The moment the press discovers you're alive, I expect they'll descend on us like locusts," Susannah said in that cool way of hers that made him wonder exactly what had changed her from the sweet little princess he recalled into this quiet powerhouse who walked beside him, out of the compound and down the mountain to where a local waited in a four-wheeled truck covered in mud. "If they discover you've been held here, that will be bad enough. But that you lost your memory? Forgot who you are and thought you were a—"

"Do not say 'god,'" he warned her in an undertone as they approached the waiting vehicle, because she wasn't the only one who worried about optics. And the press. And the consequences of these lost years, now that he could remember what he'd lost. "Not when there is the slightest possibility that someone else might hear you."

"We can't let anyone paint you as weak," she told him, with only a nod at the man waiting for them. Her blue gaze met Leonidas's and held. "That would have entirely too many repercussions."

She sounded like a perfect little bloodthirsty Betancur,

not the hesitant schoolgirl he remembered. It reminded him that while he'd been stuck in amber for years, she hadn't been. She'd been thrust into the middle of his family and all its tiresome intrigue and squabbling.

And Leonidas couldn't tell if that chafed at him—or if he liked that she was no longer so fragile. So frothy and breakable, all big white dress and wide eyes.

All he knew was that he wanted more. He wanted everything he'd missed. More of Susannah. More time with her, to probe that fascinating head of hers and take a whole lot more time exploring that perfectly lush little body. Just *more*.

He wanted back the four years he'd lost. He wanted to clear away all the shadows in his head, once and for all. He wanted to feel even an ounce as invulnerable as he had before that plane had gone down, or as he had as the Count—a man who knew his exact place in the world.

He wanted to be *certain*, and he could start with his wife, he thought. Because she was a sure thing. She was already married to him. She'd come and found him.

But first he had to play Lazarus and rise from the dead.

Just over three weeks later, Leonidas stood in Rome.

Where he belonged.

The Betancur Corporation offices were chrome and steel packed into a historic building in the bustling heart of the ancient city. He could glimpse his reflection in the glass of the great windows that rose before him, making one entire wall of his vast office a view of Rome spread out at his feet. He remembered this view just as he remembered the company and all the years he'd spent here, bolstering the family fortune and living up to his name.

But what he couldn't quite remember was the man who'd stood here four years ago, seeing what he saw.

He knew who he was now. He remembered the before, the after. His childhood, one vicious beating after the next as his father "prepared" him for life as the Betancur heir. His mother's carelessness and total lack of interest in protecting her child from these rampages, as none of it concerned her directly, she'd told him once.

"Your father is your problem," she'd said.

He was that all right. And more. Whether Leonidas had wanted everything that came with his position as the Betancur heir or not hadn't signified. No one had ever asked him what he wanted. His mother had abandoned him to his father's tender mercies, and Leonidas hadn't had any choice but to become the man his father wanted him to become.

He could remember everything now. The child who'd stopped crying out, hoping someone might save him, because no one ever had. The adolescent who had never bothered to step outside the lines drawn for him because the consequences couldn't possibly be worth surviving just to engage in a little pointless defiance. He'd grown into the life he'd lived according to his father's every harsh dictate until the old man had died—possibly after poisoning himself with his own evil, Leonidas had always thought, despite the medical authorities who'd deemed it an aneurysm.

He remembered it all.

Leonidas knew that if he turned around and sought out a mirror, he would finally look like himself again, despite the scars that told the story of that terrifying plane crash. His bespoke suits were flown in from Milan and tailored to his specifications in the privacy of his own home. He wore leather shoes crafted by hand for him by local artisans who thanked him for the honor. His hair was once more cut the way he'd always preferred it, short and neat and with the vaguest hint of the military, as if he was always on the verge of going to war.

He'd learned to sleep again in his own bed, a king-size monstrosity that sprawled across the better part of his penthouse and had been designed to work as well for intense play as sleep. Far better than the sturdy, efficient mattress in the compound.

He indulged in rich foods again instead of the bland rations of the compound. He rediscovered his family's wine labels and his own vast collection. He reintroduced himself to strong coffee and even stronger spirits.

It wasn't simply that he didn't belong in the cult—that he'd never belonged on that mountaintop—it was that the place where he did belong was almost unimaginably luxurious, and he could see that now in a way he'd never done before. He knew exactly how marvelous every bit of his life was, because he'd lost it for four years.

He kept telling himself he was lucky. That many people never got the opportunity to see life from more than one side, or if they did, it was usually a downward spiral with no possibility of return.

That notion had buoyed him for the better part of his reentry into the world. The long plane flight back, filled with phone calls to the Betancur legal teams across the planet, as well as the authorities back in Idaho about Robert's plans and goals. And then to his mother, who had performed her usual Maria Callas-like operatics at the sound of his voice but, of course, hadn't stirred herself to rush to his side from her current holiday in the South Pacific.

All excellent distractions from the fact that the last time he'd been on a private plane, it had exploded and very nearly killed him.

He'd reminded himself of his luck over and over

again during the press junket when he landed. During the speeches he gave in all the subsequent interviews, or the little myths he told anyone who asked about his time away. Every time he smiled and shaped those optics that Susannah was so concerned with—and that his board of directors had agreed were of paramount importance.

And then it had been time to go back to work, and that was where Leonidas had discovered that his memory was not all that it should have been.

He refused to admit it at first because he didn't want to believe it was possible, but it seemed as if he hadn't *quite* remembered everything when he'd regained his memory. Not everything.

He turned then, thrusting his hands into the pockets of his three-piece suit, keeping his face impassive as he looked out the glass on the other side of his office. This was the internal wall, and through it he could see the whole of the serenely lavish executive floor the Betancur Corporation offices.

More to the point, he could see Susannah.

He didn't know what he'd thought she did, back there in the States when she'd appeared at the compound. Perhaps he hadn't been able to consider it while he was so busy regaining his own identity. His own past, for good or ill. He'd first had an inkling on the flight back to Europe when she'd managed all the calls he'd had to make and had cut in when necessary with a quiet word that had always—always—stopped everyone else talking. Instantly. And he'd noticed it even more during that first press conference when they'd pulled up outside his building and she'd handled his reintroduction to life with such seeming ease. She used that smile of hers, cool and calm. She'd exuded that particular slickness, impressive and unmistakable, that seemed to define her these days—

because she hadn't dropped it when they'd finally made it past the throng of reporters and into the private elevator that whisked them from the street to the lobby of his penthouse.

Their penthouse, he'd had to remind himself. Because she lived here, too—and had, she'd informed him, ever since the wedding he'd forgotten for all this time.

"Have you taken over my position in the company, as well?" he'd asked when they'd stood in a silence he didn't want to consider awkward, not quite, in the great open room that soared up three stories and had been his pride and joy, before. His architects had made his vision real when he'd bought the building, making the top three floors of one of Rome's many ancient edifices so modern and airy within while still including elements of the historical details.

But that day, all he'd been able to focus on was Susannah. His throat had been dry from the press conference. He'd felt outside himself, as if he was recovering all over again from the accident that had struck him down in the first place. When what he really was doing was standing in the middle of what should have felt like home.

Then again, maybe nothing was going to feel like home anymore, he'd told himself. Maybe that was the trouble. There was not one single part of him that wanted to return to those Idaho mountains. But he didn't quite know how to be in Rome where he belonged, either.

In the fact that the wife he barely knew was more comfortable in his home than he was… Troubled him.

Maybe it wasn't that it troubled him. Maybe it was that it made him feel both fierce and something like lonely in a manner he didn't like at all.

"No one has replaced you," Susannah had replied in those first moments in the penthouse. She'd been standing there in another one of her sleek black ensembles. She seemed to have nothing but. The only color on her was the gold of her hair and the bright blue of her eyes. It made her something more than pretty. *Striking.*

He had the distinct impression that no one underestimated her twice.

"Do not attempt to placate me, please."

She'd raised one eyebrow, and he, in turn, had hated that he didn't know her well enough to read that expression on her face.

"You died before you could alter your will to reflect the changes everyone assured me had been agreed to before our wedding, Leonidas, which meant everything defaulted to me. And I saw no particular reason to appoint a new president or CEO, just to fill the position. There have been many candidates over the years, as you might imagine. But none have been you."

"It's been four years. That's an eternity."

She'd smiled coolly. "We've only actively been looking for replacement for…oh…the last eighteen months or so."

Leonidas had imagined he could feel the rusted gears of his mind start to grind together. "That makes no sense. Surely one of my cousins—"

"Your cousins have a great many ideas, and an even greater sense of entitlement, but what they do not have are the skill sets to back those up." She'd raised one delicately shaped shoulder, then dropped it. "And unfortunately for them, while they may be of the Betancur blood, I've been the one with the deciding vote."

No, Leonidas thought now as he had then, it would not be wise to underestimate his ever-surprising wife.

She was in the office, making her way down the center aisle of the executive floor with all its deliberate windows to let light pour into the company's highest offices. This afternoon she wore yet another dark wardrobe concoction, black boots and a dark dress he knew was an inky navy blue only because the color was slightly different from the boots. Today's boots boasted impressively high heels, but she seemed to walk in them just the same as she had when she'd been hiking up and down mountains. The dress had tiny sleeves that curved over her shoulders, somehow calling more attention to her feminine, elegant figure without actually showing too much of it.

He wanted to taste her. He wanted to test the difference between how delicate she appeared to be and how fierce he suspected she truly was.

He couldn't seem to get his need for her under control, but he told himself it was no more than a function of the time he'd spent away from the company of women. She'd reignited his thirst, that was all. It was nothing personal. It couldn't be.

Leonidas wouldn't let it be anything like personal.

He didn't do *personal*. He suspected that had been the first casualty of his father's style of parenting. Nothing was personal. Everything was the business.

He waited there as she made her way down the long hall, smiling and nodding to all she passed. Some in the hall itself, some through those walls of glass. Not quite friendly, he noticed. But cool. Direct and precise.

The Widow Betancur.

"I was barely more than a child when we married," she had told him, somewhere over the Atlantic Ocean. She'd curled her feet beneath her on the leather sofa in the private jet's living room area and managed to look nothing at all like small or vulnerable when she did it. The air steward had handed her a warm mug of something—and it ate at Leonidas that he didn't know what she drank, that he didn't know her preferences as well as the least of his employees—and she held it between her palms as she spoke in that smooth voice of hers, all those polished European vowels that could dance so nimbly from one romance language to the next. "For the first year after your disappearance, the only thing I had going for me was the depths of my grief."

Leonidas had let out a hoarse sound. A laugh, he'd told himself. "What grief? To my recollection we barely knew each other."

Her blue eyes had been frank. Assessing.

"But no one knew that," she'd said quietly. "Or if they did, it was their word against mine. And I was your widow, with your fortune and your power at my fingertips. So it didn't matter what people speculated. It mattered what I said. And I said my grief was too intense to even think about naming your successor."

He tried to imagine the company—his family—after his death. His scheming cousins would have seen it as divine intervention and a chance at last to take what they'd long believed was theirs. His manipulative mother would have moved to consolidate her power, of course, but would also have grieved him, surely. If only in public, the better to attract the attention she always craved. And Apollonia Betancur's public emotional performances tended to raze cities when she got going. Meanwhile, his greedy board of directors, each one of them so determined to squeeze every last euro out of any potential deal, would have formed alliances and tried to pulverize the competition in their race to take what had been Leonidas's.

All of them were jaded sophisticates. All of them were deeply impressed with their ability to manipulate any and all situations to their benefit. They were among the most debauched and pampered of the wealthy elite in Europe, and they exulted in the things they owned and the lives they ruined along the way.

And it seemed they'd all been bested by a nineteen-year-old.

He'd smiled at that. "So you mourned my untimely passing. You grieved for much longer than anyone could have expected after a marriage that lasted less than a day. Judging by your somber attire, you continue to do so."

"Grief squats on a person and stays until it is finished," Susannah had said softly, as much to the mug between her hands as to him. Then she'd lifted her gleaming gold head and she'd smiled at him, her clever blue eyes gleaming. "And who among us can say how another person grieves? Or when that grief should be finished?"

It had been clear to Leonidas that she'd outsmarted them all.

An impression that his weeks back here in Rome had done nothing to dissipate.

As if she could feel his eyes on her then, all the way from his end of the long hallway, she looked up. Her stride didn't change. Her expression didn't alter. Still, Leonidas felt sure that something in her had…hitched.

She pushed through his door when she reached it, letting it fall shut behind her. And then they were enclosed in the hushed quiet of his soundproofed space. A big smile took over her face and Leonidas felt that strange hitch again, but in him this time.

It took him longer than it should have to remember that his wife was entirely about *optics*. She was only putting on a show, he told himself sternly. She was smiling for the benefit of the people in the office around them who could look in through the glass of his wall and watch them interacting. This was for everyone out there who gossiped and wondered and whispered among themselves about the kind of relationship a man who should have been dead had with the wife he'd left behind.

He knew better than to give them anything. But keeping his expression impassive was harder than it ought to have been.

"Your secretary said you wished to see me," Susannah said. She didn't wait for his answer. Instead, she walked over to the sitting area nearest the big window with the sweeping views of Rome and settled herself on one of the low couches.

"I did indeed."

"I think it's going well, don't you?" She folded her hands in her lap, and Leonidas had the strangest flashback to the compound. To the way she'd sat there then, in that little cell with cameras trained on her, as calmly as she was sitting before him now. Exuding serenity from every pore. "I think your cousins found it a bit difficult to pretend they were excited by your resurrection, but everyone else is eating up the story like candy."

"By everyone else, you mean the world. The tabloids."

"Not just the tabloids. You are a major story on almost every news network in Europe. Returning from the dead, it turns out, is a feel-good crowd-pleaser for all."

He knew she was right. But something in him balked at her cynicism—or maybe it was something else. Maybe it was the fact that when she was close to him, all he wanted to do was touch her the way he had when he'd been the Count and hadn't known better.

And all she wanted to do was talk about narratives. Optics. Campaigns and complicated plots to secure his place here again.

She had been the virgin. But Leonidas was the one who couldn't seem to let go.

In all the time since they'd been back in Rome, she'd stayed out of his way. Available should he require her assistance, but back in the penthouse—where she had been sleeping in one of the guest rooms the whole time he'd been away, apparently—they hardly interacted at all. When he'd asked one night why she appeared to be avoiding him in the home they shared, she'd only smiled sweetly and told him that she was very cognizant of the fact that he needed to find his own way back into his life. That she didn't want to intrude.

The entire situation set his teeth on edge. And Leonidas didn't particularly care to investigate why that was.

"I'm glad you called me in," Susannah was saying. "Because I've wanted to speak to you, too. I didn't want to rush into this until you'd been home long enough to really feel as if you'd got your feet beneath you, but I also don't think there's any point in dragging things out unnecessarily."

Leonidas knew he needed to say what he'd wanted to say, or he wouldn't. Because he hadn't believed it was happening at first. He assumed it was stress, or that perhaps he was overwhelmed—though he couldn't recall ever being overwhelmed before in his life. Then again, his life had never included a lost four years and a cult before now.

Then this morning he'd sat in a meeting, listening to the discussion all around him and well aware that the people speaking were among those he ought to have recognized. He'd recognized the names on the memo that his secretary had handed him, but he hadn't been able to match names to faces.

"There are holes in my memory," he told her now, before he thought better of it. He stayed where he was. Tall and straight and with all that glass and Rome behind him, as if that would make a difference. As if that would make him whole.

Susannah blinked, and he thought she froze. "Holes?"

"I know who I am. I know you. I certainly knew my mother when she finally deigned to appear the other night, in all her state."

"Apollonia is not easily forgotten. Though one might have occasion to wish otherwise."

"But there is so much I can't remember. Too much."

There. He'd said it. He waited for it to hit him—for the fact that he'd admitted to such weakness to take his knees out from under him where he stood. The way his father would have taken his knees out for him, were he still alive.

But it didn't happen.

And it was because of her, Leonidas knew it. She was why he hadn't keeled over in the telling of this most disastrous of truths. She only gazed at him as if she was perfectly happy to wait as long as it took for him to tell her the rest of it.

"Faces. Names. Business decisions I clearly made years ago." He shrugged. "I don't have access to any of it."

She considered, her hands seeming to tighten in her lap. "Is this all the time?"

"No. But it's enough. I was in a meeting of vice presidents this morning and I didn't know a single person in the room. And not all of them were hired in the past four years."

"No, they weren't." She was frowning then, that gaze of hers fixed on his, and there was no reason Leonidas should have felt something like relief. That someone other than him knew. That it wasn't only his weight to carry. "Do they know you can't remember them?"

He let out a harsh sound without meaning to do it. "That would be bad optics, I realize," he said, perhaps more sternly than necessary. "I would hate to dilute the message."

Susannah didn't appear to move, and yet Leonidas was certain her back was straighter than it had been before.

"I was less concerned with the optics, or any message you might have sent, and more concerned with you." Her lips pressed together in a firm line, and Leonidas couldn't possibly have said why he felt chastened. "I expect you managed to cover it so no one could tell you didn't remember them."

"I did." He inclined his head. "But I worry it is only a matter of time before I find myself in a situation where covering it is not possible."

She appeared to mull that over. "What did the doctor say about any lingering memory loss? Did the subject arise?"

Leonidas had not been at all interested in seeing a doctor when he'd finally made it home, as it had seemed like yet another admission of weakness to him. But he had eventually succumbed to the family doctors who had tended to the Betancur family for years, because in the end, how could he not? Whether it was a weakness or not, there was no one more concerned with the four years he'd lost than him. He was the one who would had lived through them, convinced that he was someone else entirely.

There had been no small part of him that had worried he was damaged forever by that damned Count.

He blew out a breath now, and kept his gaze on Susannah. "It's possible I'll never recall the actual plane crash, but I imagine that is something of a blessing. The doctor was confident that more and more memories will come back with time, until there is very little, if anything, missing. But I don't have time."

A faint line appeared between her brows. "You have all the time you need, surely."

"Only as long as no one suspects the truth." He eyed her. "You are the only one who knows, Susannah. You and one doctor who I very much doubt would dare to disobey my order of silence. Not when his livelihood depends on me."

She no longer clasped her hands together in front of her like a latter-day nun. One had risen to her collarbone and she pressed against it, as if she was trying to leave her fingerprints against her own skin. There was no particular reason Leonidas should find that so maddeningly sexy. So alluring. It was as if he was helpless against the need to taste her. Just one more time. That's what he told himself, night and day when this craving hit him: one more time.

But not now.

"I need you," he said baldly. Starkly.

Leonidas didn't think he imagined the faint jerk of her body then. She flinched, then obviously worked to repress it.

"It's clear to me that you spent the past four years learning everything there is to know about this company," he said, as much to cover his own admission as anything else.

"I had no choice." Her blue gaze had gone stormy. "It was that or be swallowed whole."

"Then you will guide me," he told her, and he wasn't sure he was entirely concealing his relief. "You will cover for things I cannot remember."

The strangest expression flitted across her face. "Will I?"

He moved toward the sofa then, as if admitting what he needed had loosened his feet. "Under normal circumstances it would be strange to bring my wife wherever I went, but you have already served as a quasi-CEO. No one will think anything of it."

"And how will this work? Will we develop a system of touch? Will we rely on sign language? Or, I know, I will alert you to things you should know in Morse code. Using my eyelashes."

Her hands were back in her lap. It occurred to him that she did that when she was anything but serene. When she only wished to appear calm.

That shouldn't have felt like an electrical current inside him, but it did.

"Or you could simply greet the person in front of you, using the correct name, and I will follow suit." She didn't say anything. And yet somehow he had the distinct impression that that expression he couldn't quite read on her face was mutinous. "Will this be a problem for you?"

"It would be helpful if you knew the time frame for your memory to return."

"I'm told the human mind does what it will," he said coolly. Through his teeth. "I assure you, however inconvenient my memory loss is for you, I feel it more keenly." She nodded with that, and then swallowed, visibly. And something like foreboding wound its way through him. "What was it you wished to speak to me about?"

"Well," Susannah said quietly, her face calm. Serene. And yet Leonidas didn't believe it this time. "This feels awkward. But I want a divorce."

CHAPTER FIVE

Susannah was certain that Leonidas could see how she shook where she sat, as his usual arrogant, haughty expression shifted to something far more lethal and dark.

He stood there, more beautiful than any man should have been, a dark and bold thrust of impossible masculinity in the middle of this glass office with the mellow gold of Rome behind him. She'd be lying if she said he didn't affect her. If she didn't shiver every time she was near him as if she was still that overwhelmed teenage bride from four years ago.

And it had been bad enough on that mountain. She'd been beating herself up for the way she'd succumbed to him ever since it happened. What had she been thinking? How had she toppled so quickly to a man she hardly knew? She'd called it her wedding night, but it hadn't been. The Leonidas she'd found in that compound, leading that cult, was more of a stranger than the convenient husband she'd barely known years before.

She had no excuse for her behavior. She knew that. Just as she knew that she could never let him know about the dreams that woke her with their potency, night after night, until she'd had to lock herself in her own bedroom in the penthouse they shared to make sure she stayed away from him in those dark, dangerous hours when she woke up alone and so very hungry.

For him.

Leonidas's return had changed everything, just as she'd imagined it would.

The world had gone mad when the fact he'd been found alive had hit the wires. Reporters and law enforcement and his board of directors had been in fits all around him, his family had hardly known how to process it and had acted out as they always did, but beneath all of that, the truth was that this homecoming was Leonidas's. Not hers. This had nothing to do with her.

Susannah had been a widow for all of her marriage. And she'd deliberately maintained that position these past four years because it was that or succumb to a far worse situation.

But with Leonidas home, she was free.

No matter that he was looking at her now with an expression she could only describe as predatory.

"I appear to have misheard you." His voice was nothing but cold warning, but she made herself meet his gaze as if she couldn't hear it. "Would you repeat that?"

"I think you heard me perfectly well," she said, as if that trembling thing wasn't taking her over. As if she didn't feel there was a very good chance it might sweep her away. But she told herself he couldn't possibly see that, because no one ever saw her. They saw what they wanted to see, nothing more. "I want a divorce. As soon as possible."

"We've barely been married for any time at all."

"Perhaps it feels that way to you because you can't remember it. But I can." She forced a smile and kept it cool. "Four years is actually a very long time to be a Betancur."

"That sounds as if you do not wish to be part of my

family, Susannah." He inclined his head in that way of his that reminded her that there were people out there in the world who considered him a god. And it wasn't a metaphor. "No one can blame you in this, of course. They are an unpleasant, scavenging, manipulative lot, and that is on a good day. But they are not me."

"Leonidas—"

"You are married to me, not them."

"That argument might have worked four years ago," she said faintly, because the truth was, it was working now and that was the last thing she wanted. She didn't understand herself. She'd worked tirelessly all these years to find him so she could escape and now she could do just that, her body was staging a rebellion. Her breasts hurt when she was with him. They ached so much it echoed low in her belly, and the fire of it made her feel entirely too hot. So hot she was afraid he could see it all over her. "I was a very malleable teenager, but that was then."

"And this is now." She didn't think he moved or did anything in particular, and yet somehow, there was no more air in the room. As if he'd taken it all and was holding it ransom right there in front of her. "And my need of you is dire. Would you refuse me?"

"I would like to," she told him, smiling to take the sting out of it. But the way he regarded her suggested she had succeeded.

"Tell me, Susannah, why did you track me down?" he asked after a moment. When the gold of the city outside had long since blended into the gold of his eyes and she worried she'd be eaten alive by the gleam. "Why did you come all the way to Idaho and climb up that mountain when it would have been so easy to stay right here? Everyone believed me dead. You could have left me there and no one would have been the wiser. Not even me."

"I really, really want that divorce," she told him as blithely as she could, but she could hear the catch in her voice. The breathlessness.

What she didn't want was this conversation. She'd naively assumed that there wouldn't be anything to discuss. Leonidas didn't know her. He couldn't possibly want any kind of relationship with her, and the truth was, he likely hadn't wanted one back when. She doubted that he was even the same man who had left on that plane four years ago. And it wasn't as if she would note the difference, because they'd been strangers thrown together in a marriage convenient to their families, and no matter that she'd had teenage fantasies to the contrary.

This was the perfect time to draw a line under their strange, doomed marriage, and go on with their lives. Separately.

Before she was forced to face the fact that after saving her virginity all this time—after turning away Leonidas's cousins one after the next and after shutting down each and every delusional suitor who'd tried to convince her that they'd fallen in love with her smile, or heard her laughter across a room, or found her unrelenting use of black clothing seductive—she'd thrown herself at this man.

Leonidas hadn't known who he was. But she'd known exactly who she was, and that was what she couldn't forgive.

It had taken every bit of self-control she had to act as if the loss of her virginity didn't affect her. But she was terribly afraid she'd used it all up back there in that compound she fervently hoped American law enforcement had since dismantled. Because the longer she was around this man, the less she thought she would be able to keep that control intact.

She wanted out before she broke. She wanted an escape at last from what she'd never wanted to accept would be the rest of her life, and she didn't care if her parents were disappointed. She refused to be a pawn any longer. She wanted no part of Apollonia's theatrics and schemes. She didn't want to be a bargaining chip between the grasping Betancur cousins. She was tired of all this corrosive power and all the greed everyone around her had for more and more and more.

All this time, she'd believed she had a responsibility to the husband who had died so suddenly. Maybe *because* of all her girlish fantasies about what could have been. Whatever the cause, Susannah had taken that responsibility seriously, and one of the reasons she'd been so successful was because she'd felt nothing. She'd understood exactly who her parents were on her wedding night when they'd had the opportunity to try to comfort her and had instead made her feel small. Soon after, she'd come to understand the intricacies of the Betancur family and its businesses in repulsive detail. The plane crash and its wake had showed her everything she needed to know about her in-laws.

She'd filed it all away, felt nothing besides the loss of her dreams that she'd convinced herself weren't real, and that had helped her become perhaps the most powerful widow in the world.

But then she'd walked into a cult leader's compound after all these numb, safe years, and she'd felt entirely too much.

The entire plane ride back she'd tried to convince herself that it had been a geographic problem, that was all. That what had happened in that compound had been a thing that could happen only in the Rocky Mountains out there in the midst of that unnervingly huge continent. And still she woke every night to find herself barricaded in her room in the penthouse, swaddled in her bedclothes with her heart gone mad and a deep wildness between her legs, alive with too much yearning. With too much intense hunger.

It wasn't going away. It wasn't getting better.

And Susannah had realized that the only thing worse than spending the rest of her life as the Widow Betancur was this. Longing for a man who she knew, even if he didn't—not yet, anyway—would grow out of his need for her. Fast. The way her mother had coldly told her men did, in her version of "the talk" the night before Susannah's wedding.

"Leonidas Betancur is a man of tremendous wealth and taste," Annemieke Forrester had told her only daughter that night, sitting on the edge of Susannah's bed in the hotel suite where they'd all been staying in anticipation of the grand ceremony. "You would do well to assume his sexual tastes are equally well cultivated." Susannah must have made some kind of noise to match her immediate reaction, a flush of confusion and something like shame, because Annemieke had laughed. "You are an untried, untouched teenager, child. You cannot hope to interest a man like Leonidas."

"But…" Susannah had been so young. It hurt to remember how young. How sheltered. "He is to be my husband."

"You will quickly learn that your power comes from the grace with which you ignore his dalliances," her mother had told her matter-of-factly. "It will make him respect you."

"Respect?" she'd echoed.

"Your job is to produce an heir," her mother had continued. "Your virginity is your wedding gift. After that, you concentrate on getting pregnant and staying pretty. Think *grace*, Susannah. No one values a shrill, embittered woman en route to a nasty divorce. You will live a life filled with comfort and ease. I'd advise you to make the best of what you have."

"I thought that marriage would be—"

"What?" her mother had interrupted scornfully. "A fairy tale? Leonidas will tire of you, girl, and quickly. Let him." She'd waved her hand in the air impatiently. "It doesn't matter where a man roams. What matters is the home he returns to. Over time, he will return to you more than he will leave you, and he will do this far more cheerfully if you have spared him the scenes and remonstrations."

Susannah had tried to take that to heart when her brand-new husband had left her on their wedding night, apparently already tired of her, though she'd been crushed. She wasn't as foolish these days as she'd been then. And the only reason he wanted her around now, she'd thought even before he'd told her that there were gaps in his memory, was because she was the one who had found him. The only one who knew where he'd been.

Leonidas Betancur was not a sentimental man. She knew that. Neither with his memory nor without it. The scars on his body hadn't made him into someone new, they'd chiseled him into a harder sort of perfect marble, that was all. He was more beautiful, somehow, for being tested—and surviving—but he was still made of stone.

She knew. She'd felt him surge inside her and send her shattering into pieces.

And Susannah wasn't a teenager anymore. She'd grown out of the fairy tales that had colored her youth because she hadn't known any better.

She knew better now. She wanted only to be free.

"You must know there can be no divorce," Leonidas said now. Darkly, that gaze of his still fixed on her. "Not so soon after my return." His hard mouth moved into something only an optimist would have called a smile. "Think of the optics."

"I'm sensitive to optics, certainly." She was proud of how even her voice sounded. How controlled. "But I also want my life back."

"What life do you mean, exactly?" He tilted his head slightly to one side and she felt that sense of disconnection again. As if they were in two places at once, and one of them was the compound where he had ruled supreme. "If memory serves, and of course it may not, the life you led before marrying me was little better than a prison. A pretty one, I grant you. And that was the appeal, of course. Your promised naïveté. You were more sheltered than the average nun."

She'd gone stiff and she didn't even know why. "What you talking about?"

"It is amazing what things stay in the memory, even when the chief financial officer's name has gone up in smoke." Leonidas wandered across the office, and that should have taken a bit of that predatory focus off her. He wasn't even looking at her, after all. But somehow, Susannah did not feel at all at her ease. "Your father promised you to me when you were very young, you must know this."

"Of course I know it. I never forgot it in the first place."

She regretted her petulance the instant she spoke, but if it bothered him, he ignored it. Which only made her regret it more.

"Your father is not a kind man, as I'm sure you're aware," Leonidas said in that same dark way. He poured himself a measure of something from his personal bar,

dark and amber, but he didn't drink it. He only swirled
it in its tumbler and stared at it as if he was studying it.
"Nor is he a good one. He sought to sweeten the pot,
you see, when I was less interested in the match than he
wished me to be." His gaze rose from the crystal and met
hers, and it took everything Susannah had not to flinch.
"He wasn't simply selling his daughter, you understand.
He promised me you would be untouched. Completely
and wholly unsullied. That was meant to sweeten the
deal. A virgin sacrifice, all for me."

There was no reason why Susannah's mouth should
have gone dry. Why her heart should have pounded too
hard and her eyes feel too bright. It wasn't as if any of
this was a surprise, not really.

But on the other hand, he was talking about her life.
And all those years she'd spent in her overly strict boarding school, forever fielding intrusive questions about her
virtue. When there had been no moral reason for her to
remain pure, the way her parents had pretended there was.

When there had never been anything to it but leverage.

"Whatever my father is or isn't is immaterial." She
shrugged, and hoped she was managing to keep her expression clear, because there was no point mourning her
parents when she already knew exactly who they were.
"This is about me. This is not about what a teenage girl
thinks she owes her parents. It's about what I want."

Again, he didn't appear to move. And still Susannah
found it difficult to pull in a breath.

"And what is it you want?"

"Freedom," she replied at once. Perhaps a touch too
intensely. "I want my freedom."

"And what do you imagine freedom looks like for a
woman who was the Widow Betancur?" he asked qui-

etly. "Where do you think you can hide from the influence of my name?"

She heard the trap around her. It was as if she could feel iron closing in on her from all sides, and the funny part was, though she knew she should get up and run while she could, she didn't move. There was something about that sardonic lash in his voice. There was something about the way his dark gaze met hers, and held.

"I am no longer a widow," she reminded him. "You are standing right in front of me."

"And yet you are still dressed in dark clothes that might as well be fully black, as if you anticipate a second funeral at any moment."

"Dark colors are very slimming."

"The world is not prepared to let go of such an icon as their favorite widow, Susannah. Surely you must know this. Where will you go? Your past will follow you as surely as a shadow. It always does."

"Says the man who took a four-year break from his."

"I'm not going to argue with you."

She recognized that voice. It brought her back to the conversation they'd had in the car that had delivered them from the church to their reception four years ago. To the pitiless way her new husband—a perfect stranger with a cruel mouth she'd found fascinating despite herself—had gazed at her from his seat.

It was not unlike the way the Count had gazed at her from his white seat in his bright white throne room.

"There will be no honeymoon," he had told her four years ago. "I cannot take that kind of time away from my business." And when she had reacted to that, when she had allowed some or other emotion to color her face, he had only grown colder. "I understand that you are young, but in time you will thank me for giving no quarter to your childishness. We all must grow up sometime, Susannah. Even spoiled little girls must turn into women."

She hadn't thought about that conversation in years.

And he was still talking now.

"You obviously hold a bargaining chip," he was saying, but in that merciless way as if no matter what she held, he was the one in total control. "I do not wish anyone to know that I lost my memory in the first place, much less that I have not yet gotten parts of it back. For all the reasons we discussed in Idaho that make what happened there so precarious. Optics, my cousins. All of the above."

"I sympathize, but that doesn't make any difference—"

"I'm not finished."

And there was no reason Susannah should feel duly chastised, but she did. And worse for her self-esteem and the strides she'd been so sure she'd made in his absence, she fell quiet.

On command, like a dog.

"If you wish to divorce me, Susannah, I have no objection to that."

His voice was so cool, so even and without inflection, that she wasn't sure she'd heard him correctly for one jarring beat of her heart. Then another. But then his words sank in.

And she had no idea why there was some perverse thing in her that very nearly wanted to…argue, perhaps? Or make him take it back. Almost as if…

But she didn't let herself think that through. She should never let him touch her, that was all. That was the beginning and the end of it, and that was what she kept returning to while she sat here, her fingers laced together lest they take it upon themselves to touch him again.

"Oh. I mean, good. We agree."

"I will give you a divorce," Leonidas told her. "But not now."

As if it was entirely up to him. Again, as if he was the god of everything.

"You can't bargain me into staying," she said, with entirely too much intensity once more.

It was a mistake. She knew it when something flared in that gaze of his, and the way he stood there, all that arrogance in a bespoke suit, seemed to blur a bit. Less a pointed weapon, somehow.

Leonidas only shrugged, but the tenor of everything had changed and seemed...almost lazy.

"You want to be free. I want your help and am willing to free you after you give it."

"Why does my freedom come with a price tag?" she demanded, because she couldn't seem to help herself.

"Because that is the world we live in, little one." He didn't shrug again, but the look in his dark eyes seemed to suggest it, all the same. "I don't see why we can't help each other. But if that is not possible, I will have no choice but to use what leverage I have."

She didn't ask him what leverage he had. Susannah knew that it didn't matter. He would come up with something, and if he couldn't, he would manufacture something else. Hadn't she seen this in action time and again these last years? That was what these people did. It was in their blood.

"This is a good thing," she told him after a moment, when she was absolutely certain that she would sound and look nothing but in complete control. As if she was made of the same stone he was. "I was tempted to forget, you see. I was tempted to think that you were a victim. I almost felt sorry for you, but this clears it up, thank goodness. It reminds me who you are."

"Your beloved husband?" he asked sardonically. "The one you have grieved with such dedication all these many years?"

"Not just a Betancur," she said, as if it was an epithet. It was. "But the worst of them by far."

Leonidas looked more than merely predatory, then. Something in his starkly beautiful face edged toward cruel, but it wasn't intimidating. Or it was—of course it was, because this was a man who couldn't help but intimidate as surely as he breathed—but Susannah was more focused on the melting sensation that swept over her, then settled low in her belly like a greedy pulse.

And the fact that she was almost 100 percent positive that he knew it.

"It sounds as if we have a deal," he said.

And then Leonidas smiled.

CHAPTER SIX

A LONG AND exhausting month later, Susannah sat in the back of a car careening through the wet streets of Paris, wishing her head would stop feeling as if it might split into pieces at any moment.

She wasn't particularly optimistic. A long evening loomed ahead of her, and she would have given anything to leap out of the car, race through the rain and the crowds of fashionable Parisians to tuck herself up in her bed and hide beneath the covers—but she knew that wasn't possible. Tonight was the Betancur Foundation's annual charity ball that this year would serve as Leonidas's formal reintroduction to society after all his time away.

That Leonidas had survived the crash had not been known to anyone at first, they'd told the press. His funeral had been a sincere gesture of grief and mourning, not a cynical spectacle while they waited to find out if he'd live. And when his survival had become known to them, his condition had been so extreme that everyone involved had kept it quiet rather than throw the corporation into turmoil.

"Of course, I wanted nothing more than to race to his side," Susannah had told a concerned American interviewer. "But my husband is a Betancur. I knew he would want me to take care of his company while the doctors took care of him."

His assumed widow's refusal to hand over the reins looked much less stubborn through this lens, of course, which had led to any number of think pieces celebrating Susannah's "iron will" and "clear-eyed leadership" from publications that had addressed her in far less friendly terms a few months back.

But the ball was a different animal. It was overwhelming at the best of times, so filled was it with the members of the Betancur family and all their usual drama and intrigue. Susannah expected that the return from the dead of the Betancur heir himself would make it all…insane.

Surely the prospect would make anyone tired. At least this year she wouldn't have to deal with marriage proposals over canapés and several attempts at a coup before dessert. Or so she hoped.

Leonidas sat beside her in the car's comfortable backseat as the driver navigated the Paris traffic, talking into his mobile in dark, silky tones that didn't require Susannah's fluency in German to realize were menacing in the extreme. His tone did it for him. It was something about one of the resorts the corporation ran in the South Pacific, but she couldn't quite summon up the energy to care about that the way she might have normally. She stared out the window as Paris gleamed in the wet dark and plucked a bit listlessly at the dress she wore. Not that it was the dress's fault. It was a stunning creation in a deep, mesmerizing green that had been presented to her like a gift by Leonidas's Milanese tailors when she knew very well it hadn't been a gift at all. It had been a command.

Leonidas didn't have to *say* that he didn't want her to wear black any longer. That she was no longer the Widow Betancur, but his wife, and should allow her wardrobe to reflect that reality. She'd understood the message.

It was the first time she'd worn a bright color—or any

color other than the darkest of navys and the deepest of charcoals—since her wedding, which seemed appropriate for their anticipated debut as an actual married couple, a whole four years later than planned.

No wonder her head felt so tender.

The city blurred into one long gleam of frenetic light outside the car windows, and Leonidas's voice was that same low murmur, all power and command, that Susannah could feel as much inside her body as with her ears.

The trouble was, she was just so *tired* these days.

It wasn't the dress. Or the rich shade of green that flattered her so well she'd been forced to consider the fact that Leonidas had selected it because he'd known it would, which made her…uncomfortable. Restless in her own skin. She'd have liked to blame something so relatively innocuous as her wardrobe, but she knew better.

Susannah told herself it was the charade itself that exhausted her. The difficulty of keeping one foot in the Betancur world when she planned to escape it as soon as possible. That would exhaust anyone, surely. The weeks since she and Leonidas had made their bargain had seemed to creep by, every day somehow harder than the last. After all those years of playing the Widow Betancur so well, it should have been easy enough for Susannah to continue along in the same role just a little while longer. But for some reason, this last month had been more difficult than any she could remember.

It's because you know this is temporary, she told herself now, watching the city melt from shadow into dancing light and back again on the other side of the glass. *When there was no escape, when you had no choice, it was easier to simply* do *what had to be done.*

Her headaches had only gotten worse as time went on. It seemed all she wanted to do was lie down and sleep, except even when she forced herself into a long and un-interrupted night's rest, she never woke refreshed. She felt thick all the way through. Underwater, somehow.

She'd been toying with the idea that she was allergic to Leonidas.

But the thing she felt when she was close to him, doing as he'd asked and helping him navigate the cut-throat world he occupied as if he'd never been away, was not an allergy. It had a great many similar symptoms. Breathlessness. A pervasive flush. A sort of restless, itchy feeling all over...

If it was an allergy, she could take decongestants and be done with him. With this. But there was no remedy for the intensity that Leonidas exuded the way other men wore cologne.

God help her, all she wanted was to be done with this.

She'd spent her entire life training to be married off to a man like Leonidas. Then the whole of her marriage training to be as ruthless and powerful as the husband she'd lost. Susannah had no idea what it was like to be on her own.

No one had ever asked her what it was *she* wanted. Which was probably a good thing, she thought wryly, because she had no idea.

"You seem drained yet again," Leonidas said from beside her, as if in answer to the question in her head, but she knew better than to think he could read her. Or would want to read her, for that matter, as if they shared some kind of intimacy. The truth was, she might be married to him, but he wasn't hers.

A man like Leonidas would never be any woman's.

Susannah hadn't realized he'd finished his call. She turned from the rain-lined windows and the gleaming lights of Paris just there on the other side, and tried to arrange her face into something pleasant. Or calm enough to be mistaken for pleasant, anyway.

"I'm not drained," she said, because it was polite. But he was watching her, his dark eyes brooding and entirely too close, there in the backseat of the car, and she didn't feel particularly *polite* after all. "I find I am less interested in this endless game of playacting with every day that passes, that's all."

His brows rose and she thought she saw something glitter there, deep in his dark gold gaze. But when he spoke his voice was even.

"I regret that my presence is such a burden upon you."

It occurred to her that he was playing a role just as much as she was, and she couldn't have said why that realization sent a bolt of something like shame spinning through her. But she didn't let it keep her quiet.

"Yes, thank you. It always helps to be sardonic, I find. It makes everything so much better."

"As does sarcasm."

"You asked me to help you, and I agreed to do that," Susannah reminded him tightly. "I could end that agreement at any time, and whether you recall the name of every assistant in the Malaysian office or not is no concern to me either way."

Leonidas didn't look chastened. But then again, he never did. He might not remember the many people who tried to speak to him over the course of a day, but he certainly seemed to remember that he was the one in charge. Of everything. It galled her that she'd allowed him to take charge of her as well, when surely she simply could have left.

Why hadn't she left?

"Let me hasten to assure you that this extreme torture will end soon enough," he told her, and there was a note in his voice she didn't like. One that made it seem impossible that he was doing anything but indulging her, with no intention whatsoever of keeping his promises.

But there was no point debating possibilities. And her head hurt too much anyway. Susannah didn't respond. She rubbed at her temples instead, listening to the music her bracelets made as they jangled on her wrist.

"If you continue to get these headaches, I think you should see the doctor," Leonidas murmured after a moment. In that way of his that would have made an apology sound like a command.

Not that Susannah could imagine this man apologizing for anything. Ever.

"I don't need a doctor to tell me that I'm under stress," Susannah said tautly. "Or that what I need to recover from such stress is a solitary retreat. Far, far away the intrigue and drama of the Betancur Corporation."

For once, Leonidas did not respond in kind. Instead, he reached over and took her hand in his. And Susannah wanted to pull it back instantly, rip her hand from his so that she wouldn't have to sit there and fight the surging sensation that rolled through her at even so small a touch.

As if they were naked again. As if he was braced above her and thrusting deep inside her—

That was what bothered her most about this extra and intense time with him.

She didn't hate him. She wasn't disgusted with him or even disinterested. On the contrary, she continued to find her husband entirely too fascinating by half. And every time he touched her, it set off the same chain reaction. Sometimes he took her elbow as they walked down a hall or through a press gauntlet. Sometimes he helped her in or out of the car, his hand so strong around hers she imagined he could use it to lift her straight off the ground if he chose. Sometimes he touched the small of her back as they entered the room, as if he was guiding her before him. It didn't matter what he did, how utterly innocuous it was—gestures knit together by old-world manners and inbred politeness, meaningless in their way.

And yet every single time his body touched hers, Susannah…ignited.

She felt it at the point of contact first, like a burst of bright light. Then it rolled through her, making her breasts feel heavy and aflame at once. Making the blood in her veins feel sluggish. And then all of that heavy ache and thick sweetness spiraled around and around, sinking down through her until it pooled deep in her belly. Low and hot and maddening, there between her legs.

She comforted herself with the knowledge that no matter what, Leonidas had no idea what he did to her. He couldn't. Of course he couldn't, because she went to such lengths to hide it. And soon she would be far away from him and only she would ever know the true depths of her own weakness.

But as the brilliant lights of central Paris danced over his bent head from beyond the car windows, as he held her hand between his and she felt as bright as the ancient city shimmering in the rain all around her, there was a shuddering part of her that wondered if any of that was strictly the truth.

Maybe he did know. Maybe he knew exactly what he did to her, just as he'd known exactly how to touch her back in that compound…

Not that she cared, because he was pressing his big, clever fingers into her palm.

"What are you doing?" she managed to ask, and assured herself he'd think the catch in her voice was from her headache, not him.

"I was taught that massaging pressure points eases headaches," Leonidas said with gruff certainty. More to her hand than her, she thought, dispassionate and distant, like a doctor. But then he glanced up to catch her gaze, a little smile flirting with his mesmerizingly hard mouth, and her heart slammed at her.

It took her a few moments to collect herself long enough to recognize that he was right. That the pain in her temples was receding.

"Your family obviously taught you more useful things than mine ever did," she said without thinking. "My mother believes in suffering, as she'd be the first to tell you."

"My father was a mean old bastard who relished the pain of others." Leonidas's voice was matter-of-fact. He exchanged one hand for the other, pressing down into her palm and alleviating the pain almost instantly when he did. "Particularly mine, as he told me every time he beat me bloody, which he did with great relish and regularity until I got too big at sixteen, at which point, he switched to psychological warfare. And you've met my mother. The only sort of pain Apollonia Betancur knows how to relieve comes back every morning-after when the night's intoxicants wear off."

Susannah was very still, and not only because he was still holding her hand with his. But because of that searing, dark undercurrent in his voice that told her exactly what it must have been like to be born a Betancur. And not just any Betancur, ushered into a life of privilege from the first breath, but the heir to the whole of the Betancur kingdom whether he liked it or not.

Of course they'd beaten it into him. How else would these people do anything? She already knew they were monsters.

But she also knew her husband well enough by now to know that he would hate it if she expressed anything like sympathy for the childhood he'd survived, somehow.

"I was glad they sent me away to that school when I was small," Susannah said softly. So softly he could ignore it if he wanted and better yet, she could pretend she wasn't saying it out loud at all. "For all that it was lonely, I think it was better than having to live with them."

But he didn't ignore her. "I wish they'd sent me away more than they did, but you see, there were a great many expectations of *the next Betancur* and none of them could be beaten into me while I was elsewhere."

Leonidas was no longer smiling when he let go of her hand and Susannah knew better, somehow, than to reach back over and touch him again the way everything in her wanted to do—and not with a meaningless little gesture. He looked carved from rock, as impossible as a distant mountain, and she wanted to…comfort him, somehow. Care for him. Do *something* to dispel the dark grip that seemed to squeeze tight around the both of them.

But she didn't dare put a finger on this man.

She kept her hands from curling into impotent fists by flattening them on her own lap.

"My headache is gone," she told him. "Thank you. You are a miracle worker, no matter where you learned it."

"The benefits of living off the grid, far away in the woods and high up on a mountaintop," he told her after a moment, when she'd thought he might not speak at all. "No one can run out to the nearest pharmacy to fetch some tablets every time someone feels a bit of pain. We learned other methods."

"I'm stunned," she managed to say. And she was aware as she spoke that she didn't sound nearly as calm as she should have. "I would have thought it would cause a full-scale revolt if you'd healed someone with anything other than the force of your holiness."

Leonidas let out only a small laugh, but to Susannah it sounded like nothing less than a victory parade.

"It's possible I was a terrible disappointment as a resident god," he said, his voice rich with something it took her entirely too long to realize was humor. At his own expense, no less. And she felt that like a new, different sort of touch. "But in the habit of most gods, I will choose not to inquire."

And it was lucky Susannah didn't have to summon up a response, she thought as the car pulled up to the entrance of the desperately chic Betancur Hotel. They had to get out of the car and acknowledge the waiting paparazzi. She had to steel herself against Leonidas's hand at her back when she'd barely survived the car ride over. And still, she could only count her good fortune that she was able to stand and walk at all—because the sound of real laughter in her husband's dark voice was enough to make her knees feel weak.

She was very much afraid of the things she might have said—or worse, done—if that car ride had lasted another moment.

And none of that could happen, because she wasn't staying. Not only wasn't she staying, she needed to hurry up her departure, she told herself as they walked into the hotel in a flurry of flashbulbs and the typical shouting of their names. The lobby was a riot of color, golds and marbles and sultry onyxes, but all Susannah could see with any clarity was Leonidas as he led her to the grand ballroom.

She needed to hurry up and leave before she couldn't. She needed to go before she found herself addicted to these small moments with him and stayed. Like an addict forever chasing that dragon and never, ever finding it.

"You look appropriately somber at the prospect of a long night with my family and all their works," Leonidas said as they made their way toward the gala, smiling and nodding at Europe's elite as they passed in the gilded hallways.

Susannah let out a small laugh. "I can handle your family. It's mine that makes me anxious."

"I don't remember much about our wedding," he said then, angling a look down at her as they reached the doors of the ballroom. She thought she could see too much in his gaze, that was the trouble. She thought there was more in all that dark gold than there was or ever could be.

And Susannah didn't understand where the forced calm she'd wielded like a sword these last years had gone. She only knew it had deserted her completely tonight.

"I don't think that's the memory loss acting up again," she said quietly, but not at all as calmly as she'd have liked. "I think it's that you didn't much care."

"I didn't care at all," Leonidas agreed, and whatever had afflicted her, she thought it was gnawing at him, too. And there was no reason that should bring her any sort of comfort. What did it matter what happened between them? This was temporary. This had to be temporary. "But I remember you. And your mother."

"Mother prides herself on being memorable, but only for the correct reasons. Namely that she is Europe's foremost gorgon."

She'd meant that to be funny. But her words hung there between them, and even Susannah could tell that they were something else entirely.

The hand at her back smoothed down an inch or two, then rose again. And all the while, Leonidas's gaze was fixed to hers as if he could see every last part of her. Because of course, he knew what it had been like to come of age in that chilly, remote boarding school, aware at all times that her only use to her parents was as a pawn to further their ambitions. To have no sense of *family* the way others did. To be so utterly and terribly alone, always.

Until now, something in her whispered.

He knew exactly what that was like.

But she reminded herself harshly that there was no *now*. There was no *them*. Leonidas wasn't simply a Betancur, he was the worst of them. He was what happened when greed and ambition was chiseled over generations into aristocratic blood and entirely too much power. If inconceivably wealthy families could create an avatar, Leonidas was the perfect choice to represent his. Hard and dark and utterly lethal.

And now risen from the dead, as if he needed to add to his mystique.

She told herself these things over and over, until it was like cold water in her face.

But it didn't change the way he'd touched her. Or the fact that somehow, the worst of the Betancurs—her husband—had managed to comfort her when no one else could. Or ever had.

Or had bothered to try.

Somehow he'd managed to soothe her on the night of the annual gala, when Susannah was used to facing nothing but fanged smiles and knives to the back all around. She would have said it was impossible.

"Ready, then?" he asked, in that low voice that did upsetting things to her pulse. And that look in his eyes was worse. It made something deep inside her melt.

"Ready," she said, as briskly as she could, but it didn't stop the melting.

Susannah was beginning to think nothing could. That she'd been doomed since the moment she'd walked up that mountain in farthest Idaho and had demanded to see the man they called the Count.

That the Count had been easier, because he'd simply kissed her. Taken her. Done as he wished. Which had allowed her to pretend that under other circumstances, she'd have resisted him.

When what these weeks had taught her was that she didn't want to resist this man, no matter what he called himself.

Leonidas inclined his head and offered her his arm, and Susannah took it. And for the first time since they'd entered their wedding reception four years ago, she entered a glittering, gleaming ballroom packed to the chandeliers above with the toast of Europe not as the rigidly composed, much-hated, always solitary Widow Betancur.

This time, she was no more and no less than Leonidas's wife.

And he was right there with her.

CHAPTER SEVEN

THAT SUSANNAH WAS used to the endless pageant and conspiratorial drama of the Betancur clan was immediately obvious to Leonidas—and likely to the whole of the gala, he thought as he stood near the high table some time later, because she remained so composed in the face of their antics.

He was the one having some trouble adjusting to life back in the fold.

Only a scant handful of his relatives actually stirred themselves to do anything resembling work, of course, so he hadn't seen much of them since his return as he'd been focused on the company and getting up to speed on everything he'd missed. But this was a widely publicized, celebrity-studded charity ball where they could all do what they liked best: lounge about in pretty clothes, exchange vicious gossip, and carry on theatrical affairs with whoever struck their fancies—from lowly valets to exalted kings as it suited them. Usually in full view of their spouses and the press.

Leonidas was used to the offhanded debauchery his cousins practiced with such delight. He remembered it all in excruciating detail when really, his cousins' behavior was something he'd happily have forgotten.

The Betancurs gathered the way they always did at

functions like this one, sulky and imperious in turn, making Leonidas wish he could rule here as he'd done in the compound. His cousins usually did as he asked because it was bad for their bank accounts to get on his bad side, but only after great productions of pointless defiance. Meanwhile, Apollonia held court the way she liked to do, carrying on about *her only child's* return from death when it suited her, and then ignoring him entirely when it amused her to harangue the guests instead, likely in search of her next lover.

That his mother valued only the fact that she'd borne him because of the access that granted her to the Betancur fortune and consequence should no longer have had the power to hurt him. He'd gotten over that when he was still a boy, he would have said. But it rubbed at him tonight even so.

"It would not kill her to at least put on a decent show of maternal devotion, surely," he said in an undertone to Susannah at one point.

And then asked himself what the hell he was doing. The woman wasn't his friend. She wasn't even his date. She was the wife he'd never wanted who, it turned out, didn't want him, either. Whatever else she was—including the only woman he could recall being so obsessed with it was becoming an issue he feared his own hand wouldn't cure—she was certainly no confidante.

"This is no show, it's what Apollonia's maternal devotion looks like," Susannah replied in that cool way of hers that he found he liked entirely too much, all smooth vowels and that little kick of archness besides. She stood beside him as they watched his mother berate a minor duchess, and Leonidas tried to channel a measure of her untroubled amusement. "It is only that she is devoted to herself, not you."

And that was the trouble, Leonidas knew. He'd been on that mountain too long, perhaps. But he hadn't expected to *like* the sweet little virgin his mother had insisted he marry to best honor his late father's wishes that the stodgy Martin Forrester be recognized for his hard work in turning at least three small Betancur fortunes into remarkably large ones, and then adding to them every year. Even from beyond the grave, his father's orders carried the weight of his fists.

But it had not occurred to Leonidas to revolt. Not then.

"Besides," Apollonia had said while sunning herself on one of the family yachts as the Côte d'Azur gleamed in the distance, some years before his wedding, "it will make you look more relatable."

"I hope not." Leonidas had been reading complicated work emails on his mobile instead of waiting attendance on his mother, but that was when he'd still shown up when she'd called—when he'd still felt some measure of obligation. "Why would I wish to relate to anyone?"

"Most men in your position marry cadaverous actresses or shriveled little heiresses, all of whom are notable chiefly for the breadth of their promiscuity," Apollonia had told him, glaring at him over the top of her oversize sunglasses. If the fact that she had been a Greek heiress with something of a reputation when his father had met her years ago struck her as at all ironic, she didn't show it. "This one is a merchant's daughter, which makes you look benevolent and down-to-earth for choosing her, and better yet, she's a guaranteed vestal virgin. People will admire you for your keen character judgment in choosing someone so spotless, and better yet, you won't be forced to make desultory chitchat with every man who's been beneath her skirts."

In truth, Leonidas hadn't expected to spend much time

with her at all. What access he had to the offhanded memories of the man he'd been back then assured him that he'd envisioned a comfortably Continental sort of arrangement with his new wife. He'd assumed they'd handle the matter of his heirs as quickly and painlessly as possible, appear at an agreed-upon number of social events together each season, and otherwise retreat to whichever Betancur properties they preferred to live out their lives as they saw fit, with as many lovers as they could handle as long as they were reasonably discreet about it.

This was the world they'd both grown up in. People organized their lives around money, not emotion.

But Leonidas found that as he watched his spotless wife navigate the toothsome sharks masquerading as the crème de la crème of Europe—to say nothing of the far more unpredictable members of his own family—he hated it. All of it.

The notion that they were destined to end up like all these people here tonight, full of Botox and emptiness. The idea that she was one of them, this forthright creature with the cool smile and the faraway eyes. Even the faintest possibility that the woman who'd gazed at him as if he'd cured her outside these very doors tonight could ever become a master manipulator like his own mother.

He hated this.

He was nothing like these parasites any longer. That was the trouble. The compound had changed him whether he liked to believe that or not. The Count had believed in something—and no matter if it was crazy, Leonidas couldn't seem to get past the fact that he didn't.

He'd done what was expected of him. But did he know what he wanted?

Susannah wasn't like the vultures in this hard, brittle world either, he reminded himself fiercely. She'd told him who he was and given him the one thing he'd never had in his whole life of excess. Her innocence. As a gift, not a bargaining chip.

In fact, unlike every other person he'd ever known, in this life or the one he'd thought was his for four years across the planet, she hadn't bartered with it. She hadn't even mentioned it, before or since. If he didn't know better—if he couldn't see her reaction every time his hand brushed hers—he might have thought he'd imagined the whole thing.

Most people he met used whatever they had as leverage to make him do something for them. Give them power, money, prestige, whatever. In the compound, access to the Count had been doled out like currency. It was no different in the Betancur Corporation. There was literally nothing people wouldn't do to get a piece of him.

Susannah was the only person he'd ever met who didn't appear to want anything from him.

And he found he could think of very little else but keeping her, whether she wanted to stay or not.

"What a glorious resurrection," his cousin Silvio interjected then, smiling to cover the sharpness in his voice and failing miserably as he came to stand beside Leonidas. Yet his gaze rested on Susannah. "You must be so happy to have your beloved husband back, Susannah. After you mourned him so fiercely and for so long."

Leonidas understood from his cousin's tone, and Susannah's deliberately cool response, that Silvio had been one of the cousins desperate to marry her himself. To take control of the Betancur Corporation, of course—but it was more than that. Leonidas could see it all over Silvio. It was Susannah herself. She got under a man's skin.

But the only man who had touched her—*or ever will*, something dark in him growled—was him.

You agreed to let her go, he reminded himself. *Who does or doesn't touch her has nothing to do with you.*

He jerked his attention away from Silvio and looked around at the rest of his assembled family instead. His few remaining aunts were clutching wineglasses like life vests and muttering to each other beneath pasted-on smiles. His single living uncle stood with a cluster of Italian celebrities, yet looked as dour as ever.

The rest of the cousins were up to their usual tricks. Gilded swans with murder in their eyes, they all smiled to Leonidas's face, exclaimed over Susannah when they could get her attention, and hardly bothered to do him the courtesy of hiding their plotting behind a polite hand.

And Silvio wasn't the only one who'd sniffed around Susannah, right in front of Leonidas. He might have thought it was nothing more than a test to see exactly what sort of marriage he and Susannah had—but he saw the way they looked at her. He knew that every last one of them would die to get his hands on her if they could.

The frostier she was, the more they wanted her.

The trouble was, so did he.

His entire family would be ridiculous if they weren't so dangerous at times, Leonidas thought as the night wore on. Some more than others, lest he forget that at least one of the sleek relatives smiling his way tonight was more than just teeth. One of them had arranged for that plane to go down.

He'd seen the reports that had led Susannah to his compound. He knew as much as she did—that the plane had been tampered with. He didn't have to cast around for a reason when he was the head of the family, the CEO and president of the company, and he was related to all these jealous snakes. He was sure it had made perfect sense to one of the jackals he called cousin to get rid of him before he could have his own children and complicate matters—and their own fortunes—even further.

It almost didn't matter which one it had been.

"Are you enjoying all this family time?" he asked Susannah during a lull in the forced family interactions.

"Are they a family, then?" she asked, but there was a smile in her blue eyes and that eased the weight in his chest he'd hardly noticed was there. "I rather thought I was being feasted upon by a pool of piranhas."

"Never fear," Leonidas said darkly. "I haven't forgotten that one of them wished me dead. Or I should amend that. I assume they all wish me dead. But I also assume that only one of them acted on that wish."

She tipped her head to one side, still smiling. "Can you really make such an assumption? They do seem to like gathering in groups."

"Indeed they do." Leonidas inclined his head toward his aunts, who had gone from conspiratorial whispers to gritted teeth and eye daggers, visible from halfway across the ballroom. "But teamwork is not exactly a Betancur family strength."

Susannah laughed, which Leonidas enjoyed entirely too much, but then stopped abruptly. As if it had been snuffed out of her. He followed her gaze across the room and found an older couple entering the room. The woman was tall and thin, with a haughtily sour look on her face, as if she'd smelled something foul—and continued to smell it as she swept in. The man was much rounder and wreathed in as many mustaches as chins, looking so much like a staid, plush banker that Leonidas would have guessed that finance was the man's trade even if he hadn't recognized the pair of them on sight.

Susannah's parents. His in-laws.

And his wife looked about as happy to see them as he was.

The older couple picked Susannah out of the crowd and started toward her as the band began to play again after a short interval. And to Leonidas's surprise, Susannah grabbed his arm.

"We must dance, of course," she said, sounding almost offhand when he could see that frantic gleam in her gaze.

"*Can* I dance?" he asked mildly, looking down at her. And the way she was still watching her parents approach as if she expected them to strike her down where she stood. "Or is it only that I do not wish to?"

That penetrated. She blinked, then frowned at him.

"Of course you can dance," she told him, with only a hint of frost. He admired her restraint. "You were taught as a boy, like every other member of your social class. And mine."

"I can't remember one way or the other, but I feel certain I detest dancing."

"Luckily for you, I can remember that you love it." She smiled at him, and no matter that it was a touch overlarge. "Adore it, in fact."

Leonidas did not adore dancing by any stretch of the imagination. But he'd walked into that one, he was aware.

"You cannot possibly wish to dance with me in front of so many people," he said as if they had all the time in the world to have this conversation. As if her parents weren't bearing down on them even now. And what was the matter with him that he vastly preferred her family troubles to his own? "How will you possibly extricate yourself from this marriage when there will be so many witnesses to our romantic waltz on this, our first night in society since my return?"

"That is a sacrifice I'm willing to make," she replied

sweetly. "Because you love dancing so much, and *of course* I want to help you return to the life you were denied all this time."

Leonidas eyed her, and tried to keep his lips from twitching. "You are too good to me. Especially when you have so little experience with formal dancing. To think, you could make a fool of yourself so easily."

Her sweet smile took on an edge. "I know how to dance, thank you."

"You can't possibly have practiced since you were in school. What if you've forgotten all you learned?"

"I don't know why you imagine yourself an expert on my dancing prowess," Susannah said loftily, "but for all you know I danced all night and day while you were gone."

"While draped in black shrouds to honor my memory? I doubt it." He smiled at her then, a bit lazily, and was astonished to realize that he was enjoying himself for the first time since he'd entered this ballroom and started wading through too many vipers to count. "As far as I can tell, that means the only real dance partner you have ever had is me. At our wedding."

He didn't know why he said it that way—as if he was staking a claim on her where they stood. Or why she took his simple statement of fact so seriously, her blue eyes turning solemn as she regarded him. That odd electricity that had nearly been his undoing in the car earlier, then again at the ballroom doors, coursed through him again then. Making him think that if he didn't touch her right now he might char himself from the inside out.

But he managed to keep his hands to himself.

"I said *you* love to dance," she said after a moment, and the smile she aimed at him then wasn't a fake one, all polite savagery. It was real. Wry and teasing and *real*.

And all theirs, here in a ballroom that might as well have been a goldfish bowl. "I didn't say I enjoyed it, only that I could. You know how it is. A single bad experience can ruin the whole thing and then you're left with a lifetime aversion."

"I'll assume we're still talking about dancing," Leonidas said mildly.

She laughed then, and Leonidas couldn't help himself. He told himself he was indulging her, but he had the sinking suspicion that really, he was indulging himself.

He took her hand in his and he led her out into the middle of the crowded dance floor, ignoring the couples who parted to let them through—as much to gawk at them as to show them any consideration, he knew. He didn't care. Just as he didn't care that she was melting into him and holding on to him not because she was as wild with need as he was—or not only because of that—but because she wanted to avoid unpleasant conversations with her own parents.

She was doing this only because it was easier. He understood that. It was a way to hide in plain sight, right out there in the middle of the dance floor, looking for all the world like a fairy tale come to life. The Lazarus Betancur and his lovely bride, at last. It provided the damned optics she loved so much, and in as perfect a form as possible.

But when Leonidas pulled her into his arms, bent his head to meet and hold her gaze, and then began to move—none of that seemed to matter.

There was nothing but the music, then. The music and the woman in his arms, the whisper of her rich green gown and those blue eyes of hers like whole summers in the sort of simpler times he'd never known. There was nothing but Susannah and the way she gazed up at him, the same way she had that day in the compound when he'd been so deep inside her he hadn't cared what his name was.

It was almost too much to bear.

He was used to waking up in the middle of the night with wildfire dreams of those delirious, delicious moments in the compound storming all over him like some kind of attack. She'd touched him a thousand times since then in those dreams, glutting herself on the hardest part of him, and even better, letting him take his time with her. Again and again, until she fell apart the way she had then.

And he woke every time to find himself alone.

He was used to handling his hunger as best he could, with his hand in the shower and the ferocity of his self-control throughout all the hours they spent together every day. But the scent of her skin was imprinted on him now. The sound her legs made when she slid one over the other to cross them. The sweetness of her breath against his neck when she leaned in to whisper something to him in a meeting.

This was something else. This was holding her against him, as if in an embrace, and for all that it was formal and right there in full view of so many, that was what it felt like.

The kind of embrace Leonidas didn't want to end. Ever.

And even as alarms went off inside him at that, at a notion so foreign to him, Leonidas couldn't bring himself to pull away as he knew he should have. He didn't do what he knew he should. The truth was, he feared he'd lost his sanity a long time ago and the only person who had tried to save him—from the compound, from himself, from that wall between him and his memories—was Susannah.

Then she'd surrendered herself to him, and he couldn't seem to get past that.

She'd given him a gift and yet somehow he felt as if she owned him. Stranger still, he didn't mind the feeling when he knew—he *knew*—everything in him ought to have rebelled at the very notion.

He couldn't find the words to tell her that. He wasn't certain he would have said anything even if he could. Instead, he danced.

They danced and they danced. Leonidas swept her from one side of the ballroom to the other, then back again. Whether he could remember how to dance or not was immaterial, because his body certainly knew what to do while he held her. And then did it well.

And all the while he held her in his arms and against his chest as if she was precious. As if she was everything.

As if she was his.

"Susannah…" he said, his voice low and urgent.

But there was something else in her gaze then. Something more than blue heat and longing. She swallowed, hard, and he watched as emotion moved over her face, then made her generous mouth tremble.

She looked miserable.

And Leonidas was such a bastard it only made him hold her tighter.

"You promised," she whispered, and he shouldn't have found a kind of solace in the catch in her voice. "You promised me that this was only temporary."

"Susannah," he said again, and there was an intensity to his own voice that he didn't want to recognize. "You must know—"

"I need this to end," she told him, cutting him off.

Her voice was like a blow, and he didn't know how

she could have spoken so softly when it felt as if she'd hauled off and struck him. Hard.

He told himself he was grateful.

The things he saw in her eyes were not for him. He was a Betancur. The worst of them, according to Susannah. The high king of the vipers, and nothing would ever change that. Not his so-called death and resurrection.

Not her.

"Of course," he said stiffly, all cut glass and stone. "You need only ask."

"Leonidas," she whispered then, her blue eyes filling with a different emotion he didn't want to see. He could feel it in the way her fingers dug into his shoulder and her hand clenched in his. "Leonidas, you have to understand—"

"I don't," he told her, and he willed himself to stone. To granite. To something impenetrable, even to a woman like this, who still smelled like innocence and still gazed at him like he might really be a god after all. "I don't have to understand anything. We had a deal. Even the worst of the Betancurs can keep his word, Susannah, I assure you."

She flinched at that. "I didn't mean that."

"I think we both know you did. Every word." He stopped moving, holding her against his chest as if he was turning the dance into something else, right there beneath the riot of chandeliers where everyone could see them. Her green dress pooled around his legs, and he had the fleeting thought that he was the one drowning. *Steel*, he ordered himself. *Stone*. "I am everything you think I am and worse, little one. I will eat you alive and enjoy every bite. Running away from me and this cesspool I call my business and family is the best thing you could possibly do."

"Leonidas, please."

"You were my widow for four years," he said with a quiet ferocity that left marks inside him with every word. "All I need is a few more hours. Can you do that?"

She looked helpless and he knew who he was then. Not that he'd been in any doubt. Because he liked it.

"Of course. And this doesn't have to end *tonight*. It just has to end."

Leonidas did nothing to contain himself then. The wildness in him. The darkness he feared might be lethal. The need and the hunger and all the things he wanted to do to her, all wrapped up in that howling thing that didn't want to let her go. That wanted more.

That *wanted*.

He knew exactly what he wanted tonight.

"It will be tonight," he growled at her, still holding her too close against him. "Or not at all. The choice is yours. But once you make it, Susannah, there's no going back. I am not a forgiving man no matter what identity I wear. Do you understand me?"

He could see her nostrils widen and her pupils dilate. He saw her pulse go mad in her neck. There was a faint flush turning her skin hot and red at once, and she wasn't doing a particularly good job of restraining her shudders.

But she didn't speak. It was as if she knew better. As if she knew exactly what it would do to him—to them both—if she did.

Instead she nodded once. Jerkily. Her gaze fixed to his as if she didn't dare look away.

And without another word, Leonidas turned and led her from the dance floor, like the gentleman he wasn't, not anymore.

Before he threw her over his shoulder and carted her

off to his lair, the way he wanted to do more than he wanted to draw his next breath.

And might do still, he told himself grimly.

The night was young.

CHAPTER EIGHT

SUSANNAH HAD FORGOTTEN about her parents.

The truth was, Leonidas had taken her into his arms and she'd forgotten everything. The charity ball all around them. The fact they were the furthest thing from alone. That there were smiling business rivals and leering paparazzi and everything in between, with his family's treachery and the inevitable appearance of her own parents, just to make everything that much more fraught.

It had all disappeared.

There was nothing but Leonidas. The music soaring and dancing along with them. And all the sweet and terrible things that swelled between them, making it entirely too hard to breathe.

She'd felt this way only once before, and it had been far more muted in comparison. What kept racing through her like a different sort of heat was that she was positive Leonidas knew it.

She had been such a confused jumble of feelings on their wedding day. She'd still had such high, silly expectations, of course, no matter how many chilly lectures her parents had given her to prepare her—but he had taken the knees out of each and every one of them. She'd been trembling as she'd walked down the aisle, but the cool, assessing look he'd given her when he'd swept back her veil hadn't assuaged her nerves any. And then when he'd pressed a kiss to her mouth at the front of the church, it had been little more than a stamp of acknowledgment. As if he was affixing a halfhearted seal to one of his lesser possessions. The things he said to her in the car, the way he'd called her a child, had rocked her. And his total disinterest in her at their own reception, too busy was he talking to his business associates, had hurt her feelings more than she'd wanted to admit even then.

A wise girl would have armored herself a little after all these clear indications that this man did not and would not care about her, and she'd tried. Susannah really had tried—but she'd been so young. So frothy and silly, looking back.

But then there had been that dance. That single dance. When Leonidas had held her in his arms and gazed down at her, something arrested and yet stern on his face that seemed to match the wildfire raging inside her. There had been nothing in all the world but the feel of his intensely strong arms around her and the easy way he'd moved her around the floor, as if he was giving her a preview of the way their life would go. Him, in complete control. Her, a little too captivated by the way he handled her and everything else.

And all of it distressingly breathless and dizzyingly smooth.

She shouldn't remember it the way she did, in vivid and excruciating detail. And it certainly shouldn't have played out in her head the way it had all these years, over and over. That dance had made her wonder about him, the man she'd lost so swiftly, more than she'd ever admitted to anyone. It had made her wonder what would have happened between them if they'd ever had a proper wedding night. If he hadn't gotten on that plane.

Now she knew.

And this dance tonight had made her heart hurt all over again, if for different reasons. Because she knew too much now. She knew him and she knew herself and she knew that no matter how precarious it all felt when she was in his arms or how badly she wanted to stay there, she had to go.

Or she wouldn't.

She was still sorting through the clamor inside her as Leonidas led her from the dance floor. His hand was still wrapped around hers, all that fire and strength making her feel entirely too hot and something achy besides. And Susannah knew she needed to jerk her hand away and step away from her husband.

Now.

Before she spent any more time noticing how perfectly her hand fit in his and how the enveloping heat of it seemed to wrap itself around her and hold tight—

But before she could do the right thing, they stepped into the throng and the first people she saw were her parents.

Her parents, who had not supported Susannah's transformation from biddable pawn into powerful widow—because they couldn't control her and oh, how they'd hated that. They'd urged her to remarry with all possible haste, preferably to a man of their choosing, and hadn't liked it when she'd told them that one marriage of convenience was enough, thank you. They hadn't much cared for it when she'd ignored their arguments in favor of various suitors anyway.

They'd liked it least of all when she'd stopped taking their calls.

"You ungrateful child!" her father had boomed at her only a few months back when she'd refused to attend a dinner party he was throwing, where he'd wanted to use her presence to impress some of his associates as all things Betancur did, and Susannah had foolishly allowed her assistant to connect his call. "You wouldn't be where you are if not for me!"

"If I'd listened to you I would have married Leonidas's dour old uncle when he demanded it three years ago," she'd replied, happy all of Europe sat between her and her parents' home outside London. "Somehow, I can live with the consequences of the choice I made."

The conversation had disintegrated from there.

But invitations to the Betancur Ball were highly prized and fought over across the world, and there was no keeping her own parents off the list. What Susannah couldn't believe was that somehow she'd forgotten they'd be coming tonight.

You've been so consumed with Leonidas you hardly know your own name, she accused herself. And she knew it was true.

It was one more reason she had to put distance between them. Because she knew all too well that the day was fast approaching when she wouldn't want to do anything of the kind, and then she might as well lock herself away in a tower somewhere before he grew bored of her and did it himself.

Leonidas came to a stop before her parents, and Susannah didn't know if it was because he recognized them or simply because they dared to block his path.

"You remember my parents, of course," Susannah said for his benefit. She thought perhaps Leonidas was lucky to forget so many things. She'd like to forget her parents herself. Particularly on a night like tonight when she knew that they'd come with every intention of cutting her down to size. Right here in public where she was unlikely to make a scene or even respond too harshly.

Leonidas inclined his head, but said nothing when Susannah slipped her arm through his. She felt the dark gaze he slid her way, but he still said nothing, so she moved closer to him as if she intended to use him as a human shield.

Perhaps she did.

"Your husband has been resurrected from the dead," her mother said coolly instead of condescending to offer a conventional greeting to either her daughter or the man whose funeral she'd attended. "I don't think it's unreasonable to have expected a call, Susannah. Or was it your intention that your only flesh and blood should learn of this miracle in the press like everyone else?"

"What my mother means to say, Leonidas," Susannah said in mild reproof, her gaze on her mother, "is 'welcome home.'"

Leonidas gave her another swift, dark look she thought was a little too much like a glare, but he didn't say anything. He certainly didn't indicate that their relationship had effectively ended just moments before on the dance floor.

Instead, he smiled in that way he did sometimes, that made it seem as if he was bestowing a great gift upon the receiver, and then he shook her father's hand. The two men started one of those endlessly tedious masculine conversations that purported to be about business and was in fact a clever little game of one-upmanship, which left Susannah to her mother's manicured talons.

But she still held tight to Leonidas's arm.

"Imagine my surprise to discover that the tabloids knew more about my daughter's life than I did," Annemieke continued, and Susannah doubted anyone would be fooled by the little trill of laughter her mother let out as punctuation.

"Given that you and Father were exhorting me to remarry only a few months ago, I didn't think you would be the best person to take into my confidence on this matter."

Annemieke sniffed. "You knew he was alive all this time and yet you played your deceitful games. With everyone. You are a sneaky creature, aren't you?"

She raised her voice when she said it, because, of course, it was for Leonidas's benefit. And something swept over Susannah, hot and prickly. Because her mother didn't know that she was planning to leave this man who had only just returned to her. Her mother didn't have the slightest idea what their relationship was like. Even if she believed that Susannah had spent years knowing that Leonidas was alive and pretending otherwise, it was obvious they hadn't spent any time together. How could they have when the world thought he was dead and Susannah had been busy acting as the face of the Betancur Corporation?

Which meant her mother was deliberately trying to undermine Susannah in front of Leonidas. She *wanted* to malign Susannah in his eyes.

Of course she does, a voice deep inside Susannah said briskly, before that sad, silly part of her that always hoped her parents might act like parents despite years of never doing anything of the kind showed itself. *This is about power. Everything to all of these people is always,* always *about power.*

She'd had four years of it, and she was sick of it. More than sick of it. She could feel her aversion to the games these people played like a weight beneath her breastbone, doing its best to claw its way out.

But she refused to give her mother the satisfaction of seeing that she'd landed a blow.

"I haven't been feeling well," Susannah said as evenly as possible, before her mother could start in again with some new insult. "I keep getting terrible headaches. I suppose it's possible that the emotion of Leonidas's return has got to me more than I might have thought."

Leonidas moved beside her, letting her know that he was paying attention to her conversation as well as his own. She instantly regretted using the word *emotion* where he could hear it. And she hated that she was holding on to him in the first place. She'd been handling far more intense scenes than this all by herself for years. He didn't need to do anything to support her.

But before she could put the distance between them she should have, he shifted where he stood and then slid his hand to the small of her back as if they weren't strangers who happened to be married to each other, but a unit.

Suddenly Susannah was afraid of the emotions she could feel slopping around inside her as if they might flood her, then carry her away, if she gave in to a single one of them.

She needed to stop this. She needed to escape this gilded, vicious world while she still could.

And she needed to leave soon, before she forgot the way out.

Something in her whispered that the line was coming faster than she wanted to admit—and if she wasn't careful, she'd cross it without realizing it.

"Resurrection is a tricky business," Leonidas was saying to her mother, merging their two conversations into one.

"It could be that, I suppose," Annemieke said with a

sniff. "Though Susannah has never been a sickly thing, all fainting spells and fragility."

"This is where she calls me 'sturdy,' which is never a compliment," Susannah murmured, not quite under her breath.

Annemieke swept a look over her daughter, from her head all the way to her toes and then back again, in that pointedly judgmental way that always left Susannah feeling lacking. More than lacking.

Susannah reminded herself that she didn't send time with her parents for a reason. After tonight it would likely be months and months before she had to face them again and by then, who knew where she'd be? If she was divorced from Leonidas the way she planned, it was entirely likely that her parents would want nothing to do with her.

If she kept that happy day in mind, tonight didn't seem so bad. And there was no point indulging the part of her that went a bit too still at the notion of leaving Leonidas when she could feel all that warmth and strength from the hand he held at her back. No point at all.

She made herself smile. "It's only a little headache now and then," she said. "I'm sure I just need to drink more water."

"I only suffered from headaches once and it was very unpleasant." Her mother lifted a brow, and there was a gleam in the blue eyes she'd passed on to her daughter that Susannah did not like at all. "It was when I was pregnant."

And Susannah didn't hear if there was any conversation after that point, because everything seemed to… stop. Leonidas went very, very still beside her. His hand didn't move, and she suddenly felt it less as moral support and more like a threat. A terrible threat she should have heeded from the start.

A dark foreboding she wanted to reject swept over her. But she couldn't seem to speak, not even to deny what she knew—*she knew*—was completely false.

Especially not when she could feel all that lethal power emanating from the man beside her. The husband who had agreed to let her leave—but he was a Betancur. There wasn't a Betancur in six generations who'd been *laissez faire* about the family bloodline, and somehow she very much doubted that Leonidas would be the first.

Not that she was pregnant, of course, because she couldn't be.

She *couldn't* be.

"I'm nothing like my mother," she told him fiercely when he made their excuses in a gruff tone and led her away, his hand wrapped tight around her upper arm as if he expected her to bolt. "I never have been. I don't even look like her. It's ridiculous to assume that we would share anything."

He didn't stop moving through the crowd, inexorable and swift, towing her toward the doors though the party was still in full swing.

"Everyone gets headaches, Leonidas," she gritted out at him from between her teeth. "There's no need to jump to dramatic conclusions. It's as likely to be a brain tumor as it is that I'm pregnant."

But Leonidas only threw her a dark, glittering sort of look that made everything in her pull tight and then shiver. He didn't reply, he just slipped his phone from his pocket with his free hand, hit a button, then put it to his ear and kept walking.

Sweeping her along with him whether she liked it or not.

And everything after that seemed to happen much too fast, as if she was watching her own life catapult off the side of a cliff in front of her.

Leonidas whisked her from the ballroom without seeming to care overmuch that they had been expected to stay for the whole of the gala. He didn't even bother to make their excuses to his family. He had her in the back of his car and headed back to the soaring townhome he kept in Paris's Eighth Arrondissement, steps from the Avenue des Champs-élysées, without another word to her on the drive back.

And worse than that, when they arrived back in the glorious nineteenth-century dwelling in the sought-after Haussmann style, a doctor waited there in the foyer.

"This is ridiculous," Susannah all but sputtered, forgetting any pretense of calm, and who cared that the doctor was standing there as witness.

"Then it costs you nothing to indulge me," Leonidas replied, that same glittering thing in his gaze while he continued to hold the rest of his body so still.

As if he is lying in wait, something in her whispered. She repressed a shudder.

"I can't possibly be pregnant," she snapped at him.

"If you are so certain, you have even less reason to refuse."

Susannah realized he'd turned to stone. That there was no give in him at all. This was the Leonidas of stark commands and absolute power, not the man who'd touched her back, held her hand and made her heartbeat slow. She didn't understand how he could have both men inside him, but clearly he couldn't be both at the same time.

And she knew she'd surrendered to the inevitable—that it must have showed on her face—because the doctor smiled his apologies and led her from the room to take the test.

More astonishingly, she followed him.

Susannah had worked herself into a state by the time she found Leonidas again, waiting for her in his private salon filled with priceless antiques and bristling with evidence of the Bettencourt wealth at every turn. But she could hardly pay attention to that sort of thing when her life was slipping out of her grasp right there in front of her. He stood at the fireplace, one arm propped up on the mantel as he frowned at the flames, and he didn't turn to look at her when she came in.

"You are going to feel very silly," she told him. Through her teeth. And opted not to notice how absurdly attractive he looked without his coat and tie, his shirt unbuttoned at the neck so his scars showed. Or the way she melted inside at the sight of him, until she could feel that dangerous pulse between her legs. "This is embarrassing. That doctor will sell the story to every tabloid in Europe."

"I am not the least embarrassed," Leonidas replied, still not looking at her. "And if the good doctor dares, I will destroy him."

She felt dizzy at the mild tone he used, or perhaps it was the unmistakable ferocity beneath it. Either way, she took a few more steps into the salon and gripped the back of the nearest settee. She told herself it wasn't to keep her balance, because nothing was happening that should so unsettle her that she'd lose her footing. Because she wasn't pregnant. Her mother was waspish because she enjoyed it, but Susannah had long ago stopped listening to her when she was being provoking.

Leonidas would learn to do the same, she told herself piously.

Or not, a voice inside her remarked. *As you are so intent on leaving him.*

"I'm not pregnant, Leonidas," she said for the hundredth time, as if she could finally make it so if she said it fiercely enough. As if she might finally light upon the right tone that would make him listen.

Leonidas stood then. He turned from the mantel and regarded her for a moment in a manner that made every part of her shiver. And keep right on shivering.

"You are so certain, little one," he said after a moment. "But I can count."

Susannah flushed at that, as if he really had slapped her this time. She felt feverish, hot and then cold, and she gripped the high back of the settee so hard she could see her knuckles whiten in protest. She wanted to tear that damned Betancur sapphire off her finger and hurl it at him. She wanted to run down the grand staircase and out into the Paris streets, and keep on running until her legs gave out.

And while he stared at her, his gaze too dark and much too certain, she counted. The way she'd absolutely not done on the way here because it was impossible and she refused. But she did it now.

Seven weeks since that night in the compound and she hadn't bled in all that time. In fact, she couldn't remember the last time she had. It certainly hadn't been in the ten days before she'd left for Idaho to find him, because she would have remembered having to deal with that while pretending to everyone she knew that she was going anywhere but where she was really heading.

"I assumed this couldn't possibly be an issue," she said after a moment, aware she sounded more like her mother than herself. Harsh and accusing, and that was just to start. She couldn't imagine the expression on her face and wondered if she was more like her mother than she'd ever believed possible. "And I'm sure it won't be. But why didn't you make sure that something like this could never be in question?"

"Did you see a condom in that compound, Susannah? Because I did not. Perhaps I assumed you would be on birth control yourself."

"I find that hard to believe. I was the virgin in the scenario, not you."

"And I was a holy man who'd been on the top of a mountain for four years. How did I know how you'd spent your time out there in all that sin?"

"You're one to talk. My understanding is that the entire point of becoming a cult leader is to avail yourself of the buffet of attractive followers."

Leonidas smiled, and under the circumstances Susannah thought that scared her most of all.

"Did I not mention that I was entirely chaste that entire time?" His smile deepened, but it didn't touch his eyes. "Untouched and uninterested for four years. I have been entirely faithful to you throughout our marriage, Susannah. As you have been to me. Surely this is something to celebrate."

But she was sure that she could hear a steel door slamming shut as he said it.

"It was an accident," she said, but her voice was barely a whisper. "It didn't mean anything. It was only an accident."

And if he planned to answer beyond that enigmatic expression on his face, she would never know. Because that was when there was a discreet knock on the paneled door and the doctor stepped back into the room.

"Congratulations, *madame*, *monsieur*," the doctor said, nodding at each of them in turn while Susannah's breath caught in her throat. "The test is positive. You are indeed pregnant, as you suspected."

And this time, it was Susannah who turned to stone.

There was no other word to describe it. One moment she was standing there, furious and affronted and so very certain that this was all a mistake, and then the next she found herself a hard thing all the way through, as every part of her rejected the notion outright. Physically.

Because she couldn't possibly be pregnant.

But one hand crept around to slide over her belly and hold it, just in case.

She barely noticed when Leonidas escorted the doctor from the room. He could have been gone for hours. When he returned he shut the door behind him, enclosing them in the salon that had seemed spacious before, and that was when Susannah walked stiffly around the settee to sit on it.

Because she thought it was that or grow roots down into the black herringbone floor.

He crossed back to the fireplace and stood there again, watching her, while the silence grew fangs between them.

His dark, tawny gaze had changed, she noticed. It had gone molten. He still held himself still, though she could tell the difference in that, too. It was as if an electrical current ran through him now, charging the air all around him even while his mouth remained in an unsmiling line.

And he looked at her as if she was naked. Stripped. Flesh and bone with nothing left to hide.

"Is it so bad, then?" he asked in a mild sort of tone she didn't believe at all.

Susannah's chest was so heavy, and she couldn't tell if it was the crushing weight of misery or something far more dangerous. She held her belly with one hand as if it was already sticking out. As if the baby might start kicking at any second.

"The Betancur family is a cage," she told him, or the parquet floor beneath the area rug that stretched out in front of the fireplace, and it cost her to speak so precisely. So matter-of-factly. "I don't want to live in a cage. There must be options."

He seemed to grow darker as she watched, which she knew was impossible. It was a trick of the light, or the force of her reaction. He couldn't summon his own storm.

"What do you mean by that?" he asked, and this time there was something in his low, fierce voice that made her break out in goose bumps.

Everywhere.

"I have no idea," she said, sounding broken to her own ears.

Panic was so thick inside her that she was surprised she could breathe, much less speak, and scenarios drifted through her head, one more outlandish than the next. She could live abroad, in a country far from here, just her and the baby. So long as no one knew who they were or how to find them, they could live anywhere. She could raise a child in some protected mountain valley somewhere and learn how to farm—perhaps in Idaho, for a little symmetry, where it was apparently perfectly easy to disappear into the woods for years at a time. She could relocate to any number of distant, unfashionable cities she'd never seen and work in an anonymous office somewhere, raising her child as a single mother no different from all the rest.

"None?" The way Leonidas studied her did not make her goose bumps subside. She rubbed at her arms and wished she could stop that shivering thing down deep inside her. "No ideas at all?"

"Anything but this," she threw at him. "That's my idea."

"Define 'this,' please."

"*This*, damn you." She shook her head, only dimly aware that moisture leaked from her eyes as she did. "I've been a pawn in Betancur games for four years, and it's too long. I don't want to do it for the rest of my life. I certainly don't want to raise a child the way I was raised. Or worse, the way you were. This is a prison and if I don't want to live in it, I'm certain my child deserves better, too."

And she watched him change again, softening somehow without seeming to move. She didn't understand it. It wasn't as if it made him any less... Leonidas. But it was as if something in him loosened.

It occurred to her as she watched his subtle transformation that he might not have known what she'd meant by *options*.

Just as it occurred to her that it had never crossed her mind that she wouldn't keep her baby. She hadn't wanted to be pregnant, but the doctor had told her she was and all she'd thought about was escaping the Betancurs *with* her child.

She supposed that answered a question she hadn't known she had inside her. That she was already a better mother than her own, who had spent a memorable Christmas one year regaling Susannah with tales of how close she'd come to ending her pregnancy, so little had she wanted a child. Susannah had been twelve.

"You must know that I never wanted to let you go in the first place," Leonidas said now, drawing her attention back to him and that hooded, lethal way he was watching her from his place by the fire. And she should have been appalled by that. She should have railed against the idea. But instead there was something small and bright inside her, and it glowed. "I entertained the possibility because I owed you. You came to that mountain and you restored me to myself. I told myself the least I could do was grant you a wish. But you should know, Susannah, that there is no such possibility now."

He almost sounded sorrowful, but she knew better. She could see the glittering thing in his gaze, dark and possessive and very, very male.

"You might as well slam the cage door shut and throw away the key," she managed to get out past the constriction in her throat.

"I am not a cage," Leonidas said with quiet certainty. "The Betancur name has drawbacks, it is true, and most of them were at that gala tonight. But it is also not a cage. On the contrary. I own enough of the world that it is for all intents and purposes yours now. Literally."

"I don't want the world." She didn't realize she'd shot to her feet until she was taking a step toward him, very much as if she thought she might take a swing at him next. As if she'd dare. "And I understand that you're used to ruling everything you see, but I took care of your company and your family and this whole great mess just fine when you were gone. I don't need you. I don't *want* you."

"Then why did you go to such trouble to find me?" he demanded, and the force of it rocked her back on her heels. "No one else was looking for me. No one else considered for even one second that I might be anything but dead. Only you. Why?"

And Susannah hardly knew what she felt as she stared at him, her chest heaving as if she'd been running and her hands in fists at her sides. There were too many things inside her then. There was the fact that she was trapped, in this marriage and in his family and in this life she'd wanted to escape the whole time she'd been stuck in it. More than that, there was the astounding reality of the situation—that there was *life* inside her. That she'd found her husband on a mountaintop when everyone had accepted that he was gone, and she'd done more than save him. They'd made a life.

She thought it was grief that swept over her then. Grief for the girl she'd been and grief for the woman she'd been forced to become. Grief for the years she'd lost, and grief for the years he'd had taken from him.

Susannah told herself it had to be grief, this wild and unwieldy thing that ravaged her, turning her inside out whether she wanted it or not. She told herself it could only be grief.

Because the possibility that it was joy, ferocious and encompassing, might be the end of her.

"I don't know," she said quietly, her voice sounding as rough as she felt. "I didn't believe the plane could go down like that. I certainly didn't believe it was an accident. And the more I looked into it, the less I believed you'd died."

"But you don't need me. You don't *want* me."

He wasn't asking her a question. He was taunting her. Leonidas shifted then. He pushed away from the fireplace and he stalked toward her, making everything inside Susannah shake to hold her ground.

And then he kept right on coming, until he was standing over her and she was forced to tilt her head back to meet his gaze.

"No," she whispered. "I don't want you. I want to be free."

He took her face in his hands, holding her fast, and this close his eyes were a storm. Ink dark with gold like lightning, and she felt the buzz of it. Everywhere.

Inside and out.

As complicated as that mad thing that could not possibly be joy.

"This is as close as you're going to get, little one," he told her, the sound of that same madness in his gaze, his voice.

And then he claimed her mouth with his.

CHAPTER NINE

WHEN SHE KISSED him back, shifting her body so she could press closer against him and dig her hands into his chest, something deep inside Leonidas eased.

Even as something else burned anew, harder and wilder at once.

He kissed her again and again. He dug his fingers into the sweet, shining gold of her hair and he let it tumble down over her shoulders, and still he took her mouth, claiming her and possessing her and marking her the only way he could.

She was his. *His.*

And he was tired of keeping himself on a leash where his woman—his *wife*—was concerned.

She wasn't going anywhere. Never, ever again.

He had never been much of a gentleman, and then he'd become a god. He was the one who'd been acting as if he was in a cage these last seven weeks, but that time was over now.

She was pregnant. His beautiful Susannah was ripe with his child even now. A child they'd made when she'd surrendered her innocence to him in that compound where he hadn't known his own name until he'd tasted her. A child she'd already started building inside her when she'd walked with him through the gates and back into the world.

Leonidas had never felt anything like this in his life.

Triumph pounded through him, wild and ruthless in turn, and he wanted to shout out his savage joy from the rooftops of Paris until the whole world trembled before the child that he would bring into it.

And this woman whom he had no intention of letting out of his sight, ever, was a miracle. *His* miracle. She had not left him on that mountain. She hadn't left him the moment she'd delivered him home. She hadn't left when she'd wanted to do it a month ago, and despite what she'd said on the dance floor, she hadn't left him tonight, either.

And now she'd missed her chance, because he would see to it that she never would.

She was his wife. She carried his child.

Nothing would ever be the same.

Leonidas devoured her mouth, and when her sweet little moans began to sound like accusations, greedy and hungry against his mouth, he lifted her against him and then bore her down onto the thick rug that stretched out before the fire on the floor of his salon. The flames crackled behind their grate, and he laid her out there before the fire like some kind of offering, determined that this time he would go slow.

This time, he would learn her. This woman who had consented to be his right hand all these weeks, when she so easily could have left him to fend for himself. This woman who was not only the wife who had waited for him and stayed dressed in black years after his death, but who was also the mother of his child.

The child who would not grow up the way he did, with a cruel father and a selfish mother, beaten into becoming the Betancur heir they'd wanted.

He would die before he let that happen and for good this time.

But first he intended to imprint himself on Susannah.

He wanted her to taste him when she licked her own lips. He wanted her to feel him as if he was inside her, even when he wasn't.

He wanted to wreck her and redeem her, over and over, until the very idea of leaving him was what made those tears spill from her eyes.

And then he wanted to keep doing it, again and again, until this edgy hunger for her was sated at last. If it could be.

He took his time, exulting in the fact there was no barbed wire here. No followers with an arsenal and no video cameras on the walls.

There was nothing but the two of them. At last.

Leonidas moved over her, touching and tasting and indulging himself, from her lush mouth all the way down to the delicate arch of her feet. Then back again. He stripped off the stunning ball gown he'd insisted she wear, in that bright green that was so unlike the Widow Bettencourt that he expected whole tabloids to speak of nothing else come morning.

But he couldn't wait to take it off her.

He stripped her bare so that he could get to the glory beneath it, all those luscious curves he'd dreamed a thousand times since that day in Idaho. Did he imagine that they were richer than he recalled? He cupped her breasts in his palms, then tried them against his tongue. He worshipped that belly of hers that was still flat, though slightly thicker, perhaps, than it had been that last time.

He settled himself between her legs and bent to taste her fully. Sweet cream and that feminine kick, she went straight to his head. And he did absolutely nothing to stop the intoxication.

He brought her to a shuddering, rolling sort of shattering with his mouth, there where she was wet and needy.

Then he did it again. And only when she called out his name, her voice cracking, did Leonidas finally crawl up the length of her and fit himself to her center.

At last.

Then he finally thrust himself into her, sinking to the hilt, and loved the hitch in the little sound she made as he possessed her completely.

He waited as she accommodated him, wriggling her hips and flushed bright everywhere, more beautiful beneath him than any woman had a right to be.

And when he moved, it was with the knowledge that she had given him the one thing he hadn't known he wanted more than anything else in this world. Again.

His blood was all around him. His cousins, his mother, more Betancurs than anyone could possibly want. They were shoved down his throat whether he liked it or not. They schemed and plotted. They lived sparkling lives his hard work provided them and they still would have been the first to snap at him if they could. They were the part of his life he wished could have stayed forgotten, but it wasn't as if he could escape them. They were everywhere.

It had been that way all his life. His mother the worst of them, demanding and deceitful and never, ever any kind of parent in any real sense. He'd stopped expecting any better of her and he'd stopped wondering why he always felt empty inside when others clearly did not.

He knew why. This was how they'd made him. This was who his family wanted him to be, this harsh creature who felt nothing.

But Susannah hated them all as much as he did. She wanted nothing to do with his blood or what proximity to the Betancurs could do for her. If she saw the emptiness in him, she didn't shy away from it. On the contrary, she was the only person he'd ever met who treated him as if he was no better or different from anyone else.

And she had given him a family.

A family.

Leonidas would do everything in his power to make sure that he never lost what was his. Not to his own memory, and certainly not to those vultures who banked on the fact they shared his blood, assuming that would keep them safe.

He made himself a vow, there on the floor in his Paris townhome, on the night of the Betancur Ball where once again, Susannah had given him the world.

He would do no less for her—whether she liked it or not.

And then he lost himself in her, making her cry out again and again, until he finally lost his patience. He gathered her to him, then reached down between them to help her fly apart one last time.

And he followed, calling out her name as he fell.

Later, she stirred against him and he lifted her up, carrying her through the house to the room he had no intention of letting her stay in on her own the way she'd planned to do when they'd arrived. But there was no point arguing it now. He found a loose long-sleeved T-shirt and a pair of lounging pajama bottoms, and dressed her quickly. She made a face at him while he did it, but then curled herself into a ball on the bed in the last guest suite she would occupy.

And when she fell asleep, she fell hard.

With any luck, she'd stay that way until they made it to the island. Where he had every intention of keeping her until she couldn't imagine any possible scenario that involved leaving him, because that was unacceptable.

She was his.

Leonidas had led a cult for years. Whether he'd been a figurehead or not, he knew exactly how to keep one woman where he wanted her, and he had no qualms about using each and every one of the dirty little tricks he knew to make her think it was the best idea anyone had ever had.

He stood there and watched her sleep for a moment, aware that his heart was pounding at him and that he should probably be concerned that it was so easy for him to slip back into the sort of headspace the Count had always occupied. But he wasn't. The truth was that the Leonidas Betancur who had got on that plane and the man who had been dragged from its ashes weren't so different. Neither one of them had believed in much besides themselves. The Count had possessed a version of morality, but it had all been arranged around the fact he'd believed he was at the center of everything.

Susannah had changed that, as well. She'd knitted him together and made him care about her, too. It should have outraged him. Maybe on some level it did. But more than that was the deep, abiding notion that she belonged with him and anything else was intolerable.

Especially now that she was carrying his child.

It was the beginning and the end of everything, and he'd be happy to fight with her about it on his favorite private island, where she could scream into the impervious ocean if she liked and it wouldn't do a single thing to save her. If he was honest, he was almost looking forward to watching what she'd do when she realized she really was stuck there. With him.

Leonidas smiled, then tucked a strand of her golden hair behind her ear. He had to order himself not to bend closer and put his lips to her sweetly flushed cheek, because he knew he wouldn't stop if he did.

But he forced himself away from her, out into the hall.

Then he called for his staff and his plane, and methodically set about kidnapping his wife.

Susannah jolted awake when the plane touched down and she had no idea where she was.

She knew she was on one of the Betancur jets, though it took her a moment to recognize the stateroom she was in. She clung to the side of the bed as the plane taxied in, frowning as she tried to make sense of the fact that she'd apparently slept through an entire flight to somewhere unknown.

Paris gleamed in her memory. And the doctor's visit. Her pregnancy, confirmed.

And what had happened after that announcement, there before the fire.

But everything else following it was a blur. She had the vague recollection of a car moving through the city in the dark, her head pillowed on Leonidas's shoulder. Then the spinning sensation of being lifted into his arms.

She might have thought she'd been drugged but she'd felt this way before, and more than once these last weeks. This powerfully exhausted. The good news was that she knew it was the pregnancy now, not something that required a hospital stay, or that allergy she'd been half-convinced she had to Leonidas.

When the plane came to a full stop she stayed where she was for a while, then rolled out of the bed, surprised that no attendant—or confusing, breathtaking husband—had come looking for her.

She stepped out into the corridor, blinking in the light that poured in from the plane's windows in the common areas. It told her two things—that the shades had been pulled in her stateroom and that wherever they were, it was morning.

And when she looked out the windows, she could see the sea.

She made her way to the front of the plane and stepped out onto the landing at the top of the jet's fold-up steps. She blinked as she took in the soft light, then looked around, realizing after a beat or two that she was on a small landing strip on a rocky island. She saw silvery olive trees in all directions, solid hills covered in green, and the sea hovering in the distance on all sides, blue and gray in turn.

And Leonidas waited at the foot of the stairs, leaning against the side of a sleek, deep green Range Rover.

It was only then that she became aware of what she was wearing. The long-sleeve shirt she slept in and a pair of very loose yoga pants. And there was only one way that she could have come to be wearing such things, she thought, when she had no recollection of putting them on. When the last thing she knew she'd been wearing was that green dress at the ball.

Although she hadn't been wearing much of anything in front of the fire.

And maybe that was what shivered through her then. The sheer intimacy of the fact he'd dressed her. She imagined him tugging clothes into place over her bare skin, then pulling her hair out of the way…

It wasn't heat that moved through her then, though she thought it was related in its way. It was something far more dangerous. She tried to swallow it down, but her feet were moving without her permission, carrying her down the metal stairs whether she wanted to go or not.

And she could feel Leonidas's dark gaze on her all the way.

She made it to the bottom of the steps, then crossed over to stand in front of him, and the silence was what got to her first. She was so used to Rome. Paris. Great cities filled with as many people as cars. Foot traffic and horns, sirens and music. But there was nothing like that here. There was a crisp, fresh breeze that smelled of salt. No voices. No sounds of traffic in the distance. It was as if they were the only two people left on the earth.

"Where are we?" she asked, and was not surprised to hear how hushed she sounded, as if the island demanded it.

"Greece," Leonidas replied. Perhaps too readily. "More or less."

"What are we doing in Greece?" What she meant was, *Why are we so clearly not in Athens near the Betancur offices if we're in Greece?* But she didn't say that part out loud. It was as if some part of her thought the island spoke for itself.

Leonidas's hard mouth kicked up a little bit in one corner, but something about that smile of his didn't exactly make her feel easy. He did not cross his arms, or straighten from where he continued to lounge against the side of his vehicle. And something a little too much like foreboding moved through her then.

"In one sense, we are in Greece because I am Greek," he said, and his conversational tone only made the foreboding worse. Susannah felt the itch of it down the length of her spine. "My mother is Greek, anyway. This island has been in her family for many generations. There are very few staff, and all of them are some relation to me." That curve in the corner of his mouth deepened. "I mention this because you are very enterprising, I think, and you do not wish to frustrate yourself unnecessarily with fruitless escape attempts."

She blinked. "What are you talking about?"

"I will not insult you by giving you a list of rules, Susannah. That is the beauty of an island such as this. There is no way off. No ferries land here. The plane will leave tonight and you will not be on it, and there is a helicopter that flies only at my command. Do you understand what I'm telling you?"

"I assume I'm still asleep," she said tightly. "And this is a terrible nightmare."

"Alas, you are wide awake."

"Then I do not understand," she managed to say, though she was very much afraid that she did. "It sounds as if you've just imprisoned me."

"I prefer to think of it as an opportunity for you to embrace the realities of your life." Leonidas inclined his head. "An opportunity to spend some time accepting what is and let go of what cannot be."

"That sounds suspiciously like cult talk."

"If that is what you wish to call it, I cannot argue." One arrogant shoulder rose, then fell. "I would encourage you to recall that I was not a follower of any cult. I was the leader." He smiled at her. "I can be very persuasive."

"You need to take me back to civilization," she snapped at him, because that smile lit her up inside and she didn't know which one of them she hated more for it. "Immediately."

Leonidas shook his head, almost as if he pitied her. "I'm afraid I'm not going to do that."

And it was as if everything that had happened and everything she'd seen since she'd stepped off that plane into the wilds of Idaho slammed into her then. The compound itself, after that steep climb. The barbed wire, the cameras, the ugly weapon pointed at her with a few threats besides. Not to mention what had happened inside with her long-lost husband.

There'd been the press storm when they'd left, when Leonidas had been returned to the world that had thought him dead. And these weeks of close proximity, always so scrupulously polite and careful not to touch too much, as if she wasn't spending entirely too much time with the man she meant to leave. The Betancur Ball. His cousins and his mother and then worse, her parents.

And that dance in the middle of all the rest of it, like some bittersweet nod to a life she'd only ever dreamed about but had never seen. It had never existed and it never would, and the fact that she discovered she was pregnant and then fell all over him like some kind of wild animal didn't change that.

She wanted her baby. She didn't want the Betancur baby and the circus that went along with that. She didn't want Leonidas.

Because she couldn't have him, not the way she wanted him, and all of this was just delaying the inevitable. Why couldn't he see that?

"I told you that I didn't want to live in a prison," she said when she was sure that she could speak again, and she didn't care if she sounded distinctly unlike her usual serene self. She didn't care if he saw her fall apart right there in front of him. "I told you that our marriage already felt like a cage. Your name is the key in the lock. I told you. And your response to that was to pack as I was sleeping and strand me on some island?"

Leonidas finally stood. He straightened from the side of the Range Rover, unfolding to his full height, and then loomed there above her. His arms dropped to his sides and his face took on that granite, lethal expression that she somehow kept forgetting was the truth of him. She'd seen it when he was the Count. And she'd seen it last night in Paris. And there been glimpses here and there, across these past seven weeks, of a different side to the man—but she understood now that they were flashes, nothing more.

This was the truth of Leonidas Betancur. Susannah had absolutely no doubt. Ruthless, bordering on grim, seeming practically to burn with all that power he carried around so effortlessly inside him.

This was the man she'd married. This was the man she'd given her innocence to, then made a baby with.

And she had no one to blame but herself, because he'd never hidden any of it. He was a Betancur. This was who he was and always had been.

"I am your cage," he told her, in the kind of voice it didn't surprise her at all had led men to abandon their lives and follow him up the side of a mountain "The marriage, the Betancur name, all of that is noise. The only prison you need worry about is me, Susannah. And I will hold you forever."

She wanted to shake. She wanted to cry—put her head down and sob until her heart felt like hers again. She wanted to scream at him, beat at him with her fists, perhaps. Pound on him until something made sense again, but she didn't do it. That same impossible grief—because it couldn't be joy, not here, not now—rocked through her again.

She sucked in a breath and tried to straighten her shoulders. "If that was meant to make me feel better, it failed."

"You are carrying my child," he blazed at her, and it took everything she had not to jump. "I don't know what kind of man you think I am, but I don't give away what's mine, Susannah."

It was possible the top of her head exploded. She

surged forward, recklessly taking her finger and poking him in the chest with it. "I am not yours."

Leonidas wrapped his hand around hers, but he didn't pull her finger away from him. He kept her hand trapped against his chest.

"I will not debate you on that, my little virgin. But it doesn't change the fact that only I have ever had you."

"I was the widow of one of the most famous men in the world." She tugged at her hand, but he didn't release it. "I couldn't exactly pop into a club and pick someone up to have sex with, could I?"

"But you would have, you think. Had you been a less identifiable widow."

She frowned at his sardonic tone. "I would have divested myself of my virginity before the end of your funeral if I could have. Happily."

She threw that at him, but he only laughed, and she hated him for it. Or she hated herself for feeling so unsteady at the sound.

"I don't believe you," he told her. "You pride yourself on your control, little one. It's obvious in everything you do. The only place you cede it is when you are beneath me."

She shook at that, and she knew he saw it. Worse, he could likely feel it in the hand he still held against the steel wall of his chest.

"I'm an excellent actress. Ask anyone in your company. Or your family."

"Deny it if you wish, it makes no difference to me." This time when she tugged on her hand, Leonidas let her go. And it didn't make anything better. He regarded her with that dark stare of his that she was sure could see all the things she wanted to hide. All those feelings she didn't want to name. "But do not imagine for even one second that I will let you wander off with my child. Do not fool yourself into some fantasy where that could ever happen, prison or no prison. It won't."

"You can't keep me here." Her voice didn't even sound like hers. Susannah supposed she sounded the way she felt—frozen straight through.

Or at least that's what she thought she felt. The longer she spent around this man, the less she seemed to know. Because there was a perverse part of her that almost liked the fact that he wasn't letting her swan off, out of his life. The way everyone else in her life had if she'd proved less useful than they'd imagined she'd be.

"I can," he said quietly.

"You'll have to spend your every waking hour trying to keep me locked up if you want me to stay here," she warned him. "Is that really what you want?"

"I think you'll find that I won't need to expend any energy at all," Leonidas told her. Almost happily, Susannah thought, which she knew damned her even before he went on. "The geography takes care of that. It is an island, after all, in an unforgiving sea." He shrugged, clearly amusing himself. "All I have to do is wait."

CHAPTER TEN

SUSANNAH DIDN'T SPEAK to him for a week.

In that time, she explored every inch of the island. She had access to one of the vehicles parked in the garage if she wanted, but it wasn't as if there was anything to do but drive back and forth along the same dirt road that led from one end of the island to the other, about a fifteen-mile round-trip. There was a dock or two, but they were clearly for swimmers when the weather was fine. No boats were moored at them, or even pulled up on the beaches.

Nothing that could make it across the brooding Ionian Sea, anyway, even if Susannah had been a sailor.

There were olive trees everywhere, growing too wild to be considered a grove. There were beaches, more rock than sand. It was a sturdy island, with no village to speak of and only a few homes clustered together around one of the coves. What few people lived on the island worked in the big house that sprawled over the top of the highest point of the island. It rambled this way and that, a jumble of open atriums and windows that let the sea in and then flirted with the nearest cliff.

She might have loved it, wild and raw something far more intense than the usual whitewashed Greek scenes that cluttered up the postcards, if she hadn't wanted to escape so badly.

"You cannot keep this up forever," Leonidas said a week into her prison sentence.

She'd wandered into the villa's surprisingly well-stocked library without realizing he was within. He usually worked in the office that was tucked away on the far side of the house, which meant she'd gotten used to avoiding him easily when she was inside.

Susannah spent her days driving aimlessly around the island as if she expected a magical bridge to the mainland to appear at any moment. She sunned herself on the rocks if the weather was fine, though it was always too chilly for swimming. Or she took quiet walks among the olive trees, trying to keep her head clear. When she felt sufficiently walked out, she usually moved inside and rummaged around the books that were packed onto the library's shelves, smelling faintly of age and water.

If she hadn't been trapped here, this might have been the most relaxing holiday she'd ever had.

Today she'd gone straight for the huge stack of German novels that had caught her eye yesterday. And she cursed herself for not looking around before she'd wandered into his vicinity.

Leonidas was sprawled back in one of the deep, comfortable chairs, his feet propped up on the table before him and a cup of coffee at his elbow. He had a laptop open on the wide arm of the chair, but he wasn't looking at the screen. He was studying Susannah instead, with an amused, indulgent look in his eyes that drove her mad.

"Why would I speak to you?" she asked, making no particular attempt to keep the challenge from her voice. Or the dislike. "What can you imagine I could possibly have to say to the prison warden?"

Leonidas shrugged. "I told you before that you can

be as stubborn as you like, Susannah. It will make no difference."

"I know you think you can wait me out," she seethed at him. "But you have no idea who you're dealing with. You never actually met the Widow Betancur."

He laughed at that, raking a hand through his dark hair and reminding her, against her will, how much she'd liked sifting her fingers through it herself.

"I'm not afraid of my own widow, little one."

And she didn't know why the way he said that, his gaze trained on her though he didn't rise from that chair, should have echoed in her like a promise.

"You should be," she told him coldly, snatching up her book and heading for the door again—and faster than she'd come in. "You will be."

But the truth was, she thought that evening as she readied herself for another one of the long, dangerous nights she tried so hard not to think about during the day, she was very much afraid that he could indeed wait her out. That he was already halfway there.

Because Leonidas was relentless.

He didn't argue with her. If he saw her throughout the day, he rarely said anything. Maddeningly, he would most often offer her a slight smile, nothing more, and leave her to it while he carried on running the Betancur Corporation remotely. The staff served food in the villa only at specific times, so there was no avoiding him when she wanted to eat, but if she didn't speak to him he did nothing about it. He only smiled and ate, as if he enjoyed his own company immensely.

More, as if he already knew how this would end.

Every night, Susannah readied herself for bed and resolutely climbed into the four-poster in the guest suite she'd tried to claim as her own. And every night she would fight to stay awake, but she never managed it. She fell asleep, and sometimes dreamed of being lifted into a pair of strong arms. Or being carried through the villa with only the moon peeking down into the open atriums to light the way. But the dreams were never enough to wake her.

And every morning she woke up in Leonidas's bed, because they weren't dreams at all.

Not just in the same bed, another massive king bed like the one she'd never slept in back in Rome, but curled around him as if she couldn't get enough of him. As if she wanted to be a part of him.

It didn't matter what she told herself the night before. It didn't matter what promises she made. Every morning it was the same. She woke up feeling rested, warm and safe, and only gradually became aware that she was sprawled over him. Or curled on her side, with him wound tight around her, holding her to him with one heavy arm.

And every morning she fled as soon as she woke. And he let her go, his arrogant laughter following her as she went.

It was an insidious kind of warfare, and he was far too good at it.

Tonight, Susannah sat on the edge of the bed in her room she kept trying to sleep in, but she was running out of steam. More to the point, she was growing tired of her own defiance.

It did nothing to Leonidas if she ignored him, or tried. He didn't care if she stormed off or if she snapped at him. He was like a mountain, unyielding and impassable, and she'd been battering herself against him for much too long now.

Meanwhile, all he did was smile and go about his business, and he got what he wanted anyway. What was the point?

She moved over to the French doors that led out to her terrace, and threw them open. It was too dark tonight to see the sea, but she could hear it, crashing against the rocky shore down below. She'd always loved the waves. She'd always admired the inexorable push of the sea, over and over, tide after tide. But tonight she found that she felt significantly more sympathetic to the shoreline. Battered over and over by a ruthless, unyielding force, whether it wanted it or not.

She let the night air slap at her, chilling her from the stones beneath her bare feet all the way up to where her hair moved against her shoulders. She hugged her arms around her middle, noticing with a touch of awe and wonder the changes that were happening to her every day. She was a little thicker. A little bit different all over despite her best efforts to pretend none of this was happening.

As if her body had picked sides a long time ago.

She turned back toward the bedroom and stopped, the buttery light from within gripping her. She could see the rest of the villa, built to look almost haphazard as it claimed the top of the cliff with bright windows glowing against the dark night, too cloudy for stars. But she didn't need light to see the island any longer.

It was one more thing that was becoming a part of her no matter how little she wanted it. She remembered when that had happened four years ago. The first day she'd walked into the Betancur Corporation offices had been intense. Awful, even. She'd been a nineteen-year-old with nothing going for her but her ability to hold the gazes of angry men and smile politely until they finished ranting. But every day she'd gone back had been easier. Or she'd gotten used to it.

And one day she'd found herself sitting in the office she'd claimed, going through some files, and it had struck her that it was all…normal. She'd made the impossible *normal*.

Leonidas was right, she realized then, pulling in a breath of the cold night air. He was going to win. Because she could apparently adapt to anything, and would without thinking about it.

That night she fell asleep almost before her head hit the pillow the way she always did. But when she felt his strong arms around her, lifting her up and carrying her through the dark halls, she forced herself to wake up. To become more alert with every step. And when he laid her down in his wide bed, she waited for him to sprawl out beside her, and then she propped herself up on one hand and gazed at him.

"Sleeping Beauty is awake at last," Leonidas said in a low voice. "That's when the trouble starts, I'm told. Historically."

There were no lights on in his bedroom, only the last of his fire glowing in the grate. Susannah was grateful for the reprieve. In the almost total dark, there was no need to worry about what expression she might have been wearing. There was no need to hide if he couldn't really see her. So she forgot about her own masks for a moment, and let herself marvel at the lack of his.

In the dark, he seemed approachable. Not soft—he could never be soft—but all those bold lines and harsh edges seemed muted, somehow. And though she knew his scars were there, stamped into his rangy body, she couldn't see them either.

It was as if the shadows made them both new.

"If you didn't want trouble," she whispered, "you should have let me go."

"At some point, Susannah, you will have to face the fact you didn't really want to leave," Leonidas said, his voice barely more than a thread in the dark. "Or why go to such lengths to find me at all?"

"I thought it was what you would have wanted," she said before she thought better of it.

But she knew the truth then. When her words were lying there between them, so obvious once spoken. It was what *she* would have wanted if her plane had gone down. She would have wanted someone to find out what had happened, and when the answers didn't make sense, to dig deeper. She would have wanted someone to send investigators. She would have wanted someone who refused to give up until the truth came out.

She would have wanted someone to care. Just once.

"I always get what I want," Leonidas said, his voice as dark as the room around them. "Sooner or later."

And Susannah had spent entirely too much time working this through in her head. On all those drives, walks through the olive trees, and afternoons on the rocks with a wool sweater wrapped tight around her to ward off the cold while the sea spray made her face damp. Or when she'd sat out by the heated pool near the house and had pretended the sun might warm her more than it did, there where she could smell flowers and dirt and the salted crispness of the bright Greek air. She'd been so furious, and she hadn't wanted to see what was on the other side of it, because fury felt like a destination all on its own.

The island slowed her down. It made her think even when she didn't want that. It had defeated her even if he couldn't.

But it had also given her a new resolve.

"Always?" She reached across the wedge of space between them and traced that hard, unsmiling mouth of his with her fingers. "I know that's what you tell yourself. But I think we both know you don't always get what you want. I saw the compound, remember. I know how you lived there. And how quick you were to leave a place they worshipped you outright."

"Eventually," Leonidas said, but there was an edge to his voice then. He stilled her hand, drawing it away from his mouth. And he didn't let go. "I always get what I want, eventually."

And this was what had happened to her four years ago. First the shock, and a kind of grief that the life she'd been training for all those years was no more. She'd let it take her down. But then she got up again, and when she did she'd taken action.

It was what Susannah always did.

So she would do it here, too. And if there was a part of her that mourned the man who'd held her in his arms while they'd danced at that gala, well. That had only been a fantasy, after all. A fairy tale. This was gritty. This was a baby she hadn't planned for and a complicated life with a husband whose name she knew better than she knew him.

She'd had a fairy-tale wedding with a man who'd scoffed at all her silly dreams and crushed them while he did. She'd lived through widowhood, pretending to mourn a man she'd hardly known and a love that had never existed, except possibly in her head. She'd hunted down a stranger who hadn't known her when he'd seen her, and she'd won back the husband she barely knew with a kiss. And her virginity. Then she'd spent seven short weeks pretending to be a devoted wife and business partner while sleeping by herself in a lonely guest room.

But she had never done *this*.

Susannah had never been his wife in act and deed as well as word. And she decided that she was tired of punishing herself. She was tired of hiding. Most of all, she was tired of fighting wars she wasn't sure she even wanted to win.

If he could do exactly as he pleased, kidnap her and confine her on this island simply to make a point, there was no reason she couldn't do what she liked, as well.

And it was time to stop pretending that she didn't like him, because she did. He was a flame and she was a desperate sort of moth, but there was no need to batter herself to pieces when she could choose instead to simply land. And burn as she wished.

"Eventually will be a long time coming," she told him softly. She moved closer to him then, tangling her legs with his. "If at all."

He let out a laugh that was more warning than anything else.

"I'll have you eating out of my hand sooner than you can possibly imagine," he promised her, perhaps a little roughly. "It's inevitable, little one. You might as well fold now."

"You can't have me," she told him then, her voice as simple as it was stark. A part of the shadows, somehow. "That's how this works, don't you understand? When you keep something against its will, you can hold on to it, but it's never yours."

Then she leaned in close, because it was what she wanted. Because she could do as she liked, surely, since he always did. Because she was much too fascinated with him and her heart went silly whenever he was near, and she'd resolved to embrace that.

To burn of her own volition on that lethal flame of his, again and again, until he tired of her and this game and all the rest of it. The way she knew he would.

She got even closer, pressing herself against him in the dark, and sealed her doom the only way she knew.

With a kiss.

CHAPTER ELEVEN

"I TRUST YOUR cage grows more comfortable by the day," Leonidas said, his voice hardly more than a growl, shoving his mobile into his pocket as he strode out to the pool in the atrium. "You almost look as if you're enjoying it."

Susannah looked up from where she sat in the bright sunlight, wrapped up against the cool breeze in an oversize sort of shawl that looked as if it could double as a duvet, thrown over the flowing, casual dress she wore. Her blond hair was twisted back into the makeshift chignon she preferred, looking messy and yet somehow as impossibly chic as she always did, as if it was effortless.

He thought he couldn't want her more. Every day he thought this. Every night, he was sure.

And then she did something unforgivable, like sit out in the sun on a cold winter's day to read a book with her sunglasses on and her bare feet exposed. What defense was he expected to have against such a thing?

"Comfortable or not, a cage remains a cage," she replied, almost merrily. The same way she always did. As if it was all a joke when he knew very well it was not.

None of this was any kind of laughing matter at all.

The anger that had beat at him all through that last call he'd hated making didn't disappear, but the sight of his wife somehow...altered it. She reminded him that no matter who had acted against him or why, *she* had stepped in and saved him.

He reminded himself that she was what mattered to him. Susannah and the child she carried. This, right here, was all that mattered.

And someday he would find a way to bring back that dancing sort of light he'd glimpsed in her only briefly, now and then. Usually while they were naked. He would make her happy, damn it. Leonidas was always successful at what he did. He would succeed here, too.

Susannah wanted to keep a part of herself separate, and he couldn't abide that—but he could wait. He told himself that he could wait her out, wear her down…and no matter that he was finding that harder and harder to tolerate.

Everything had changed.

She'd kissed him that night and altered the world again, and for the most part, he liked it.

He liked an end to the charade of separate beds. She stopped the pointless theater of marching off to the guest suite every night and took her place in his rooms instead. She stopped giving him her icy silent treatment and simmering anger at every turn.

And she gave herself to him with a sweet fire and wild greediness that might have humbled him, had he let it.

"I am your husband and you are my wife," he had said that first night, after he'd reduced her to a boneless heap. He'd carried her into his expansive bathroom to set her in the oversize tub set in an arched window to look out over the quietly seething Ionian Sea. "And I have no intention of being the sort of husband who creeps down the cold hallway when he wishes the company of his wife. I do not believe in twin beds. I don't believe in anything that gets in the way of you and me, not even a damned nightgown." He'd watched her as she'd settled in the steaming water. "I trust we are finally in accord on this."

"I don't think you know what you believe about marriage," Susannah had retorted, though she'd been sleepy and satiated and had watched him as if she might like to take another bite out of him. He'd climbed into the tub with her, then had shifted to pull her against him, her back to his chest. "Since you've only been married to one person in your lifetime and I remember more about those years than you do."

"I intend for both of us to remember this part of our marriage," he'd murmured into her ear, raking his teeth over the tender lobe to make her shudder. "Vividly."

And there had been no arguing after that. He didn't bother with that anymore. He picked her up when things got a bit fractious, then expressed his feelings about whatever minor disagreement it might have been all over her delectable body. He showed her exactly how little space he wanted between them. Over and over again.

She had spent seven weeks filling in the gaps in his memory. Now, having met her parents, he took it upon himself to fill in any gaps she might have had in her own life thanks to the things they'd obviously not given her. Such as nurturing of any kind. He tended to her headaches. He made sure she ate. He took care of her.

He'd never taken care of anyone in his life, not directly, but he took care of Susannah.

And he taught her that she'd been very silly indeed to imagine that one stolen afternoon in a faraway compound meant that she had the slightest idea what sex was. Because there were so very many ways to tear each other apart.

And Leonidas happened to know every last one of them.

She learned how to take him in her mouth and how to

make him groan. She learned how to crawl on top of him where he sat, and settle herself astride him, so she could take control and rock them both into bliss.

Sometimes when they were lying an exhausted heap, barely able to breathe, he would slide one of his hands over her belly and hold it there. And allow himself to imagine things he'd never imagined he'd want. Much less this badly.

"You haven't had one of your headaches in some time," he said today, coming over to stand at the foot of the lounger where she sat. She set her book aside and peered up at him. Then she swept her sunglasses back and anchored them on the top of her head, narrowing her eyes at him in a way he couldn't say he liked.

"What's the matter?"

Leonidas didn't want to answer that. Or acknowledge that she could see into him like that.

"Perhaps the worst of them is over," he said instead.

Susannah stood, pulling her shawl around her and tilting her head slightly to one side as she regarded him.

"You're not all right," she said softly. "Are you?"

"What can that possibly matter to you?" It was ripped from him. Too raw. Too revealing. And yet he couldn't seem to stop. "As you keep telling me—as you go to great lengths to make sure I never forget—I can never have you. What does it matter whether I am all right, whatever the hell that means, or not?"

Susannah didn't flare back at him. She didn't do anything at all for a moment but stand there and study him, and only when he thought he might come out of his skin did she move. Even then, it was only a small thing. She reached over and put her hand to his jaw, then held it there.

Small. Meaningless, he wanted to say.

But it felt like the world.

"You have this, Leonidas," she said quietly. "And maybe this is enough."

It shouldn't have felt like a storm. It shouldn't have rocked him the way it did, deep and wild, razing what had been there and leaving nothing he recognized in its wake.

But he would think about that later. He would piece himself back together later.

He would try to rebuild all the things she'd broken then.

If he could.

Here, now, he took what she was offering.

"It's my mother," he said gruffly, and tried to hold on to his anger. Because he was very much afraid that what was beneath it was the pointless hurt and grief of the child in him who still, all these years and bitter lessons later, wanted Apollonia to be his *mother*. Just once. "She's the one who had the plane tampered with. She's responsible for the crash."

Susannah's brow creased, but she didn't say anything. She only waited, dropping her hand to her side to hold her shawl to her and keeping her gaze trained to his. And somehow that made it easier for him to keep speaking.

"I never stopped investigating the plane crash. Your investigators led you to me, but I wanted more. Because, of course, if someone tried to assassinate me once it stood to reason that they would do it again."

"What's frustrating is that there are so many possibilities," she murmured. "And so many lead in circles."

And Leonidas felt his lips thin. "Indeed. And it warms the heart, I must tell you, to realize the extent to which I am hated by my own blood."

Susannah's gaze sharpened on his, and her blue eyes were serious. Intent.

"They don't hate you, Leonidas," she said fiercely. "They don't know you. They are tiny, grasping people who long for things to be handed to them, that's all. They are victims forever in search of someone to blame. They look around a world in which they have everything and see nothing but their own misfortune." She shook her head. "Being hated by these people says nothing about you, except perhaps you are a far better person than they could ever dream of being."

"Careful, little one," he said roughly. "You begin to sound as if I might have you after all."

She looked away, and he felt that like a punch to the gut, even when she smiled. Was it his imagination or his guilt that made him think that soft curve of her mouth was bittersweet? And why should he feel that like it was the worst of the blows he'd taken today?

"The truth is that your mother is the worst of them," she said, and he didn't want to do this. He didn't want to talk about his mother. He wanted to trace the curve of Susannah's mouth until her smile felt real. He wanted to wash himself clean of all of this. His name, his blood. "I mean no disrespect."

Leonidas let out a short laugh with precious little humor in it.

"I doubt you could disrespect my mother if you tried." And the air was so clear here, bordering on cold but not quite getting there. The island was quiet. The riot was in him, he knew that. "And still, I didn't think it could be her. Not her. I didn't want it to be her."

Susannah whispered something that sounded like his name. Leonidas forged on.

"My cousins made sense to me as suspects. All they do is congregate and plot. Why not the biggest plot of all?" He shook his head. "But not one of them would actually want the things they claim have been taken from them. They don't want to be in charge. That's responsibility, and they would hate it. They just want money. Money and stature and power. They want the appearance of power, but certainly not the work that goes with it. My mother, on the other hand…"

Susannah's eyes were wide. "Apollonia doesn't like to work. She likes to talk about working and claim she's exhausted from some other sort of work that can never be performed when anyone can see it…" He held her gaze until she trailed off and blew out a breath. "Are you certain?"

"The investigators reached this conclusion some weeks ago," he said bitterly. More bitterly than he should have, because what had he imagined? That a woman like his mother could change? She'd always been selfish. He'd always known that. The only surprise was *how much*. "But I refused to accept it."

"Do they have proof?"

"They didn't," Leonidas said. His jaw clenched tight. "Now they do."

And for moment, they only stared at each other, out in the bright Greek sun, held tight in the grip of that horrible truth.

Susannah didn't apologize for his mother. She didn't express her sorrow for what could not have been, in the end, that much of a surprise to her. Just as it hadn't been for him. Loath as he was to admit that, even now.

It wasn't a surprise. But that didn't make it hurt less.

She didn't apologize, but she didn't look away, either. And he thought that this, right here, was why he was never going to get over this woman. This was how she'd wedged herself so deep inside him that he could no longer breathe without feeling her there, changing everything with reckless abandon whether he wanted it or not. Because she simply stood there with him. As if she was prepared to stand there all night, holding a vigil for the mother he'd never had.

"And now I must face the fact that she is far worse that I could have imagined," Leonidas said, forcing the words out because he was sure, somehow, that it would be better that way. He couldn't have said why. "It is not bad enough that she has never displayed the faintest hint of maternal instinct. It doesn't matter that when she could have protected me from my father's rages, she only laughed and picked herself another lover. It all follows the same through line, really. There is not one single thing surprising about this news." He shook his head slightly, almost as if he was dizzy, when he was not. Not quite. "And yet."

"And yet," Susannah echoed. This time when she reached over, she placed her palm in that hollow between his pectoral muscles and held it there, pressure and the hint of warmth. That was all. And he felt it everywhere. "What will you do?"

"What can I do?" He didn't grimace. He felt as if he'd turned to stone, except it wasn't the stone he knew from before. It was as if he'd lost the ability to harden himself, armor himself, the way he wanted. And he knew it was the fault of the woman who stood there, keeping her hand on him as if her palm was a talisman crafted especially for him. He knew it was her fault that he cared about anything. Because losing the things that had made him harder in that other way felt worth it, he realized, if this was what he gained.

If Susannah was what he had, he couldn't care too much about the things he'd lost.

Something dawned in him then, deep and certain, that he didn't want to know. And not only because he'd imagined himself incapable of such things. But because, as the phone call he just had had proved beyond a reasonable doubt, he didn't know a single thing about love. He never had and he doubted he ever would.

"I cannot haul her before any authority," he pointed out, fighting to sound dispassionate. Analytical. "I don't want that sort of attention on the plane crash, much less what happened afterward. Even if I wanted her brought to justice, it would be nothing but a fleeting pleasure. And on the other side of it, more instability for the company. More questions, more worries. Why permit her to cause any more problems than she already has?" He tried to hold his temper at bay. "She took four years of my life. Why should she get another moment?"

Susannah's eyes flashed. "I admire your practicality. But I want her to pay even if you don't."

And he thought he would remember that forever. Her hand on his chest and her blue eyes on fire while she defended him. He'd never felt anything like the light that fell through him then. He'd never have believed it existed.

"Making her pay is simple," he said, his voice a little gruffer than he'd intended. "She only cares about one thing. Remove it and she'll act as if she'd been sent to a Siberian work camp." He shrugged. "I will simply cut her off. No money, no access. Nothing. She should be humbled within the week."

"Apollonia?" Susannah shook her head, and her gaze was hard. "I don't believe she can be humbled."

Leonidas stepped away then, before he couldn't. Before he took his wife into his arms and said the things he knew he couldn't say. There was no place for that here. That wasn't who he was, that certainly wasn't what he did, and he couldn't allow that kind of weakness. Not now, when all he had in this world was betrayal on one side and a captive spouse on the other.

And a baby who would come into this world and know only a father who had imprisoned his mother on an island.

He had never wanted to be his own father, a brute dressed in sleek clothes to hide himself in plain sight as he went on his many rampages. And yet it had never occurred to Leonidas that when all was said and done, he was more like his mother than he wanted to admit.

What he was doing to Susannah proved it.

His father would simply have beaten a defiant woman. This sort of game was in Apollonia's wheelhouse. Manipulation and treachery were her life's blood.

How had he failed to see it?

"I hope you let her know that you know what she did," Susannah said, frowning. "That she hasn't gotten away with it. That there will be consequences, whether she likes it or not."

But Leonidas was looking past her then. He looked out toward the rocks and the sea beyond. The wild Greek sea that stirred something deep in his bones. It always had. He liked the rawness of these islands, unmanicured and untamed. They spoke to something deep inside him, and he understood in a sudden flash that Susannah did the same.

She had warned him. He couldn't pretend she hadn't. He could keep her, but he would never have her. A cage was a cage was a cage.

And he recognized that now only because he'd broken out of his. At long last, he'd finally seen his mother for who she was. Not an amusing socialite, flitting here and there as the whim took her. But the woman who had ordered the murder of her own son. On a whim.

She hadn't even denied it.

"You were being so tiresome about my allowance,"

she'd told him when he'd called, her voice shifting over into that nasally whine she used when she thought she could plead her way out of a scrape. She didn't seem to understand that this was no "scrape." That Leonidas was done. "What did you expect me to do?"

Some part of him—most of him—might have preferred to stay imprisoned in the last gasp of the lie he'd built a long time ago to explain Apollonia's behavior, because it was easier. It was what he knew.

But this was better. It had to be. There had to be a point to this sort of bleak freedom, he was sure of it, even if he couldn't see it now.

"I have never loved anything in my life," he told Susannah, out where the air was fresh and the sky was blue and none of the stink of his family could taint her. "I doubt I am capable, and now I know why."

"You are not responsible for the things that woman did," Susannah retorted, instantly drawing herself up as if she intended to go to war with Apollonia there and then. "Not a single thing."

"I fear it is in my blood," he confessed. "It's not only the Betancurs. It's every single part of me. Venal. Malicious. Scheming and vile. Those are my bones, Susannah. My flesh. My blood."

"Leonidas," she began.

But he couldn't stop.

"I have been a god and I have been a king, of sorts. I have acted the lover, but I have never felt a thing. I can run a company and I can lead a cult, but I have no idea how to raise a child. How to be a father." He shook his head, not sure if he was dazed or this was what it felt like to finally have perfect, devastating clarity. "I'm not entirely certain I know how to be a man."

"Stop it." Her voice was ragged. A scrape of sound,

and then she was moving toward him again. He hadn't realized he'd stepped away. "Just stop this."

Susannah didn't wait for him to argue as she must surely have known he would. She crossed the distance between them, dropping her shawl at her feet and not bothering to look back. She leaned in and wrapped her arms around him at his waist, then tilted her head back to scowl up at him.

"I want you to stop talking," she told him.

And he heard it then. All the power and authority of the Widow Betancur herself. A woman who had every expectation of being obeyed.

But he had never been anybody's underling. "And if I refuse?"

She studied him for a moment, then she stepped back again. Keeping her gaze fixed to his, she reached down to gather up the loose, flowing dress she wore. It was long and deceptively shapeless while managing to emphasize the sweetness of her figure, and she simply watched him with that challenging glint in her eyes while she pulled it up and off. And then she stood before him in nothing at all save a pair of panties.

She was already so ripe. Her breasts had grown heavier in these weeks, round and sweet. Her belly was beginning to curve outward, reminding him of the baby she carried even now. And the fact that she was his.

No matter who he was, no matter what he'd done, she was still his.

"You can refuse me if you like," she said, all womanly challenge. "Or you can take me. I know what I would choose."

And Leonidas might not be much of a man, but he still was one. And when it came to this woman he had no defenses left.

He hauled her to him, crashing his mouth to hers, and taking her with all the wild ferocity that stampeded through him.

Raw. Hot.

Perfect.

She was fire, she was need, and he was nothing but greedy where Susannah was concerned.

He couldn't get close enough. He couldn't taste her enough, touch her enough.

Leonidas took her down onto the lounger where she'd been sitting, and let himself go. It was a frenzy, it was a dance. It was madness and it was beautiful.

And she was his.

Right here, right now, she was his.

And as he thrust into her, for what he understood even then was the last time, he let himself pretend that he deserved her.

Just this once. Just for this moment. Just to see what that felt like.

He made her fall apart. He made her scream his name. He made her beg, and he knew he'd never hear anything so beautiful again as the sound of her voice when she pleaded with him for more. And then more still.

When he finally let himself go, Leonidas toppled over the side of the world, and he carried Susannah with him one final time.

And later that afternoon, while the bright Greek sun was still shining and the air was still cold, he put her on that helicopter and he sent her away.

CHAPTER TWELVE

IT WAS NOT a good week.

Leonidas spent most of it in his office, because he couldn't bear to be in that damned penthouse, filled as it was with the ghost of the wife he'd sent away.

For her own good, he snarled at himself every time he thought about it—but he never seemed to ease his own agitation. He was beginning to imagine it couldn't be done.

It had amazed him at first that a space he'd lived in with her for only seven short weeks should feel haunted by her, particularly when she'd gone to such lengths to avoid him. But Susannah was everywhere, filling up the soaring levels of the penthouse as if she was some kind of aria he couldn't bring himself to shut off or even turn down. He didn't understand how she could manage to inhabit a place when she wasn't even in it, especially when he hadn't spent the kind of time with her in the penthouse as he had on the island.

They had never shared his bed in Rome. He'd never touched her the way he wanted to here.

And still he lay awake as if, were he only to concentrate enough, he might catch her scent on pillows she'd never touched.

He'd spent his first night back from the island in the

penthouse, restless and sleepless, and he'd avoided it ever since. It was easy enough to spend twenty-four hours a day in the office, because there was always a Betancur property somewhere in the world that required attention. Leonidas had poured himself into his work the way he'd done so single-mindedly before his wedding. And he had his staff pack up all the things Susannah had left in the guest room she'd stayed in while she was his widow, and he'd forwarded them on to her new home across the world from him.

Just as he'd wanted, he reminded himself daily.

He had not asked his staff in the Betancur Corporation's Sydney office to report in on how she was settling into life in Australia. She wasn't to be tailed and watched, or have any security above and beyond what was necessary for a woman in her position. He had vowed to himself that this would be a clean break.

"You wondered why you couldn't have me," she'd said back on the island when he'd informed her that they needed to separate. That this was over, this thing between them. That their marriage worked, clearly, only when they were apart. Her voice had been thick with emotions he didn't want to recognize or even acknowledge, and she'd swayed slightly as she stood, as if he'd dealt her a body blow. "This is why. There was never any question that you would leave. It was only a question of how and when." Her gaze had nearly unmanned him. "I expected tawdry affairs I'd be forced to read about in the papers, if I'm honest. That's usually how the people we know send these messages, isn't it?"

He'd wanted to answer her in a way she could not possibly mistake for the usual vicious games of the kinds of people who glittered in Europe's most prestigious ballrooms and viewed the tabloids as their own version of social media. But he'd kept himself under control. Barely.

"It is a big world," he'd said coldly. Hoping he could turn them both to ice so neither one of them could feel a thing. "All I ask is that you choose a place to live that is within reach of one of the Betancur Corporation offices."

"So you can monitor my every move, I presume?"

"So that if the child or you are ever in need, help can arrive swiftly," he'd replied. Through his teeth. "I am trying very hard not to be the monster here, Susannah."

But he'd felt like one. His scars had felt like convictions, pressed into his flesh for all the world to see.

"I want to live in Sydney," she'd told him, her voice a rough sort of whisper. "I not only wish to be on a different continent from you, but across the international dateline whenever possible. So we won't even have a day in common."

He hadn't responded to that the way he'd have liked to, either. Instead, he'd sent her on her way and had a plane meet her in Athens for the flight to Sydney. She'd been as far out of his life as it was possible for her to get without him retreating back to the compound in Idaho.

And now he had exactly what he'd wanted.

Leonidas reminded himself of that as he stood at the window in his immaculately furnished, quietly intimidating office, where he could look out over Rome and feel like a king instead of a monstrous wild man who'd thrived in the wilderness for years. Centuries of rich, powerful men had stood in positions much like this one, looking out at the same view. Rome had been breeding emperors since the dawn of time, and what was he but one more?

An empty king on an empty throne, he thought with

more than a little bitterness today. But that was what he'd asked for.

He hadn't been lying when he'd told her that he always, always got what he wanted. It was only that it had never really occurred to him what a pyrrhic victory that could be, and the truth was, the world without her felt entirely too much like bitter ash.

It will fade in time, he told himself now. *Everything does.*

Leonidas realized he wasn't paying attention to the conference call he was meant to be on, the way he hadn't been paying attention to much these last days. His memory was as good as it was going to get, he'd decided. Too good, since all it seemed to want to do was play out every moment of every interaction he'd had with Susannah since she'd found him in the compound. On an endless, vivid loop.

"I want this settled," he interjected into the heated conversation between several vice presidents scattered around the world, because he had no patience left. Not when he had to spend his every waking moment *not* flying to Sydney. The call went quiet. "Quickly."

Someone cleared his throat. He heard the shuffle of papers, echoing down the line, and what sounded like traffic noise in some or other distant city.

"Of course," the Philippines vice president began carefully. "But it will take a little more time to really—"

"I want the matter dealt with," Leonidas said again, more brusquely this time. "I don't want any more discussion. If you cannot do it, I will find someone who can."

He ended the call with perhaps a bit more force than necessary, and when he turned around to look out through the glass at the rest of the executive floor, he froze.

He thought he was hallucinating.

On some level, he welcomed it.

Leonidas was already starting to think of his time in Idaho as an extended hallucination. It already seemed more like a dream than a reality he'd known for four years—the only reality he'd known at all while he was in it. He'd decided that perhaps he needed to simply accept that he was the sort of person for whom reality was malleable. So it made perfect sense that he should see Susannah marching down the central corridor of the executive floor of the Betancourt Corporation dressed in her trademark inky black.

His widow had been resurrected. And was headed straight for him.

And Leonidas told himself that what he felt as he watched her stride toward him in impossible shoes with an unreadable expression on her lovely face was fury.

The way his pulse rocketed. The way his heart kicked at his ribs. That pounding thing in his head, his gut, his sex.

Fury. He told himself it had to be fury that she had dared contradict his wishes and show up here.

Because he wouldn't let it be anything else.

Susannah nodded imperiously at his secretary, but didn't slow. She swept past the outer desk, then pushed her way into his office as if he'd issued her an engraved invitation to do just that.

And then she was here. Right here. And it had been only a week since he'd last seen her on that island. A week since he'd said the words he knew would hurt her, and so they had. A week since she'd stood before him, her mouth moving in a way that told him she was working her hardest to keep her tears inside. She hadn't let one fall. Not a single one.

He'd felt that like a loss, too.

But today he told himself that his response to her was fury, because it should have been. He didn't move as she kept coming, bearing down upon him where he stood as if she was considering toppling him straight backward, through the window and down to the streets of Rome far below.

A part of him thought he might let her try.

Before she made it all the way to the window, she veered to the left and to his desk. Her blue eyes met his and he felt himself tense, because the look that she was giving him was not exactly friendly. She held his gaze and stabbed her finger on the button that made the glass in all his windows that faced the office go smoky. Giving them exactly the sort of privacy he didn't want.

"You are supposed to be in Sydney." His voice sounded like steel. Harsh and very nearly rude. "Sydney, Australia, to be precise, which is a good, long way from here. A good, long, *deliberate* way from here."

"As you can see, I am not in Sydney."

This woman made him…thirsty. His eyes drank her in and he wanted to follow his gaze with his hands. The deep black dress she wore fit her beautifully, and called attention to that tiniest of swells at her belly. So tiny that he very much doubted anyone but him would know what it signified.

But he knew. Oh, did he know.

And this time, when a new wave of fury broke over him, he knew it wasn't masking anything. He knew it was real.

"Do you think I sent you away for my health?" he demanded.

She let out a noise. "I don't care why you sent me away, Leonidas."

And he had never heard that tone from her before. Not

at all cool. Not remotely serene. Not calm in any way whatsoever. It was so surprising—so very unlike the Susannah he knew—that it almost knocked him back a step.

He frowned at her, and realized abruptly that while she looked as sleek and controlled as she usually did, it was only the surface. The effortless chignon to tame her blond hair, the stunning dress that called attention to its asymmetrical hem and its dark color, and the sort of shoes that most women couldn't stand in upright, much less use to stride across office buildings. All of that was typical Susannah.

But her blue eyes were a storm.

And this close to her, hidden away behind smoky glass in his office, he could see that she was trembling besides.

"Susannah—"

"I don't care," she said again, more sharply this time. She took a step toward him, then stopped as if she wasn't sure she could control herself. "For once, I just don't care about you or your health or your feelings or anything else. My God, Leonidas, do you realize that my entire life has been about you?"

"Hardly." Leonidas scoffed at her. At that notion. At the heavy thing that moved in him, entirely too much like shame. "I doubt you could have picked me out of a lineup before our marriage."

And the laugh she let out then was hollow. Not much like laughter at all. It set his teeth on edge.

"You're thinking of yourself, not me," she retorted. "A rather common occurrence, I think." When he only blinked at her, astonished, she pushed on. "I was a teenager. My parents told me that I was promised to you long before we got married, and believe me, I knew exactly who I was saving myself for. You were Leonidas Betancur. I could have found you blindfolded and in the dark."

He told himself there was no reason that, too, should settle on him like an indictment.

"I am not responsible for the fantasy life of a schoolgirl," he gritted out at her.

Susannah nodded, as if he'd confirmed her expectations. Low ones, at that. "On our wedding day, you took great pains to tell me how little the things that mattered to me matter to you. Like my schoolgirl fantasies that you might treat me the way any man treats his bride. And I accepted that, because my mother told me it was my place to do so."

Leonidas couldn't tell if he was affronted or abashed by that. He didn't much care for either. He decided he preferred affront, and stood taller.

"You were nineteen years old and I was an extremely busy—"

"But then you died," she continued, and there was a shaking in her voice, but it didn't seem to bother her in the least. She advanced another step. "Has it ever crossed your mind how much easier it would have been for me to marry someone else after that?"

"It would make you a bigamist, but I sense that is of no matter in this remarkably slanted portrayal of our relationship."

"I'm not sure *relationship* is the word I'd choose to describe a distant engagement, a circus of a wedding during which you spoke only to your business associates, your death and resurrection, my unwise attempt to help you—"

"Susannah." His lips felt thin enough to cut glass. "I am still an extremely busy man, as you must surely be aware. This harangue could have been put into letter form and sent by post, surely. Why did you fly some sixteen thousand kilometers to do it in person?"

She studied him for a moment, and there was still

that fine trembling all over her. Her mouth. Her fingers. He could even see it in her legs. But she didn't appear to notice.

"Everyone was deeply invested in my remarriage, Leonidas. I was bullied and manipulated, pushed and prodded. No one took me seriously. No one wanted to take me at all, unless it was to the altar. But I persisted."

"Yes, and your persistence makes you a great hero, I am sure," Leonidas said drily. "Given that it made you perhaps the most powerful woman in the world. My heart bleeds for your sacrifice."

"I persisted because of you, you arrogant—" She cut herself off. He watched her pull in a breath, as if she needed it to steady herself, and then her blue eyes were hard on his again. "I persisted because of *you*. Because I had an idea of you in my head."

"Based on tabloid nonsense and too many fairy tales, I have no doubt."

"Because you danced with me at our wedding reception," she corrected him, her voice as quiet as it was firm. "You held me in your arms and you looked at me as if I was…everything. A woman. Your wife. Just for one moment, I believed I could be. That it would all work out."

Leonidas could say nothing then. He remembered that dance, and he didn't know if it was memory or longing that moved in him now. The urge to hold her again, to sweep her into his arms without having to pretend it had anything to do with dancing or weddings or galas, swept over him. It was like an itch, pushing him to the limit.

But Susannah was still coming toward him, that wildness in her blue eyes.

"I carried this company for four years," she told him matter-of-factly. "I made myself into an icon. The untouchable widow. A Betancur legend. And all the while, I looked for you."

"No one asked you to do this," he growled back at her. "You should have left me on that mountaintop. No one could possibly have blamed you. Hell, they would have celebrated in the streets."

"I looked for you and then I found you," she continued, as if she hadn't heard him say a word. "I took you out of there. I even sweetened the deal with the virginity I'd been holding on to for all these years. But like everything else, you didn't seem to realize that it was a gift."

"I beg your pardon." He stood as tall as he could without breaking something, and his voice was so scornful he was surprised it didn't leave marks. And he couldn't seem to stop it. "Have you come all this way to remind me that I owe you a thank-you note? I'll instruct my secretary to type one up as soon as possible. Is that all?"

Susannah shook her head at him, as if he'd disappointed her. Again. "You know your cousins. You can imagine the lengths they were willing to go to get control of me, and by extension the company."

The truth was, Leonidas did know. And he didn't want to know.

"I refused to drink out of an open glass that wasn't first tested by someone else for years," she told him. "Because I didn't want to wake up to find myself roofied and married to a random Betancur, then declared unfit and packed off to a mental institution before ten the next morning so I couldn't object. Do you think that was fun?"

"So that's a yes, then," he said after a moment, feeling more and more certain that if she didn't leave, and soon, he was going to do something he might truly regret. Like forget why he'd sent her away in the first place. "You do want a thank-you note."

But this time, Susannah closed the distance between them. And then she was standing there before him, within touching distance. She was still trembling, and it slowly dawned on Leonidas that that faint little tremor that shook all over her wasn't fear or emotion.

It was temper.

She was furious. At him.

"I wanted to leave when we brought you home from Idaho, but you begged me to stay," she reminded him.

"Begged?" He laughed. Or made himself laugh, more like. "Perhaps your memory has as many gaps as mine."

"The funny thing is that I knew better. I knew that nothing could come of it. That we would always end up in the same place." That storm in her eyes seemed to get wilder. More treacherous. "Right here."

He said nothing. He could only seem to stand there before her, undone in ways he refused to investigate because he didn't think he could be fixed. He didn't think he'd ever put himself back together—but he didn't want to think about that, either.

Because it doesn't matter, something in him asserted. *Nothing matters once she's gone.*

He told himself that life—frozen and haunted and consumed with the company—was better. It was much, much better than this.

"I'm pregnant, Leonidas," she said then, as if the very words hurt as she said them. "Don't you understand what that means?"

"Of course I understand," he bit out.

Then Susannah did something extraordinary. She punched him.

She balled up her hand into a fist and whacked it against his chest. Not enough to hurt, or move him backward even a little, but certainly enough to get his attention.

The way no one had ever dared do in all his life.

Leonidas stared down at her, at that fist she held there between them as if she planned to punch him again, and felt something roaring in him. Loud and long. Raw and demanding.

"I would suggest that you rethink whatever it is you think you're doing," he said. Very, very quietly. "And quickly."

"I am your wife," Susannah said, in very much the same tone. "And I'm the mother of your child. Whatever else happens, those two things remain."

Her fist seemed to tighten, as if she was contemplating hitting him again.

"I take it you have never heard of the divorce you asked for," he said, not exactly nicely. "Perhaps they didn't teach that in your strict little convent where you dreamed of wedding dances and were met with only cruel disappointment."

Susannah punched him again. Harder this time.

"You're a coward," she said, very distinctly.

And that roaring thing in him took over. It was as if everything rolled together and became the same searing bolt of light. Leonidas reached down and took her fist in his palm and then held it away from his chest as if it was a weapon. As if she could do him real harm, if he let her.

And he had no qualm whatsoever pulling her closer, reaching down to wrap one hand around her hip and haul her the extra distance toward him so he could keep her locked down.

"Say that again," he invited her, getting into her face so his lips were a mere breath from hers. "I dare you. And see what happens if you punch me again when you do."

But she had married him when she was a teenager and she'd stayed his widow for years when anyone else would have folded. Maybe it wasn't surprising that she didn't back down.

If anything, her blue eyes blazed hotter.

"You're a coward," she said again, and with more force this time. "It took me too long to recognize this for what it is. I was so certain that you would behave exactly the way my mother said you would behave. Like all the men she knows, my father among them. Faithless and unkind because they don't think they're required to be anything more than the contents of their bank accounts. I assumed you were the same."

"I am all that and more," he promised her.

"Those men are weak," she threw at him, and if she was intimidated by the way he held her, pulled up against him as if he might kill her or kiss her at any moment, she gave no sign. Her blue eyes flashed and she forged on. "If any one of your cousins went down in a plane, they would have died. And not from the impact. But because they wouldn't have it in them to fight. Every single scar on your body tells me a story about the real Leonidas Betancur. And every one of those stories is a tale of overcoming impossible odds. It isn't accidental that you ruled that compound. They could have killed you when they found you, but they didn't. They could have put you to work as a cook. A janitor. Instead, you became their god."

"A god and a janitor are much the same thing in a place where there is no running water and winter lasts ten months," he told her, his voice a harsh slap.

"I told you that you couldn't have me, but I was only protecting myself," she whispered.

"Something you would do good to think more about right now, Susannah."

"But you never told me the truth," she accused him.

"That no one can have *you*, Leonidas. That it's not about me at all."

That struck at him, and he hated it. "You have no idea what you're talking about."

"You are so filled with self-loathing and this terrible darkness you carry around inside of you that you think you have nothing to give anyone. Leonidas. You do."

And her words sat there like heavy stones on his chest. Her blue eyes burned into him, accusation and something else. Challenge, perhaps. Determination.

Not that it mattered.

Because she was right.

"I don't," he heard himself say, as if from far away. "I don't have anything to give. I never have."

Susannah made a sound, small and raw, and the look in her eyes changed. Still electric, though the storm seemed to deepen. Soften.

She stopped holding herself so tightly upright and apart from him, and melted against him. And it was only the fact that it might hurt her that kept Leonidas from hurling her away from him. Throwing her across the room, before that melting softness could tear him apart the way he knew it would.

He knew it.

"You do," she told him, as if it was a self-evident truth, blazing like a fire in the corner of his office. "You have everything to give. You're a good man, Leonidas."

He let out a laugh, harsh and short. "Not only is that not true, but you wouldn't know it if it was. You don't know me, Susannah. I might as well be a stranger on the street."

"I do know it," she retorted, fiercely. "Because I walked into a room in a scary compound on the side of a mountain and met a stranger who had no reason at all to treat me kindly. You could have hurt me then. You didn't."

"I took your virginity."

"I gave it to you and even then, you didn't hurt me," she said hotly. "You didn't remember me and you weren't abusive. And you could have been. Who could have stopped you?" She shook her head at him. "I want you to think about that, Leonidas. When you thought you were a god, you didn't abuse your power. You tempered it."

He felt his grip tighten on her and made himself loosen it. "None of this matters now."

"Of course it matters." She sounded something like frustrated. And raw with it. "You think that you're the same as your parents. Leonidas. But you're not. You think you're just like your cousins, but there's no comparison. You're nothing like any of the people we know."

"That is nothing but a mask," he gritted out.

"The mask wasn't the Count, who lived by his ideals and stayed true to his vows," Susannah retorted. "The mask is this, here. The Betancurs. Not you."

He let her go then, before he did something else he'd never be able to forgive or undo. Like pull her closer.

He put the distance between them then that he should never have allowed her to close and straightened his suit as if he was making sure his costume still fit—but no. She was wrong. This was his life, not a mask. That was the trouble.

"I will support you and this child," he said briskly, ignoring the thickness in his voice. "Neither one of you will ever want for anything. If you wish to remarry, nothing will change. If you wish to retain the Betancur name, you can do that as well with my blessing. It is entirely up to you, Susannah. All that I ask is that you do it far from here, where there is none of...this." And his voice was too rough then. He knew it. But he couldn't seem to stop it. "None of these lies, these games. Make the child a better class of Betancur."

"Him," Susannah said. Very distinctly.

When Leonidas only stared at her, as if everything in him had turned to ice where he stood, she aimed that heartbreaking smile of hers at him. Straight at him as if she knew, at last, what a weapon it was.

"It's a boy, Leonidas. We're having a little boy." And she didn't wait for him to process that. Instead, she twisted the knife and thrust it in deeper. "And you have a choice to make. Will you treat your own son the way your father treated you? Or will you prove that you're the better man? Will you behave like your mother—so terrible that when her only son found out she'd arranged to have him killed he wasn't all that surprised? Or will you make certain that your own child will never, ever believe that you could be capable of such a thing?"

"You're making my point for me, Susannah. Look at where I come from."

"I know exactly where you come from, because I come from the same place," she said fiercely. "And I've been in love with you since the moment I learned that I was to be yours."

And it wasn't the first time in his life that Leonidas had shattered, but this time, he thought the damage might be permanent.

"That's nothing but a schoolgirl's fantasy," he managed to say past the noise inside him.

"Maybe so. But it's still here. And it's only grown, you foolish man. I don't think it's going anywhere."

"You need to go," he said, but his voice hardly sounded like his own.

"I'm going to do something radical, something our

parents never did for either one of us, and love this baby.
Our son." Susannah's gaze held him as if she was pinning him to a wall. "Will you?"

He staggered back as if she'd hauled off and hit him.
Some part of him wished she would. He knew how to take
a blow. He'd learned that young, at his own father's hand—

And the thought of a son of his own taking the kind of
beatings he'd weathered sickened him, down deep into
his bones, until he felt something like arthritic with the
force of his own disgust at the very idea.

"I told you before," he threw at her. "I don't know how
to love. I don't know what it is."

But she kept coming. This woman who had saved
him. This woman who never saw a monster in him. This
woman who called him the worst of the Betancurs, an
unparalleled monster, but made love to him as if he was
only and ever a man.

"Neither do I," she told him as she drew closer. "But
I want to try. Try with me, Leonidas."

He didn't mean to move, but he found himself down
on his knees, though he was a man who did not kneel. He
was on his knees and she kept coming, and then he was
wrapping her in his arms—or she was the one wrapping
him in hers—and he kissed her belly where their future
grew. Once, then again.

And when he looked up into her face again, tears were
leaving tracks down her cheeks and her eyes were as blue
as all the summers he wanted to show his son. As clear
as a promise. As perfect as a vow.

"I will try, Susannah," he whispered. "For you—for
him—I will spend my whole life trying."

"I will love you enough for both of us, Leonidas," she
told him, her voice rough with emotion. "And this baby
will love you even more than that."

"And I will love the two of you with every part of me," he replied, aware as he said it that she'd changed him. That he was a different man.

Not the invulnerable Leonidas Betancur who had gone down in that plane. Not the Count who'd believed himself a prophet at the very least, but more likely a god. But both of those men and more, the husband who had been loving this woman since he'd kissed her in a faraway compound and she'd brought him back to life.

Life. Love. With Susannah, they were the same thing.

"I will try until I get it right," he told her. "No matter how long it takes. I give you my word."

"As a Betancur?" she asked, but her mouth was curved as if she already knew the answer.

"As the man who needs you, and wants you, and never wants to be apart from you," he replied, smoothing his hands up the line of her back as he knelt there before her. "As the husband who cannot imagine a world without you. As the fool who lost his memory and now sees nothing at all in the whole of this world but you."

And he tugged her mouth down to his, his beautiful Susannah, and showed her what he meant.

Forever.

CHAPTER THIRTEEN

Adonis Esteban Betancur came into the world with a roar.

He had a shock of dark hair and fists he seemed to think were mighty as he waved them all around him in a great fervor.

And Susannah had never seen anything more beautiful, heartbreaking and gorgeous at once, as the way one tiny baby boy with an outsized personality wrapped his ruthless, intimidating father around his perfect little fingers.

Though their life together came close.

Leonidas found he didn't much care for running the Betancur Corporation alone, and especially not when he could have Susannah by his side to do it with him. Leonidas on his own had been a force to be reckoned with. The Widow Betancur had wielded her own inexorable power.

Together, there was nothing they couldn't do.

She was pregnant with twin girls when he came to her, late one night after he'd put four-year-old Adonis to bed with tales of brave Greek gods and stories of grand adventures. Susannah watched him from where she sat, out by the quiet pool in the soft Australian night, in the same Darling Point house in Sydney where he'd sent her to live on her own once upon a time.

Leonidas smiled as he came to her, lit by the soft lights that hung in the trees, and sat beside her on the outdoor couch that was tucked up in the shade during the hot days and offered a fire pit for the cooler evenings.

He rested one arm on the back of the sofa and twisted to kiss her as he rested his other on her huge belly, laughing against her mouth when one of his daughters kicked at him. This was how they danced now, Susannah thought. This was the best dance of her life.

"When you tell Adonis stories of gods, do you mention that you were one?" she teased him.

Leonidas took the kiss deeper for a moment, letting her taste that hunger that had only intensified across all these full, bright years. And when he pulled back his smile had gone wolfish in a manner that boded well for the rest of the evening.

"That is a story he will appreciate more when he is older, I think," he murmured. "When he has forgotten how much he looked up to me when he was small."

He did not mention how little he'd looked up to his own father. He didn't have to; it was obvious every time he did not beat his own son to a pulp. Every time he did not go off on a rampage and use his fists as punctuation.

Every time he did not have to *try* to love his son and his wife—he just did, and well, despite the lack of any parental role models in that area.

Because when Leonidas Betancur decided to do something, he did it well.

Susannah had stood beside him as he'd handled his mother these past years after he'd cut her off from the Betancur fortune, as promised. The world had watched Apollonia's dramatic response to that, played out in as many tabloids as would listen to her tales of woe.

"If you want to see your grandchild," Leonidas had

told her the last time she'd showed up where she wasn't welcome, "you have a great deal of work to do to convince me that you deserve it."

The names his own mother had called him then had been disgusting, but unsurprising. And the last they'd heard of Apollonia, she'd shacked up with one of her many lovers in Cape Town. Where Susannah hoped she'd stay, nicely hidden away, for as long as possible.

Meanwhile, the arrival of Adonis had cracked something open in the heart Susannah would have said Martin Forrester didn't have.

"I suppose you don't have to be a good man to love a baby," she'd said to Leonidas in wonder not long after Adonis was born, when her father had not only insisted on a visit but had chastised Annemieke for her dour attitude during it. Because if she wasn't mistaken, her crusty father had fallen head over heels in love with his grandson.

"No," Leonidas had agreed. "But if you're lucky, loving a child can show you how to be a better one."

Leonidas was more than a good man, Susannah thought. He loved his son so wholly and obviously that it could have lit up the world, if he'd let it.

He loved her the same way.

So much, so deep, it was almost funny to imagine that five years ago, they'd stood in the Betancur offices in Rome and vowed to *try* to love each other.

"Do you know what today is?" she asked him now.

"A Tuesday," he replied at once, drawing patterns on her belly as if sending secret, encoded messages to the twin girls within. "In Sydney, Australia, where I am happy to say we are both on the same side of the international dateline."

"Five years ago today I hunted you down in your office in Rome, pregnant with Adonis and very, very unhappy with you," she reminded him.

"Surely not, when I am in all ways the very best of men. Isn't that what you were moaning into your pillow just this morning?"

Susannah made a face at him. Then reached out to put her hand on his rock-hard thigh beside her, letting his heat and strength seep into her. He made her feel safe and strong. He made her feel as if they were dancing, around and around, when they were sitting still. She was huge with this pregnancy, ungainly and slow, and he made her feel beautiful.

"If all of this is you *trying* to love me, and our son, and these babies we haven't met yet, I can't imagine what succeeding at it will look like," she told him softly. "Or how my heart will take it."

Leonidas turned to her then, his hard and beautiful face in shadow—but she could see him. She could always see him.

"I love you, Susannah," he said, very gravely, so it lodged in her heart like the best kind of steel. "You saved me five years ago. And you've saved me every day since. And your heart can take it, I promise. I'll make sure of it."

"I love you, too," Susannah whispered, as his lips claimed hers.

She felt him smile against her mouth.

"I know that," he told her. "Haven't you heard? In some places, I am worshipped as a god."

But no one could possibly worship this man as much as she did, Susannah thought, even as she laughed. This remarkable, formidable, perfect man. Her husband. Her other half. The man she'd loved since she was a girl, and loved so much more now she was a woman.

So she showed him, right there on their patio while the wind blew in from the water with hints of summer in it.

The way she showed him for the rest of their life, day after day.

It turned out Leonidas was right. Her heart was just fine, if bigger and brighter than she ever could have imagined when she'd walked up the side of a mountain so long ago and located the husband she hadn't lost, after all.

And never would again, as long as they lived.

* * * * *

SENSIBLE HOUSEKEEPER, SCANDALOUSLY PREGNANT

JENNIE LUCAS

To Kimberley Young, the best editor in the world.

Thanks for making my first ten books the
best they could be!

CHAPTER ONE

THE gray sky dripped rain like mist, fine as cobwebs, across the dark minarets of Istanbul as Louisa Grey cut the last autumn roses from the garden. Her hands, usually so steady, trembled around her pruning scissors.

I can't be pregnant, she told herself fiercely. *Can't be!*

Could she…?

Abruptly Louisa sat back on her haunches, wiping her forehead with her sleeve in the cool twilight of early November. For a moment, she stared at the red and orange roses of the lush garden of the old Ottoman mansion. Then her hands fell into her lap. She felt the weight of the pruning shears against her gray woolen skirt.

Blinking fast, she turned her head blindly to stare out at the red sunset shimmering across the Bosphorus.

One night. She'd worked for her ruthless playboy boss for five years. One night had ruined everything. She'd fled Paris the very next day, demanding a job transfer to his neglected home in Istanbul. She'd tried to put their night of passion behind her. But now, a month later, she had one terrified thought. One question that kept repeating itself in her mind. Every day, the question became louder and more afraid.

Could she be pregnant with her boss's baby?

"Miss? The cook's taken ill," a girl said in accented English behind her. "Please, may he go home?"

Louisa's shoulders instantly became steel-straight. Pushing her black-framed glasses up on her nose, she turned to face the young Turkish maid. She knew she must reveal no weakness to members of her staff who looked to her for leadership. "Why does he not ask me himself?"

"He's afraid you'll say no, miss. With so much to be done for Mr. Cruz's visit—"

"Mr. Cruz is not expected until the morning of the dinner party. Tell the cook to go home. We will manage. But next time," Louisa added sharply, "he must ask me himself and not send someone else because he's afraid."

"Yes, miss."

"Also tell him he must be completely well by the day of the party, or he will be replaced."

With a timid movement like a curtsy, the maid departed.

Once Louisa was alone, her shoulders sagged. Leaning forward, she gathered two fallen roses from the grass and placed them in her basket. She picked up the pruning shears and rose heavily to her feet. She forced herself to go through the household checklist in her mind. The marble floors and chandeliers were sparkling clean. Her boss's favorite foods had been ordered to arrive fresh from the markets each day. His bedroom suite was ready, needing only these fresh roses to sweeten the dark, masculine room for whichever beautiful starlet he might choose to bring home with him this time.

Everything must be perfect for his visit. Mr. Cruz must have no reason whatsoever to complain. No reason, Louisa thought as she clipped the stem of the bush's very last rose with rather more force than necessary, to speak to her alone.

She heard the wrought-iron gate open with a long scraping sound behind her. She'd have to get that oiled, she thought. She turned, expecting to see the gardener, or perhaps the wine seller with the large delivery of champagne she'd ordered for the dinner party.

Instead she sucked in her breath as a towering figure stepped from the shadows. Except this man didn't just step out of the shadows.

He *was* the shadow.

"Mr. Cruz," she whispered, her mouth suddenly dry.

His eyes glittered in the twilight as he looked at her. "Miss Grey."

His deep, husky voice echoed across the garden, causing her heart to pound in her chest. She clenched her fingers tightly around the basket and pruning shears so her suddenly clumsy hands wouldn't drop them. He was three days early. But when had Rafael Cruz ever done what was expected?

Handsome, ruthless and rich, the Argentinian millionaire had the darkly seductive charm of a poet—and a heart like ice.

Tall and broad-shouldered, with a latent power in his thickly muscled body, he stood out from all other men with his strength, his masculine beauty, his wealth and his stylish appearance. But today, his black hair was tousled. His usually immaculate black suit looked rumpled and his tie was loosened and askew at his neck. His jawline was dark with shadow below his sharp cheekbones and Roman nose. Light gray eyes stood out starkly against his tanned olive skin.

Disheveled as he was, today he looked barely civilized, half-brutal. And yet he was somehow even more handsome than she remembered.

A month ago, Louisa had been in his arms. For one night, he'd taken her body, he'd passionately taken her virginity—

She cut off the thought and took a deep, steadying breath.

"Good evening, sir." Her voice betrayed nothing of her emotion. It was dignified, almost cool—the perfect manner for the valued servant of a powerful man. Her training held her in good stead. "Welcome to Istanbul. Everything is in readiness for your visit."

"Of course." His lips curved into a sardonic smile as he came closer to her. His dark hair was windblown and damp. "I would expect nothing less from you, Miss Grey."

She tilted her head back to look up into his brutally handsome face.

There was something dark in his gaze. Something indescribably weary. The smoothly ruthless playboy looked strangely troubled in a way she'd never seen before.

Against her will, worry and concern for him smothered her heart as the mist deepened into rain, splattering noisily against the dark trees above.

"Are you…are you all right, Mr. Cruz?"

He stiffened.

"Perfect," he said coldly. He clearly resented her intrusion.

Louisa tightened her hands against the basket handle, furious at herself. What was she thinking? She knew better than to ask a personal question. If her ten months of house management training hadn't taught her that, living for five years as Rafael Cruz's housekeeper in Paris certainly should have!

He never showed his feelings. She'd tried to do the same. It had been easy for the first year or two. Then somehow, in spite of her best efforts, she'd started to care….

Looking at him now, all she could think about was the last time she'd seen his face, the night she'd realized she was hopelessly, wretchedly in love with her playboy boss. She'd been sobbing alone in the kitchen when he'd come home unexpectedly early from a date with yet another impossibly beautiful woman.

"Why are you crying?" he'd asked in a low voice. She'd tried to lie, to tell him she just had something in her eye, but when their eyes had met she'd been unable to speak. Unable to move as he walked directly to her. He'd taken her in his arms and she'd known, down to her bones, that it could only end in her own heartbreak. And yet she couldn't push him away. How could she, when she loved him, this untamable, forbidden man who could never truly be hers?

In his penthouse near the Champs-Élysées, against the backdrop of the sparkling city and the Eiffel Tower lit up like a beacon in the night, he'd exhaled her name in a growl. He'd grabbed her wrists and pushed her against the kitchen wall, kissing her so savagely that all she could do was gasp out his name in the first shock of explosive, mutual need and the joint hunger of their embrace.

She'd wanted him with desire she'd repressed for years. But how could she have ever allowed herself to surrender, knowing it could only end badly?

And that was before she'd even started to worry she might be pregnant…

Don't think about it! she ordered herself desperately. She couldn't be pregnant. If she were, Rafael would never forgive her. He'd think she'd done it on purpose, that she'd lied to him!

She licked her lips. "I'm…glad you're well," she faltered.

His dark slate eyes traced her face, lingering on her mouth before he abruptly turned away, slinging his overnight bag over his shoulder. "Bring dinner to my room," he barked.

He stalked into the house without looking back.

"At once, sir," she whispered as the rain fell faster.

Heavy droplets pounded against her face and body, plastering her hair to her head and smearing her glasses.

After her boss disappeared into the mansion, she was able to breathe again. Protecting the basket of roses from the rain with her gray woolen blazer, she fell into step behind the two male assistants carrying his suitcases from the limousine now parked in the carriage house.

The fading ribbons of sunset streaked red across the low clouds as Louisa entered the grand foyer of the nineteenth-century mansion. She carefully wiped her feet before noting her boss's wet footprints across the marble that would now need to be meticulously re-cleaned. Her eyes followed the dirty footsteps up the sweeping stairs. She saw his dark head and broad-shouldered back disappear behind the landing to his bedroom suite.

The house felt so different now he was here. Rafael Cruz electrified everything. Especially her.

The men followed him up the stairs with the suitcases, and once she was alone, Louisa leaned against the wall, her legs sagging with relief.

Their first meeting was over. It was done.

It seemed that Rafael—*Mr. Cruz,* she corrected herself angrily. His first name kept sneaking into her mind!—had already forgotten all about their night of passion in Paris.

Now if only she could do the same.

Her eyes looked again toward the second-floor landing. But why had he seemed so troubled? Something was very wrong, and she knew it had nothing to do with their one-night stand. Women were interchangeable to him. Easily forgotten. Completely replaceable. No woman could ever touch Rafael's heart.

So if not for a woman, what had brought him to Istanbul three days early—and in such a black mood? She stared up the empty stairs toward his room. She suddenly yearned to know what troubled him. Yearned to offer him solace, some kind of comfort…

No!

She stomped on the thought angrily. Every woman thought Rafael needed comforting. It was part of his seduction, something he used ruthlessly to his advantage. Women were drawn by his brutish, brooding charm, imagining him a modern Heathcliff with a darkly haunted past. They all yearned to comfort the world-weary Argentinian millionaire with the handsome face and whisper of a broken heart. Louisa had already seen endless women delude themselves into thinking they, and only they, could save his soul. Only Louisa knew the truth.

Rafael Cruz had no soul.

And yet she loved him. She was a fool! Because she, of all women, knew the kind of man he really was— cold, ruthless and unforgiving!

Swear to me you can't get pregnant, Louisa, he'd said to her that breathless night. *I cannot get pregnant,* she'd said.

If it turned out she'd lied to him…

I'm not pregnant, she repeated to herself furiously. *It's impossible!*

And yet, she was afraid to take the test that would tell her for sure. She told herself she was just late. Very late.

Leaving her wet shoes at the front door, she carried the basket of roses into a little mudroom near the large modern kitchen. She filled an expensive crystal vase with water, then arranged the roses carefully inside it. She cleaned the pruning shears and put them away in their drawer. Going up to her room upstairs, she removed her wet clothes, replacing them with a new gray skirt suit as plain and serviceable as the first. She tidied her brown hair back into a severe bun, dried the rain off her glasses with a towel, then gave a single glance at herself in the mirror as she passed. She looked plain and orderly and invisible—just as she wished.

She'd never wanted Rafael to notice her. She'd prayed he wouldn't. After what had happened at her last job, invisibility felt like her only protection. But somehow, it had failed her. Somehow, he'd noticed her anyway. Why had he taken her to his bed? Pity? Convenience?

She took a deep breath, squaring her shoulders. Then she carried the vase of roses into the kitchen.

Almost immediately, her spirits lifted. The kitchen, along with the rest of the mansion, had changed quite a bit in the month since Louisa had arrived here. Her constant attention, working eighteen-hour days to hire staff and oversee cleaning and remodeling of the once-faded house, had turned it into a well-run home. Louisa gently touched the polished wood of the door frame, smiling down at the colorful, gleaming mosaic floor. Overseeing this mansion's restoration to its former glory had been a huge amount of work, but had given her a great deal of pleasure.

Once, it had been neglected. Now it was loved. *Treasured.*

Louisa set her jaw stubbornly. So she wouldn't allow one moment of weakness to force her out of this job she'd loved with such passion for five years. She'd been a convenient woman for Rafael to take to his bed, nothing more. She loved him, but she would try her best to kill that love.

She would do her job. Keep her distance. *Try to forget how he'd taken her virginity.*

She'd forget the way his lips had pressed against hers, so hot and hard and demanding. She'd forget the sensation of his powerful body pressing her to the wall. Forget his strength and the dark hunger in his eyes as he'd lifted her up in his strong arms, and carried her without a word to his bed....

Louisa stood for a moment, alone in the kitchen. Then she started. What had she been doing here? Right. Making his dinner. The cook had gone home sick. She only hoped he had the same hideous stomach flu she'd had in Paris six weeks ago, so he'd be right as rain in three days, in time for Rafael's birthday dinner. She could make simple dishes, but she was no chef. Her cooking skills tended more toward baking cakes and brownies than preparing *chimichurri* sauce for flank steak or preparing a piquant *cazuela de mariscos,* a seafood stew in tomato broth, for a party of twelve!

But like the captain of a ship, she had learned to do nearly every task that running a vast home required. She quickly put together a simple but delicious sandwich using sliced ham and her own freshly homemade bread from the well-stocked pantry. She looked down at the tray and carefully smoothed the linen napkin beneath the silver utensils. She hesitated, then added a small bud vase, in which she placed a newly budding red rose.

There was nothing wrong with adding a rose, she told herself. It was not the act of a lover, but of a house-keeper who cared about details. Nothing had changed. *Nothing.*

She summoned a maid. "Take this tray to Mr. Cruz, please."

The newly hired maid shifted weight from one foot to the other as she picked up the tray. She looked nervous.

With an inward sigh, Louisa patted her on the shoulder encouragingly. "Do not be afraid. Mr. Cruz is…a kind man." She was surprised a lightning bolt didn't strike her dead for that lie. "He will not hurt you." That, at least, was true. He liked his homes and businesses to run smoothly, so he did not ever seduce members of his staff—ever.

At least not until a month ago, when he'd thrown Louisa against his bed and ripped off her clothes. When she'd reached for him so urgently as he fell upon her naked body, and they both were devoured by their hunger and urgent need—

No! *No!*

"Please take it at once," Louisa choked out.

With a nod, the maid took the tray and left the kitchen. But Louisa had barely started washing up the dishes when the girl returned, covered with ham and Dijon mustard smeared down her apron and the rose hanging precariously from her newly wet hair!

"What happened?" Louisa gasped.

The young maid looked close to tears. "He threw the tray at me!" She held the silver tray in one hand and a cracked plate in the other. The accent of her schoolgirl English thickened in her stress. "He says he'll only have you serving him, miss!"

Louisa sucked in her breath.

"He *threw* the *tray?*" Louisa was shocked at the thought of her boss losing control. For heaven's sake, what had happened? Had he lost a business deal? Lost a lot of money? What was wrong with him? For him to be so violent and uncivilized as to actually *throw a tray*—

Louisa's eyes narrowed. Whatever had happened— even if he'd lost the entirety of his fortune—that gave him no excuse to be vicious to a member of her staff! "Give me the tray, Behiye. Then go home."

"Oh, no, miss, please don't sack me—"

"You have just been given the rest of the week off with full pay." She gave a brief smile, covering up her internal rage. "A vacation courtesy of Mr. Cruz, who regrets his brutish behavior very much."

"Thank you, miss."

And if he doesn't regret his behavior yet, Louisa thought furiously as the girl left, *he soon will.*

Louisa's rage built to burning point as she tossed the ceramic plate, once a beautiful specimen of antique İznik blue-and-white porcelain, into the trash. She washed the silver tray and reassembled the entire meal on a new plate, grimly adding a fresh rose in a silver vase. She made another sandwich, exactly the same as the first, and carried it up the sweeping, curving stairs to the second floor.

She gave a single hard knock on his bedroom door.

"Enter," his voice said harshly.

Still furious, Louisa pushed open the door. Then she stopped.

His bedroom was dark.

"Miss Grey." She heard his low, sardonic voice unseen from the darkness. "So good of you to follow my orders."

His voice was deep, combative. *Hostile.*

Peering into the darkness, Louisa saw him sitting on a chair in the shadows, in front of the cold fireplace. She set down the tray on a nearby table and, crossing the room in her sensible two-inch heels, she pulled down a switch to turn on the small lamp.

A circle of yellow light illuminated the darkness, revealing a bedroom that was masculine, Spartan and severe.

"Turn that off," he growled, his gaze whirling on her. The blast of angry heat in his gaze nearly caused her to stagger back.

Then, straightening, Louisa clenched her hands into fists. "You won't intimidate me like you did poor Behiye. How dare you attack a maid, Mr. Cruz? *Throwing a tray at her?* Have you quite lost your mind?"

His eyes narrowed as he slowly rose to his feet.

"It is none of your business."

But she stood firm. "Oh, but it is. You pay me to oversee this household. How do you expect me to do that when you terrorize the staff?"

"I did not throw the tray at her," he growled. "I knocked it out of her hand to the floor. She is the one who tried to catch it. Foolishly."

Spoken like a man who'd never cleaned his own floor. "You frightened her!"

His gray eyes gleamed at her in the shadowy light. "An accident," he bit out. "It was…careless of me." Turning away, he set his jaw. "Give the girl the rest of the day off."

She lifted her chin. "You already did, sir. In fact, you just gave her a week's vacation with full pay."

There was a pause in the darkness. "Miss Grey." His voice sounded suddenly odd, almost wistful. "You seem to always know what I need. Sometimes even before I do."

The look he gave her made her heart catch in her throat. As if he needed something very much right now and wished she knew what, without him saying a word.

She felt his look with a flood of heat. Against her will, she was reminded of how it had felt when he'd kissed her… No. She wouldn't think about that night. Couldn't!

"It's my job to know what you'll want," she said evenly, folding her arms. "You pay me to know."

The words *you pay me* hung between them, dividing them.

"Yes," he said in a low voice. "I do."

He turned away, but not before she caught the stark look in his eyes. The same look she'd seen on his face when he'd first come through the garden gate. It wasn't anguish, exactly, but a flash of vulnerability. Of weariness. Loneliness. But that was ridiculous. How could the most ruthless playboy in Europe ever be lonely?

"You never should have sent the maid," he said in a low, dangerous voice. "I told you specifically I wished for *you* to bring me dinner. Not some maid. You."

He wanted to be alone with her?

Exhilaration flooded through her. Then fear overwhelmed everything. She couldn't allow herself to be seduced again, couldn't!

She kept her expression unmoved, hiding her emotions behind layers of her training as she'd been taught. Formality was her strongest weapon. Her only weapon.

"I regret I did not correctly understand your request, sir," she said stiffly. "I have brought up a newly prepared sandwich for your dinner." She gave him a little bow. "Now, if you please, I will leave you to the peace and tranquility of your own company."

"Stop."

Something in his voice made her obey. Slowly she turned back to face him.

His face was dark. He came close to her, almost touching. "I never should have done it."

"Thrown the tray?" she agreed.

His dark eyes seared through hers. "Made love to you in Paris."

For a moment, she couldn't breathe.

Her desire for her boss threatened everything she held dear. Her career. Her self-respect. *Her soul.*

She forced herself to straighten. "I don't remember any such incident, sir."

"Don't you?" he said in a low voice. He reached down to stroke her cheek. His fingertips were feather-light as he turned her chin to meet his gaze, and she shivered at his touch, at the intensity of his dark eyes. "If you cannot remember it, then I must have been mistaken," he whispered. "I didn't kiss you, then. I didn't feel your body trembling against mine."

"No, you didn't." She could hear the rasp of her own breath, was choked by the frantic beating of her heart. "It never happened."

He leaned forward. "Then why," he said, "have I thought of nothing else?"

Her knees shook. She was so close to surrender. So close to acting like all the others, to flinging herself at him. But there could be only one end to that. She'd seen it played out too many times.

Rafael Cruz was ruthless. He broke women's hearts with careless pleasure.

If she let herself want him—he would be the poison that killed her.

She shook her head desperately. "I don't remember you so much as kissing me."

"Perhaps," he said softly, "this will remind you."

Lowering his head, he kissed her.

His lips seared hers, scorching her entire body with

that one point of contact. She felt his arms around her, pulling her close, closer still until his large, muscular body seemed to surround her on all sides. She was lost, lost in him. His tongue swept hers, causing every nerve ending from her nipples to her earlobes to her toes to sizzle and contract.

He kissed her, and against her will, she surrendered.

CHAPTER TWO

RAFAEL CRUZ had broken many hearts, and he did not feel particularly bad about it.

He wasn't being arrogant. It was simply a fact.

Every woman he'd ever taken to his bed had objected when he'd inevitably ended the affair. They always wanted more. They turned from flirtatious, seductive, powerful women into clingy shrews sobbing for another chance. No wonder he so rarely slept with a woman more than once or twice. Because once he'd possessed them, the women inevitably changed and lost every quality that had originally attracted him in the first place.

He never lied to any of them. He always told them the truth—that their affair would not last long or be based on anything but physical attraction. If women surrendered their bodies and hearts in a way that ultimately caused them pain, well, that was not his fault. They were adults. They made their own choices. He was not to blame.

But he'd sworn long ago never to seduce an

employee. Not out of any concern over a workplace harassment suit—he laughed at that idea—but because the fallout would have made his life inconvenient. And Rafael Cruz must never be inconvenienced.

The world was full of beautiful women to fill his bed. But good employees were hard to find.

Louisa Grey was not merely a competent employee; she was exceptional. She'd become indispensable in his life. She made all his homes run smoothly. After five years, he couldn't imagine his life without her.

She'd never once tried to lure him. Unlike the often clumsy attempts of every woman from his elderly secretary to the cocktail waitress at the bar to gain his notice. Louisa had barely seemed to notice he was a man. *That made him want her most of all.* She was so mysterious. She never spoke of her feelings; never spoke of her past. She had a cool reserve, and hid her beauty beneath glasses and awful clothes.

Still, he'd promised himself he'd never seduce an employee, and he never had once been tempted to break that vow.

Until a month ago.

A mistake. His seduction of Miss Grey had been momentary lapse of willpower. From now on, he had promised himself he would have some self-control.

She was his lead house manager. She coordinated between all his homes around the world. He could not afford to lose her. And women always fell apart when he ended affairs—even previously independent, strong women always turned clingy, whining and desperate in the end. If their night together turned into a full-blown affair, the only end would be the termination of Louisa's employment. Either she would quit, or he would be forced to fire her.

His only hope of keeping her where she belonged— directing his home and satisfying his needs before he was even half-aware of them—was to keep her at a distance.

But his resolve had disappeared from the moment he saw her today.

He'd had a horrible day. Arriving in Istanbul—too late, too late!—his whole body had been knotted up in tension and grief and fury.

Returning from his father's funeral, the father he'd never known, he'd felt so tense his muscles had ached with his rage and failure. His chauffeur had opened the door, and as Rafael had gotten out beneath the drizzling rain, he'd loosened his tie and headed for his house, intending to seek a tall glass of whiskey and perhaps to send his private jet to Paris to collect his latest French flirtation and deliver her to Istanbul. He'd told himself his one-night-stand with his housekeeper had been a mistake that must never be repeated. *It must be forgotten.*

Then he'd seen Louisa in the twilight of the garden behind the mansion. Standing beneath the cypress and fig trees, she'd been holding a basket of freshly cut roses. She looked even more beautiful than he remembered, more sensual and desirable than he could bear. Looking out at the dark waters of the Bosphorus toward

Asia, she'd had an expression of wonderment and wistfulness.

Louisa Grey was an oasis of calm and comfort in this chaotic, cold world.

Rafael had promised himself he wouldn't touch her. But when she'd turned to him with her wide, black-fringed eyes, he'd looked at her slender body beneath those shapeless, ugly clothes. He'd known from that moment that he would have her again, no matter what it cost him.

He'd ordered her to come up to his bedroom. Tense and pacing, he'd waited for her. Then he'd been surprised by the maid with the tray. Later, when Louisa had deigned to come up to his room, she'd defied him as no one else dared. She'd tormented him—provoked him. Finally, when she'd drawn up her shoulders and said in a voice full of bravado, *I don't remember you so much as kissing me,* something inside him had snapped.

He'd seized her.

Now, kissing Louisa was heaven. Her lips were so soft and sweet and yielding beneath his. Her skin smelled like soap and spring flowers. His whole body tightened with the force of his desire.

It was more than desire. He knew this was wrong—forbidden—but he longed for her in a way he'd never felt for any woman. The elusive Miss Grey. When he felt her surrender in his arms, a growl rose in the back of his throat. He wrapped his arms around her more tightly and started to pull her back toward the bed.

With a gasp, Louisa wrenched away from him. "No!"

"Louisa—"

"No." She stumbled back from him violently. "We can't do this!"

He reached his arms out for her. "We must."

She jumped back another two steps. With a shuddering intake of breath, she put her fingertips on her lips as if she could still feel him kissing her. "I can't," she whispered. "I work for you."

He knew she was right. That just made him more angry, more determined to have her.

"It doesn't matter," he said fiercely.

"Oh, but it does. You have a rule, Mr. Cruz," she said, lifting her chin. Her beautiful chocolate-colored eyes glittered. "You never seduce your employees. That's the one line you don't cross!"

He craved her desperately. She was the one tonic that would make him forget everything he'd lost today. But he could not tell her that. He must never appear vulnerable to anyone—not to any woman on earth, let alone one of his employees!

"It is my rule, not yours," he said coolly. "I can choose to make an exception."

But she stepped back, out of his reach.

"I choose differently," she said. "What happened between us in Paris was a mistake. It will never happen again. I can't lose my career, my reputation, my life," she whispered. "Not again!"

He frowned, trying to read her expression.

"What do you mean, *again?*"

She blinked fast as she looked away. "Nothing."

"I don't believe you." He knew little about her past beyond what was spelled out on her résumé. She'd always deflected personal questions with cool, dignified reserve.

She turned to him sharply. "Paris," she muttered. "I meant Paris."

"You didn't mean Paris."

"What else?"

Another deflection. He narrowed his eyes. "There was another man before me," he guessed.

"You know there wasn't!"

"You were a virgin. That doesn't mean there wasn't another man." The thought made his shoulders feel tighter still.

She set her jaw stubbornly. "You checked my references. You know all about me."

Rafael didn't know half what he wished he knew. He'd been so impressed by her at the interview that he'd done only the barest measure of due diligence above and beyond what the exclusive employment agency had provided. He never liked to rely totally on underlings. He'd spoken to the wife of her last employer, and the woman had raved up and down the moon about Louisa Grey, calling her "amazing" and a "treasure." It seemed very unlikely that she would have spoken so highly about Louisa if she'd suspected her husband of having an affair with her.

It didn't make sense.

"What are you hiding?" Rafael said, his eyes searching her face. "You never mention family or friends back home. Why? Why do you never want to go home?"

He saw her eyes widen, heard her intake of breath. Then she smoothed her oversize gray woolen skirt beneath her trembling hands. "It doesn't matter." She turned away. "If there will be nothing else, sir, I will leave you now—"

"No, damn it." He crossed the room in two steps, blocking the doorway so she could not leave. "I won't let you go. Not until you answer me. I…" *I need you,* he almost said, but the words caught in his throat as sharply as a razorblade. He hadn't said them to anyone for years. He'd created his whole life to avoid saying them.

Through the open window, he could see the lights of Istanbul flickering in the dusk. Black silhouettes of minarets plunged like daggers into the dying red sunset. He could hear a muezzin's broadcasted call to prayers echo across the sea.

His eyes locked with hers in the shadowy room. The tension between them changed. Electrified. Desire for her swept through him, negating all else.

"Get out of my way, Mr. Cruz," she whispered.

He could hear the quickness of her breath, see the rise and fall of her chest. "No."

"You can't keep me here!"

Rafael almost shook with the force of his need for her. "Can't I?" he said softly.

He wanted to bury himself in her so deeply that he would forget everything—everything that threatened to break him apart. He heard the quick pant of her breath. He took a deep breath of her, smelling her fragrance, soap and clean cotton and freshly cut roses.

If he were smart, he would let her go. He would find a different woman to fill his bed. The pouting French starlet he'd been flirting with for the last few days. Her. Anyone.

Anyone but Louisa Grey.

His eyes fell to her mouth. Her beautiful bow-shaped lips were pink and bare of makeup. Something about Louisa intrigued him beyond his understanding. He wanted her in a way that almost felt against his will. He craved the mind-numbing pleasure he'd felt making love to her. The best sex of his life.

The pleasure of her body would help him forget his pain. She would be the drug to distract him from his grief and despair. He would ravish her in his bed, hard and fast, until the fire in his blood was sated. Until the pain in his heart was obliterated into ash. Then, and only then, would he let her go….

Rafael looked at her from beneath heavily lidded eyes. He saw the tremble of her body in the shadows.

She wanted to escape him—to deny them both what they both wanted.

But this inexperienced girl was no match for his will. She'd been a virgin when he'd first taken her in Paris. She would not be able to resist him now. He would possess her until he was utterly satiated, until he felt her writhe and shake beneath his body.

Slowly, implacably, Rafael pulled her into his arms.

She tried to resist, but he would not let her go. She trembled, tilting her head back to look up into his face. Tall as she was for a woman, he still towered over her.

Her beautiful brown eyes glistened in the faint golden light.

"Please," she said in a low voice. "Let me go."

His hands tightened on her. "Are you so afraid?" he said quietly.

She drew a shuddering breath. "Yes."

He cupped her face. "Of me?"

"No," she said in a low voice. "If you kiss me again, if you take me to your bed, I'm afraid…"

"Afraid of what?"

She blinked fast, her full lashes black against her pale skin.

"Afraid I'll die of wanting you," she whispered.

He nearly gasped.

Reaching up, Louisa put her hand on his rough cheek. "I've missed you," she said in a voice full of anguish. "I've missed you so…."

He shook beneath her touch. Taking her hand in his own, he fervently kissed the palm, then pulled her into his arms. Lowering his mouth to hers, he kissed her. Deeply. Hungrily.

He kissed her with all the repressed desire of the month they'd been apart—and of all the wasted years before that.

Louisa trembled.

Rafael's touch burned her. It frightened her. *Seduced her.*

He kissed her, his powerful lips moving over hers. Guiding her. Giving her such explosive pleasure, causing electricity to sizzle down her limbs beneath her gray woolen suit until she thought she might die of this ache like fire.

Too many years of repressed desire could no longer be contained. It was all she could do not to blurt out the two devastating secrets that would destroy everything.

She was completely, irrevocably in love with a man who never wanted to be either husband or father. And she might be pregnant with his child....

Rafael's hand on the back of her head, stroking through her hair and the bare skin of her neck, created a spark that seared up and down her body. Her breasts became heavy, her nipples tight. She tingled with painful awareness all over her body. She wanted him so much it drove her to despair.

"Forget I'm your boss," he murmured against her skin. She felt the warmth of his breath, the roughness of his jawline against her cheek. "Stay with me tonight."

She was overwhelmed by the sensuality of his hands on her body, his fingers stroking her back down to her hips.

He pulled back from her and golden light flickered in his dark eyes like the hot flames in hell. "Stay with me," he commanded.

Her gaze fell to his lips. She could barely breathe. She wanted to say yes. Wanted it so badly she thought she'd die. But...

"I can't," she gasped, even as her fingers tightened on his black shirt. She licked her lips. "If the rest of the staff ever found out I'd been your mistress...they'd lose all respect for me."

"It's no business of theirs—"

"I'd lose all respect for myself!"

For answer, he touched her hair. Pulling out the pins that held her hair in a tight bun, he let it tumble down her shoulders. "So beautiful," he whispered, moving his fingers through the long chestnut waves. He looked into her eyes. "Why don't you ever let it down?"

Her hair? Or her guard?

His fingers felt so deliciously light moving through her hair. She held her breath. Her scalp tingled as he stroked whisper-light touches against her earlobes and neck then cradled the back of her head in both of his hands. He looked down at her.

"You work miracles." He looked around the newly remodeled bedroom with wonder. "No one could ever feel anything for you...but respect."

She exhaled. His words were balm to her.

But she knew how the world truly worked. Her spine snapped straight.

"Reputations are destroyed by affairs like this. No one would ever hire me for a respectable job again."

"Why would you ever leave me?" He lifted a dark eyebrow. "No woman ever wants to leave."

He spoke the words as a joke, but Louisa knew they were true. She also knew that she couldn't possibly remain his housekeeper as his discarded mistress. That she'd already given him her body once was bad enough—it had forced her to flee to Istanbul.

She was still able to work for him, barely. But she did have some pride. If she gave herself to him completely, if she admitted that she was in love with him, she knew she'd never recover from his scorn. She'd never survive loving him, working for him—and seeing him move on to another woman.

Especially if she was pregnant…

I'm not pregnant, she repeated to herself, but the words had become hollow and metallic. She gritted her teeth. All right, fine. She would take the test. *Tonight.* As soon as she was alone. Then she would know for sure that she had nothing to fear. Or else she'd have some shocking news for Rafael Cruz—the heartless, ruthless, charming playboy—and she'd have to tell him she was going to make him a father against his will.

He would never forgive her. He would never believe something had gone wrong with the Pill, that her cycle must have been thrown off by those two days of bad flu she'd had a week or two before their affair. She'd given him her word of honor she couldn't get pregnant. He'd be furious. He'd think she'd lied.

Or worse: that she'd gotten pregnant on purpose to trap him. Louisa had overheard more than one of his cast-off mistresses plotting cold-bloodedly to get pregnant in a stupid, selfish attempt to marry him. He'd evaded their plots easily. So how would he feel being unintentionally trapped by his own housekeeper?

"You're shivering," Rafael murmured. He pulled her closer into his arms. "Are you cold?"

Unable to answer, she shook her head.

He stroked her cheek.

"Let me warm you," he whispered.

His head lowered toward hers.

"No!" She pushed away from Rafael with strength she hadn't known she had. From across the room, they stared at each other, not touching, in the shadows. The only sound was the ragged pant of her breath. She turned away.

"I need you, Louisa," he said behind her. "Don't go."

Not turning around, she closed her eyes. "You don't need me," she replied hoarsely. "There are women aplenty to fill your bed. You have your pick of them. You don't need me."

"I found him," she heard Rafael say behind her. "My father."

She froze in the doorway. With a gasp, she whirled around.

Across the large bedroom, Rafael stood like a statue chiseled in ice. His handsome face was stark and strange, half-illuminated by the window's slanted beam of moonlight.

"You found your father?" she choked out, clasping her hands. "Oh, Rafael, I'm so glad! You've been looking for him for so long!"

"Yes."

His voice was harsh and jagged as a rusty knife. Louisa frowned at him in bewilderment. Why did he not look pleased? Why did he still look so frozen and strange?

Rafael had been looking for his father for twenty years, ever since the Argentinian man who'd raised him had revealed on his deathbed that Rafael wasn't truly his son. His stepfather had told him before he'd died that, the week before he'd married her, Rafael's mother had returned from Istanbul—pregnant.

"Is your father here?" Louisa breathed. "In Istanbul? Have you talked to him?"

"His name was Uzay Çelik," Rafael cut her off. He looked toward the window. "And he died two days ago."

"Oh, no," she whispered, her heart in her throat. Against her will, she walked back across the bedroom toward him as he stared into the flickering lights across the dark waters of the Bosphorus. "Your investigators found him too late."

Slowly he turned to her.

"They never found him at all. My mother is the one who finally told me. After twenty years of silence, she overnighted a letter to Paris that I received this morning. After he was dead."

The hurt in his voice, the pain like a boy's, caught at her throat. And Louisa could hold herself back no longer. Reaching out, she placed her hand on his back, rubbing his tight muscles and his strong, powerful, hunched shoulders. "Why did she wait so long to tell you?"

He gave a harsh laugh. "To hurt me, I suppose," he said. "She doesn't know that it's impossible. I'll never be hurt again—not by her or anyone."

The bleakness of his tone belied his words.

"But surely," Louisa persisted, "your mother loves you—"

His lip curled. "She sent me a letter and a package

that arrived in Paris today." He held up a gold signet ring. "She'd saved it for thirty-seven years, since before I was born. Now she sends it to me. Now, when it's too late."

Louisa's heart turned over in her chest at the pain in his handsome face. She knew what finding his real father had meant to Rafael.

"I barely made it to the funeral. There were only five mourners, and they seemed to have shown up with the thought of asking surviving family members for money. Debts are all my father left behind. No wife. No other children. No friends. Just debts."

"I'm so sorry," Louisa whispered, desperate to take the pain out of his eyes, feeling helpless. "I'll contact your guests and tell them the birthday dinner is canceled."

His gaze became hard. "Why?"

"Because, because," she stammered, "you're in mourning."

He shook his head. "The dinner party will go on as planned."

"Are you sure? You don't have to do this."

He didn't answer. Instead he looked around the beautiful room. He gave a low laugh. "I bought this palace for my father, for when I found him. Now all I have left—" his hand tightened into a fist around the gold ring hanging on a chain "—is this."

She pressed her hand against his rough cheek, looking up into his face. "If only there was something I could do, if only—"

"There is."

And he kissed her.

His lips were fierce, demanding. She could not stop him or pull away; all she could do was surrender to his strength, and the force of her own desire.

His hands moved over her clothes in the soft circle of pale golden light amid the shadows. He stroked her arms, her belly. Pulling off her woolen blazer and dropping it gently to the floor, he cupped her breasts through her thin cotton shirt. She gasped. Then, with a soft moan, she wrapped her arms around his neck and pulled him closer.

He pushed her back against the bed, still kissing her. He moved with increasing urgency, pulling up her blouse, reaching beneath her silk bra to caress her breasts. Her nipples hardened to small pebbles beneath his muscular fingers as she held him close, aching for his touch. But it wasn't enough…wasn't nearly enough!

With sudden impatience, he pulled open the blouse in a single swift movement, popping the buttons. He ripped her flimsy silk bra in half easily, pushing the cups apart and lowering his head to suckle her.

She gasped, arching beneath his mouth. As he licked and bit one nipple, his powerful hand squeezed the other breast, sending sparks of longing down her body, between her legs.

Lifting his head, cupping both her breasts in his large hands, he gave her a hard, possessive kiss that bruised her lips. But amid the pain was an intensity of pleasure, the need of her own longing that drove her almost insane.

She had to stop this.

She would die if she stopped this.

As he kissed her, she felt the weight of his body, fully clothed and so much larger than her own, pressing her heavily into the firm mattress. His mouth plundered hers, his tongue tantalizing and mastering her. She felt his powerful hands move down her body. Grabbing her skirt's hemline at the knee, he pulled it up until her legs were bare all the way to her hips.

He continued to kiss her fiercely, holding her body to the bed with his weight. One hand moved between her legs, caressing between her naked thighs. She sucked in her breath. She tried to move, to push him away from her, but she could not. Her mind was no longer in control of her body. Her body wanted what it wanted—*and it wanted him.*

His hand cupped between her legs, and she gasped. He cut off her gasp with a hard kiss, stealing her protest away, leaving her beyond the ability to fight what they both wanted. He moved his hand beneath her white cotton panties, caressing her slick folds like molten heat with a thick finger, caressing her sensitive core with his thumb.

She gasped, arching off the bed.

He pulled away, looking down at her. His eyes were dark.

Then he yanked her panties off her body in a swift movement, tossing them to the floor. Before reason could start to return, before she could remember she should tell him *No, please, we must stop,* he knelt before her on the bed. Pushing her legs apart, he moved his head between her legs and took a long, languorous taste.

She gave a high-pitched cry, gripping the pillow beneath her head with both hands.

Holding her hips firmly, refusing to allow her to move away, he held her to him. He licked her, lapping her one moment and suckling her the next. His tongue flicked inside her. Then fingers followed, with rough sensuality she could not deny or escape.

With all his experience, he knew just what to do. He played her like an instrument. He knew how to make her sing. The pleasure was so intense she nearly wept.

She felt the first waves of aching fulfillment start to crest, building inside her. Just as her hips started to lift of their own volition against his mouth, just as her whole body started to tremble and shake, he released her. As she cried out in frustration, he rose to his feet. He pulled down his pants. He did not wait to remove the rest of his clothes before climbing on top of her and covering her body with his own. She felt his hardness seeking entry between her legs for one brief second and he brutally thrust himself inside her. A sharp explosion of agonizing pleasure ripped through her as she felt him impale her so deeply. Pinning her with his massive size and weight, he thrust again, more deeply still and her whole body hummed, tense as a bow. The sweet agony coiled inside her, climbing higher…then still higher… until she could not breathe, until she thought she could bear no more, until she thought she would break.

He pulled back and rode her, holding her hips with his big hands to penetrate her so deep and wide and hard she felt split in two. She moaned, holding her hands against the black headboard, writhing from side to side as he shoved inside her again and again. She had to bite her lip to keep herself from moaning his name, from begging him to not stop, from begging him to love her and never leave…

With a growl, he pushed one last time inside her so deep it shattered her apart into a thousand glimmering pieces. He nearly pierced her heart, and as her world exploded, from a distance she heard herself scream his name.

The next morning, Rafael woke up to find his lead housekeeper, the most prized member of his staff, naked and sleeping beside him in bed.

He nearly groaned aloud. He'd done it. *Again*. After promising himself he'd never touch Louisa again!

Sunlight was shining bright through the tall windows of his bedroom. The dark wood and new furniture, with shining steel fixtures and stark glass lights, had an oddly warm appearance beneath the soft golden light pouring from the windows. Or maybe the golden glow came from the woman now sleeping beside him. She made everything beautiful.

He looked at her lovely face, surrounded by brown hair tumbling over the pillow in waves. A tender smile still curved her pink lips. Sleeping and naked, she looked so vulnerable. So young.

He cursed himself in low, guttural Spanish.

He'd thought he had some self-control. He'd done everything to try to forget his night with Louisa Grey, and the fact that it had been the single most amazing sexual experience of his life. Which with all his experience, was incredible.

Perhaps that was why he'd been unable to forget. Uninterested in other women. Unable to think of anything else.

He still didn't know why she'd been crying that night in Paris. He'd been shocked when he'd returned from another dull date to find Louisa overcome with emotion. Louisa, who never showed her feelings. He hadn't known how to deal with it, so he'd taken her in his arms. And then he'd done what he'd longed to do for months. He'd kissed her. He'd done more than kiss her. He'd made passionate, reckless love to her—and discovered to his shock that his beautiful, self-contained housekeeper was, at twenty-eight, still a virgin.

Even now, when by all rights he should have been well satisfied, his body tightened at the memory of making love to her in Paris. Of making love to her last night. He felt the heat off her skin as she lay sleeping beside him, naked in his bed, and he wanted her anew.

He looked at her in the morning light. She looked so beautiful. So impossibly young. So lush and desirable.

He'd tried to rid himself of his inconvenient desire for her. He'd allowed her to transfer to his Istanbul house, though he did not want her to leave. He'd busied himself with work in Paris. He'd tried to move on with another woman, specifically Dominique Lepetit, though the truth was that the amoral actress was no longer of any interest to him.

Louisa, however...

With a low groan, he rolled over in bed and sat up, holding his head in his hands. He could still not quite believe he'd slept with her without a condom again, something he'd never done with any other woman. Oh, other women had told him they were on the Pill, but he'd never trusted them completely. In the past, he'd either been well-prepared with condoms, or he'd walked away from the situation. Simple as that. He never wanted to have a wife or child or be pinned down in any way. He took freedom even more seriously than he took pleasure.

Rafael glanced back over his shoulder at Louisa, who was still sleeping peacefully, like a child. He immediately felt comforted. Louisa Grey would never lie. If she'd said she was on the Pill, then she was.

He trusted her. In fact, she was the only woman he trusted. She'd been a virgin the first time he'd taken her, for God's sake. That had been an amazing discovery during an incredible night. And last night had been even better....

He had the sudden memory of her naked body beneath his, the way she'd felt when he'd pushed inside her. The image of her ecstatic face as he'd possessed her as their sweaty bodies pressed together urgently in the heat of the night.

He'd thought the first time he'd taken her, in Paris, had been the best night he'd ever had with any woman. But last night had been even better. Something about the feel of her skin—or the smell of her hair. Perhaps it was the way she moved, the combination of sensuality mixed with innocence. Or her elusiveness. She always held something of herself back. Always.

Except in his bed.

Whatever the cause, some chemical reaction took hold of his brain whenever he was near her. He, who'd slept with so many women, who had his choice of heiresses and princesses and models, could not stop wanting his housekeeper. Louisa was like a drug to him.

Because she was forbidden?

His smile fell. And he cursed himself anew.

Rising to his feet, he put on a robe and left the well-kept bedroom. He went out to the veranda. He looked down at the garden and the Bosphorus beyond. In a short time, she'd turned this neglected mansion into an exquisite home.

His hands gripped the wrought-iron balcony railing. And now, because of his lust, he would lose her—his most prized employee!

He glanced back at the beautiful woman sleeping in his bed. He had to find a way to return to a simple relationship of boss and employee. But he wasn't sure he could.

From the moment he'd first interviewed her in Paris for the head housekeeper position, he'd been intrigued by her—this pretty young woman who went to some lengths to appear plain, wearing black cat's-eye glasses and oversize, unflattering clothes, pulling her chestnut hair back into a tight bun from which no tendril could hope to escape. She'd left her first position in the household of a financier in Miami, at a very good rate of pay, because apparently she wished to see Europe.

"You will be allowed no vacations," he'd told her at that first interview. "I need a house manager who will have no other desires other than to smoothly and perfectly run my home."

He'd waited for Miss Louisa Grey, a modern young woman, to tell him he was out of his mind with such expectations and to leave his office; instead, she'd just looked up at him with her cool brown eyes.

"Of course."

"I don't think you understand," he'd said evenly. "You won't be able to leave. Not for vacations. Not for Christmas. And do not think I will eventually transfer you to New York. I like stability in my home life. If you start in Paris you will stay here."

"Fine," she'd repeated, frowning up at him with her brow furrowed.

"Fine?" he barked.

"I do not need to go back home."

He'd lifted his eyebrows in disbelief. "Never?"

"Correct. For…for reasons of my own which I do not care to explain." She lifted her chin. "I will do excellent work for you, Mr. Cruz."

And she had.

Efficient, dedicated Miss Grey had never taken a day off. Never asked for a vacation. Never complained. She'd never asked for a transfer.

Until he'd seduced her.

For the first few years she'd been his housekeeper, she'd acted as if she could barely distinguish Rafael from an intemperate child to be tolerated and tended. Gradually he'd taken it as a challenge. He'd coaxed her out of her shell in the evenings, as he'd eaten a late supper in the kitchen. He'd gradually lured Louisa's warm heart out from beneath her dignified reserve. It had been an amusement. Even—a friendship.

Until he'd seduced her.

He cursed himself again under his breath.

She wasn't just his valued housekeeper, she was the extremely competent manager who coordinated between all his homes in New York, St. Barts, Buenos Aires, Istanbul and Tokyo.

And this would be the end of it. *Qué fastidio!* Now that he'd slept with her twice, it would end badly—as it always did. She would cease to be sensible, useful Miss Grey and become a woman without a shred of reason in her head. She'd be clingy to her fingertips.

Or would she?

Louisa Grey, clingy? The thought was almost laughable. She was so different from all other women. Was it possible, then, that their affair could be different as well?

He still wanted her. Was it possible she could be that legendary creature—a reasonable woman—and they could continue their affair until he was satisfied? Could they enjoy the passion of a love affair—then simply return to their regular lives that were already so convenient and perfect, as employer and employee?

He ached for her as he did for no other woman. A few days and he'd certainly be done with her. That's how all of his affairs ended. If he could just enjoy her in his bed for just a few more days....

"Good morning," he heard her say behind him.

He turned to face her and sucked in his breath.

Louisa stood on the veranda wearing his white oversize robe. The pink sunrise dawning over the minarets of the east brought such beauty to her face. Her smile was quiet and resolute.

He'd never seen anyone more beautiful, with so much sweetness and dignity. She was the most intriguing woman he'd ever met. No woman came close, he realized. Even now, remembering how he'd taken her the night before, he was throbbing with need for her. He wanted to lift her up in his arms, drag her back into his bedroom and throw her on the bed. He wanted to take her again and again, fast and hard, until he'd had his fill.

"Come away with me," he said abruptly.

She laughed playfully, looking around the Ottoman mansion and the incredible view of the Bosphorus. "To get away from all this?"

He frowned, trying to think. He had a hard time thinking straight when she was smiling like that. He remembered suddenly an offer made by an acquaintance selling him real estate in Paris. Xerxes Novros was a coldhearted bastard but the man had offered the use of his island. "Greece?" he suggested.

She saw he was serious and blinked. Then she shook her head. "Your dinner party is in two days."

"Knowing you, the arrangements are already completed."

She took a deep breath. "But still…"

"I am done with Istanbul," he said harshly. "After the party, I intend to put this house up for sale. I am done here." His dark eyes looked down into hers. "But not done with you."

"I should go." Her voice was small. Unhappy.

"Go?"

"Work for someone else."

He stared at her, dumbfounded. Then his eyebrows lowered. "You can't," he said in a low voice. "I need you."

"What you mean to say is that you like having me work for you. That you find it *convenient*."

"Yes," he said gruffly. "I do. And it is. I see no reason why that should stop."

She gave a low, bitter laugh. "No. Why would you?"

He placed his hands persuasively on her shoulders. "*Mira!* So we've fallen into bed. I've been through this many times. A few days together, and we'll come back and no longer feel this way. Our lives can return to normal. I promise you."

She looked at him, her brown eyes so deep and tender, and for a moment he thought he convinced her. Then she shook her head. "Sure, that is how it works. *For you.* Your mistresses have nervous breakdowns."

"Not you. You would never be like that, Louisa," he said. "You have far too much dignity. Too much sense. That's what I love most about you." He gave her a sudden wicked grin. "Along with your luscious body."

She stared at him for a moment. Then she turned her head, staring off at the Bosphorus, flooded with the brilliant pink light of sunrise.

He took her hands in his own, looking down at her.

"Forget I'm your boss. Forget that you work for me. Take two days and go away with me. Let me pamper you in luxury where no one else knows you. Let someone else serve *you* for a change. Let me give you pleasure," he whispered, stroking the bare skin of her inner wrist, "such as you've never known."

He kissed her lips before she could answer. When he finally pulled away, he whispered into her ear, "Give in. You know I'm going to take you, Louisa. You know you won't be able to resist me. You will be mine."

You will be mine.

Louisa couldn't breathe, she wanted him so much.

She looked into his handsome, ruthless dark gaze and knew she should tell him off—tell him in her devastatingly formal way that she was his housekeeper, nothing more, and she existed to keep his homes organized and well-staffed. To tell him that she had no feelings for him whatsoever as anything more than her boss. But when she looked into the darkness of his eyes, she could not lie.

His touch felt like fire to her.

"All right," she said in a soft voice she almost couldn't recognize as her own.

He pulled back, his fierce eyes searching hers. "Yes?"

"I'll come away with you," she whispered.

He kissed her fervently on the palm, then the back of her hand. A shiver of longing went through her, a shiver that shook her to the core.

She couldn't deny them what they both wanted.

No matter what it cost. She would have two days—two days to be his mistress and know how it felt to be his adored lover. Two days to live on for the rest of her life, when she would love him from a distance, with a broken heart, knowing he would never love her in return.

She only prayed he was right, and that two days of pleasure would cure her of this desperate, hopeless love. She prayed it would satiate her, ending all her longing for Rafael, so she could once again enjoy the job she loved, supervising the housecleaning, managing the staff and arranging his life.

Would she really be able to watch him move on to the next woman and feel nothing? Apparently Rafael thought so. And he knew so much more about love affairs than she. She prayed he was right, and when she returned to Istanbul, she would no longer want him, that she'd no longer love him.

She would be able to take back her heart. She would no longer cry out for him in the cold loneliness of night. This two-day affair could save her.

Unless she was pregnant. Then…it was already too late.

CHAPTER THREE

"ANOTHER iced tea, Miss Grey?"

Shading her eyes from the hot Greek sun, Louisa looked up from where she was stretched out on the poolside lounge chair. "Yes," she said, blushing. Being served, rather than the server, still shocked her. "That would be lovely. Thank you."

The Greek servant, who was young and very handsome, handed her the cool drink in a tall glass with a flourish and a respectful, admiring bow before he departed back inside the white walls of the sprawling hillside mansion.

Sipping her drink—which was, incidentally, her third one that afternoon—Louisa stared around her for a moment with shock. She'd been on this private Greek island since yesterday morning, but she still couldn't quite believe that she was the one relaxing, instead of the one rushing around like a madwoman trying to satisfy her employer's wishes. Instead of cleaning and organizing, she was lazily sunning herself in a bikini as her handsome lover did laps in the infinity pool over-looking the blue Aegean Sea.

Taking another sip of her tea, Louisa set it down on the table with a happy sigh. Lifting her arms over her head in a yawn, she glanced at the white mansion behind her. It was huge and luxurious, clinging to the rocky hillside above the sea. She leaned her head back against the lounge chair cushion. The sky was a cloudless, limpid blue. Reaching for her sunglasses, she put them on and picked up her paperback novel. Holding the book over her head to block out the sun, she tried to focus on the page.

She was distracted when she saw Rafael rise from the water. As he climbed out of the pool, she couldn't look away. His tanned skin glistened in the sun as rivulets of water poured down the hard muscles of his body, down the dark hair of his chest, disappearing beneath the small swim trunks slung low across his slim hips.

Her lips suddenly went dry.

"Are you bored, *querida?*" Rafael said huskily, looking at her across the pool deck.

"Yes, very," she managed to tease him.

"Put down that book." He walked slowly across the white stamped concrete floor. Like a lion stalking a gazelle, he never looked away from her. "If you need distraction, I will entertain you."

"I like to read—" she protested weakly, but she could not resist as, for the third time since they'd arrived on this island, he took the book away from her. She had bought the book, a deliciously trashy novel, with high anticipation. But she had yet to finish the first paragraph. Perhaps because her life had taken a sudden turn and was full of more luxury and passion than she could have ever imagined in any fantasy.

Rafael pulled the sunglasses off her face and set them down on the table. He placed both hands on the soft white cushion around her. For a moment, he looked down at her and she was overwhelmed by anticipation, by the scent of him, by the cool feel of his wet skin against her warm body.

Then he lowered his mouth to hers.

She closed her eyes with a sigh of pleasure as he kissed her, searing her bruised lips with the magnetic force of his own. She felt his bare skin against her body, the rough dark hair of his chest pressing against her warm, naked belly. They'd already made love at least a dozen times since they'd arrived here yesterday morning, at this beautiful private island compound borrowed from one of Rafael's wealthy tycoon friends whom she'd never met. Two days of pleasure, of being served cocktails and hors d'oeuvres, of being waited on hand and foot. Two days of nothing but admiration and adoration.

Was this what it felt like to every woman, to be a rich man's mistress?

Or was it just because the man was Rafael, and she blossomed beneath the miracle of his full, devoted attention?

Whatever the reason, Louisa had never felt so beautiful or so desired. She'd never felt so happy. She felt like a different woman. Everyone here treated her as if she were some gorgeous young creature who deserved to be spoiled, her every whim catered to. They treated her as if luxury and admiration were her birthright, and they did it in such a convincing way that she almost was starting to believe it herself. Especially when Rafael kissed her like this…

He pulled away abruptly. His gray eyes were the color of slate, dark with need.

"You look beautiful in this bikini," he growled. "You'd look even better without it."

She looked up at him. Bright sunlight traced the sharp edges of his cheekbones and jawline with shadow. He was so impossibly handsome. So impossible to resist. And here, in this fantastic place, she had no reason to resist him. She wasn't a housekeeper here.

She was Rafael's mistress.

"I'm glad you like the bikini, since you're the one who insisted on buying it—along with the other four." She gave a sudden laugh. "Honestly, Rafael, how many swimsuits do you think a girl needs for a two-day vacation?"

He put his hand on the naked skin between her breasts, barely covered with small triangles of fabric. "If you're the girl, I'd prefer none."

He slowly undid the tie of her bikini. Pulling it off her body, he dropped the top to the floor.

She tried to cover herself with her hands. "The staff," she whispered.

He stopped her, pulling her hands away.

"They will see nothing," he said between kisses. "They are paid not to see."

He cupped her breasts, then suckled each nipple beneath the bright Greek sun. Slowly he licked his way down her belly before he lazily untied the strings of her bikini bottom. The reflection of the sunlight from the pool dazzled her, causing sparkles like diamonds in her vision. Or maybe it was just the way Rafael touched her....

She closed her eyes. She felt him stroking her, as if she were a precious treasure. *His desired, adored mistress.* He kissed and licked down the length of her tanned belly, his skin now warm against hers. She heard him move, heard his swim trunks fall to the floor, and then he was on top of her....

For just a moment. Her world turned upside down and she opened her eyes in surprise, realizing that he was now beneath her on the lounge chair, and he'd placed her astride him. His hard erection was jutting between her naked legs.

Rafael met her eyes steadily.

She took a deep breath. Then, with some trepidation, she touched him, stroking his shaft gently. He moved beneath her fingers, expanding somehow to even greater size in her hand until she wondered how it was possible he would ever fit again inside her.

"Kiss me," he commanded. She wondered for an instant exactly where he meant her to kiss him, then she felt him drag her shoulders up so he could plunder her mouth with his own. Below, she felt his hardness move against her soft belly, then between her legs, seeking entrance. He kissed her deeply, entwining his tongue with her own, and she involuntarily swayed her hips against him. She felt him jump beneath her, rock hard and huge. Her breasts felt heavy against his dark-haired chest, her nipples tightening to painful intensity as she swayed. The hot Greek sun beat into the naked skin of her back, against the warmth of his smooth skin.

She ached for him. *Ached.* But he wouldn't take her. Though she could see how greatly he desired her, he seemed to be waiting, to be taunting her and luring her to be the one to initiate. He wanted her to be the one to take him.

With an intake of breath, she lowered herself over him, taking him a single inch inside her.

She heard him gasp—or had the sound come from her own lips?

She moved and swayed against him, wrapping tighter and lower in a circular motion, moving the tight molten core of her liquid need against his taut muscular body. With each circle, she moved lower, bringing his shaft deeper and deeper still inside her. She felt him tremble and gasp with his own need but he did not try to force the rhythm or roll her beneath him. He let her control the pace, and when she looked into his face, she could see what that cost him, how close and grimly he was hanging to the ragged edge of his desire.

She finally took him all the way inside her, all the way to the hilt, and for a moment she could not move. She closed her eyes, savoring the feel of him inside her, wishing she could make the moment last forever.

Then she heard the hoarse gasp of his breath and

knew how she was torturing him. She smiled. She moved against him, riding him slow and deep, and the first shuddering wave almost immediately hit her. She gripped his shoulders and held on for dear life as her hips rode him harder and faster. She felt him shudder and shake and he cried out her name. Hearing his name on her lips, her own world exploded, blinding her with a million shards of light and darkness, of white sun and blue sea.

She exhaled.

When she came back to herself, she was lying on top of him. In wonder and amazement, she stared down at her pale hand splayed across his dark-haired chest. Though she'd been sunning herself all day, her skin was still pale and fair compared to his darkly tanned olive hue. Both his strong arms were still wrapped possessively around her body, holding her against him. Rafael's eyes were closed as he slept, a smile of amazed joy still tracing his sensual mouth.

She loved him.

Staring at him, she could not deny it. Deny it? She gloried in it.

She loved him.

Then as she stared at his beautiful face, her smile faded.

She still hadn't taken the test.

With an intake of breath, she lowered her head back against his bare chest, closing her eyes. She hadn't had a single moment alone, and there wasn't exactly a twenty-four-hour drugstore on this island. There was nothing here except the sprawling mansion…and tennis courts…and two pools…and stables…and a vineyard. This entire island was nothing but a rich man's fantasy.

Tomorrow, they would return to Istanbul. She would cease being Rafael's cosseted mistress, and return to being his plain, efficient housekeeper. She would serve the guests at his dinner party, then begin preparations to assist the real estate agent in the sale of the house Louisa had created with such love. *That she'd created for him.*

With her cheek pressed against the rough dark hair of his muscular chest, she stared out blindly at the shimmering blue sea beneath the swimming pool. She'd just started to feel at home in Istanbul. But now, just like Paris—just like Miami—the rug was being pulled out from beneath her.

When would she finally have a home of her own, a home no one could ever take from her?

Louisa blinked fast, staring out at the bright blue sea blending into eternity with the endless blue sky. Memories raced through her, memories she'd tried to avoid for five years. Memories of Matthias…and Katie. *I'm sorry, Louisa. I never meant to get pregnant.*

Would she ever have enough distance in space and time that her past would no longer haunt her?

She felt Rafael's hand brush against her cheek. She looked up at him.

"What is it, Louisa?" he said softly. His gray eyes seared her, searching her soul. "What are you thinking about?"

With an intake of breath, she looked away. She hadn't told him about her past. She hadn't spoken of it to anyone.

Five years ago, she'd been stabbed to the heart by the two people she loved most in the world. She'd fled the United States for a fresh start. She'd changed her bright, formfitting clothes to plain, serviceable gray ones, boxy, shapeless suits. She'd lost her appetite. She'd lost weight. She'd started wearing glasses instead of contacts and pulled her brown hair back in a tight bun. She'd done everything she could do to make sure no man would ever notice her again.

She found a new job in Paris. She hadn't feared to work for Rafael. She knew she would be safe from any playboy's charms. She'd worked constantly, literally lived at her workplace, and hadn't taken a vacation—not so much as a single Saturday off.

She'd tried not to love Rafael. She'd tried. But somehow, he'd snuck past all her defenses….

Rafael's hand stroked her cheek. "You won't answer. You never answer," he said softly. "Someday you will." He looked down at her. "Someday, you will tell me everything."

But as he pulled her once more into his arms beneath the bright Greek sun, Louisa knew she would never tell him about the last man she'd fallen in love with. Her last boss. At least, she'd thought it was love at the time. She'd been so young then, so young and naive…

Thinking of the pain in her past, she looked at her future and was very, very afraid.

"Do you like this place?" he said softly, twisting a tendril of her hair around his finger.

She looked at him.

"So much that maybe I should get a job here," she said, only half-joking. "Does your friend who owns this island need a housekeeper? What is his name?"

Rafael glowered at her. Irritation emanated off him in waves.

"He is not a kind man. Especially where women are concerned."

She'd been trying to lighten the mood, but it seemed to have failed miserably. Why was he taking her comment so seriously? Lifting herself on one elbow, Louisa reached up to rub his shoulder. "The same could be said about you," she teased.

His jaw clenched. "Yes," he said shortly. "It could."

Was it possible he was jealous? No, surely not! "You know I'm not serious, Rafael!"

"I do not care for such jokes of you mentioning other men," he said stiffly. "You belong to me."

She stopped rubbing his shoulder. She looked at him. "I belong to you?"

He shook his head. "You know what I meant. You are a valued member of my staff. You—"

"No," she interrupted. She pulled back her hand, sitting up. Suddenly she was so furious she couldn't think straight. "You had it right the first time. You think I *belong* to you. That you own me. That I'm your possession." So much for imagining herself to be his adored mistress! "You think I have no feelings." She slapped down on the nearby table. "Like this!"

"Do not be dramatic. I pay you well. There is no

question of you being my possession. You stay in my
employ because you appreciate your situation."

"And now?" She looked around them at the luxurious place that had suddenly lost its glamour. "Am I
working for you now?"

He ground his teeth. "No. You know you are not!"

"Then who am I to you?"

"Here, you are my mistress. Beyond this island, you
are the best servant on my staff. You oversee all of my
homes, coordinating with the other housekeepers. I
could not manage without you."

He might as well have slapped her across the face.

"Perhaps it really is time for me to move on," she said
slowly, feeling numb. Why did she feel so betrayed,
when she'd known all along how this would end?

"No," he said furiously. "You won't go work for
him—or any other man. You belong to—*with*," he corrected himself as he caught her glare, "me."

His hands grasped her naked waist in the bright
sunlight. She looked down into his gray eyes. His face
was dark, almost savage. She could hear the hoarseness
of his breath. Their eyes locked.

His fingers tightened on her almost painfully.

Then he reached up and kissed her.

His kiss was hard and deep, a plundering of her
mouth, as if he'd held something back for far too long,
as if the master had himself been enslaved by an unwilling passion he could no longer control. His kiss abruptly
became more persuasive, wistful and sensual in a way
she could not resist. She wrapped her arms around his

neck as, with a low growl, he pulled her back against his naked body on the lounge chair. She could feel how he already wanted her again.

"You belong to me," he whispered. "Say it."

"Never," she said.

But her defiance only seemed to increase the force of his passion. He made love to her again beneath the hot Greek sun, hard and fast and with a brutality that matched her own passionate desire.

"You're the only woman I trust," he said in a low voice afterward, caressing her cheek as he looked down at her cradled in his arms. "The only woman I've trusted in a long, long time."

But as he held her and closed his eyes, dozing in the sun, tears streaked unheeded down Louisa's sunburned cheeks.

She was well and truly caught.

She had to face it. Though she knew it was nothing more than a fantasy, though she knew it was foolish, stupid and dangerous, she could no more stop loving him than stop breathing. No two-day idyll would cure her of loving Rafael.

She did belong to him. Completely.

CHAPTER FOUR

BACK in Istanbul the next afternoon, Louisa stumbled as she came out of the private hospital northeast of Taksim Square. Blindly she stepped into the street.

A loud honk made her fall back as she was nearly run over by a taxi driver who shouted at her in fluent, expressive Turkish. Gasping, almost crying, Louisa stood trembling on the sidewalk, shivering with shock.

Pregnant.

She was pregnant with Rafael's baby. Pregnant with the child she'd promised him she could never conceive!

Over the last week, she'd tried to mock her own fears, tried to convince herself she was being foolish to worry. But she hadn't been foolish at all. The doctor had just confirmed her worst fears had been right on target.

What would Rafael say when she told him?

She walked down the street, took deep breaths until she stopped trembling, then climbed back into the tiny car that was used by the staff. She drove north through the thick traffic to the outskirts of Beyoğlu.

They'd been back in Istanbul for only a few hours,

but already everything had changed between them. Rafael had immediately gone to his home office and barked out orders to various assistants about the upcoming real estate deal he was hoping to have signed tonight. And all the house staff had rushed to her with their questions about the final preparations for the dinner party.

Louisa had become his employee again. Rafael had become her boss.

They'd left the lovers behind on the island. Left them behind forever.

Now, Louisa stared out at the busy traffic, colorful billboards and old buildings of the city through the grimy glass. The car needed to be washed, she thought dimly. She'd have to tell the chauffeur's assistant when she got back....

Should she even tell Rafael she was pregnant?

Her great-aunt's words came back to her. *Always be honest, child. Tell the truth, even if it hurts. Better to hurt now than twice as much later.*

But Louisa wasn't so sure. She'd saved five years of her salary in Europe, since she'd never taken time to travel or see the sights. She'd always told herself she mustn't be selfish—Mr. Cruz's needs must come first. She'd told herself she would see the sights of Europe later. Somehow, that time had never come.

And what did she have to show for it? She was just five years older. Pregnant. Alone!

The shaking vibration of the little car as she drove north on the old road was hypnotic.

Pregnant.

As she drove past the mansion's gate, she barely noticed the security guard's respectful greeting. She parked the car, informed the chauffeur's assistant that the car needed attention, then went into the house.

Everything looked beautiful for Rafael's birthday dinner tonight. Every room was filled with flowers, autumn roses from the garden supplemented with pepperberry stems and dark orange Asiatic lilies. As this was his first dinner party at his home in Istanbul, Louisa had planned it with care, choosing a menu rich with the exotic flavors of the city. Even now, the Turkish cook, who'd fortunately recovered from his earlier illness, was rushing around the kitchen and barking orders to his assistants to prepare the *midye dolmasi,* mussels stuffed with spiced rice, the sea bass stew, lamb kebabs and a variety of fruits and pastries for dessert.

She herself had made one of the desserts. It was not a traditional Turkish recipe, so it did not fit in with the menu, but she knew it was Rafael's favorite and so she'd made it that morning anyway. For his birthday. Because she loved him. It had taken her an hour, but she'd carefully prepared her specialty dessert, caramel macadamia brownies with white chocolate chips.

She'd wanted to make his first dinner here special. But since he intended to put the house on the market tomorrow, it would also be his last. Now, looking around her, she felt a lump in her throat.

She'd wanted everything to be perfect for him. She'd made his home beautiful, made his life comfortable and full of ease. She'd sacrificed her every need for his. And now it was over. Now it was done. Once she told him she was pregnant, she would lose everything.

The job she loved. The man she loved.

Where would she go, without him to be both her albatross and her star? What would she do without him, all alone?

Slowly, heavily, she started to go up the stairs to her room. As she passed the study, she heard one of his assistants say, "Mademoiselle Lepetit is on the phone for you, sir."

Louisa froze on the stair.

Dominique Lepetit was a beautiful French starlet famous mostly for her time spent pouting while topless, posing for the paparazzi during the Cannes Film Festival. Blond, curvaceous and cruel—she was everything that most men seemed to want in a woman.

"Tell her I'm busy," came Rafael's curt reply, and Louisa exhaled. She hadn't realized until then how very much, in spite of everything, she wanted him to be faithful to her.

Rafael Cruz, faithful to any woman? She mocked herself as she climbed slowly up the stairs to her room. Had the pregnancy hormones kicked in already? She must really be out of her mind!

But he'd refused Dominique Lepetit's phone call. Could a man change?

Could he understand that sometimes fate changed people's lives in unexpected ways—for the better?

When she reached her room, she closed the door

behind her, leaning against it for strength. She looked down in wonder, putting her hands on her belly as a new realization occurred to her.

Pregnant. A new life was growing inside her—Rafael's child. A smile lifted her lips. A *baby*. A sweet-smelling baby to cuddle in her arms, to love forever. Her parents had died long ago, and she'd been estranged from her younger sister for five years. But with this baby, she would finally have a family of her own. A reason to create a real home, after so many years alone.

Had Katie felt like this when she'd first found out she was pregnant?

Louisa pushed away the unbidden thought. She didn't want to think about Katie. Didn't want to think about the niece or nephew she'd never met. The child must be almost five now, probably with brothers and sisters. And Matthias Spence as their father...

She'd tried not to think about Matthias for years. But to her surprise, the thought of him no longer hurt her the same way. Because she'd never really cared about him? She'd worked for him for only a few months before he'd proposed to her. She hadn't known him half so well as she knew Rafael.

Or perhaps it was because her relationship with Matthias seemed so laughably in the past, the crush of a schoolgirl long ago, compared to the enormity of being pregnant with Rafael's baby.

How could she tell Rafael the news?

Straightening her shoulders, Louisa went to her closet. She pushed through all the plain, serviceable clothes and pulled something out of the back, covered by plastic. Taking it out, she stared down at a sexy black bustier dress.

The last time she'd worn this, she'd been an engaged woman. Her sister had been visiting for a month from college, and had insisted they go shopping. "You're so lucky," Katie had said wistfully. "Going from a live-in housekeeper to a rich man's wife." "I love him," Louisa had replied, smiling. But she'd allowed Katie to talk her into spending an entire paycheck in one splurge on the dress for their engagement party. Louisa had hoped to look pretty for Matthias, and try her best to impress his friends. Then a few weeks later, an hour before their engagement party began, her nineteen-year-old sister had asked to speak to her privately.

"How could you?" Louisa had gasped a few moments later. "You're my sister. How could you do this to me?"

"I'm sorry!" Katie had cried. "I never meant to get pregnant. But I can't believe you even love him. If you did, you wouldn't have kept him at arm's length, refusing to sleep with him until you were married! Who does that anymore?"

"I do," Louisa had choked out, and grabbing her purse, she'd run from the house. She'd run as far away from Miami as she could, all the way to Paris.

She'd nearly thrown the dress in the trash five years ago. But instead, for some reason, she'd kept it. Now, the sexy black dress was the one item of clothing from her old life, before she'd been afraid of love, before she'd disappeared from the world to walk the earth like a ghost.

As she put on the dress, Louisa told herself she had no illusions that Rafael would love her; he would certainly never marry her. She only prayed he might love and accept their coming child. And that was the reason—the only reason!—that she put it on.

It was a little loose from her weight loss over the last few years, all the time she'd spent without time to exercise or sit down and eat meals or take care of herself properly. But when she added a belt, the dress still looked nice. She brushed her dark hair, leaving it tumbling and lustrous down her shoulders. She took off her black-rimmed plastic glasses and put in contact lenses. She was out of practice after wearing glasses for so long. She added some mascara to her lashes and some deep red lipstick on her mouth, then surveyed herself in the mirror for the effect.

After so many years, she almost didn't recognize herself.

She looked pretty.

Louisa prayed it would help. Because she was terrified.

As she went downstairs, she could hear the first guests starting to arrive outside. She saw Rafael at the base of the stairs and stopped, gripping the polished wood of the railing. She closed her eyes as she took a single calming breath, her hand on her belly. Could this night be anything like her deepest dreams?

"I'm pregnant, Rafael," she would say.

His gray eyes would widen. He'd gasp. Then he'd take her into his arms. "I am glad," he'd say fiercely. "Of course I want this baby. And I want you. You are the only woman for me, querida." Looking down at her, he would lift her chin and whisper tenderly, "I love you, Louisa."

"Louisa."

She opened her eyes to see Rafael looking up at her from the bottom of the stairs. He was frowning at her as if she'd dyed her hair purple and dressed like the Easter bunny.

"Why are you dressed like that?" he demanded, coldly surveying her from head to toe.

It wasn't quite the reaction she'd been hoping for, but she tried to smile as she walked down the stairs—carefully, on her four-inch black patent high heels.

"For the party," she said. She stopped one step above him. He still wouldn't smile back at her. "For your birthday," she tried again.

Instead of looking pleased, Rafael scowled. "You are going to attract attention like that."

A servant should always be invisible. The rule had been drummed into her for ten months. After her parents had died, Louisa had given up her chance at a college scholarship to stay home and take care of her little sister and ailing great-aunt. But her aunt had left Louisa a small inheritance, which she'd used to attend butler school to become a certified household manager. *You are not a person to your employer. You are a tool in his service. Serve invisibly. Never invade your employer's privacy or force yourself upon his notice. To do so will cause embarrassment to you both.*

Now, Louisa stiffened. "You don't like my dress?"

He glared at her. "No."

It seemed almost impossible to believe just that morning, she'd been in his arms. They'd been naked together in the amazing Greek mansion overlooking the Aegean. Now, when she needed his attention the most, he'd suddenly become distracted. Distant.

Was he already thinking about Dominique Lepetit, who was already on her way? Had he already forgotten Louisa completely?

"Go change," he said coldly. "The guests will arrive any moment."

He seemed completely disinterested in her. Just as he'd promised two days ago, their little affair had apparently cured his desire for her. He'd had his fill of her. He was done. He was ready to move on.

With a deep breath, she told herself it was irrelevant if he cared for her. She had to think about their unborn child. Rafael had to know she was pregnant. *For their baby's sake.*

As he turned to leave, she grabbed his wrist. It took every ounce of her courage. "I need to talk to you."

He stared at her hand on his wrist. She released him as if he'd burned her.

"I want you on the plane to Buenos Aires tomorrow," he replied icily.

"Buenos Aires?" she whispered, staggered. He no longer wanted her in Paris? "Why Buenos Aires?"

"You'll take over my house there." He gave a single dismissive nod, already turning away. "Now go change your dress."

Louisa felt a stab of pain.

He could not have said it more plainly. He no longer saw her as anything but a servant.

And the truth was that even in Greece, when she'd imagined herself his cosseted mistress, she'd still been his servant. Serving his needs in bed, rather than in the household. And now that he was done with her, he expected her to simply return to being invisible, to being the plain gray ghost that vanished into the hundred-year-old woodwork of the mansion.

So he cared nothing for her but as his invisible servant? She gritted her teeth.

So be it.

She had no intention of going to Buenos Aires. She wouldn't go meekly off to serve him forever in exile, while he enjoyed a succession of other women!

Having him love her—what a ridiculous fantasy that had been!

Her head pounded. She felt almost physically sick. But she pushed the pain aside. She would deal with that later. Tonight, she had a job to do.

She'd make his dinner party perfect. He would never have reason to complain she'd been anything less than an exemplary housekeeper.

Then, afterward, she would tell him she was accidentally pregnant. Not because she still hoped he might care. But because her baby deserved a father, and Rafael deserved the truth. He deserved that much, and no more.

The doorbell rang, and she lifted her chin.

"I'm sorry, your guests are already arriving," she

said sweetly. "I have no time to change my clothes. Excuse me."

Pushing past him, she opened the door.

That night, as the guests arrived, Louisa personally stood near the door to take their coats. The house was all in readiness; she'd supervised everything. As she took each coat, she saw that each guest was more powerful, wealthy and beautiful than the last. She watched Rafael greet each of them, some with handshakes, some with slaps on the back.

But not the women—no. He greeted each of them with a kiss on both cheeks. The five women were all so beautiful, and every single one of them looked up at Rafael with longing. No wonder. Impeccably dressed in a tuxedo with a black tie, he was beyond handsome. He was the spectacular angel of his namesake.

He didn't look at Louisa. He seemed not to notice she was there, any more than he noticed the grandfather clock or the antique hat rack that she'd lovingly chosen for this mansion. All his possessions, *including her,* were to be used and then discarded at will when he no longer found them useful.

She clenched her hands, trying to ignore the pain.

"Dominique," he purred, pushing past Louisa to help the beautiful blond starlet remove her white fur coat. He pulled it off her shoulders himself, smiling down at her seductively. "I am glad to see you."

"Rafael." The infamous French beauty reminded Louisa of a pampered white Persian cat, with her tiny button nose, big blue eyes and fluffy bleached-blond hair. Her sparkly gold minidress barely covered her nipples on the top and upper thighs on the hemline. She smiled up at him with her curved red lips. "I wouldn't miss your birthday, *chéri.*"

Looking at them together, Louisa suddenly felt how plain she was, how tall and ungainly and skinny in her five-year-old black dress. A sharp pain rose in her throat. Twenty minutes earlier, she'd thought she looked rather pretty in the mirror but now she felt as drab as a sparrow. Why hadn't she just stayed in her gray smock and glasses? At least then no one would have snickered at the plain girl who was actually trying to look pretty, who was apparently under the delusion she could compete with someone like Dominique Lepetit!

Rafael and Dominique were suited for each other in every way, both physically and by reputation. The French starlet was as well-known for discarding love-tortured suitors as Rafael was known for crushing women's hearts. Louisa swallowed, looking down at the floor.

Suddenly a fur coat was thrust into her arms. She nearly coughed at the weight and sensation of something so huge and fluffy—like a dead animal beneath her nose.

"Take care of that, won't you?" Rafael murmured to Louisa, not looking away from Dominique.

"Of course, Mr. Cruz," she replied miserably.

The dinner party was sparkling. The company was served *mezes,* starters like stuffed vine leaves and dip, cooked artichokes and hummus with *pide* bread, along with cocktails and Argentinian wine. Louisa supervised

the entire night, calming down the chef who though recovered from his earlier illness, seemed dangerously
unhinged emotionally as he rushed around the kitchen.
Realizing how many famous people were sitting in the
dining room for Rafael's birthday, the man seemed to
abruptly disintegrate under pressure and, while shouting
at one of his poor assistants, he nearly cut the end of his
thumb off with a sharp knife.

She'd prepared for this. She'd gone to the famous
butler school in Miami when she'd realized she had no
skills except taking care of people. And organizing homes.
And, she thought dully, falling in love with her boss.

Louisa managed the cook, calmed down the kitchen
and then organized the waiters who brought out each
course of the meal. Each time she went into the dining
room she was involuntarily dazzled by the beautiful
guests, by their sparkling conversations and witty rep-
artee. She tried not to listen, but she could not help it.
Just as she could not help noticing how Rafael looked
into Dominique Lepetit's lovely, wicked eyes with such
apparent fascination as they leaned their heads together
and she whispered something in his ear.

She'd known Rafael would move on—but she'd
never thought it would be at such lightning speed!

She swallowed, feeling increasingly hot as she
returned to the kitchen. How could she tell him she was
pregnant?

Should she even tell him?

What if he rejected their baby? What if he not only
blamed Louisa for the pregnancy, but he was never

able to love the child they'd created, the child he'd never wanted?

As the interminable dinner was finally drawing to an end, she went into the dining room and announced heavily that dessert and coffee would be awaiting them on the terrace. When one of the toothpick-skinny actresses asked her to list the desserts Louisa couldn't stop herself from looking at Rafael when she mentioned the caramel macadamia brownies. Across the room, from where he sat beside Dominique Lepetit, Rafael's slate-gray eyes suddenly locked with hers.

The pouting French beauty abruptly knocked over her wineglass. "Oh! *Mon dieu,* but how clumsy of me!"

With an intake of breath, Louisa hurried forward with a hand towel to clean up the mess. She saw Dominique's feline smile as the beautiful girl leaned forward on the table, blocking Rafael's gaze from her.

One of the other guests, a very handsome dark-eyed man sitting across the table, watched the scene with interest. As Louisa straightened from the table with hot, flushed cheeks and the wine-soaked towel, her eyes met the stranger's. His lips curved, as if he knew everything. Her cheeks, already red with humiliation, became hotter still.

"Novros," Rafael said, rising from the table with sudden sharpness. "We have business to discuss. It is time."

"Yes," the other man said to him, his black eyes gleaming.

"Excuse us," Rafael said more smoothly to the other

guests at the table, pausing for a particular smile at Dominique. "We will join you on the terrace in a moment. Miss Grey, will you show them the way, if you please?"

"Of course, sir," Louisa said over the lump in her throat.

Once outside in the moonlit night, upon the high stone terrace overlooking the garden and the sparkling Bosphorus below, the guests scattered in pairs into the shadows. Louisa directed several maids in setting up the pastries, including the *kadayif,* the shredded puff pastry filled with nuts and honey, along with strong Turkish coffee, brandy and other liqueurs, serving them on sterling silver trays filled with antique copper goblets.

As the maids bustled around her, Louisa paused in the moonlight. Blinking fast, she stared up into the inky-blackness of the sky twinkling with distant frozen stars.

Just yesterday, she'd been his mistress. Just yesterday, she'd been free. Just yesterday, she'd had everything she'd ever wanted.

A lot could change in just one day.

By early autumn next year, she would be a mother. She would have a baby to love and care for.

But would her child have a father? Would Rafael have any love for their baby—or would he just resent and despise the innocent child for being forced upon him?

A shudder went through her body. She was afraid she already knew. He did not want a wife. Did not want a child. She had been a fool to ever dream otherwise.

Louisa stared across the garden, yearning to run away and not even give Rafael the chance to despise and abandon them.

Why had she not kept to her original plan and waited to become a wife, before she'd ever risked becoming a mother?

Because she'd been in love with Rafael for years. And at twenty-eight years old, she hadn't felt principled and idealistic. Her virginity had started to feel like a burden. She'd started to feel like she would never be wanted—never be loved.

She took a deep breath when she heard the guests flirting and laughing among each other out in the shadows of the garden. As soon as she could get Rafael alone, she would be the idealistic, principled girl that she'd been raised to be. She would be strong. She would force herself to tell him the truth, even if it did nothing but hurt her.

Wouldn't she?

Rafael was in hell.

He'd been distracted all night. By returning to Istanbul. By his guests. By his birthday. By the business deal he was about to make.

Most of all, by Louisa.

He was trying his damnedest to push her away. To keep her at a distance. He was desperate to return to simply being boss and employee. He'd promised her it would be easy, hadn't he? He'd promised her when they returned to Istanbul, everything would fall back into place. But his plan that never before failed—had failed.

Somehow, after two days of making love to her, he still wanted her more than ever.

And if that weren't bad enough, Louisa had come down the stairs looking like some kind of damned sex symbol in a tight black dress. Was she trying to torture him? Or was it possible…she already knew his plan had failed, and so she was looking for a new employer?

His hands tightened. From the moment he'd seen her in that dress, he'd hated the thought of any other man looking at her. One man above all—his business rival, Xerxes Novros. He'd invited his Greek rival to the party in his determination to finally close the real estate deal in Paris; but the two men were far from friends. Novros was such a callous womanizer, he made Rafael look like a damned saint. That was why Rafael had ordered Louisa to change clothes before the party. When she'd come down the stairs, looking so shockingly, glamorously beautiful in a way he'd never seen her before, he knew at once that she would attract the wrong attention.

"By the way," the Greek said coolly as they walked down the hall, "I never wished you a happy birthday."

"Thanks." At thirty-seven, Rafael no longer felt young and invincible. His soul was starting to feel brittle around the edges. He was ready to leave this city, with his failure and the memory of his father's funeral, far behind him.

Rafael had hundreds, perhaps thousands, of friends around the world. They were amusing. They were witty.

The women were beautiful and eagerly gave themselves to his bed. The men were all business rivals who placed bets and smiled through their teeth like wolves. He didn't really give a damn about any of them, including the guests who were here tonight. He craved distraction.

He craved...*her.*

"You have a beautiful house," Xerxes Novros said as he followed Rafael down the hall to his private study. "You said your housekeeper supervised the refurbishment? That lovely creature in the sexy black dress?"

"Yes," Rafael growled as he snapped on the light. He closed the door behind them then picked up papers from his desk. "Your lawyers sent their corrections this morning. Sign these and we'll be done."

"Does she have a lover?"

"Who?"

"Your housekeeper."

"None of your damned business."

Flashing him a smile, Novros flung himself down in a high-backed chair and looked idly through the contract.

Rafael sat down at his desk, watching him. He never should have borrowed the man's private Greek island the last two days, he thought grimly. It gave him the vague sense of being in the man's debt. A dangerous feeling as he finished the negotiations of purchasing the real estate in Paris, a prestige property in the business district of La Défense. A dangerous feeling, as it brought Louisa to the other man's notice.

"It all appears to be in order." Novros looked up with

a lazy smile. "Throw in your housekeeper to seal the bargain, and we have a deal."

Rafael's hand tightened on his pen.

"Careful," he growled through his teeth. He lifted his head, and his eyes glittered dangerously at his rival. "Don't talk about her. Don't even look at her."

Novros lifted a dark eyebrow. "I see," he said mildly, and looked back at the papers. He shook his head and threw them back on his desk. "Sorry. I'm going to need more time to think about it."

Rafael clenched his jaw. He needed to break ground on the hugely expensive property at once in order to meet his schedule, and they both knew it. He wished to build a new headquarters for his international conglomerate in Paris. They'd already agreed on a price. He was tempted to smash the man's face in.

Instead he smiled.

"Shall we throw in a sweetener?" Rafael suggested. "Sign it. Finish the deal. And this house—" he indicated the study with a generous sweep of his hand "—will be thrown into the bargain."

Xerxes Novros stared at him for a moment.

Then with a nod, he signed the papers with a flourish.

"You gave in too easily," the man said, handing the contract back to Rafael with an insolent grin. "I would have accepted less money for the property in Paris."

Rafael took the signed contract and put it in his safe. "And I would have sold this house for a single euro."

The other man stared at him, then snorted. "So we've both done well, then." He lifted his chin, looking around the study. "How long will it take your people to get your possessions out of my house?"

"A week."

"Fine." Novros rose to his feet, then stopped at the door. "I suppose your little housekeeper is the mistress you took to my island?"

Rafael tensed. It irritated him that the man guessed that—and that he'd even noticed Louisa! "You find that so hard to believe?"

"Not now that I've seen her." Novros paused, then said evenly, "Just be careful."

"What?"

"With her history."

Rafael stared at him. Novros knew something about Louisa that he, Rafael, did not? "What about it?" he bit out.

"Do you not know? Your Miss Grey used to work for a friend of mine in Miami. She lured him on, got an engagement ring out of him by keeping him out of her bed. Then when he started to lose interest, she invited her younger sister to come stay with them. The sister immediately seduced him into her bed. He was so sex-starved, he didn't even think to use a condom. She got pregnant, as they'd planned, and the man felt he was honor-bound to marry her." An admiring grin spread across his lips. "It was quite a clever plan, really."

A cold chill went down Rafael's spine.

"I'm just telling you this," Novros said casually, "from one free bachelor to another. Be careful."

Rafael felt cold. Then hot.

This was Louisa's secret? This was the big mystery of her past? Something so sordid—and clichéd—as gold diggers getting their hands into wealthy men by deliberately trapping them with a pregnancy?

He sucked in his breath as he remembered calling to check Louisa's references. Of course her employer's wife had given Louisa an excellent reference. The woman he'd spoken with was her *sister!*

"Get her pregnant, and she'll play you for a fool," Novros said lazily. He stroked the polished wood of the door frame thoughtfully. "She did do excellent work overseeing this house. A very clever girl—and beautiful to boot. Send her to me, won't you, when you're tired of her?"

After the man left, Rafael sat still at his desk, staring blankly at the wallpaper across the study.

Louisa had said she was on the Pill. He'd blindly believed her. He'd told himself Louisa Grey would never tell a lie. He, who trusted no woman, had trusted her!

Cold rage slowly built up inside him. Was everything Novros had said true? Had Louisa been *trying* to become pregnant?

She'd had ample opportunity. He hadn't used a condom in Greece, either. In fact, she could already be pregnant now.

Placing his hands on his desk, he pushed himself to his feet. He took a deep breath, briefly closing his eyes as he clenched his fists. Then he went out into the garden.

He found Dominique waiting for him in the moonlight, pouting and smiling.

"Darling, I've been waiting for you for so long," she purred. She shimmied toward him in her tiny gold dress. She reached up her arms, barely able to reach his shoulders as she gave a seductive laugh. "It took you so long."

Coldly he pushed her away.

"Go home, Dominique," he said. "The party is over."

And leaving the pampered French starlet gaping behind him, he strode toward the terrace, where he saw the source of his desire, his suffering and his fury. *Louisa.*

CHAPTER FIVE

COLORFUL paper lanterns swung across the trees in the breeze, illuminating the dark garden above the black shimmer of the Bosphorus far below as Louisa cleaned the dishes from the terrace.

Dessert was over. Most of the guests had swiftly disappeared, returning to their rented villas or to nearby hotels, gorgeous women and wealthy men pairing off, seduced by each other and the exotic sensuality of Istanbul.

Louisa looked up when she heard a trill of low, feminine laughter. Dominique Lepetit's laughter. She heard the murmur of Rafael's low voice in answer.

For a moment, Louisa stared out blindly into the night. She blinked back cold tears beneath the cool breeze of wind coming off the water.

Then with a deep breath, she bent over to continue scrubbing the stone table. She gathered the silver coffeepot and dirty dishes back onto a tray. Some of the puff pastries remained, but all of her specialty caramel-macadamia brownies had been devoured down to the last crumbs. Rafael had never gotten his birthday brownie after all....

Louisa heard footsteps on the terrace and looked up.

A tall, dark-haired man stood alone on the other side of the terrace. He looked her over with an appreciative glance.

"You are Miss Grey?"

"Yes."

"I enjoyed those bars you made. What were they?"

She swallowed. "My secret recipe."

"A secret. How delightful." He wasn't entirely handsome; he had a slightly crooked nose, and a cruel twist to his lips as he said carelessly, "And if I offered to pay you a million dollars?"

She lifted her chin. "I still wouldn't give it to you. It's mine."

For a moment, he stared at her. Then he smiled. "Good for you."

And with those incomprehensible words, the man left her. She stared after him for a moment, frowning as she lifted the tray full of all the dirty dishes, whiskey and brandy bottles and small plates of half-eaten desserts.

"What did he say to you?"

Rafael's voice was harsh behind her.

Louisa almost dropped the tray as she whirled around. He took the tray from her grasp and set it back down on the stone table. His gray eyes flashed.

"What did Novros say?" Rafael demanded in a low, dangerous voice.

She shook her head, frowning in confusion. "Nothing."

"You're lying. I heard him speak to you. Did he offer you a job?" He grabbed her wrists and suddenly the expression on his handsome face was so hard and full of repressed fury, she felt afraid. "Did he offer you something more?"

Bewildered at his strange reaction, she shook her head. "No."

"Then what?" he demanded.

She swallowed. "He didn't make sense."

His grip tightened on her. "Tell me," he ordered.

She whispered, "He offered me a million dollars for my brownie recipe, then when I wouldn't, he just said... 'Good for you.'"

Rafael's jaw clenched. His impossibly handsome face looked like stone in the moonlight.

"Do you know what he meant?" she asked.

With a coldly furious expression, he shook his head.

She licked her lips nervously. Why was Rafael acting so angry? She felt a lump in her throat, a nausea right beneath her ribs.

He wouldn't release her wrist, and a hard knot of anger grew in her own throat. She thought she'd known him—known all his faults. But she'd never seen Rafael so dark, so altogether brutal.

Ripping her hand away, she demanded, "Why are you acting like this?"

"You know why," he growled.

Grasping at straws, she asked, "Did something happen to your business deal, Mr. Cruz?"

His lips twisted into a harsh, ironic smile at the *Mr.*

Cruz. "An interesting suggestion. It's always about money to you, isn't it?"

He wasn't making any sense—any more than that Greek man had! Louisa's hand tightened into a fist as she picked up the wet, dirty towel she'd been using to scrub the stone table. She took a deep breath. "Miss Lepetit is no doubt looking for you."

"Miss Lepetit," he ground through his teeth, "is gone. All the other guests have gone. We are—" his lips curved "—alone."

"Oh," she whispered, licking her suddenly dry lips. So this was her chance, then. Possibly her only chance to tell him she was pregnant…

But how could she tell him now, when he was acting so dark and strange?

She twisted the wet towel in her hands as she looked up at him nervously. "There's something I need to tell you, Rafael," she whispered. "It's important."

He grabbed her shoulders. Startled, she dropped the towel heavily against the stone terrace floor.

"What is it?" he demanded in a low voice.

She sucked in her breath, searching his gaze. Did he already know she was pregnant? Had he somehow guessed?

She licked her lips. "It's not something I thought could happen. I denied it, even to myself…"

"Let me guess," he said sardonically. "You're desperately in love with me."

She nearly gasped. Then, looking up into his face, she told him the truth.

"Yes," she whispered.

His face hardened. "For so long, you've been such a mystery. An intriguing problem to solve." He brushed back tendrils of her dark hair the wind had blown across her face. "But now I understand you. At last."

She shivered beneath his touch, closing her eyes.

Was it possible that everything she'd dreamed of for so long was about to happen? Was it possible he was about to tell her he loved her as well, and in a moment, when she told him shyly about their coming baby, he would take her into his arms and kiss her?

She could barely breathe....

"You've been setting me up," he said harshly. "Just like you and your sister did with your last employer."

Her eyes flew open.

"My...my sister?"

She felt Rafael's fingers clench into her shoulders, and she gasped. He looked down at her with something close to hatred in his eyes.

"I thought I could trust you," he said in a low voice. "But it was all just a trick, wasn't it?"

"No," she whispered. She shook her head. "You're wrong."

He gave a harsh, cruel laugh.

"I trusted you. Trusted you as I trusted no other woman alive. But have you spent the last five years of your life setting me up for a con?"

"What?" she gasped. Unshed tears stung her eyes as she shook her head fiercely. "I don't—"

"Tell me the truth!" he said coldly. "Was I a fool to trust you? *Did you lie when you said you were on the Pill?*"

Horrified, Louisa sucked in her breath.

For a moment, silence fell. The cool breezes from the sea caused the colorful paper lanterns to sway amid the darkness of the garden.

Rafael's jaw was set in a grim line as his hands tightened on her.

"I thought I'd done due diligence by calling your last employer personally. I spoke to his wife, not realizing she was your *sister.* Of course she gave you a glowing recommendation—she wanted to help you get your wealthy man, as you helped her!"

Louisa drew back, tears suddenly in her eyes as she thought of all the pain. "That's not how it was!"

"No?" His lip curled. "Then how was it?"

Louisa took a deep breath. She didn't want to speak of the past, but she had no choice. For their child's sake, she had to make him understand that her pregnancy was an accident—not a trap!

"Five years ago, I fell in love with my boss," she whispered, then stopped.

Rafael gripped her shoulders. "Go on."

"I'd only been working as his housekeeper for a few months when Matthias asked me to marry him." Every low, hoarse word felt painfully ripped from her. "But I wouldn't go to bed with him. I told him I wanted to wait for our wedding night. I was so young, so young and idealistic. Then my little sister came to visit from college." She looked up at him, blinking back tears.

"The night of our engagement party, Katie told me Matthias was going to marry her instead. Because…she was pregnant with his baby."

Staring down at her, he took a deep, shuddering breath. For a moment, she thought he meant to comfort her. Then his dark eyes looked at her with the fire of betrayal.

"Just as the two of you planned all along. You left him sex-starved, your sister lured him into her bed and he fell into her trap. Just as I fell into yours," he said in a low, cold voice. "I trusted you, Louisa. Although I should have suspected something when I first took you to bed. There would be no reason for a virgin with no boyfriend to be on the Pill—"

"I told you, it was for cramps, to regulate my cycle—"

"I thought it was just an unfortunate coincidence," he spoke over her ruthlessly, "that when I came home that night and found you crying in Paris, the apartment was out of condoms. You set me up so methodically, and I wanted you so badly, I was blind."

Louisa stared at him in shock and grief.

She'd shared something of her past she'd never spoken about with anyone—but he didn't give a damn. He was just determined to use her own words against her!

A slow burn of anger built inside her.

"I forgot to restock the condoms, but that wasn't on purpose! Perhaps I had trouble—" she lifted her chin defiantly "—because you were going through boxes so rapidly."

His jaw twitched. Abruptly releasing her, he folded his arms. "You lured me by acting distant, knowing that would intrigue me. Then you made sure I found you weeping, needing comfort, knowing there was only one kind of comfort I would offer."

"I never thought you would come home early from your date and seduce me!"

"So you're not pregnant?"

She sucked in her breath.

This was worse, so much worse than she'd thought. Why hadn't she realized that her two-day stomach flu had totally ruined the effectiveness of the birth control? She'd never thought he might look at her past and imagine that she could be so devilishly clever.

If she were, she thought bitterly, she wouldn't have slept with a heartless, suspicious playboy like Rafael Cruz!

Dark shadows and swinging red lights moved over his hard expression, making him look devilish. She sucked in her breath, trembling at the dark promise she saw in his eyes. It made her take an involuntary step backward.

She had to lie. There was no way she could tell him the truth now.

But the thought of denying the existence of her unborn child, the weight of telling such an awful lie, beat down upon her like golf-ball-size chunks of ice.

She felt incredibly hormonal and exhausted from being pregnant and traveling back from Greece. She felt tearful and emotionally drained from the roller-coaster ride of the last few days. Just yesterday, she'd been his adored mistress; today, she'd been ripped apart by the discovery of her pregnancy, and yet she'd been forced to hide her emotion, to serve him and his fancy guests while watching him flirt with another woman.

And suddenly, she'd *had it*.

Louisa took a deep breath. Slowly she looked up at him. She could live without his love. She could ball up her heart into a block of ice. She could ignore her feelings. She'd done it before.

But he had to love their baby.

If Rafael was cold to their innocent child and treated him badly through his whole life, letting their son or daughter know they were never wanted... No, she couldn't let that happen. She would deny their child's existence before she would risk causing her baby such endless grief!

He gently stroked her cheek. But his gaze was anything but gentle as he raked her soul with his fury and rage. She had the sudden feeling of being trapped. His body, his darkness, towered over her.

The heat between them felt like a cold burn. Like ice. *Like a threat.*

"There's only one thing I need to know," Rafael said in a low voice. "One thing that will determine if I was a fool to believe you were the last honest woman on earth. So tell me." His dark eyes glittered in the swaying light of the red paper lanterns. "Are you pregnant, Louisa?"

Rafael's muscles were painfully tense as he waited for her answer.

She wouldn't meet his eyes.

"Could you love a baby?" she whispered.

He nearly growled at her. "Don't change the subject. Answer my question."

"If I accidentally got pregnant," she faltered, "don't you think it's possible it could have nothing to do with money, and everything to do with…with…"

"Love?" He sneered.

Wordlessly she nodded. Her eyes were wide, limpid pools in the night. Wild. Desperate.

For a moment, his body instinctively wished to comfort her. It was the same way he'd felt when she'd revealed how she'd loved her last boss then lost him— to her sister. He'd almost pulled her into his arms, until he'd reminded himself that this might be part of her con. Her innocence, her pain, her supposed *love*—was it all an act to get him to marry her?

His stomach clenched. "A mere housekeeper does not go to all the trouble of getting pregnant by a wealthy man without expecting a payout."

Turning pale, she gasped.

Then her lovely face hardened, in that aloof, cold expression he knew so well.

"So I'm a *mere housekeeper* now, am I?" she said in a low voice. Her dark eyes glittered. "Just what sort of payout do you think I want?"

He set his jaw. "Marriage."

She sucked in her breath. *"Marriage?"*

"You know very well," he said grimly, "if you were pregnant, I would have no other choice."

They stared at each other in the shadows of the garden.

Looking down at her beautiful face, Rafael's body hurt with tension and fury.

He'd always vowed he would never get trapped by any woman. It had happened to him once, and that was enough. At seventeen, he'd fallen for an older woman who'd callously dropped him to marry a wealthy man. When Rafael had pleaded with her to marry him instead, she'd laughed at his tiny diamond ring. The faded Cruz fortune wasn't nearly enough to tempt her, she'd said. She liked his body well enough, but money was what mattered most to her.

At eighteen, he'd made it his mission in life to get rich. Ten years later, he'd ruined the woman—and her husband—in payback.

Rafael would never feel desperate over a woman again. It was why he could never have children. He would never give a woman that kind of power over him. Never feel vulnerable again. *Never.*

He looked at Louisa. *Especially* her. She had too much power over him already.

Against his will, Rafael's gaze dropped to her lush mouth. Even now, wondering if she'd tricked him, wondering if she were the most accomplished liar he'd ever met, Rafael couldn't stop wanting to kiss her. His body ached for her.

"So if I were pregnant, you would really wish to marry me?" she whispered.

In spite of all her defiance, he saw that she wished

to marry him. She wanted to pin him down. *She was no different from all the rest.*

He said evenly, "There's no way I would allow my child to be raised by some other man. So I would make you my wife. Is that what you want, Louisa?" he said dangerously. "Is that what you've wanted all along?"

With a deep intake of breath, she looked away from him, staring out at the view of Istanbul across the Bosphorus. So close across the water, but it was another continent entirely—Asia.

Clenching his hands into fists, he stared at her. Louisa was like that. So close, and yet so far. She was standing beside him. He could feel the warmth of her skin. And yet she was so far away. He realized he'd never really known her at all.

"Would you be a good father?" she whispered into the night, still not looking at him. "Would you love our child?"

His eyes narrowed as he looked at her lovely face, so different without glasses. Her eyes were wide and deep as the night. Her long dark hair brushed against her creamy shoulders in the soft breeze. She was the most beautiful, elusive woman he'd ever known. *And he hated her for her beauty.*

When he spoke, his voice was low and even.

"I would marry you for the baby's sake. But I would make you pay for trapping me into marriage," he continued in a low voice. He reached out and brushed a tendril of hair off her cheek with his fingertips. He felt her shiver beneath his touch as he leaned forward to whisper in her ear, "I would make you pay…and pay… and pay."

"What do you mean?" she gasped, shuddering.

He gave a cold, cruel smile as he straightened. "I would take pleasure of you in my bed until I had my fill." He stared down at her. "I would own you, as you would never own me."

She sucked in her breath.

She looked up at him, her eyes troubled in shadow. "But would you love our baby?"

Suddenly he was done with her endless evasions. Setting his jaw, he reached into his pocket for a cell phone. He dialed a number and spoke into the phone. "Dr. Vincent, please."

"What are you doing?"

He looked at her coldly. "Since you refuse to tell me if you're pregnant, I will have you examined by my doctor in Paris."

Louisa ripped the phone from his hands and ended the call. She took a deep breath.

"Well?" he said coolly.

"I'm…" She licked her lips.

He stared at her, his heart full of darkness and fury.

"I'm…" she said in a low voice. She took a deep breath, briefly closing her eyes as she said, "I'm not pregnant."

He exhaled in a rush. "You're not?"

She stared at him. Her eyes were pools of darkness.

Relief coursed through him, almost making him stagger.

He hadn't been wrong about her! She could be trusted! He hadn't been such a fool as he'd feared!

Then, staring at Louisa's tight shoulders and barely concealed fury, he reconsidered that statement. If she was innocent, he'd just treated her very badly indeed.

Looking at her with sudden regret, he rubbed the back of his head wryly. He'd let Novros's suspicions get to him. The Greek bastard had probably made it all up, he thought in irritation, spinning the facts for his own reasons, hoping to cause friction between Rafael and his housekeeper. Hoping he could get Louisa for himself!

He sighed. So who was a stupid fool after all…?

"Sorry," he said, spreading his hands wide and giving her his best smile. "Forgive me. I let my suspicions get the best of me. I should have known I could trust you, Louisa…"

But as he reached out for her shoulder, she backed away before he could touch her.

Rafael ground his teeth, silently cursing both his own untrusting nature and the Greek business rival who'd so easily managed to cause such trouble in his household.

"So, Miss Grey," he said in a determinedly jocular voice, "your housekeeping skills are desperately needed at my apartment in Buenos Aires. Please go fix it up, just as you've done here. There's no reason to stay in Istanbul any longer, as I just gave this house away in a business deal—"

"You did what?"

"You'll fly to Argentina in the morning. I will follow in a week or two, after I've completed the Paris deal."

For a moment, she was silent. Then she said a single cold word.

"No."

He tried again. "You will, of course, receive a much-deserved raise. I intend to double your salary."

"No," she bit out. She lifted her chin, and her eyes glittered. "I've done nothing, nothing to deserve the humiliating treatment you've given me. My only mistake was sleeping with a heartless playboy, knowing what kind of man you were!"

He set his jaw. "Louisa, you must believe I never meant—"

"I'm not finished!" she nearly shrieked. "For the last month, I've asked myself again and again how I could have slept with you in Paris. Then I did it again, letting you convince me to be your mistress on that Greek island. I wanted you so desperately. For years, I've made excuses for your bad behavior. I told myself you had some goodness deep inside you. I've devoted every moment of the last five years to making your life comfortable. But now, I see you how you really are. How could I have ever let myself love you? A coldhearted, selfish bastard like you?"

"I never asked you to love me." He gritted his teeth. "And I paid you well—"

"You'll never pay me another penny," she interrupted in a low, cold fury. "I won't take one more dime from you. Ever."

He took a deep breath. "Louisa, you're just upset," he said in a reasonable voice. "I admit I was rude to jump to conclusions, but surely you can see how your past looked to me? I am sorry I accused you of trying to trap me. I should have known you would never try to purposefully get pregnant with a child neither of us want. Forgive my stupidity," he said humbly. "Let's forget all this unpleasantness. Leave it behind and return to how we were. Boss. Valued employee."

She shook her head, her face a mask of repressed fury and some other emotion he could not read. Disgust? Grief?

"I will never work for you again," she whispered. "God help any woman stupid enough to be completely under your control. I'm done with you, Rafael. I never want to see you again." She lifted her chin, and her eyes glittered. "*I quit.*"

CHAPTER SIX

Sixteen months later

THE bakery had been busy all day amid the hubbub of the early spring season in Key West. Outside, the sun was warm, glimmering off the turquoise sea and a cruise ship docked nearby. It was only early afternoon, but Louisa guessed that she'd already served nearly every tourist on that ship. As she worked the counter, she glanced at the ship briefly through the storefront window that proclaimed Grey's Bakery.

Then, as the family of six left with their arms full of doughnuts and cookies, Louisa turned with an apologetic smile to the last customer. "Good afternoon. I'm so sorry for the wait—"

Then she finally got a good look at the man who'd been behind the throng of tourists. She sucked in her breath. The tongs she'd been holding dropped to the floor with a clang.

Rafael looked down at her, smiling with his dark eyes.

"Hello, Louisa," he said. "How are you?"

She stared at him in shock, unable to speak.

It had been almost a year and a half since she'd left him in Istanbul, this selfish, coldhearted man who hadn't wanted either a wife or a child. He looked at her now with the exact same gray shade of eyes as her baby son, who was now almost eight months old. The baby who was right now sleeping in the tiny office behind the counter. *The baby he didn't know about.*

Involuntarily she moved a little to the right, blocking his view of the office door. What was Rafael doing in Florida? Had he somehow found out about Noah?

"What are you doing here?" she choked out.

"You don't look pleased to see me." He rubbed the back of his dark hair and glanced up at her with a sheepish half smile. "I guess you're not the one who sent the letter. I hoped you were."

"Letter?" She hid her shock by leaning down behind the counter to pick up the tongs from the tile floor. She turned and dropped them into a sinkful of soapy water. Bracing her hands against the sink, she closed her eyes and took a deep breath.

"Not exactly a letter," he clarified. "It was a flyer advertising your bakery. Someone sent it to my office in Paris."

A chill went through her. She knew just who'd sent it. *Damn Katie!*

Fear pierced her heart.

Don't be afraid, she told herself desperately. Why should Rafael Cruz frighten her? She was no longer his employee. No longer his lover. This was her bakery, hers and her sister's, and if Louisa chose, she would throw him out onto the street!

He had no power over her, she told herself. None whatsoever.

But she knew that was a lie. She thought of her baby in the darkened room behind her. If he knew about Noah…

Could he possibly know?

Sucking in her breath, she turned to face him. Her eyes searched his face.

Then she exhaled. He didn't know. He couldn't. If he'd known, he wouldn't be looking at her with an expression that was so open and friendly and warm. He would have come in here with all guns blazing.

"What do you want, Rafael?" she bit out. She would never call him Mr. Cruz, ever again.

"I've missed those caramel brownies of yours," he said. "I'll pay for them, of course."

She heard the echo of his long-ago words. *I would make you pay…and pay…and pay.* She lifted her chin. "I thought I made it clear that I never wished to see you again."

"You did," he admitted. "But when I got that letter, I realized that I wanted to see you." He smiled at her. "Can we go somewhere to talk?"

The smile he gave her would have melted the heart of any woman.

But not hers. Never again. She glared at him, then turned with an elaborate smile to help a new customer who'd just come in her store. He waited with unusual patience as she served the other customer. After the tinkle of the bell as the customer went back onto the boardwalk with a bagful of doughnuts, Louisa finally turned to him coldly.

"I have nothing to say to you. Please leave."

"I had to find you, Louisa. To tell you," he said, "to tell you I'm…sorry."

She stared at him.

He was sorry.

"You have nothing to be sorry about," she said coldly. "I'm glad you forced me to quit. My life now is exactly what it should be." After she'd fled Istanbul, she'd returned to Miami, where she'd been stunned to discover Katie was a widow, living in a mobile home and barely able to support her five-year-old daughter. They'd hugged and cried in each others' arms. Now, they were sisters again. *They were a family.* Louisa lifted her chin. "You did me a favor."

He looked at her ruefully. "I did?"

Louisa nodded coldly. She'd used her savings to start this bakery on Key West, a place she'd visited long ago. This bakery wasn't just a family business, it was a labor of love. Even her little niece, who was now in first grade, helped out. The two sisters worked here during the day, and lived upstairs with their children in a small apartment above the bakery.

She had the perfect life now. She had her family, a successful business she loved and friends on this island. And if she still sometimes dreamed of Rafael, hot dreams of longing in the night—well, what of that? She didn't want him. She was better off without him!

Rafael looked at her. His eyes were as deep and dark as the Caribbean at midnight. He shook his head. "Ever since you left Istanbul, I've regretted my behavior that day. I never should have let my suspicions get the better of me."

"Forget it," she said shortly.

"I cannot." He looked at her regretfully, then with a sigh, he clawed back his dark hair. "I accused you of trying to get pregnant with my child. You! Of all women on earth, I should have known you would not do such a thing!"

She surreptitiously glanced back at the room where their baby was sleeping. She heard the soft snuffle of Noah's heavy breath. He would be hungry and waking soon. Katie had gone to pick up her daughter from school, but any moment now she'd be back to take her turn working the counter.

Her interfering, well-meaning sister would no doubt be thrilled to see Rafael. *Curse her.*

"Forgive me," Rafael said humbly, bowing his head. "I am sorry for how badly I treated you."

She heard her baby shift in his playpen, heard his snuffle as he started to wake up.

"I forgive you," she said abruptly.

"Just like that?"

"Just like that." She had to get Rafael out of her bakery—fast. She moved behind the counter, using fresh tongs to pick up some of her caramel brownies, the most popular item at the bakery, and put them in a white bag. "Here," she said. "Take these as a peace offering. On the house."

"Thank you." He took the bag, but he did not leave as she'd hoped. Instead he hesitated, propping the bag on the side counter as he slowly looked around the shop. "It's a beautiful store."

"Thanks," she said unwillingly.

"How did you end up here? At this remote island?"

Not remote enough, she thought, looking at him. "My sister was still living in Miami with her daughter. Her husband had died the year before."

"Yes," he said quietly. "I just heard about that."

"Right." Matthias Spence, the handsome, wealthy older man the Grey sisters had once fought over, had died of a heart attack shortly after the government had seized his remaining fortune for milking his investors in a money-making scheme. "But we're all doing fine now."

"Really?" he said softly.

"Yes," she ground out. Except she was going to kill Katie for sending Rafael the flyer. Her sister had been pestering her for the last year to tell Rafael about Noah. Louisa folded her arms. How could Katie have gone behind her back like this?

"I'm glad you're doing well," Rafael said in a low voice. "You deserve to be happy."

"Yes." But her success came at a price. Between caring for the baby and the bakery, Louisa only slept six hours a night at most. She was so tired. So, so tired. And Rafael looked more devilishly handsome than ever, well-rested and well-groomed in his black button-down shirt and slim-fitting jeans. "We work hard," she said. "Matthias left nothing to my sister. The bakery needs constant attention, as do the children."

"Children?" he asked.

Louisa bit her tongue, furious at her mistake. But before she could come up with an explanation, the bell chimed at the door.

"Sorry I'm late." Her sister came in with her niece, who was carrying a backpack and several large sheets of artwork. "The line at the school was so long. It seems all the parents wanted to pick up their kids today.... Oh." She stopped, staring at Rafael. "Hello."

Louisa glared at her. "Look who dropped by for a visit. My old boss."

Katie had the audacity to smile and hold out her hand. "Nice to meet you, Mr. Cruz."

"Call me Rafael."

"Rafael."

Behind them, Louisa simmered with fury. Then she jumped when she heard her baby give a soft mewling whimper from behind the office door. She glanced at Rafael, but by some miracle, he hadn't heard it. *Yet.*

"I think I'll give him a quick tour around the island," Louisa interrupted abruptly. She looked at Rafael. "Would you like that?"

He looked startled, but instantly said, "Yes."

Louisa untied her apron. "Take over the counter for me, Katie. Feed the little one with what I left in the fridge." She gave her sister a hard look. "I'll talk to you later."

Looking abashed, her sister nodded. Katie would make sure to feed Noah some of the milk she'd left in the fridge.

Hanging her apron up on a hook, Louisa came around the counter. Kicking off her sturdy shoes and shoving her feet into flip-flops, she pulled out her bun and shook out her hair, letting it tumble down her bare shoulders over her tank top. "Have you seen Key West?"

"No," he said, looking at her shoulders and hair. His gaze lifted slowly from her chest to her neck to her lips to her eyes. "When my plane landed, I came straight here."

"You're in for a treat," she said grimly. "Come with me."

Rafael couldn't stop looking at her.

Louisa had changed so much in sixteen months, he thought. How much had changed? Her hair? Her face? Her clothes? Yes, but it was more than that.

For the last year and a half, when he'd dreamed of Louisa, he'd pictured her either naked or in a gray shapeless skirt suit, wearing black glasses over her pale skin with her brown hair pulled back into a tight bun.

This new Louisa looked nothing like the tight, prim, aloof housekeeper he remembered.

Now, her face was tanned, bringing out the natural beauty of her bare face. He could see the intense color of her eyes in the sun. Her lips were deep pink. Her hair no longer was pulled back into the tight bun, but now fell down her shoulders, highlighted by the sun into the color of dark honey. She'd put on a few pounds in all the right places. His eyes traced the shape of her body beneath the aqua-colored tank top and madras shorts. What was different?

Color, he realized. She was in color.

She'd been beautiful as his employee, but had always been in the background, almost invisible, the capable Miss Grey in her black-framed glasses, sensible shoes and gray suit.

Here in this little town, on the edge of the turquoise Caribbean Sea, Louisa was vibrant with her youth and energy. She shone with color and life.

As they walked toward the beach, he couldn't take his eyes off her. He hadn't come just to ask for forgiveness. He'd come to offer Louisa her old job back. He'd missed her. His houses were all disorganized, half in shambles since she'd left. He'd intended to quadruple her salary, to give her two months of vacation a year, to invite her family to come along—whatever it took to lure her. He needed her. Not just as his housekeeper, but as his mistress. As his lover and friend.

The flyer in the mail had been the sign he needed. He'd given her over a year to cool off. He'd come to Florida, confident he could convince her.

But from the moment he'd walked into the charming, busy bakery, he'd started to have doubts. As they went down the street, everyone they passed seemed to know her. Young mothers pushing baby strollers, gray-haired retired couples holding hands, children, teenagers— they all greeted her with enthusiasm. Including—Rafael growled beneath his breath—some men. Young men in their twenties, carrying surfboards and scuba gear. Older men with expensive wristwatches and expensive cars. Young or old, every time one of them smiled at Louisa, his eyes lingering on her face and body, Rafael had to restrain himself from punching a stranger.

As he and Louisa walked by Mallory Square, Rafael set his jaw. He'd been so arrogant, so sure he could get his way on the journey from Paris. But now, he looked down at her from the corner of his eye. What did he have to offer that would compete with the vibrant life she'd created here for herself?

She had her own business, a life with her sister and her niece, friends of her own. And for all he knew, she had a lover. Or worse: more than one…

"Key West," she began, "is the southernmost settlement in the continental United States…." She continued to describe the island like a tour guide, but Rafael barely understood the words. He heard only the lovely sound of her beautiful voice. Only saw the movement of her lush pink lips. He couldn't look away from her as they walked down the sidewalk, then crossed the busy street.

"Are you hungry?" she asked suddenly.

He'd been openly staring at her, he realized. He forced himself to look away, to not look at her gorgeous face, her high cheekbones tanned by the sun. To not look at her sensual mouth, or the full shape of her breasts in her clingy blue tank top. To not notice how tiny her waist looked, barely the span of both his hands, above the wide sway of her hips and her impossibly long, tanned legs.

"Well?"

He swallowed, forcing himself to meet her eyes and only her eyes.

"I'm starving," he muttered.

"Come on, then," she said, giving him a brief, impersonal smile. "We can't let you leave on an empty stomach."

He followed her to a nearby food stand near Mallory Square. After placing her order, Louisa turned and thrust a piping hot fried pastry, wrapped in a napkin, into his hands.

"What's this?" he said, staring down at it.

"It's a conch fritter," she said, taking a bite of it. "Try it."

He tried not to watch the way her mouth moved as she chewed the greasy fried pastry. She licked a spot of grease from her lips, and he nearly shuddered.

Then he realized she was waiting expectantly. He reached for his wallet.

"No. My treat," she said brightly, stopping him. "You came all the way from Paris. It's the least I can do to feed you before you leave."

It was the second time she'd made the not-so-gentle hint about him leaving. But could he blame her, after the way he'd treated her? "Right." He cleared his throat. "Shall we go sit down?"

She shook her head. "I'd rather just walk as we eat."

"It's crowded." He felt the stares of passing tourists,

and other people, locals who greeted Louisa by name with big smiles. Some of them were men. It irritated him to no end. He glanced at the wide vista of the beach. "How about we walk by the beach?"

"By the boardwalk? Sure. There's a path. Come on."

They walked in silence, the only sound the soft crunching of sand beneath their feet as they crossed the path. He felt the hot wind blow against his skin.

He looked at her out of the corner of his eye. He'd missed her. Dreamed about her. And now, seeing her like this, wearing almost nothing over her curvaceous body…

He wanted her.

So much he shook with it.

She ate with gusto, swiftly finishing her fritter. Lifting her eyebrows, she looked at his own fritter. He hadn't even taken a bite yet.

"Don't you like it?" she asked, her eyes glinting at him in the sunshine. She was daring him to say no. Taunting him to admit he only liked fancy gourmet food, the kind she'd prepared for him while she was his housekeeper in Paris.

She didn't know about all the years he'd barely existed in New York, where he'd started his commodities trading firm while still in college. He'd poured all his money into investments, barely surviving on the cheapest food he could get.

But he hadn't had to live that way for long. Success had come easily for him. He'd found that all it took to do well in the world was charm and confidence, and never, ever admitting when he had no clue what he was doing.

And the same was true of love affairs. No matter what women said, they did not want a man who was vulnerable. Kindness? They saw it as weakness. Whatever they said, women were attracted to one thing only: power.

Looking straight into her eyes, he took a bite of the conch fritter.

"It's good," he said. He took another bite, though he barely tasted the food. How could he explain that he had no appetite? He wanted only one thing.

He wanted Louisa in his bed.

"I'm sure it's not what you're used to," she said mockingly. "It's not exactly caviar and steak tartare."

He stuffed the rest of the fritter in his mouth, not tasting it at all. He put the napkin in his coat pocket. He stopped halfway across the beach and looked at her.

Wind swirled her dark honey-colored hair around her face. Behind her, he could see the green leafy palm trees and brilliant bougainvillea. But the pink of the flowers was nothing compared to the roses in her cheeks, to the deep red of her lips.

He reached out to push back the dark blond tendrils of hair from her face. His fingertips brushed her warm skin. Touching her burned his fingertips.

She looked up at him, so close beneath the bright Florida sun, and he noticed for the first time that the eyes he'd always believed to be a regular brown were actually hazel, gleaming with a thousand tiny slivers of green and blue and brown like an explosion of light and color.

He took a deep breath.

"Come back to me, Louisa," he whispered.

She sucked in her breath, staring at him.

"I miss you." Reaching down, he took both of her hands in his own. Her fingers were slender and gentle and warm. He looked down at her intently. "I want you."

Their eyes locked. "You do?" she whispered. "Why?"

He couldn't tell her the full truth. Couldn't tell her how much he needed her. Right here. Right now. Being weak would never win him what he wanted; so he told her half the truth.

"My homes are in shambles," he said honestly. "The various housekeepers do their best, but no one organizes things like you. No one oversees things. I need a firm hand, I need your intelligent command. I need *you*."

She stared at him. Then she looked away, blinking fast. "You want me to work for you," she said dully. "That's what you need from me. You want me to be your housekeeper again."

"Yes." He paused. "I will quadruple your pay. Give you all the vacation time you need. Whatever you want."

Her lips curved. "You are generous," she whispered, but her tone was bitter. Then she turned to face him, her eyes suspiciously bright. "But I'm afraid I have no interest in being your housekeeper ever again."

Rafael clenched his hands into fists. From the moment he'd seen her in the bright bakery, looking so vibrant and happy as she served customers, it was just what he'd feared she would say.

But he couldn't accept that—couldn't!

"I told you I was sorry about what I said to you," he said quietly, "and I am. I overreacted. Can't we put it all in the past?"

"It *is* in the past." She looked past him to the brightly colored booths across the road, to the single roving chicken squawking as it walked freely on the beach, flapping its wings. In the distance, children were laughing as they flew a kite in the breeze. Turning back to him, she gave a brief smile that didn't reach her eyes. "I'm not leaving Key West. I like it here. With my family…"

"I'll buy your sister an apartment near us in Paris."

"No, thank you."

Why was she being so stubborn? Was it truly because she loved this island so much—or was it because she'd already given her heart to another man? But he wouldn't think about that possibility, couldn't allow himself to think about it! He set his jaw. "I could offer you a great deal of money—"

"No!" She whirled on him fiercely. "We are *not* having a hard time with money. My little bakery is doing just fine, for your information. I don't want or need your help. I can support my own family. Without you." She gave him a hard look. "You'll have to find someone else to sort out your messy life." Her whole body seemed tight as she turned her back on him. "I need to get back to my bakery now."

"Louisa, wait!"

But she started walking away, so he had no choice but to hurry after her. His mind was spinning with ways to convince her to come back to him. But he could not think of anything he hadn't yet offered. They crossed back through the town where everyone seemed to know her, where everyone was glad to see her.

What could Rafael possibly offer her to compete with the life she'd created for herself?

"Here we are," she said briskly as they reached the door of her gingerbread-style shop beneath the over-hanging awning on the wooden sidewalk. She held out her hand. "Goodbye."

Slowly he took her hand. But when he felt it in his own, he knew he could not let her go. He shook it, then instead of releasing her, pulled her hand closer, pulling her toward his body.

"Come back to me, Louisa," he said in a low voice. His eyes searched hers. "Not as my employee...but as my mistress."

Her jaw dropped. "What?"

"I've never tried to be faithful to one woman before," he said. "But since you left I haven't been able to forget you. I want to be with you, Louisa. Not as your boss. As your, your...lover." The word was pulled from him painfully. "I was a fool to let you go. A fool to push you away. You are the one woman who's never lied to me." He gave her a crooked smile. "The one woman who defied me when I deserved it, who dared to tell me when I was making an ass of myself. I need you."

She stared at him. "What are you saying?"

"I can't offer you marriage. But for as long as we're

together—" he took a deep breath "—I promise I will be faithful to you."

He heard her intake of breath, felt her tremble in his arms.

Suddenly an explosion of happiness went through him. *He knew he had convinced her.*

Lowering his mouth to hers, he gave her a long kiss full of passion and tenderness. He held her tightly, kissing her until he felt her surrender, until he felt her sigh in his arms. Until she started to kiss him back.

When he finally pulled away, he was smiling. He'd never been so happy.

"So you'll come?" he whispered, feeling more sure of himself now. Caressing her face, he smiled down at her. Louisa's eyelids fluttered open. She blinked in apparent bewilderment as he stroked her cheek and added, "My plane is waiting to take us to Buenos Aires."

She looked up at him. Then she sucked in her breath.

"No," she said. "Damn you! No!"

His jaw dropped as he stared at her, unable to believe her answer. He couldn't even fathom what he was hearing. For his whole adult life, he'd been the legendary elusive playboy. He'd never offered any woman as much as he'd just offered Louisa.

So now to have her actually refuse him!

"Why?" he demanded over the lump in his throat. He thought again of the men they'd passed on the street who'd been so delighted to see her. All those surfer boys looking at her with longing, all those wealthy yacht-owners who'd eyed her with lust. Rafael's expression hardened. "Is there someone else?"

He heard her intake of breath as her eyes flashed up at him.

"Yes," she said in a low voice. "There is someone else. I'm sorry." She pulled her hand out of his grasp, and he had the sudden feeling of the warmth of her slipping away, slipping away forever. "Goodbye," she whispered.

Turning in a whirl of vibrant color, she pushed open the door into her bakery. He heard the bright tinkle of the bell, and then he was left alone on the wooden boardwalk, beneath a cloudless sky stretching to the brilliant blue sea.

CHAPTER SEVEN

LOUISA'S legs wobbled with emotion as she went back into the bakery.

She felt the sudden blast of warmth and light as she entered the shop, smelled bread baking in the oven, heard the laughter of her six-year-old niece talking to her baby son in his bouncy chair. She was home again, and safe. She'd kept her secret and left Rafael behind forever. She'd put her child first. He was the only one who mattered.

So why didn't she feel happier? Why did she feel so broken inside? She blinked her eyes fast, barely able to keep from crying, staring down at the floor.

The floor needed to be mopped, she thought dimly. She would do that first. And as her heart turned over in her chest she pushed away the memories of the man she'd tried for over a year to forget, the father of her baby. She tried to focus on her business, her child, the rest of her daily schedule. Anything but the man she'd just pushed away...

I can't offer you marriage. But for as long as we're together, I promise I will be faithful to you.

"Did you have a nice visit?" her sister said innocently as the last customer left carrying a box of caramel macadamia brownies. "I didn't expect you back for hours."

"Didn't you?" she said hoarsely.

"To be honest I'm glad to see you," Katie said with a sigh. "This is the first lull in traffic we've had since you left. A minute ago five people were waiting in line wanting cookies and tarts, and then the baby started to cry, and I thought I would lose my mind either laughing or crying…"

Louisa slowly lifted her head. Her eyes glittered at her sister.

"You sent that anonymous letter, didn't you? You brought him here."

Her voice was even, revealing nothing of her turmoil inside.

Katie stopped. Then she slowly nodded.

"Why?" Louisa said. She heard her baby give a snuffling cry and walked swiftly behind the counter and lifted him from his bouncy seat, jiggling him on her hip as she continued to glare at her sister. "Why would you try to hurt me? Do you want him to take my son from me? Do you still hate me so much?"

"No!" her sister gasped, her expression horrified. Tears rushed into her eyes, the hazel-colored eyes so similar to Louisa's own, though her sister was several years younger and her hair was lightened into a luscious light blond color. She swallowed. "I once took away the man you loved. I am trying to make it up to you."

Louisa blinked at her in shock.

"I'm so sorry for what I did to you," Katie choked out. "I thought I loved Matthias. I thought you didn't. But I was wrong. So wrong to sleep with him. And I should have known. A man who would betray one person in his life would betray others…" Her voice trailed off bitterly. She looked up, openly weeping. "You've done so much for me. Always. I'll never forgive myself for taking Matthias away from you."

Matthias. The truth was that Louisa could barely remember him now. How could she have ever thought she loved the man, when she'd barely known him?

Unlike Rafael, whom she knew so well in so many ways.

The way he played the piano at night when he was lonely, the way he would carelessly eat five of her caramel brownies before dinner. The way he loved the smell of roses in the springtime. The way he ate dinner at three in the morning, then rose for his coffee and newspaper three hours later. The way he ruthlessly cut people out of his life before they could disappoint him.

Louisa shook her head. "You were right all along. I never loved Matthias," she said in a low voice. Lifting her head, she gave a shuddering breath. "But Rafael…"

"You have to tell him," her sister said. "He has to know."

Louisa looked at Katie. "It's too late."

"It can't be," she whispered. "It can't be too late. I need to do something, something to make you forgive me…."

Six-year-old Madison, her blond hair in pigtails, reached her arms up anxiously around her weeping mother. "What's wrong, Mommy? Why are you crying?"

It had been almost two years since her father's death, and the little girl already had forgotten almost everything about her father.

"Nothing's wrong, sweetie," Katie said, wiping her eyes and trying to smile.

But so much was wrong, Louisa thought. She and Katie had had such a happy childhood in northern Florida, beloved and protected by both their parents. Then, all too young, their mother had died of a long, lingering illness, followed by their father six months later when he simply seemed to lose the will to live. They'd lost their parents. Her niece had lost her father. But that had been beyond their control.

Louisa was deliberately choosing to deprive her baby of his father, and though she tried to remind herself why she'd had no choice, suddenly pain ripped through her. She looked down at her baby. What if she'd made the wrong choice?

"Can you ever forgive me?" her sister whispered.

Reaching over, Louisa hugged Katie fiercely with one arm. She realized she was crying, too. "There is nothing to forgive."

"I love you," Katie whispered. "And I want you to be happy. Do the right thing while you have the chance. Give your child a father."

"I can't tell him," Louisa said over the lump in her throat as she pulled away. "Rafael would be furious. He might try to take Noah away from me...."

"He wouldn't!"

"You didn't hear him last year when he said he would

force me into marriage and make my life hell as his wife. If he ever knew I'd had his baby…"

She looked down at Noah. At almost eight months, he was a happy, chubby baby with fat legs and a smiley disposition. Other than his dark hair and the slate-gray color of his eyes, he was nothing like the man who'd fathered him.

"Whatever he said to you, he said in anger," Katie argued. "He wouldn't take Noah away from you. You're a good mother!"

"You don't understand," Louisa cried, wiping her tears away fiercely. "If Rafael knew I'd had his baby… *he would destroy me.*"

The words were still coming out of her mouth when Louisa heard the chiming bell of the door. She froze. Then, with her baby still against her hip, she turned.

Rafael stood in the doorway. He'd been reaching for the bag of caramel brownies that he'd left on the counter. But by the wide look in his eyes as he saw Louisa with the baby in her arms, she knew her worst fears had been realized. He knew everything.

"Rafael," she breathed. "I can explain."

He looked at the baby.

"Who is that?" he asked in a low voice.

"Rafael…he is…I wanted to…"

His eyes narrowed. His shoulders straightened, and his body seemed so tall and strong and powerful. His face was dark as he took a step toward her, and it took all of her courage to remain rooted in one spot.

"Is that baby mine?" His voice was cold. Dangerous.

The panicked thought raced through her brain that she should lie, say the baby was her sister's, or that she was babysitting for a neighbor—but as she looked up into his hard, gray eyes, her heart pounded in her throat. And she found she could not lie.

"Tell me." His voice was deceptively soft as he took another step toward her. "Who. Is. That. Baby."

Her teeth chattered. "He is…my son."

Coming very close to her, looking down at her without touching either her or Noah, he said in a voice low as a whisper and dark as night, "And who is the father?"

Lie! A voice inside her screamed. Lie!

But she could not. Even after everything she'd done, she could not look into his face and deny him the truth that was obvious. Everything about their son looked exactly like Rafael, from his black hair to his beautiful gray eyes.

"Is he my son?" Rafael said in a low voice.

Closing her eyes as if bracing for a blow, she took a deep breath.

"Yes," she whispered.

The simple, clipped word from her lips—*Yes*—nearly caused Rafael to stagger back, as if struck by a mortal blow. Even though he'd known the truth from the instant he saw the baby on Louisa's hip.

But hearing the word, beads of sweat broke out over his forehead. His entire body felt like ice.

She'd had his baby. And she hadn't told him.

Louisa had caused him to unknowingly abandon his son.

His hands tightened as he stared at her across the warmth of the bakery. A large group of tourists entered the shop behind him with a happy chime of the bell.

With a snarl, Rafael opened his mouth to speak, to accuse. Grabbing his arm, still holding her baby against her hip, Louisa pulled Rafael up the flight of stairs behind the counter.

At the top of the stairs, he looked grimly at the second-floor apartment around him. It was a small, pretty, feminine home. Anxiously tugging on his arm, Louisa pulled him into a bedroom and closed the door behind him.

"Please understand," she said desperately, turning to face him. "You left me no choice!"

He stared around the small room. It contained a single bed, a crib and a changing table. The bed was covered by a handmade quilt. On the wall over the crib, soft fabric letters spelled out N-O-A-H beside a framed picture of a giraffe that looked like it was from an old children's book.

There was no lavish luxury here. This apartment wasn't a palace, but it was homey and cozy. It was bright and warm. The bedroom was decorated with warmth and simplicity—and kept absolutely clean.

Warmth. Love. Care. Everything Louisa had denied Rafael for the last year and a half. Along with the truth. *Along with his child.*

The rage of betrayal ripped through him.

"Rafael, please. Won't you talk to me?"

Slowly he turned back to stare at her. He'd thought

Louisa Grey was different from any woman he'd known. He'd thought her an intelligent woman with a bright mind and a rare sense of dignity—of loyalty. In the years she'd worked for him, he'd looked forward to seeing her every night after he returned from a date. He'd become accustomed to seeing dark eyes gleam through her glasses as she made him a late-night turkey-and-baguette and listened with some amusement to his latest dating woes, which always involved some woman going to pieces after he dumped her.

"It's your own fault, you know," she'd chided him gently. "You treat them badly."

"I make them no promises," he'd protested. "I tell them our affair cannot last. I am not a man made for marriage."

"You might tell them that, but your eyes say something else," she'd said quietly. "I've seen you. You look at every woman as if she, and only she, might be the one to make you faithful."

Rafael exhaled. She'd been right, of course. Louisa saw through all of his lies—even the ones he hadn't realized he was telling. She'd made herself indispensable in his life. Unique.

And now this. Her vengeful cruelty took his breath away.

Had Louisa Grey always been a liar? Or had Rafael turned her into a liar—when he'd slept with her?

No! He wasn't going to think that way—wasn't going to give her any excuse to say he was the one at fault for her crime. He wasn't the one who'd done this!

All these months, he'd felt so guilty, thinking he'd treated her badly. And all along, she was the one who'd lied to him. *She'd stolen his child.*

If not for the anonymous letter, he might never have come here. His baby might always have grown up believing Rafael had abandoned him.

His hands clenched into fists. He'd once thought Louisa a gold digger. Now he wished she were. A gold digger would have at least contacted him for a payout. This was far worse. Louisa Grey was a vindictive, cold, ruthless woman.

Rafael looked at the child in her arms. What kind of woman could keep a baby a secret from his own father?

"What is his name?" he said harshly.

She looked at him with pleading eyes. "You told me you never wanted a child, Rafael. You said—"

"That's your excuse?" he bit out furiously. "You use my own words against me? I also told you that if you were pregnant, I would marry you."

"But I didn't want to marry you!"

He stared at her, then shook his head in fury. "No, you didn't, did you?" he said. "You wanted revenge for the way I treated you. And you knew this would hurt me as nothing else ever could."

"That's not true!" she gasped. "You made it clear you never wanted a wife or child! Do you think I would share my precious baby with a man who didn't even want him?"

He narrowed his eyes. "It wasn't your decision to make."

She took a deep breath, shifting position from her left leg to the right as the baby squirmed in her arms.

Without warning, Rafael took the baby away from her. He saw Louisa choke back a protest, saw her clench her hands at her sides, as if fighting her initial instinctive reaction to snatch the baby back into her own arms.

He looked down at the baby. "My son," he whispered. "You are my son."

"His name is Noah, after my father," she said unwillingly behind him. "Noah Grey."

Holding the baby tenderly, he whirled to face her in a swift and decisive motion. "Noah *Grey?* You did not even give him my name?"

She shook her head stubbornly.

"You lied to me, Louisa," he said softly. He looked from his precious young son to the lying woman who had given birth to him. He saw her tremble, but kept himself from touching her—from raging at her, from shaking her—by an act of fierce will. "You are a far greater liar than I ever imagined." He gave a low, harsh laugh. "And to think you said you *loved* me," he sneered. "That's what your love was worth!"

Her cheeks went hot. "I did love you," she said quietly. "It nearly killed me."

He narrowed his eyes at her. "So that is why you lied to me about being on birth control? Because you thought you were in love with me?"

"I didn't lie!"

"Then how did you get pregnant?"

"I was on the Pill in Paris, like I told you," she whispered, then shook her head. "The whole staff ate some bad fish from the market. I threw up for days. I never thought that it might make the Pill useless, but then," her cheeks colored, "I never paid much attention to the birth control aspects of the medication. I never expected you to seduce me!"

Silence fell. Through the sheer curtains at the large sash window, with its brightly painted open shutters, he could see clouds trailing across the blue sky, above the distant turquoise sea. He took a deep breath.

"Perhaps you're not lying," he said quietly. "For if you were truly a gold digger, you would have jumped at the chance to marry me. The pregnancy must have been an accident." He set his jaw as he looked down at his son. "But your lie to me for the last year and a half was not."

"You're not being fair!" she cried. "You told me you never wanted a child. If I'd told you I was pregnant, you'd have insisted I was a gold digger who'd purposefully set out to 'trap' you!"

"Like the devil, you twist my own words against me," he said, then gave a low laugh. "You are the most cold, heartless woman I have ever known. Which is a high mark indeed."

"I'm not," she whispered.

"You looked into my face and lied to me. *I'm not pregnant,* you said." He nearly choked on the words. "When were you planning to tell me the truth, Louisa? After he was a grown man? Or did you mean to punish our son as well as me," he said harshly, "by only telling him the truth after I was dead?"

She went pale. "I would never do that to you."

"You already have."

Pain racked his body. Louisa had hurt him in the most devastating way possible.

And when he thought of how, just a half hour ago, they'd walked along the beach, he'd humbly held his heart in his hands and asked her to be his lover…

He shuddered with humiliation and fury. Then, still holding the baby, he turned without a word.

"Where are you going?"

"I'm taking my son home."

"No!" she shrieked. Racing ahead of them, she blocked the door. "You can't take my baby away from me—you can't!"

"We'll come to a custody arrangement." He had the satisfaction of seeing her shoulders sag with relief before he mercilessly continued, "You've had Noah for the last eight months. I will take him for the next eight months." Cradling his baby son against his shirt, he turned to go. "You will hear from my lawyers sometime before next Christmas."

"No!" she screamed, pulling on his arm. "You can't take him from me—his mother! Not for eight months!"

He glanced back at her coldly. "Can I not? But that is what you have done to me. You've had your time. I will have mine. Is that not 'fair' enough for you?" he said mockingly.

"No," she wept freely. "Please. It would kill me."

Rafael looked down at her. Somehow, in her abject grief and surrender, even with her nose red and tears streaking down her cheeks, she was still beautiful. He still wanted her. It infuriated him.

He heard the baby start to cry, his loud wailing mingling with Louisa's. Rafael awkwardly tried to comfort the baby, but could not. He had no experience with babies and no idea how to comfort Noah. He did not know his own son. The injustice of it raged in his heart as, setting his jaw, he gently handed the baby to Louisa.

"Noah. Oh, Noah." Louisa's weeping only intensified as she cradled her baby against her, whispering words of love, kissing his chubby cheeks again and again. "Oh, my sweet baby."

Rafael stared down at them. He took a deep breath. And came to a sudden decision.

"*Vale*," he said through clenched teeth. "I will not separate you."

"Thank you," Louisa whispered.

He stared at her coldly. "It's for my son's sake. Not yours."

She rocked the baby in her arms, her breath still uneven between sobs and hiccups. Rafael looked at her, then looked slowly around the room, from the sheer curtains over the window to the giraffe on the wall above the crib.

She was, he thought grudgingly, a decent mother. What she would not be—what she could never be again—was a woman he could trust.

But that didn't stop Rafael from wanting her.

There is someone else, she'd said.

Who was the man? Rafael's hands clenched. How many lovers had been in Louisa's bed over the last year, while he'd tossed and turned, tormented by longing for his fantasy of her as he'd believed her to be—honest, loving, chaste?

For all these years, Louisa Grey was the one woman he'd never been able to completely possess.

Now, he wanted to punish her. To break down her elusiveness. To own her.

Then discard her like the rest.

An idea occurred to him. A cruel, perfect idea.

It would be a neat, tidy, perfect revenge.

He smiled grimly. Walking across the nursery, he placed his hand on her shoulder.

"There is just one condition," he said brutally.

"Anything," she whispered. "Just don't separate me from my son."

Lowering his head, Rafael gave her a seductive kiss. He possessed her mouth with his, luring her with his tongue. He felt her shiver in his arms. He felt her sigh, then surrender.

When he pulled away, he saw the haze of longing in her eyes, and hid a smile.

She thought she'd beaten him, but he would make her pay. He was the master of the coldhearted seduction. Soon, his possession of her would be complete.

"You will be completely mine," he whispered. He stroked her cheek as he looked down at her, his eyes glittering in the shadowy room. "You will marry me, Louisa."

CHAPTER EIGHT

"WELCOME to Buenos Aires, Señora Cruz."

As the doorman greeted her, Louisa barely had time to wonder how he already knew about the marriage before bodyguards hustled her inside the *Belle Époque* high-rise in the exclusive Recoleta district. In two seconds, they'd crossed the lavish marble floor and were in the elevator.

Tall, hulking men clustered all around her, making Louisa feel small as she cradled her baby nervously in her arms. Worst of all: the tallest and most powerful of the men around her was Rafael. *Her new husband.*

When she'd woken up in Key West that morning, Louisa had never imagined she could find herself taken to Buenos Aires as the wife of a man who hated her. He kissed her so well that she almost imagined, in his arms, that he could forgive her. But when he pulled away from her, he could not hide the coldness in his slate eyes.

Within minutes after he'd demanded marriage, he'd dragged her to the courthouse. He'd somehow managed to convince the clerk Louisa was not a Florida resident and to skip the three-day waiting period. Before they'd even left Key West, Louisa had been his lawfully married wife. He'd spent the long flight on his private jet working. Ignoring her.

Now, in the elevator, Rafael's dark eyes gleamed at her malevolently. What did he intend to do to her?

I would make you pay for trapping me into marriage. I would make you pay...and pay...and pay.

At least she still had her baby in her arms, she comforted herself. That was what mattered. When she'd thought Rafael meant to take their son away, she'd been so frightened, she'd known she would do anything—*anything*—to stay with Noah. And so she'd said farewell to her sister and niece, telling her she was eloping with Rafael.

Katie had been ecstatic for her. "We'll be fine with the bakery until you get back," she'd said joyfully. "Have a wonderful time!"

If only her sister knew the truth. Louisa feared she was never going back to that warm, loving home in Key West. Rafael would never let her go.

When the elevator reached the top floor, Rafael pushed open the double doors.

"Welcome home," he said sardonically.

"Home?" Louisa looked around her in dismay. The old luxury apartment was old, musty and desperately in need of cleaning and refurbishment. All the furniture was covered with white sheets, which gave it a ghostly appearance. But in spite of her anger and fear, she could not help but observe the space with a professional eye and see the loveliness beneath the neglect. It had high Edwardian plaster ceilings and a view of the city through wide windows. Against her will, she could almost see how to make this apartment beautiful again. How to make it a home.

"I had no idea it was in such disarray," she whispered.

He shrugged. "I'm not here often."

She looked at him out of the corner of her eye. "I could make it nice," she offered.

"Don't bother," he said shortly. "We won't be here for long."

Louisa shivered. Now that she was his bride, now that they shared a child, he had more power over her than ever before. After five years of obeying his orders as his housekeeper, it would have been easy to return to the habit of trying to please him. But her time living in Key West had changed her. She had finally found her voice.

"This house could be so lovely," she said softly.

His lips twisted. "Do not fall in love. We will be here only a few days." He pushed open a door. "You will sleep in here."

This bedroom, at least, had been neatly tended. A small crib had been set up in the darkest corner near the large, modern bed.

With an intake of breath, Louisa turned back to him, her eyes shining. She'd wondered if he had any goodness left in his soul, but he must. Or why else would he have been so kind? "Thank you for letting me sleep in the same room as the baby. I promise you can trust me. I won't take Noah anywhere without your permission."

"I know you won't." His eyes were dark. "Because you and I will be sharing a bed."

She looked sharply at the bed. The enormous bed. And imagined what he planned to do to her there.

She'd thought she would do anything to keep her baby…but this?

Give her body to the man who hated her? Who had such power over her? Who wanted revenge for the way she'd kept his son a secret?

She repressed a shiver, remembering the last time they'd been in bed together on the private Greek island. She'd been so happy then. He'd made her light up with joy from without and within, given her such pleasure she hadn't even imagined it possible.

If she gave him her body ever again, how much longer would it be before he owned every inch of her soul?

Any woman who loved Rafael Cruz would ultimately be destroyed by that love. Because he had no love to give. He offered only seduction, not love. He had a heart of ice.

And if at times he seemed to care, if he seemed to be vulnerable after all, that was the most dangerous illusion of all.

Straightening her shoulders, she turned to face him. "I won't sleep with you."

"You will," he said, a sensual smile tracing his mouth. "You are my wife."

She licked her lips. "Just because we are legally married does not mean you own me!"

"Does it not?" he said softly.

He approached her, and for a moment she thought he intended to kiss her. Then the baby started to whimper and squirm in her arms. He stopped.

"Take care of my son," he said. "When you are done, I will be waiting."

Cuddling Noah in the bedroom, she fed him once they were alone. When he was asleep, she tucked him tenderly into the crib. The only sound was the quiet, even breathing of their sleeping baby as she finally left the bedroom, closing the door softly behind her.

She looked up with an intake of breath when she saw him waiting for her at the end of the hall, a dark, towering figure in a house full of shadows.

Rafael's eyes never left hers as he came slowly toward her. He put his hands on her shoulders, and she shivered.

How long could she resist him?

God help her if he ever reverted to the charming, seductive man she'd once known, the man with a gift for words and a light in his dark eyes that could convince any woman that she, and only she, could bring out the good in his heart.

God help her if Rafael decided to make her love him again.

"Come," he whispered.

Taking her hand, he pulled her down the hall. Dinner had been catered in and served on the massive oak dining table overlooking the wall of windows and the view of the city. The servers set up the food, then departed, along with the bodyguards.

Louisa was alone with Rafael, with no chaperone but their sleeping baby down the hall. She looked out toward the windows, past the ghostly white furniture covered with sheets. He opened a bottle of Argentinian red wine and poured it into two crystal goblets.

It should have felt intimate, and yet in the neglected penthouse it felt cold. Soulless. The food was delicious, but this place didn't feel like home. It felt dead. It felt like a prison.

And Rafael was her jailer.

She thought of the snug little apartment she'd left behind in Key West, of the sunshine and sound of the sea and her niece's laughter, and felt a lump in her throat. She set down her fork with a clang against the china plate.

"Don't you like the *empanadas?*" he asked.

"They're delicious," she murmured. "But it doesn't feel like home."

"Still a housekeeper at heart?" he said mockingly.

She lifted her chin. "I'd rather cook for us. For our family."

"Just take care of Noah. That is enough. We won't be here long." His eyes narrowed, and the darkness in his gaze scared her. "I have some business in Buenos Aires. A payback that has been a long time coming." He smiled. "Once that's done, *querida,*" he said, "we will return to Paris."

Paris. She thought of her memories there with a

shiver. Back to Paris. Where she'd first surrendered to her desire for her playboy boss. Where she thought he'd opened up his soul to her.

She couldn't let herself fall for him again—couldn't!

He might have some kind of sensual power over her that she could not fight—but she wouldn't let him have her soul!

She took a deep breath, squaring her shoulders.

"I cannot just live with you, doing nothing," she said quietly. "I married you and came to Buenos Aires because you left me no choice, but you must see that this cannot last. Let me at least act the part of your housekeeper. Because you do not want me as your wife."

"And you?" he said mockingly. "Do you want me as your husband?"

She swallowed, trying not to remember the ridiculous dreams she'd had after she'd first found out she was pregnant, when she'd dreamed of Rafael falling in love with her. When she'd imagined him changing somehow into a good father, a good husband. Then, she'd wanted…

She shook her head. She wouldn't think of it! "I was doing fine on my own. Noah and I were happy in Key West."

"Too bad." He took a drink of the expensive red wine from the crystal glass. "You're never going back."

It was exactly what she'd feared he would say, but she lifted her head defiantly. "Of course we're going back. I have a business to run, and a family that needs me—"

"Consider the bakery a gift to your sister," he said carelessly. "She now owns it."

She stared at him in shock, then narrowed her eyes.

"You are *out of your mind*," she said tersely, stabbing her fork toward him in midair for emphasis, "if you think I'll let you just give away the business I love, the business I built and created with my life savings after I worked for you for *five hard years—*"

"Yes, I am certain that was a fate worse than death," he said coolly, taking another sip of the red wine. "But your sister and her daughter will do well with the bakery. They will be happy and secure. That is what you want, is it not?"

She ground her teeth.

"Of course it is. But I want to be there with them! I've missed too much time with them already," she said softly, then shook her head. "Florida is my home. You cannot take me away from a place where I've made friends—"

"*Sí,*" he said sardonically. "I saw your many *friends* when I was there. Why don't you admit the truth about why you're so desperate to return?"

"Because I hate the sight of you?"

To her frustration, he seemed untouched by her jab. He only gave her a cold smile. "Who is he?"

"He?"

"The man you have been seeing. Or was there more than one? I might have been your first experience in bed, but how long did you wait for your second and third and fourth?" His cold eyes met hers over the table.

"Tell me, Louisa. How many men did you invite to your bed while you were still pregnant with my child?"

She stared at him in horror. Then, she rose from the table. Looking down at him, she raised her hand but he grabbed her wrists. He was so strong she could not pull away.

He stared at her for a moment in cold fury. She felt the pounding of her own heart, heard the soft gasp of her own breath. Felt the electricity in the air suddenly change between them.

Then, lowering his head to hers, he claimed her mouth in a punishing kiss.

Louisa tried to fight. Tried to push him away. He was bruising her, hurting her—

Then his kiss suddenly gentled. His hold on her became seductive, his arms caressing her softly, so softly, that her shirt and shorts disappeared as if blown off her body by a light warm breeze. His lips moved against her so tenderly, so lovingly, that she could not resist.

She wrapped her arms around his neck as he lifted her up into his arms and carried her, not to the bed, but to the nearby couch covered with a white sheet. There, he made love to her with such amazing tenderness that she wept.

Afterward, as she held him and he slept in her arms, she looked out at the view of the city and was suddenly reminded of their first night together, in Paris. The night she'd admitted to herself that she was in love with him.

Now, she looked at him in the slanted light from the

windows, curled up beside her on the long, wide sofa covered with the white sheet. She listened to the rise and fall of his breath, felt the warmth of his skin against her cheek, heard the beat of his heart with her head against his chest.

And knew she still loved him.

She'd been in love with him secretly, hopefully, desperately for years. The sixteen months they'd spent apart, where she'd tried to convince herself she didn't love him anymore, had changed nothing.

She loved him.

And, from the way he'd touched her in the night, was it possible he could love her…?

No, she told herself fiercely. *It's just his nature. His body promises what his soul cannot deliver.*

And yet…

They had a child together. Could somehow, by some miracle, Louisa be the one to reach Rafael's heart, to make him whole, to heal his soul so they could be the real, loving family she longed for them to be?

She heard Noah cry. Quietly, so she wouldn't wake her husband, she crept out of his arms and went down the hall. Pulling on her clothes, she padded softly across the apartment to feed the baby and rock him back to sleep.

She returned to the living room with her heart in her throat, full of dreams and plans and hopes to help Rafael be the man she needed. The man she loved. The man she was convinced he was born to be. She could hardly wait to sleep in his arms….

She stopped abruptly when she saw the sofa was empty.

He came up behind her. She whirled around to discover him wearing a white terry cloth robe, clearly just come from the shower.

"That was enjoyable," he said coolly, drying his wet hair with a towel. "I think I may like having a wife."

She tilted her head, her heart pounding with hope. "You think so?" she whispered.

His lips curved. "Of course. You're in my bed. At my service. And apparently wishing to cook and clean for me whenever you're not satisfying me in bed. I'm saving a great deal of money, since I don't even have to pay you. You are—" he reached out to stroke her cheek "—every man's dream wife."

She swallowed, trembling as she looked up into his cold gray eyes. "You are trying to hurt me. Why?"

"I said I will enjoy our marriage. And you—will not." Pulling his hand away, he leaned forward until his handsome face was inches from her own. "Nothing has changed," he whispered. His eyes were a mesmerizing gray. "You will regret the day you stole my son away from me."

Pain stabbed through her. Was that all their night together had been for him? She'd thought—dreamed— it could be some kind of new start for them, the sweet promise of forgiveness and a new life, raising their son together.

He'd fooled her yet again. His tenderness, his sensuality, had been the weapons he'd used to punish her!

She had the sudden image of the pain he could inflict on her, this man she loved, this man she'd once known so well.

I can't offer you marriage. But for as long as we're together, I promise I will be faithful to you.

She sucked in her breath. He'd cared for her. He still did. It was only his anger that was making him try to hurt her!

But she wouldn't let him. She wouldn't let him destroy their chance of being a family. Somehow, in spite of everything, she would break through his anger and make him forgive her!

It was their only hope….

She looked up at him. She could tell he was waiting for her to get upset, to yell, to cry.

Instead she took a deep breath. "I'm sorry."

"Sorry?" he ground out. "For stealing my son? You think an apology is enough?"

She nodded. "I thought I had no choice," she said simply. "If I'd told you I was pregnant in Istanbul, you would have insisted I was a gold digger—and punished me. Instead I tried to raise our son on my own, without any help from you. So you accuse me of being vindictive—and you want to punish me." She lifted her eyes to meet his. "Have you ever considered that you are an impossible man to please? Have you ever considered," she said quietly, "that the problem might be *you?*"

He stared at her.

"Are you joking?" he growled.

She folded her arms over the paper-thin fabric of her

tank top, wishing she had more clothes than her little shirt and shorts, more armor to protect her as she faced him. If only, she thought, she had one of her old gray woolen suits, her old thick black-framed glasses!

But all she had was herself. That would have to be enough.

She took a deep breath. "I still love you, Rafael," she whispered, then gave him a tremulous smile. "There. I said it. In spite of your faults, in spite of your weakness, I love you."

"My weakness?" he exploded.

She shivered at the danger in his dark eyes. But she still forced herself to be brave enough to speak the truth in her heart.

"A strong man," she said, "allows himself to be vulnerable. He shows his love at any cost. A truly strong man gives everything he has—everything he is—to his family. He loves with all his heart and holds nothing back!"

"And where did you learn that? Housekeeping school?" he sneered.

"No," she said simply, facing down his sarcasm. "I learned it from my father, who though he never made a fortune, he made us feel every day like we were valued and loved."

Rafael sucked in his breath through his teeth.

"Forget it," he barked. Pulling on some jeans and a black T-shirt, he stuffed his feet into black Italian-made shoes and headed for the door.

"Where are you going?"

He looked back at her just once. His face was dark in the shadows of the apartment.

"Out," he said.

"Out? Out where? It's midnight!"

He gave a hard laugh. "The night is young—for me. I guess I'm too *weak* to stay." His eyebrows lowered as he ordered her, "Be ready for me upon my return. Perhaps I will want you again." A cold smile curved his mouth. "Perhaps not."

She stared at him, her heart throbbing painfully in her throat.

"Don't do this, Rafael," she choked out, blinking back tears. "Stay and talk to me. Please. I want so much for us to—"

"I've had enough *talk* for one night," he said coldly. Opening the door, he walked out. She saw him have a quiet word with the huge bodyguard outside as the door closed behind him.

Louisa shook with humiliation and despair. She went to the window and stepped out onto the wrought-iron balcony, staring out into the twinkling lights of Recoleta and all Buenos Aires beyond it in the warm, humid night.

Looking down, she watched Rafael leave the building, watched him with her heart in her throat and tears streaking her face.

He glanced up. Their eyes met.

Then he coldly turned away. He climbed into the yellow sports car his bodyguard had brought to the curb. Stepping on the gas, he drove off into the night.

Where was he going? Louisa wondered with anguish. To meet another woman?

She stayed on the balcony for a long time after he left, feeling trapped, feeling helpless. The city at her feet still seemed to be busy and alive, noisy and young. All of the things she no longer felt.

Louisa was so tired, but she knew she would not be able to sleep. Not when her emotions were so wound up. Not when pain and love and helplessness made her shake.

Then she had an idea.

If Rafael couldn't stand a direct discussion, she would come at him sideways.

She would lure him into their marriage through the weak point he would never think to guard. She would seduce him with her skills. She would give him a home.

A small smile traced her lips as she left the balcony. Crossing the apartment, she flung open the front door. She spoke directly to his head bodyguard outside, an American named Evan Jones who rose respectfully to his feet.

"I need your help," she told him coolly, in her housekeeper voice that no staff member could ever resist. And neither did he.

As she gave him her instructions, Louisa suddenly felt a surge of optimism. She might no longer be Rafael's housekeeper, but she still had power in his life. More than she'd ever had before. And though he did not know it, Rafael himself had given it to her. He'd done it when he'd made her his wife.

CHAPTER NINE

RAFAEL didn't return to the apartment until noon the next day.

He'd met some old school friends for a drink, but when women had come up to them at the bar, he'd found himself bored. Not just bored—uncomfortable. And so he'd left.

But he couldn't go home. Not after what Louisa had said.

In spite of your faults, in spite of your weakness, I love you.

His hands clenched to remember it. How did she dare? His weakness? No woman had ever said such a thing to him before! He'd intended to punish her, and yet somehow she'd gotten one step ahead of him!

His weakness.

Louisa knew him too well. She'd lived with him, day in and day out, for five years. No other woman had had such an opportunity to see beneath the facade. Or so thoroughly get under his skin. *She knew him.*

Rafael didn't like it. It made him feel weak, like she claimed him to be. And so he'd checked into the Four

Seasons hotel to teach her a lesson; to prove to them both who was in control, and how easily he could hurt her. Let her suffer the same suspicions he himself had suffered in Key West with her. Let Louisa wonder what other lovers might be taking her place!

He had her ring on his finger. And as long as he did, he would never cheat on her. His honor would not allow it. As long as he was with her, he would be faithful.

But she didn't have to know that. She already had too much power over him.

A strong man allows himself to be vulnerable. He shows his love at any cost. A truly strong man gives everything he has—everything he is—to his family. He loves with all his heart and holds nothing back...! Have you ever considered that you are an impossible man to please? Have you ever considered that the problem might be you?

He was the problem? Him?

Rafael growled to himself in the elevator. She was the one who'd stolen his son!

Ignoring his bodyguard's cheerful greeting, Rafael pushed open his front door. And froze in the doorway.

For a moment, he thought he'd wandered into the wrong house. This surely could not be his apartment. It did not look remotely like the same place!

The old apartment had been thoroughly scrubbed, and all the old dusty knickknacks had been swept away along with the ghostly white covers. Fresh flowers were on the kitchen table. He could smell something delicious baking in the oven.

And how the hell had she managed to replace the old, heavy-set wooden furniture with new modern sofas, sleek chairs and a huge big-screen TV—all in the space of just a few hours?

"Welcome home, Rafael," he heard Louisa say behind him warmly, and he whirled to face her.

His wife looked incredibly pretty, smiling up at him, wearing a sweet, demure dress. He was immediately attracted in spite of himself. Taking a deep breath, he looked away—only to have his eyes fall upon the platter of caramel macadamia brownies cooling on the counter.

Louisa Grey—Louisa Cruz—was indeed everything any man would want. Sexy, strong, smart as hell. A good mother and a good cook. She was everything he'd ever wanted.

Except he hated her. Didn't he?

"How did you do all this?"

"I have my ways." She smiled mischievously, and love shone in her eyes. "I made the house a home. For us. For our family."

"I see," he said faintly.

He'd come home expecting a scene. He'd expected Louisa to scream and yell at him and wail, as other women had done when he'd pushed them away. Staying out all night was the swiftest, most convenient way he'd found to end a relationship.

But Louisa didn't even ask him where he'd been all night. It was as if she weren't even worried, as if she had complete confidence that she was the only woman he wanted.

And it was true, damn her.

She had too much control over him by half. She knew him too well. And he couldn't simply end their relationship and walk away, no matter how much easier that seemed. They were married. They had a child.

But Rafael knew what she wanted. She wanted his soul. No matter how beautiful she was. No matter how tempting. He wouldn't give it to her. He would never let himself be vulnerable again.

He took a deep breath, keeping his expression cold.

"I did not give you permission to do this," he said. "I liked the house left how it was. I told you."

"Well, I didn't like it."

"It's not for you to choose—"

"It wasn't a healthy environment for the baby." She held out the platter. "Brownie?"

Caramel macadamia nut with white chocolate chips. His favorite. He narrowed his eyes. Did she truly think him so weak that he could be bought so simply?

"I'm not hungry."

She shrugged, then cut herself a big piece. Her smile spread into a joyful grin. He watched her bite into the gooey caramel brownie, with its layers of butterscotch and macadamia nut. Melted white chocolate smudged her lip. He watched her lick it off. His mouth watered.

But it wasn't the brownie he wanted anymore. He hungered for Louisa.

Her body.

Her laugh.

All of her.

Making love to her last night had been incredible. He'd seduced her to punish her but in the end, he was the one who'd been caught. He'd woken up, bereft of her in his arms. He hadn't liked the feeling. He'd jumped in the shower. He'd tried to pretend to them both that finally having her in his arms again, finally making love to her after sixteen months of yearning, had meant nothing.

But he could not lie to himself. Not anymore.

Rafael watched her pick up the baby from his bouncy seat and lift him on her hip. As she sang songs to Noah, swinging him in her arms as they twirled around the kitchen, her eyes danced with laughter.

He watched Louisa laughing with the baby in her arms. He looked at them, his heart in his throat.

He'd married her yesterday intending to discard her in Paris. Now, he realized his plans had changed. Louisa brought so much to his life. Why should he ever let her go?

He could still get the revenge he'd planned. Then he could take Louisa to Paris and they could start a new life….

"By the way," he said abruptly, "my mother is coming for dinner tonight."

Louisa stopped, clearly startled. Then her eyes lit up. "Your mother? How lovely!" she exclaimed. She tickled the baby, making him squeal with laughter as she cooed, "And she'll get to meet her sweet new grandbaby, won't she?"

Yes, she would. For the first and last time.

Grabbing the knife, Rafael cut himself an enormous

piece of brownie. He took a huge bite. It was delicious. Like the taste of vengeance.

Louisa beamed up at him as he ate. He could see that she thought he was starting to bend, to break, beneath her influence. Well, let her continue to think so.

He smiled at her.

She would soon learn the truth. Rafael would neither bend, nor break, for any woman. He would be the last one standing.

He'd once begged Louisa to remain his housekeeper. He'd once pleaded with her to become his mistress.

Marrying her had changed everything.

The marriage license would hold her as no employment contract ever could. Louisa would warm his bed, take care of his child and prepare his meals. The fact that she was now his wife meant he would never have to pay her. He'd never have to give her a vacation. And he'd never have to fear losing her again.

She was his wife. He owned her now. Forever.

"Welcome, *Mamá*."

Louisa watched Rafael kiss the stooped woman on both cheeks as he welcomed his mother to their home. Agustina Cruz was nothing like Louisa had expected. She'd thought Rafael's mother would be a slender, severely elegant socialite. Instead she was plump, gray-haired and had a timid, hopeful smile on her bright coral lips as she looked at her tall, handsome son.

"*Buenas noches, mi hijo,*" she said to Rafael. "I am so happy to see you," she said in Spanish, standing on her tiptoes to embrace him. Louisa's high school Spanish was rusty after so many years in France, but she could still understand as Agustina continued tearfully, "It has been too long. I haven't heard from you since I sent you the letter after your father died."

"I remember," Rafael said coolly in English. "Come in."

Why was he being so strangely cold? Louisa thought. This woman was his mother! Whoever his father had been—she was the one who'd given birth to him, loved him, raised him!

She'd hoped that Rafael was starting to forgive her, that he was starting to allow the goodness of his heart to shine through. But now...she didn't know what to think.

Holding her own baby against her hip, Louisa smiled at the older woman.

"Welcome to our home, Señora Cruz," she added warmly in English. "I am so happy to meet you at last."

The other woman blinked at Louisa in her white cotton tea-length dress, peering at baby Noah in a white shirt and black pants with a little tie. Louisa had chosen their clothes with care. Meeting Rafael's mother was important to her. And yet—she glanced over at Rafael. He was casually dressed in a black shirt and dark jeans. Why had he, alone in the group, made no effort?

Agustina blinked at Louisa and the baby. "Thank you, my dear. But who are you?"

"I am Rafael's new wife."

Agustina turned reproachful eyes upon her son, still

standing grim and silent behind them. "Rafael, you are married?" she chided gently.

He shrugged.

"And this," Louisa added quickly, to cover up for her husband's coldness, "is our baby. Noah."

Agustina stared at the baby. "Your…your baby?" she gasped. Tears filled her eyes. "My grandson?"

Louisa nodded. Smiling, she placed the baby in his grandmother's arms.

"Oh *mi nieto, mi pequeño angelito,*" the woman whispered. Tears fell unheeded down her face as she held the baby in her arms.

Watching her joy, tears filled Louisa's eyes as well. She looked back at her husband with a smile, expecting to see the same emotion in his face. Instead his dark eyes were blank. Expressionless. *Dead.*

"Come," he said in a low voice. "Let's sit down for dinner."

The meal was a joyful one—at least for the baby, mother and grandmother. Agustina Cruz was a lovely, warm, charming woman. She reminded Louisa of her own mother, whom she missed very much.

"That was delicious," Agustina said at the end of the meal, when she'd finished the last bite of Louisa's brownies covered with vanilla ice cream and butterscotch crumble.

"Thank you." Louisa had insisted on preparing the meal herself, as an expression of respect and care. Rafael had scoffed at that idea, then shrugged and let her do it.

Louisa had thought, when he'd come home at noon after being out all night, that she'd done everything she could to make him happy here. She'd worked on the house most of the night and all of the morning between caring for the baby. She'd dressed with care. She'd baked his favorite foods. She'd really thought she was starting to get through to him...especially after she'd been able to learn from the bodyguard, to her intense relief, that Rafael had spent the previous night alone at a hotel.

It had killed her to pretend she didn't care. But she knew Rafael too well. She couldn't play by the same rules as his other women had done. She had to keep him guessing. Keep him off balance. It was her only hope of gaining what she truly wanted.

His happiness—and her own.

Agustina set down her fork. "What an amazing meal."

"Louisa made it. To honor you," Rafael said coldly.

Gratitude and joy washed over his mother's face.

"Thank you. Both of you," Agustina said tearfully. "I was so afraid you'd never forgive me, Rafael. You must believe that I never meant to hurt you when I wouldn't share your father's name...."

"Hate you? Why would I hate you?" He took another drink of brandy then set the empty glass hard against the table. "Just because you waited until he was dead—just because you made sure I never had a real father and left me begging you for answers for twenty years—why would I hate you?"

Her plump cheeks had gone pale. "Rafael," she whispered, "I thought you understood."

"I do understand. And now—" he rose to his feet "—you will finally understand as well. You will know how it feels." He stared down at her. "You've met my family. For the first and only time. Now, you will never see them again."

"What?" Louisa gasped.

He picked up Noah. "We are never coming back to Buenos Aires. My son—" he looked down at the happy, smiling baby "—will never remember he has a grandmother. He will never even know you exist. You will die as my father died," he said harshly. "Alone."

His mother looked as if she might faint.

"Rafael—you cannot do this," Louisa gasped, pushing herself to her feet. "I won't let you do this!"

"It's your choice," he said evenly. He gave her a hard look. "Choose my mother, a stranger to you—or choose your husband and child."

Still holding the baby in his arms, he left the room.

Louisa started to run after them, then abruptly stopped. She looked down at Agustina, who was still sitting at the table, alone and forlorn.

"I'm sorry," Louisa choked out. "I will try to talk to him!"

The older woman looked at her, then sadly and steadily shook her head. "It will do no good, my dear," she said softly. She gave a trembling smile. "It was lovely to meet you. Take good care of my boys—both of them. *Adios*. Go with God...."

Tearfully Louisa rushed out the door. The elevator was gone so she ran down six flights of stairs. She barely made it outside the building, pushing open the door with a bang, before she saw the limousine pulling away from the curb with her husband and child inside it.

"Wait!" she screamed. The car stopped.

"Cutting it close," Rafael observed coolly, as she wrenched open the door.

Panting, she scrambled into the back beside the baby seat. She kissed Noah tearfully on his downy head then, as the car pulled away from the curb, she turned on Rafael.

"How could you do that to your own mother? She loves you! How could you be so cruel?"

"Now you know what I do to people who betray me," he said evenly. "It's taken almost twenty years, but I finally got justice for what she did to me. And to the father I never knew," he said coldly. He leaned forward. "To the airport."

"You are more heartless than I ever imagined," she whispered, suddenly frightened.

"I am not heartless." Abruptly Rafael leaned toward her in the backseat. He cupped her face with one hand. "For I am willing to forgive you, *mi vida,* for one mistake. One." He caressed her cheek. "But never cross me again."

"What do you mean?" she whispered, trembling beneath his touch.

"Never lie to me again. And I will allow you to remain my wife and raise our son. You will be honored and respected forever as my wife. But if you ever betray me again…"

Their eyes locked.

"If I do?" she whispered.

He abruptly pulled his hand away. He picked up the newspaper in his lap and unfolded it, creating a wall of newsprint between them. "Then you will lose everything."

CHAPTER TEN

You will lose everything.

A few weeks later in Paris, Louisa couldn't stop shivering in the cool spring morning as she sat outside at a riverside café overlooking Notre Dame across the Seine. Baby Noah was sleeping, tucked snugly into blankets in the baby stroller beside her. Louisa took another sip of coffee so hot and strong it scalded her tongue, but still she continued to shiver. Even in a black cashmere sweater, dark skinny jeans and knee-high boots, she felt cold down to her toes.

Closing her eyes, she turned her face toward the sun.

If Rafael ever learned what she'd just done…

I had no choice, she told herself fiercely. She couldn't allow him to so callously, cruelly hurt his mother, not when his desire for revenge would hurt everyone—grandmother, grandson, and most of all: Rafael himself!

Just a few moments ago, Agustina had been here at this café, sitting beside her. She'd been so happy to see her grandson again. A lump filled her throat. And

Louisa had finally learned the truth about Rafael's past. She understood at last why his mother had protected him all these years.

Rafael thought his mother was cold-blooded and controlling. He was wrong. But Louisa could not tell Rafael about his father, any more than Agustina could. It would hurt him too much. Louisa couldn't rip his heart out with the truth. No matter how badly he lashed out.

"*Merci, madame.*"

Louisa looked up, blinking fast and trying to smile at a waiter who left the bill. She put down her euros, then drank the rest of her *tasse* of hot black coffee. She glanced down at her sleeping baby in the stroller, feeling warmth and adoration swelling her heart.

"I'll find a way to break through to him," she whispered to her sleeping child. She'd find a way to make him forgive his mother…but how?

"*Mi vida.*"

Louisa nearly jumped in her chair when she heard Rafael's voice behind her. With a gasp, she turned and saw him climbing out of the limousine that had pulled to the curb. "What are you doing here?"

He slammed the door closed then walked toward her.

"Are you and Noah having a nice morning?" he said, smiling.

She rose to her feet so quickly all the blood rushed from her head. "We were just leaving."

She'd chosen this café in the *Quartier Latin* because

of its distance from their penthouse, which was in the more exclusive eighth arrondissement across the river. She'd known he had a full schedule today, meeting a new stockholder who owned a château to the south of the city. She'd never imagined he might drive right by the café. Of all the quirks of fate…

She was suddenly sweating in the cool spring air. If Rafael's car had driven past this café just ten minutes ago, he would have actually seen his mother sitting beside her!

Their marriage, their building trust, could have been destroyed forever. She glanced down at her sleeping baby. Noah was so precious to her. Was she being a fool to risk a decent life, in hopes of having a happy family?

Rafael smiled at her. He looked so handsome in his dark suit and blue tie. His jawline was sharp and shaved, his eyes bright in the sunshine.

"Before I met with my stockholder, I went up to La Défense," he said. "Our new building is perfect."

"Is it done? Ahead of schedule?"

"Next week we'll start moving our people in. Then I'll take you to see it."

But would she still be his wife next week? Louisa's hands tightened on the handle of the stroller.

"Shall we walk back to the apartment?" he said.

Her eyes widened. "You have time? Now, in the middle of the day?"

Rafael shrugged. "It is a beautiful morning. I'll make time."

She swallowed. Of all the days she'd wished he

would spend time with her, he was choosing now? Now, when she was racked with guilt and fear over what she'd done, bringing his mother secretly to Paris? She took a deep breath and tried to smile. "That would be lovely."

They walked together along the river. She gave him little glances. He'd been busy constantly with work since they'd arrived in Paris. He'd had time only to give his baby son a kiss each morning before he left—and when he came home late at night, he'd climbed into bed beside Louisa and made passionate love to her in the dark. But this was the most they'd spoken together in weeks.

In many ways, nothing had changed since the last time she'd lived in this city. She still based her whole world around Rafael Cruz, running his home and trying to gain his approval.

But in other ways, everything had changed. While she still oversaw the house, Rafael wanted her to spend her time as mother to their son—and as his wife. Which meant far too many shopping trips to the designer boutiques of the nearby Rue du Faubourg St-Honoré. In fact, in a few days, she would attend her first society ball on his arm.

The thought of attending the soirees she'd once organized for him, not as his housekeeper but as his wife, terrified her. The thought of facing all the various women he'd once slept with—and for all she knew, might someday sleep with again—made her ill.

She'd tried to create a loving home. But it wasn't

enough, not nearly enough. He still didn't allow himself to be vulnerable. He still wouldn't allow himself to love either her or the baby.

Springtime in Paris was lovely. The flowers and trees were starting to come back to life. The baby was awake and chortling happily, kicking his feet in the air as Rafael pushed the stroller, by the time they reached the eighteenth-century building near the Champs-Élysées. Rafael owned the entire building, but only used the top two floors to live in. The floor beneath was for his bodyguards and assistants, and the several floors below that were being used as office space until the new headquarters was finished.

As the elevator opened to their spacious penthouse, Louisa took a deep breath at the beauty of the home and the view of the city. She could see the Eiffel Tower across the river. Even as housekeeper, she'd loved this home; and now she was not only its mistress, but the mistress of all Rafael's homes around the world.

But if he knew the truth about how she'd brought his mother to Paris and allowed her to spend time with Noah behind his back…

It was wrong. Louisa knew she shouldn't have done it. But he was so caught up in his ideas of revenge.

How could she ever make him forgive his mother, how could she ever get him to open his heart, without causing him irreparable harm?

A sudden thought occurred to her.

She could tell him the truth. Rather than wait for him to find out what she'd done—rather than avoid conflict, as she always had—she could take the bull by the horns and tell him all about it.

But the thought terrified her. No. She couldn't risk it!

Later that night, with their baby sleeping in his lavish nursery, a few hours after Louisa had gone to bed, she felt Rafael climb in beside her. She always slept naked, as he preferred. Before she was quite sure whether she was dreaming, he was kissing her. She felt him on top of her, felt his body hot and hard against hers. Within moments, she was crying out her pleasure, and she heard his shout as he collapsed on top of her.

Afterward, he held her close in his arms in the darkness.

"I have a gift for you," he murmured against her skin.

She looked up at him in the shadows, her heart in her throat. "What is it?"

He purred in her ear, "Do you remember that private Greek island?"

How could she forget? Those were the happiest two days of her life. "Of course."

He kissed her temple and whispered, "I bought it for you today."

She sucked in her breath. "You—bought it?"

"Novros wasn't sure he wanted to sell." She heard his smile in the darkness. "But I convinced him."

"Thank you," she said softly. Her eyes filled with tears as she held him tightly to her.

His hand moved toward her naked breast. "Anything for you, *querida*."

Anything?

Suddenly she knew she had to take the gamble. She wanted him to trust her. She didn't want to lie to him.

She loved him. He gave her everything she could want when it came to money, but so little of himself except his lovemaking, which was very inventive and satisfying. Now he'd given her an entire island, but it was still not enough. Not nearly enough.

She wanted *him.*

She wanted him to be the man he was born to be. The good, kind, loyal man she knew he had inside him, beneath all the calloused armor.

She entwined her fingers in his. "I have…a favor to ask you."

"A favor?"

Her teeth chattered. Was *favor* the right word to describe her request that he give up all thoughts of revenge, give up all his other women, and love her madly, as she loved him? "It's bigger than a favor."

"Ah. It takes more than a Greek island to impress you, does it?" He gave her a wicked half smile as he slowly moved his hand over her naked belly. "I will see what else I can do."

Though he'd just barely brought her to gasping fulfillment, she could feel that he already wanted her again. She felt the same. But before his touch could utterly distract her from taking the risk she must take, she put her hand over his own, stopping him.

"I have to tell you something," she whispered. "But I'm afraid."

"You can tell me anything," he said. "You've started to earn back my trust, *querida*," he says softly. "I am glad of that."

A huge jolt went through her.

"I brought your mother to Paris," she blurted out. "I spoke with her at the café today." Her teeth chattered as she looked up at him and whispered, "You have to forgive her."

Rafael felt sucker-punched as he stared down at her.

"You brought my mother to Paris?" he said in a low voice. "You allowed her to see Noah?"

"Yes," she said, staring up at him, her hazel-brown eyes wide.

He ripped his hand away from her. As he rose naked to his feet from the bed, the world seemed to be spinning around him. "You disobeyed me."

She shook her head desperately. "I'm trying to save you!"

"Save me?" he ground out.

"Your mother loves you. You have to forgive her. She had a good reason for not telling you about your father!"

He sucked in his breath. "What was it?"

"I…I…" She hesitated. "I can't tell you."

His heart beat rapidly inside his hollow chest. There was a metallic taste in his mouth. "You betrayed me."

She grabbed his hand. "I could have lied to you. But I'm telling you the truth. I'm telling you now, rather than doing it behind your back. I—"

He was beyond listening. "I told you what would happen if you ever betrayed me."

She looked stricken, as if he'd just slapped her.

"Please," she whispered. "I was only trying to make us a real family."

He reached for his clothes and swiftly got dressed. "I told you what would happen," he repeated.

His words were cold and even, but inside, he felt sick.

He'd never thought she would betray him like this. He'd never thought he would have to carry through on his threat, but now he had no choice.

"But, Rafael," she whispered, "I love you."

"Love? All that you've proven," he said harshly, "is that every time I start to trust you, you stab me in the back."

"But I didn't—I told you the truth!"

"Yes, after the fact." How smug they must be right now, both the women in his life who'd conspired against him and made him look like a powerless fool in his own house! "I told you what would happen if you ever crossed me. Get out of my house. I'll be filing for divorce."

"I'm not leaving you, not now, not ever! But you can't treat your mother so shamefully, not when she is innocent of what you think she did—"

"She told you that, I suppose?" He sneered.

Louisa started to speak, then cut herself off. She took a deep breath. "She didn't have to tell me. I saw it in her eyes! She loves you, she would die to protect you. The same as I feel about Noah!"

"You'll have to love him from a distance," he said coldly. "Because I'm cutting you out of his life."

"I won't leave him—or you! If you want me to go, you'll have to throw me…" she flung her arms toward the wide tree-lined boulevard of the Champs Élysées "…out that window!"

"Very dramatic," he said acidly, following her gaze. "But your little act won't save you."

Now fully dressed, he strode out of the room and headed straight for the nursery. He heard Louisa rush to follow him, scrambling for a robe.

But Rafael didn't pause. He didn't stop. He simply collected his sleeping son from the crib. Noah immediately started to cry when he was woken up. His wails matched Louisa's screams and sobs as she abandoned her attempts at tying her robe and clutched wildly at his arm.

"No!" she screamed. "You can't take him away from me!"

He stared at her, feeling unmoved. Feeling absolutely nothing.

Or so he told himself.

"My lawyer will be in contact," he told her coldly. Ripping his arm away, he carried his son downstairs and had two words with the bodyguard in the small apartment below.

Louisa tried to follow him, but at his orders, his bodyguard held her back as Rafael left.

When Rafael arrived at his favorite hotel ten minutes later, he felt guilt and pain threatening to bubble up inside him as he climbed out of the chauffeured limousine. He pushed the emotion away. He told himself Louisa was no decent mother, no decent woman. She'd lied like all the rest.

She didn't deserve either Rafael—or their son.

By the time Rafael had checked into the penthouse suite at the hotel, and their part-time nanny had arrived after his assistant's frantic call, the baby still was crying. But even after the plump, motherly Frenchwoman had come up to the suite and taken the baby tenderly in her arms, Noah wouldn't stop crying. He cried until his little face was red.

And slowly, Rafael realized he was the liar.

Louisa had made him a liar.

Because he could not follow through with his threat. Damn her! He could not separate his son from her. No matter how she'd betrayed him, no matter if she deserved it, he could not see his son suffer without his mother.

Cursing her, cursing himself, he realized he would have to allow her access to their child. But their marriage was over, he told himself furiously. It was done. But as he reached for his phone to call Louisa, it rang in his hand.

"I never thought you could do something like this. Ever."

He frowned. *"Mamá?"* he replied slowly, almost not recognizing her voice.

"Louisa called. How could you take her baby from her? How could you! You are not the man I thought you were!"

He ground his teeth. Of course Louisa had called her! "What happened between my wife and me is no concern of yours."

"I am downstairs. I have something to tell you. Come down now."

"Why should I?" he said stiffly.

"See me this one last time, *mi hijo*. One last time before I go back to Argentina."

The phone clicked softly in his hands.

Rafael set his jaw. Fine. One short conversation would be a small price to pay to get the woman out of their lives forever. Rafael made sure his son was tucked away in the second bedroom with the French nanny, then went downstairs.

He found Agustina at the bar. He expected her to try to immediately look at him with timid love and a pleading smile, as she always had for the last twenty years.

But this time, she'd changed. She was no longer the soft, anxious woman he remembered. Her face was stern. She started speaking the instant he sat beside her at the darkened hotel bar.

"I've tried to protect you for all your life," she said without preamble. "But you are a man. At a certain point, no parent can protect their child. And now that I've heard what you've just done, I fear my protecting you has done you more harm than good." She pushed some pages toward him on the smooth polished dark wood of the bar. "Here."

A sneer twisted his lips as he reached for the pages. The sneer soon dropped off his mouth as he read the old faded words. His eyes widened. He turned the page. He couldn't stop reading it. Five minutes later, he got the final stab in his throat when he read who'd signed the letter. His whole body felt cold when he finally looked up into the eyes of his mother.

"My father wrote this letter," he whispered, then shook his head, trying to get some warmth back into his body. "You told him you were pregnant with his child. And he told you to get rid of me."

His mother's eyes, so much like his own, looked at him steadily. "Yes. When I wouldn't, he sent me his gold ring. He said that was all I would ever get from him."

"Why?" he said over the lump in his throat. "Why didn't he want me?"

"He disliked children. And he'd never been in love with me. I found out he'd never even been faithful to me." She took a deep breath. "I was so young. I had no way to support us. I went back to Buenos Aires and married the man my parents had wanted me to marry all along. Arturo said he would be a good father to you…but he did not follow through on that promise."

"But, *Mamá*," Rafael said slowly over the ragged, sharp pain in his throat, "why did you never tell me the truth? Why did you let me blame you for all these years? Why wouldn't you tell me my father's name?"

"You'd already suffered enough from having one father who didn't love you, and all those years you never knew why—until Arturo broke his word and told you the truth as he died." Her eyes went dark, then with a sigh, she dropped her hands into her lap and became the gentle mother he'd always known. "You were so young and so hurt. When you found out you weren't his true son, you imagined all these wonderful things about your real father. I couldn't let another father disappoint you. I couldn't let your heart be broken all over again."

Rafael sat back with shock in his chair.

Everything he'd thought was true—was wrong.

"I'm sorry," he whispered, turning to his mother. He put his hand over hers as he felt tears rise unbidden to his eyes. "I'm so sorry."

His mother smiled through her own open tears. "I'm sorry I couldn't give you the father you deserved," she whispered. "But you can be that father for Noah. You can give him the family I tried and failed to give to you."

Family. Rafael sucked in his breath.

Louisa.

All he could suddenly think about was what he'd done to his wife. The woman who tried so hard to love him.

"Does Louisa know?" he said faintly.

His mother nodded. "But she wasn't going to tell you. She didn't want to hurt you."

Rafael stared at her.

Louisa hadn't wanted to hurt him? Even when he'd done the cruelest thing possible to her, taking their child away, *she hadn't wanted to hurt him.* She'd been trying to protect him.

In spite of everything, in spite of knowing his faults

so well, Louisa truly loved him. The generosity and loyalty of her love took his breath away.

And this was how he'd treated her. She'd risked everything to tell him the part of the truth that would not hurt him, and he'd made her pay for it. She'd openly offered him her heart, not once but twice, and he'd wantonly ripped it apart, stomping on the pieces.

He stared blindly across the dark shadows of the exclusive bar.

"She'll never forgive me," he said.

He felt his mother's hand on his shoulder. "She will."

He looked up, no longer trying to hide the sheen of tears in his eyes. "How can I ever win her back? All this time I've thought I couldn't trust her. The truth is, how can she ever trust me?" He thought of his son crying upstairs. He'd done everything wrong from the start!

What could he do?

How could he ever make it up to her?

Louisa had tried to save his soul, and he'd repaid her by nearly destroying hers.

He loved her, he realized.

He loved her.

He'd been trying to fight it for years. Even as he'd told himself he just wanted her in his bed, or needed her skills in his home, the truth was that he'd loved her for years. Not just what she did for him, but *her.* Her smile, her gentleness, her feistiness. The way she looked all mussed in the morning. The way her eyes glinted with tenderness when she saw him across the room.

He loved her.

Clenching his hands into fists, he slowly rose to his feet.

He loved her. Even if it made him weak. Even if it made him vulnerable. He loved her, and he would make her love him.

He'd win this fight, or he would die trying.

CHAPTER ELEVEN

COLLAPSED on the floor, Louisa lay curled up on the priceless Turkish carpet. She'd run out of tears hours ago. The bodyguard who'd restrained her, Evan Jones, had seemed disgusted with his job that day, but he'd done as his boss had ordered, keeping her a virtual prisoner in the luxury penthouse.

After Rafael had left, Louisa had thought desperately of calling the police, then despaired. Rafael was, after all, Noah's father! So instead, she'd called Agustina, who'd cried with her over the phone. The older woman had promised to try to help. But what could she do, really?

Now, Louisa was numb. She shivered and shook in the cold, then rose and put on a T-shirt and pajama pants before her knees became weak and she collapsed back on the carpet. She stared up at the ceiling, staring blankly at a long, thin crack in the plaster.

She had cried until there were no tears left. She was numb. No: she was dead. When Rafael had left her, taking their sobbing baby with him, she had died inside.

Now nothing was left of her. She rose slowly to her feet. Opening the screen door, she went out to stand on the balcony. She stared out at the night. She felt the cold breeze against her hot face.

Across the river she could see the lit-up Eiffel Tower. She looked down into the darkness beneath the balcony. It would be so easy, she thought. So easy to end all the grief and pain with just one easy jump. She gripped the railing of the balcony, looking down at the street.

But she had to believe there was some chance she might see her husband and child again. She had to live in the hope someday she would hold them both in her arms.

She felt something cold and stinging against her face and realized she'd been wrong. She did, after all, have some tears left.

A hard knock sounded at the door.

Who could it be at this time of night? Who would the bodyguard even allow to come to her door?

For a moment, she didn't move. She stayed outside in the darkness. Then she heard something that ricocheted through her like a bullet.

Her son's cry.

With a choked gasp, Louisa ran inside, rushing across the apartment to fling open the door.

"Madame Cruz," she heard the elderly French nanny say, "your husband sent me…"

But Louisa heard no more. With a sob, Louisa took her son from the other woman's arms. She whispered words of love to her baby as she cradled him close, kissing his plump cheeks, his downy head, his fat arms. Noah hugged her desperately, and in a few moments, he ceased crying. He finally became calm, then abruptly fell asleep in her arms.

"Ah," the French nanny said tenderly, looking down at the baby in Louisa's arms. "*Enfin,* he sleeps."

For the first time, Louisa looked at her. "What are you doing here?" she said, feeling like she was in a dream. "Why did Rafael send Noah back to me?"

The Frenchwoman shook her head. "I do not know, madame. But he wanted the baby brought to you immediately, even though it's the middle of the night." Stretching, she gave a discreet yawn. "If you please, I will go home now."

"But—he isn't demanding I send him back?"

"No," she replied quietly. "Monsieur Cruz said I was to make it particularly clear that he would never try to take Noah away from you again. He did ask if you would meet him for breakfast tomorrow."

Louisa's eyes narrowed. Meet Rafael for coffee and croissants, pretending nothing had happened, after all he'd done to her? Or worse—a preliminary meeting to discuss their imminent divorce? "No."

The other woman nodded with a rueful shrug. "I will relay your answer to him, madame. Now, if you will excuse me, I must go home to my bed."

Louisa cradled her sweet baby in her arms all night. She slept slumped on the rocking chair, unwilling to be apart.

When she woke the next morning, she heard a knock

on the door and answered it, her heart in her throat. She expected to find Rafael on her doorstep, demanding in his cold way for her to come with him to breakfast so they could meet with his lawyers.

Instead she saw a delivery boy staggering beneath the weight of a huge arrangement of roses, hundreds of them in every color.

"Flowers for you, madame," he gasped.

"Who sent these?" Then, behind him, Louisa saw the bodyguard smile, and she knew.

"Send them all back!" she thundered, and slammed the door.

But for the next three days, the gifts kept coming. No matter how firmly she sent them back, they didn't stop arriving. First there were the flowers, then after that came a team of manicurists and masseuses from the day spa. She received packages of clothes from all the top French designers. Handbags, exotic shoes, ball gowns. The capper was when a sports car in hot pink, with a big bow on the hood, was dropped off at the curb.

She refused them all.

Next came multiple deliveries from the finest jewelers in the city. Long ropes of priceless pearls. An emerald bracelet. A necklace of hundreds of sapphires. And finally: a diamond solitaire, as big as a robin's egg, set in platinum.

Louisa sent them all back.

For one long morning, her doorbell was silent. She spent her morning playing with the baby, baking a chocolate cake and trying not to think about Rafael. He wanted her back. That much seemed clear. But when was he going to stop sending her gifts? How long would it take to show him that her trust and forgiveness couldn't be bought?

Was Rafael ever going to come to her himself?

Then, the doorbell finally rang at last, and she braced herself to open it, knowing it would be Rafael.

Instead there was a messenger holding only a single rose—and a note.

I have something to tell you. Meet with me. Please.
Rafael

She took a deep breath. Then, she nodded. *"D'accord,"* she told the messenger. She was curious, she told herself. That was the only reason. That, and the fact that Rafael had actually written the note himself. She supposed she should be flattered!

The messenger nodded with a smile and said in French, "There is a car waiting outside to escort you and your baby to the airport. No need to pack anything for either of you. Monsieur Cruz, he has arranged for everything."

But Rafael wasn't waiting for them on his private jet. By the time the plane touched down at the private island, the Greek island she remembered all too well, Louisa could not pretend to herself anymore that she felt only curiosity. She wanted to see Rafael. No matter how she tried not to feel it, she missed him. Wanted him.

And some part of her still wished he could love her. Though she now believed he never would love anyone.

But Rafael wasn't waiting for her on the tarmac. He wasn't waiting for her in the beautiful whitewashed house on the private island.

This was her island, now.

Had he changed his mind about meeting her here? Had he given up his pursuit? Was he just going to leave her in sole possession with the baby, the lonely queen of this island?

The house was empty. A strange disappointment went through her as she passed empty room after empty room.

She tucked her sleeping baby into the lovely elliptical crib she found in the newly decorated nursery. Closing the door softly behind her, she looked out at the orange and scarlet sunset. She walked across the empty house. She opened the screen door and went out on the terrace beside the infinity pool. Blinking back tears, she looked around her and remembered all the places where they'd once laughed, where they'd shared meals, where they'd made love. Past happiness surrounded her like the echo of ghosts.

Folding her arms, blinking back tears, she lifted her chin and stared out at the red twilight over the darkening blue sea. How had everything gone so wrong?

Her love hadn't been enough to save him.

It hadn't been enough to make him love her back.

But as she wept, Louisa suddenly heard a voice behind her.

"Forgive me."

With an intake of breath, she whirled around and saw Rafael. He was coming toward her. His figure was dark as a shadow in the deepening night. Only his eyes seemed like pools of light, gleaming at her with the intensity of fire.

"Forgive me," he said again. She was frozen by his gaze, unable to move as he came toward her. He took her in his arms. Holding her with his gaze, he brushed tendrils of hair back from her cheek. "I was so wrong."

She opened her mouth to speak, but he stopped her by placing a finger on her lips. He looked down at her, and she realized he had tears in his eyes as well.

"I love you," he whispered. "I love you, Louisa. You and only you. Since the day I took you to my bed, there has never been another woman for me. You are my lover. My friend. The mother of my child. Most of all—you are my wife. I love you."

She stared up at him, unable to breathe.

He lowered his head toward hers as his hand stroked her face. "Can you ever forgive me?"

She shook her head, unable to speak.

"You sacrificed so much to protect me. I know everything now. My mother told me everything. I cannot live without you. Not just for Noah's sake, but for my own. Everything I am, everything that's good, is because of you."

"Oh, Rafael…"

He gave a ragged intake of breath. "I know you can't forgive me for taking Noah from you like I did.

But I swear to you I will spend the rest of my life trying to earn your love back again. I can think of nothing but you. I want you, love you, need you and I always will…."

Louisa stopped his words with a kiss. When she pulled away, his handsome face was dazed with joy.

"Louisa…"

"I love you," she whispered tenderly. "And I never stopped loving you."

Pulling her back into his strong arms, Rafael kissed her fiercely beneath the dark sky, beneath the stars that fell into the deepness of the sea, twinkling light into eternity.

"We're engaged!"

Six months later, Louisa looked up from the poolside chair to see her sister holding out her left hand with a shyly joyful smile.

"Engaged?" Louisa exclaimed. "To who?"

Katie grinned back at Rafael's chief bodyguard. "All the times Madison and I have visited this island…I never thought I'd come back with a souvenir like this!"

"A husband is your idea of a souvenir?" Evan Jones said with a grin, then took Katie's hand in his own and said earnestly, looking into her eyes, "This time, I wasn't going to let her go back to Florida without me."

Louisa leaped to her feet, clapping her hands. "I'm so happy for you both."

All this time, she'd hoped her little sister would find true love…and now she had. She looked out toward the surf, where Rafael was playing with his little niece,

Madison, and his son, Noah, who at fourteen months old was now running like crazy all over the sand as fast as his chubby little legs would carry him. "Does Rafael know yet?"

"Not yet," Evan said with a rueful grin. "We thought we'd better tell you first. We might need you to smooth things over. You know how Mr. Cruz hates staffing changes. He's not going to like getting a new chief bodyguard."

The three of them looked down at the beach. The sun was shining against the white sand. Baby Noah had picked up a little pail and shovel, and was running frantically in pursuit of his cousin Madison across the sand. Louisa heard her husband laugh as he scooped his son up, swinging him around. His deep laughter, along with the higher-pitched giggles of their son, was Louisa's favorite sound in the world.

"But it's too bad for him," Evan Jones said, turning back to Katie with a smile. "I've decided to quit the bodyguard gig to become a baker."

"So don't make Louisa do your dirty work," Katie said, nudging her new fiancé with her shoulder. "Go on, tell him you quit. You're the one with the gun!"

"Actually I don't have..." he started, then squared his shoulders. "All right. I'll do it."

He marched off toward the beach.

Once Evan was out of earshot, Louisa asked softly, "Are you sure about this? He's so different from Matthias...."

"I know." Katie looked at her, her eyes shining with

tears of joy. "Evan is better than rich. He's an honest, loving man with a good heart."

"Not to mention brave." From a distance, Louisa saw her husband scowl at Evan, folding his arms as he received his now ex-bodyguard's news. She gave a little laugh. "Uh-oh. We'd better get down there!"

Once Louisa joined her husband on the beach, the situation was easily managed. Within three minutes Rafael was congratulating the man and wishing him all the best with a hearty clap on the back.

Afterward, Louisa took her husband's hand. Rafael turned to her, kissing her palm, looking down at her with eyes shining with love. Her heart turned over in her chest. Was any woman ever so lucky, to be so adored?

Then, with a laugh, she picked up their giggling baby and ran off into the surf to frolic. They were swiftly chased by the man she loved: her former boss, her forever lover, her beloved husband who'd had a good heart all along but just needed a little help to find it.

A housekeeper always knew just what to do. Just what her boss needed most.

And sometimes, Louisa thought, smiling as she looked back at the most handsome ex-playboy on earth, she knew it even before he did.

EXPECTING HIS
SECRET HEIR

DANI WADE

To the Worshams, Tates, Nelsons, Schafers and Raymos, for teaching me all that family can mean during the highs and lows of life.

One

From her crouching vantage point, Sadie Adams sized up the composition before her with an artistic eye.

Wide, straight shoulders of a towering man, silhouetted against the smoking buildings and rubble. A small strip of dead cotton plants in the foreground. The sun lightening the top of his thick head of hair, leaving the rest of him in shadow. Standing in profile, hands on his hips, head hung as if in despair.

As the shutter clicked, she wondered about his story. Had he been an employee of the ruined mill behind him, or was he there to help? As several men approached, he raised his head, giving her a clearer view of his rough-cut features.

I should have known.

Those broad shoulders, clothes that fit a tight, strong body in all the right places—he was the most capable man she'd ever known. The most incredible lover she'd ever had. The one it had almost killed her to walk away from.

Zachary Gatlin was the reason she was back in Black Hills, South Carolina. But he could never know that.

She took a few more pictures, surreptitiously inching in the other direction, as he talked with the men surrounding him. Yet she kept Zachary Gatlin in her line of sight. Five years ago, he had blended in with the crowd. A worker bee. Now, he was clearly in charge, directing those around him with decisive gestures and a firm tone that reached her even though she couldn't make out the words.

Had he worked his way up into management at the mill? Would that change how he treated her? Would it change how he saw her?

Moving along the edge of the parking lot, she attempted to get closer to the ruined buildings. Her high-quality camera had some amazing close-up capabilities that she was eager to test. The piece of equipment was a luxury she couldn't afford—but her employer could, and he was pulling out all the stops to ensure she got the information he needed. She should feel dirty for accepting the camera, but it was the one thing—the only thing—she didn't regret in her current situation.

If Zachary knew the truth, he'd make sure she deeply regretted ever coming back here. He wouldn't rage or get physical. He wouldn't need to. That dark stare and hard features would be enough to make his point. At least, that was the Zachary she'd known—or thought she'd known.

Would he be the same now?

Turning to the smoking ruins, she focused on the things she knew. Angle, lighting, depth, perception. Her circumstances had prevented her from pursuing photography at a professional level, even though she'd had a few photographs published, thanks to a friend. But if her life had been different, with fewer obligations, maybe she could have followed her own dreams instead of lying awake at night wondering how her family would all survive.

Lost in her art, she'd almost blocked out her surroundings until a masculine voice spoke near her. "Ma'am?"

For just a moment, her heart jump-started. Had Zach finally spotted her? But she turned to find a generic security guard by her side. "Yes?"

"If you'll come with me, please?"

Though it was a question, his firm gesture in the direction he wanted her to go brooked no arguments.

After ten steps she had no doubt where he was leading her. Desperate to delay the inevitable, she paused. "Excuse me? Could you explain what happened here?"

Possibly fooled by her innocent expression, the man stopped, too, and cocked his head to the side. "You aren't from around here, are you?"

She shook her head. "No. I've visited before, and really wanted to come back. But I didn't think I would find the quiet place I remembered in such an uproar."

That was the truth. The single hotel in the area had been booked full. Sadie had managed to get the last room in the last B and B with an opening. From the types of people she saw coming and going, most of the influx consisted of firefighters and construction crews. From the looks of the half-full parking lot, quite a few of those guys were out here today.

"I kinda guessed, based on the accent," he said with a smile.

Yep. No matter how she tried to tame it, her Texas breeding colored her every word.

The guard went on, "Well, the admin building on this side of the plant had a bomb go off in it."

Sadie made herself look surprised, even though she'd picked up this tidbit of information around town already. "Really? Who would want to do that? This is the main source of employment for the town, if I remember right."

"It sure is," the man said, shaking his head. "They say they have a suspect in custody but haven't released any names yet." He stared up at the building for a moment, looking confused. "I have no idea why someone would want to ruin the mill, but after all the bad stuff that's happened around here in the last year—"

"Steve," Zach barked from over a dozen feet away.

"Oops. Better get movin'," the guard said.

Each step felt like a final walk down death row, but Sadie forced herself to move. After all, making contact with Zach was the reason she was here. She needed to spend as much time with him as possible—and she hoped their previous one-night stand might give her a bit of an in, even if the fact that she'd disappeared after it wouldn't make it a positive in.

Zach still had a group of workers around him who parted as she drew near. She expected them to skedaddle now that the boss had new business, but no. Not a single one moved away.

Her petite five-foot-five stature had been the bane of her existence ever since she'd realized she wouldn't be growing anymore, and being surrounded by a bunch of six-foot-tall men did not set her at ease. She felt like David approaching Goliath against his will.

Not that she had any sort of righteousness on her side.

There was only a moment to study Zach up close.

His thick jet hair was a little longer than it had been the last time she'd seen him. Remembering that night long ago, she couldn't help the itch to bury her fingers in those silky strands again. Or to run her fingertips over the weary lines of his chiseled features until the tension melted away.

Her sensual memories were dimmed by the current hard look on his face. There was no glimmer of recognition or softening as she stood before him, even though she could remember every detail of the body that now towered over her. No smile of welcome softened his sculpted lips as he asked, "What are you doing?"

"I'm just taking some pictures," she said quietly, lifting the camera still in her hand.

If anything, his dark eyes hardened more. "On private property."

She glanced around, uncomfortable under the stares of the other men. "This is…was a business, right? There aren't any signs posted about private property or trespassing."

"That's because they were all blown down by the bomb."

Really? She wanted to challenge him, push past that stony facade to find out if he was simply making that up. Was he trying to punish her for walking away? Or did he really not recognize her? Had she been that unmemorable? The thought made her slightly ill.

She settled for a simple, "Sorry, I didn't realize."

Zach stared her down. What would he do next? She had a feeling this wasn't going to end as a friendly little chat. Her cheeks started to burn. Inwardly cursing her fair skin, she tilted her chin up to counteract the feeling of inadequacy. So what if he didn't remember her…she'd still find a way to get what she needed.

But she couldn't force her gaze back up to his.

"As you can see, this is still an active fire zone, and we've got a great deal to investigate before we know how safe it is."

She smirked at the lame excuse. "I wasn't anywhere near the fire. I was in the parking lot with a bunch of other people."

The crowd around her shifted, as if uncomfortable with her spark of courage. But Zach didn't back down. "Do you have a press pass?"

"What?"

"A press pass," he said, enunciating each word with careful control. "Do you have permission to be taking photos of the scene?"

She seriously wanted to roll her eyes at his show of dominance but held herself in check. "No."

"Steve, please escort this lady back to her car."

Startled, she snapped her gaze up to meet his eyes once more. Surely he wasn't throwing her off the property?

He stepped closer, close enough for her to catch the scent she'd missed all too often, mixed with perspiration from his work despite the cool October air. His fingers— the same ones that had explored her body that long-ago night—caught her chin, tilting it up just a touch more until it was uncomfortable. Then she had no choice but to meet his gaze, despite their height difference. Her heart thumped hard, though she didn't know if it was from his nearness or fear.

"I suggest you stay away from where you don't belong."

As the guard escorted her back to her car, she had only one thought.

Guess he does remember me after all...

* * *

Zach Gatlin stood behind his desk, lost in thought as he stared at the large monitor. Where had she come from? Did he really want to know?

Unfortunately, he did.

As much as he wished he could forget the red-haired beauty he'd taken to bed five years ago, the memory of her eager passion had resurfaced all too often. As had the memory of her love of sunsets and people and nature—her artistic eye had taught him to see the gentler world he'd forgotten in the midst of war.

Then, with no warning, she was gone. He'd consoled himself with the thought that if she hadn't been willing to say goodbye, she wouldn't have stayed in the long run anyway. Probably for the better, since Zach's responsibilities were a heavy load.

Sometimes he wondered if that inner voice lied.

Shaking off the memories, Zach focused on the present. The question was: Did he look into her or not? Running a background check would be all too easy, especially now that he ran his very own security business. The tools were within close reach. Close enough to make his fingers twitch. He could know all he wanted within minutes, every small detail of her life within days.

But was it the right thing to do?

Maybe he should have asked himself that before he threw her off mill property yesterday. He'd had a gut reaction to seeing her there, so close but seemingly oblivious to him. He wished he had controlled himself, but what was done was done. He couldn't go back.

With his life, he knew that all too well.

Turning away from the computer, he decided to confront this problem head-on rather than hide behind snooping. Security might be his business, but it didn't have to be his life.

Thirty minutes later, he wondered if he should have taken the easy way out. Figuring out where Sadie was staying had been easy—this was, after all, a small town. Getting past the nosy owner of the B and B? Well, that was an altogether different problem.

"Gladys, I know she's here, I just need to know what room she's in."

"Is she expecting you?"

"Probably." At least that much was the truth. If Sadie remembered anything at all about him, it should be that he was a man of action.

Gladys leaned against the high desk in the foyer. "Now, why would Black Hills's newest hero want to see some strange woman who just came into town?"

Lord, this woman wanted a pound of flesh, didn't she? "I haven't always lived here, Gladys."

"So you met her somewhere else?" Was that a gleam of excitement in her eyes? How sad that his life had gone from daily drudgery to full-on gossip mill fodder.

He'd met Sadie right here in Black Hills, but it had seemed like another time and place. "The room number?"

Probably recognizing the obstinate look on his face and realizing she wasn't getting any gossip from him— outside of his very presence here—Gladys relented. "Room three."

Back straight, he refused to look over his shoulder to see her watching him as he climbed the stairs. He hesitated before knocking, but luckily there was no one to see it.

The door opened, revealing Sadie. She was just as he remembered her, with smooth, translucent skin, an abundance of fiery red hair and green eyes that appeared guileless. A trap he wasn't falling for this time.

"Zachary," she said.

He stalked through the doorway. The suite was more spacious than the tiny hotel room she'd occupied the last time she'd been here. This was open and airy, with a lightly feminine touch. His gaze bounced away from the bed in an alcove and came to rest on the laptop in a low sitting area in front of a fireplace. He made his way forward with measured steps.

"It's been a while, Sadie," he finally said.

"Five years," she murmured.

He paused, giving away the fact that he'd heard her when he would have preferred not to show any reaction at all. He was ashamed to admit, even to himself, that he'd often thought about what he would say if he ever saw her again. He'd pictured himself as calm, slightly condescending as he asked her why she'd left without a word, without any explanation.

Nothing in that scenario came close to the amped-up emotions he was experiencing at the moment.

Eager for a distraction, he paused in front of the open laptop. Several pictures shared space on the screen, showcasing the smoldering mill from different angles. He'd never had much time for art, but to his inexperienced eyes, these looked pretty good.

Which for some reason made him even angrier.

"You weren't authorized to take pictures there."

"Did you tell that to every bystander in that parking lot with their cell phones in their hands? Or just me?"

He glanced in her direction, mildly surprised by her return salvo. He hadn't known her to be very confrontational. Not that they'd spent much time arguing, but they had talked—a lot. He wouldn't have called her a doormat, exactly, but she'd shown a lot more spirit in the last twenty-four hours than he'd seen in the week he'd known her five years ago. A week that had ended in a night he couldn't forget.

She raised one fine brow. "There were no signs posted. No one said I couldn't be there...at first."

He studied the images a bit longer. Damn if she didn't have him stumped. What exactly had he wanted to accomplish by coming here? To go over the same territory as at the mill? To find out why she had returned? To get information without having to ask any direct questions?

To put himself out there to be hurt again?

Gesturing toward the screen, he asked, "So you came back just for pictures?"

It was as close as he'd let himself get to addressing the elephant in the room. He really wanted to know why she hadn't come back for him. She was the one woman he'd ever felt he could actually let into his life, have a real relationship with. And she'd walked away without looking back.

"I was in the area and heard about the explosion. I wanted to check it out."

She looked too calm, acted too casual. And she just happened to be in the area? He shook his head. When had he gotten so suspicious?

"What about you?" she surprised him by asking. "What were you doing there?"

That's when he realized she wasn't the only one who had changed in five years. "I'm head of security for the Blackstones—"

She smiled. "Wow. That's really great. Going from maintenance to head of security is a big jump."

He knew he shouldn't, but he said it anyway. "I'm not head of security for the mill. I handle security details for the entire family and all of their interests. I run my own security firm." Bragging did not come easily to him. Not that he'd ever had much to brag about. But somehow it felt good to rub his success in Sadie's face.

He wasn't the same man she'd met then—recently returned from combat in the Middle East, fighting the nightmares while maintaining a strong facade for the women in his family he'd spent a lifetime supporting.

Then one night he'd let her in, and he wished she'd never seen that side of him.

"Until we can get a good look inside and evaluate the damage, the mill is a huge security risk. So the Blackstones have asked me to oversee this initial part of the investigation."

"I heard it was a bomb."

He nodded. Yep. A bomb set off by a crazy man.

"Any suspects?"

It was a natural question. Simple curiosity. So why did his muscles tense when she asked?

"Yes, but that information is not being released to the public."

The words came out in a more formal tone than he would have normally used, but it was all for the best. Keeping their distance meant keeping himself sane. Instead of leaning in to see if her hair smelled the same as it did before.

He did not need to know that.

He eyed the bright waves dancing around her shoulders. He definitely didn't need to know.

"So it would be better to stay away from there right now." *And away from me, so all these emotions will respond to my control.* "Wait until we can guarantee it's safe."

"In the parking lot?"

"Right." He didn't care if she wasn't buying it. A man had to do…

Suddenly realizing he'd accomplished nothing but torturing himself during this visit, he stalked back to the door. Unfortunately, she followed, until she was within arm's reach. He was too far away from the door to escape.

It all flooded back—all the memories he'd struggled to hold at bay since that first moment he'd seen her again at the mill. The way his heart pounded when she laughed. The way her soft voice soothed his nerves as she told him a story. The way his body rose to meet the demands of hers.

So many things he couldn't force himself to forget.

But he could force himself to walk away this time. "I'll be seeing you, Sadie," he said, as casually as he could.

She pulled the door open and smiled. "Definitely."

Something about her tone, that confident edge, ruffled him, pushed him to throw her off balance. He couldn't stop himself. He stopped in front of her, bending in low to place his mouth near her ear. He sucked in a deep breath. "So…" he said, letting the word stretch, "aren't you gonna tell me why you really left?"

Her gasp left him satisfied…for now.

Two

Sadie's entire body instantly snapped to attention. She might not have moved, but every nerve ending was now awake and focused on the man before her.

She hadn't thought he'd directly address her leaving. Indeed, he'd seemed to do everything but ask the all-important question: Why? She'd thought she was prepared. Her flippant answer rattled around in her brain for a moment, but she couldn't force it out.

Instead she stared up into his brooding dark eyes and lost her breath. She'd known she would hurt him, leaving like that. He'd never tell her so, but she couldn't help but wonder if it were true from his somber gaze.

His body seemed to sway a little closer, and her mouth watered at the thought of his lips on hers once more. Then the trill of her phone broke the moment of silence.

Suddenly he was back to arm's length, leaving her

to wonder if she'd imagined that moment. Wished it into being.

His eyes grew wider, reminding her that her phone was still ringing. She ignored both him and the phone. Her mother called late in the evening, when her duties for the day were done. Only one person would be calling her at this time of day, and she wasn't about to speak to him in front of Zach.

Her heart pounded. She licked her lips, trying to think of something to say.

Instead of waiting for an answer, Zach gave a quick smirk and then walked out the door without another word. She waited until he was down the stairs and out of sight before pushing the door closed. Then she dissolved against it like melting sugar.

Tears welled, along with the wish that things didn't have to be this way. She quickly brushed both away. Her life had been one long lesson in dealing with reality, not dreaming of fairy tales.

At least he hadn't forgotten her.

Forcing herself to her feet, she crossed to the sitting area and picked her phone up off the low table. The very name she expected flashed across the screen. She sucked in a deep, bracing breath, then touched the screen to call him back.

"I'm listening."

She hated when he answered the phone like that. The part of her that rebelled against what she had to do forced her to hold her words just a minute longer than necessary, garnering some petty satisfaction from making him wait.

"What do you need, Victor?" she asked.

"Ah, Adams. Where were you?"

The impersonal use of her last name grated on her

nerves, but she was, after all, simply a servant. "Away from my phone."

"Don't get uppity with me, Adams. Just because you're hundreds of miles away from Texas doesn't mean you're off the leash."

Right. Remind her of the dog she was—that would make her work harder. But it was an apt description—she was a hunting dog. Sent to search for and fetch exactly what her owner wanted.

"I apologize," she said, hoping he couldn't tell her teeth were gritted. "But I didn't think you wanted me to answer the phone and give you an update in front of Zachary."

"Very good, Adams. I knew I could trust your judgment."

As if it had been all his idea. If Victor Beddingfield had an original idea ever in his life, she'd be shocked. Of course, this little expedition was his idea—and here she was. But the idea wasn't original to him. His father had tried it first.

"So you've already made contact? Good girl."

Yep, she was definitely a dog to him. "I have, but he's not happy about it."

"You simply have to make him like it. You know how to do that…don't you?"

She wished to goodness Victor had never found out the truth about her last visit to Black Hills. Not that he cared about her choice to deceive his father, telling him that Zachary couldn't possibly be the son he sought. The longer Zach had been out of his life, the more of their father's money Victor could spend. Still, the knowledge had given him a weapon to use against her—but not the biggest one.

"This might take some time." Although, even if she

had all the time in the world, Zach would probably never forgive her—then or now.

"Well, we don't have time, remember?" he said, his voice deepening in a way she perceived as a threat. "I need money. Now. And I'm sure you do, too—or rather, your sister does."

Not really. Amber didn't worry about that sort of thing. The hospital treated her cancer, that was all she knew. It was all Sadie wanted her sister to know. The practical aspect—bills, scheduling, medical decisions—all of that was handled by Sadie. Some days, it was enough to make her feel like she was drowning, but she did it anyway. It kept her sister alive, for now. It allowed her mother to be at her sister's side for however much longer they had her. That was all that mattered. Still, the reminder struck home.

But Victor wasn't done. "So get me the dirt I need to disinherit him, and we will all be in a much better position. Got it?"

How could she not? "I understand. I'll do my best."

"Good girl."

One of these days, Sadie's teeth were going to be worn to a nub, just from the irritation of listening to this guy. "He's not giving me much to work with," she said, consciously relaxing her jaw.

"Then get creative," Victor said. Without another word, he disconnected the call.

Get creative.

Sadie sighed. Easy for him to say. Victor had always had someone to do the dirty work for him. Her role in his father's household made her a convenient option. Her role in his father's investigation of his older son five years ago told Victor she wasn't just convenient, but experienced.

Now he wanted the investigation into Zach reopened so he could discredit the man who didn't know he was Victor's older brother.

Time for Sadie to earn her keep.

Plopping down onto the couch, she stared at her computer screen. Get creative. How? She couldn't think of any way to get around Zach's present uncooperative state. She needed to get close to him, learn everything she could about him. But he wanted her nowhere near him.

Glancing around to remind herself that she was alone, Sadie clicked on the computer folder she'd closed when Zachary had knocked. Instantly the screen filled with images of him. There were pictures from all different angles, taken while he wasn't looking. Not for Victor's benefit. Not because she had to. Because she wanted to.

Because the single photo she had of him from her last visit wasn't nearly enough to last her a lifetime.

She hadn't dared take home any more, certain that her employer, Victor and Zach's father, would discover them and realize she was lying about how much she'd found out about Zach.

She studied the haunting image she'd gotten of Zach silhouetted against the smoking building from yesterday. The contrast of his strength with the ruins of the mill reminded her of his conscientious care for his family, his quiet way of watching those around him until he saw a need that he could fill. If only he could fulfill her needs, free her from this mess of a life so she could be with him once more.

No, she couldn't think like that. This was her problem to solve, as always. If Zachary knew what she was involved in, he'd lead the mob running her out of town. The town didn't know her, either. They'd protect their own.

At least, that was the perception she had from watching him at the mill. But did she really know? What could the town tell her about Zach that he wouldn't tell her himself?

She studied the picture once more. She needed to find out, and she had an idea how she might make that happen.

I need more information.

And she wasn't going to get it moping in her room. Grabbing a light jacket against the autumn chill, Sadie threw a quick glance at the computer to make sure it was off, then headed out the door.

She shouldn't worry about her laptop. But Victor had taught her that people did all kinds of things that served their own ends—and invaded other's privacy. She never wanted to be caught off guard again.

Not that she had many secrets, but Victor had managed to find a doozy.

She paused on the stairs. Zach had said he owned a security firm now. Would he have checked her out?

Even now, had he figured out who she was? How long after that would he find out who her employer was, and what he meant to Zach?

Once that happened, her mission would be over before it even began. The ticking time bomb had been set.

Luckily, the overly friendly proprietress of the bed-and-breakfast was at the front desk when Sadie reached the office. The woman's husband was as reticent as she was open, so he wouldn't have been nearly as helpful. For now, luck was with Sadie.

The woman even started the conversation in the direction Sadie wanted it to go.

"Wow! New to town and already getting visits from the local hero."

Technically it was a statement, but Sadie could hear the question beneath the words. And Gladys wasn't finished. "Of course, not everyone feels that way…"

Interesting.

"Why is that?" Sadie didn't feel the need to beat around the bush. Subtlety wasn't Gladys's forte.

"Oh, there was a big to-do when he came home. He graduated to officer in the military, survived combat. Then came home to take care of his family after his mama's heart attack."

Sadie murmured a few encouraging words, even though Gladys didn't need them.

"But then all those plants got poisoned earlier this year—"

That made Sadie's ears perk up. "What plants?"

"Cotton fields." The older woman leaned toward Sadie over the high desk in what Sadie had learned was Gladys's favorite position. "One of the things Zach did to earn money was crop dust. Early this spring he dusted nigh on half the county in a day. By morning, the plants were dead. Boy, did that cause an uproar."

"I bet." Probably more like a riot. Killing the cash crop of choice for the area… "Did the police get involved?"

"You bet. Quite a spectacle it was, though I wasn't there. Handcuffs and all. But they released him the same day."

Gladys lowered her voice, though they were the only two around. "Them Blackstone brothers got involved. And they obviously believe in him, because he's the biggest news story around here…besides the bomb, of course."

"You mean his new job?"

The woman nodded, her tight gray curls bouncing.

"He don't have to work three jobs now, that's for sure. I hear his business is taking off like hot cakes."

See, he doesn't need the money.

Sadie pushed away the seductive thought. She wouldn't sugarcoat what she was doing. Regardless of his current circumstances, Zach deserved the inheritance her late boss had wanted to give him. The one she had denied him because she had lied and told Victor's father that Zach wasn't, in fact, the son he sought. She'd been afraid he would corrupt Zach the same way he had everything else around him.

Still believing his firstborn was out there somewhere, Beddingfield Senior had willed him his inheritance. The only way for Victor to get it was to ruin Zach. Because he knew the truth…the truth behind the lies she'd told.

Desperate times called for desperate measures.

Gladys had just given her a place to start looking for Zach's dirty laundry. And if Sadie succeeded in her mission, she'd steal away every last dime.

From Zach.

Three

"I heard there was an incident at the mill yesterday."

Of course she had. Zach glanced over at his sister. Despite her engagement to the richest man in town, KC had kept her bartending job, and she heard everything. "You mean besides the fire?"

"Well, this was a bit more interesting than a bomb, in my opinion. It was about you…and a woman."

Only KC would find that more interesting. But since there was never any gossip connecting him to any women in town, he could see her point of view.

Zachary hated that he paused before answering, practically admitting his guilt. "You heard about that?" His sister was too smart for him to bother pretending he didn't know what she was talking about.

Her sassy attitude was displayed in a raised brow and hand on her hip. "Seriously? This is a bar. In a small town. People in here have nothing to do but talk all day…" She studied him in a way that made him want to squirm. "Did you really throw her off the property?"

"You make it sound so much worse than it was."

KC's eyes widened. "Zach! Why would you do that?"

He wanted to use his lame security excuse again, but he seriously needed better lines. Instead, he focused on pulling a beer. "Let's talk about it later—we're kinda busy right now."

"That we are," KC said, filling her tray with drinks for a rowdy table of off-the-clock firefighters. The dinner hour was just approaching, and Lola's bar was already filled to capacity. "But you're not off the hook," she warned him.

He wanted to let his rare bad temper loose and tell her to mind her own business, but knew his sister's fiancé, Jacob Blackstone, wouldn't pull any punches putting him in his place if Zach made his own sister cry. Besides, it wasn't KC's fault.

It was Sadie's.

He hadn't been able to stop thinking about her, to the point that he wished his brain had an off switch. Even sleeping hadn't given him any relief. Ever since seeing her two days ago, he'd dreamed of the single night they'd been together, and the glorious sensuality of her body.

The images in his brain were not calming him right now. Any part of him...

He distracted himself by checking on his orders in the kitchen, along with the two new hires he'd put in place a month ago. One was a veteran chef from the military who'd put in ten years of duty before losing a leg in Afghanistan. The other was a hardworking kid who reminded Zach a lot of himself at his age, with a single mom and baby sister at home to support. Only Miguel's dad had been killed in a car accident. Zach's had simply walked away when supporting a wife and child got too boring for him to handle.

Despite the rush, he found everything moving along smoothly in the kitchen. There was no need for Zach to be working at Lola's. In fact, he refused to let his mother pay him anymore. The last thing he needed these days was money—a concept he couldn't quite absorb. But he couldn't stay away.

Taking care of his grandmother, mother and sister was a way of life for him. He'd only been away from them while he was in the military. No matter what his job was now, his day still wasn't complete until he'd touched base with them. And he wasn't the kind of man to sit around while the women worked. He wasn't like his father—uncaring enough to walk away from the people who needed him. Nor KC's father, who'd done the same when the going got tough. Zach had never let down the women in his life, and his new millionaire status wasn't an excuse to start now.

So here he was on a Friday night, carrying a tray of appetizers out to a table surrounded by several couples eager to eat before hitting the dance floor. Lola's was crowded tonight. Lots of people were in town needing to blow off steam, especially those who worked out at the mill. Too many probably thought about the disaster they would have faced if it hadn't been a mandatory shut-down weekend when the bomb had gone off.

Zach talked to the customers for a few minutes about the damage, then left them to their food. As head of security, he'd done his best to spread the most positive outlook. He hoped he was having some effect, because the last thing this town needed was for the people living here to give up. Regardless of the damage, the Blackstone brothers were not going to let the mill close and the town disappear. They'd all worked too hard to have that happen to the people they cared about.

Hearing some boisterous laughter, Zach glanced at the table of firefighters only to spot an unexpected red-headed beauty in their midst.

Well, look what snuck in while I was in the kitchen.

He should stay away—he really should—but knew he wouldn't. Casually making his way across the room, he stopped to check in at a few tables while keeping Sadie in view. Her laughter, her smile were beautiful things, though she wasn't overtly flirting. Still, a surprising surge of anger streaked through him. He found himself circling slowly, almost like a lion studying his prey from all angles.

Coming in from behind, he could no longer see her face, but he could finally hear her words.

"So, did they know someone was sabotaging the mill before this?"

Every cell in his body went alert at the question. Why was she asking?

"Oh, yeah," one of the locals eagerly replied. "Of course, those of us who work there knew it way before any manager did. But we needed proof, right?"

She nodded, which caused the muted lighting to glint off her ruby curls.

"They say they got someone in custody," the man continued. "Whoever it is, they're gonna get a sh—oops, not supposed to say that in front of a lady."

Was that a hint of a blush on the curve of her cheek he could actually see?

"But the whole town, they're already up in arms."

"That will just give them a target," she murmured, nodding her understanding.

Standing right behind her, Zach felt a moment of evil satisfaction that he stood so close, yet she seemed unaware. One by one the men at the table spotted him. Oddly enough, none gave away his presence to the lamb in their midst.

Every time he was around this woman, his hackles rose. He told himself it was because he'd found her at the mill, where she didn't belong, but he was afraid the reason was much, much deeper.

"Why would you want to know?" he finally asked.

Sadie jerked around to face him, causing her drink to slosh over the rim and drip from her fingers. "What are you doing there?" she asked before lifting her hand up and gently sucking the moisture away.

Zach ignored the tightening in his groin, ever aware of his surroundings and a half dozen pairs of eyes glued to their interactions…and that was just at this table. Zach gave a short nod in the direction of the men, then cupped Sadie's elbow with his palm. "Let's get you a fresh drink."

Without waiting for a response, he ushered her around a dozen tables to get to the less crowded, more utilitarian end of the bar. The whole time his heart pounded with intensity, though he wasn't sure why the conversation affected him that way. He forced himself to speak quietly. "Why are you asking all those questions?"

Sadie didn't jerk away, but she kept up a firm pressure with her arm until he let her free.

Zach ignored KC's curious glances from several feet away, grateful that there were enough customers to delay her interrogation. He turned back to his prey. "What was that all about?" he demanded again, letting anger seep through his self-control.

At first, he thought she would cave and spill her guts.

His stomach churned as he realized he wanted to know everything about why she was here, why she'd walked back into his life and turned his emotions on their head.

Then her thick lashes swept up, revealing those gorgeous green eyes, and somehow he knew he wasn't getting what he wanted tonight.

She wiggled her glass. "I thought I was here for a fresh drink?"

He wasn't sure whether to shake her or kiss her, but he felt relief as he moved behind the bar. Being that close to Sadie only encouraged his circuits to misfire.

So he tried a different tactic. He let his fingers slide slowly over hers as he lifted the glass from her hand. Her lowered lashes told him she had something to hide. At least that secret he could guess, if her reaction was anything like his.

"You know those guys?" he asked as he refilled her Coke. He wanted to grin at her drink of choice. As far as he'd been able to tell, she didn't drink, smoke or get into trouble. Her innocence simply hinted at an incredible sensuality that he'd never been able to forget.

She shrugged delicate shoulders. "A couple of the guys are staying at the B and B. The hotel ran out of room."

They'd been lucky with all the crews that had come in to help fight the fire and pull debris. Unfortunately, Black Hills wasn't very well equipped for visitors. Every last vacant room was in use at the moment. There were even a couple of fire chiefs bunking out at Blackstone Manor.

"I told them there was a great place for food and drinks out this way. They invited me to join them when I was free. I hope that was okay?"

The glance from under her lashes didn't seem to be seeking permission so much as a reaction.

It was his turn to shrug. "I've always been easy to find."

Her petite body stilled. She glanced around, as if making sure no one was close enough to listen. "Look," she said, "I'm very sorry about leaving. I just got... scared."

He stepped closer, bypassing the safety of the counter. "Why?"

She swallowed, hard. His instincts were to follow the movement with his mouth, taste what he could only see.

Reaching out, he forced her chin up with demanding fingers. "Why?"

"It was just too much for me," she whispered.

Without thought, he found himself murmuring, "Me, too."

Startled eyes met his. He could drown in all that fresh green color. Five years ago, her eyes had been just as vibrant. Just as alluring. He'd fallen for her seductive pull and received the rudest awakening in his life for it. But he still couldn't forget the night spent drowning in her green gaze.

Suddenly Sadie was bumped from behind, breaking the hold she had on Zach. Quickly he shuttered his expression.

He stepped back once, twice, until he found his breathing distance. "Now, what's with the questions?"

"Why? Do you see me as a threat?"

In more ways than one. But he wasn't giving her more ammo, so he bit his tongue. "Should I?"

Her gaze dropped at his question, causing his hackles to rise once more. Why was getting any information from her like pulling teeth?

"Just don't stir up trouble." He turned away, lifting a tray of dirty glasses off the counter and stepping through the opening behind the bar.

Only then did he hear her say, "And how's a busy guy like you gonna stop me?"

"Don't you know you don't have to do this anymore?" a male voice from right behind Sadie asked.

Zach turned back toward her, focusing over her shoulder with a grin that she wished was directed at her. But it was better than the glower she'd been sure to receive after her challenge.

"My mama doesn't care how much money I make," Zach said. "She simply points at a table and tells me to get busy."

When Zach came back out from behind the bar she was forced to step to the side, giving her a good look at the newcomer.

Or rather, newcomers. The trio looked like the epitome of wealth…and exhaustion. Zach shook hands with the blond man before turning to do the same with a man whose dark hair had a mind of its own. The woman between them received a light, social hug.

Based on her discussions with people in town, these must be the Blackstones.

If she remembered her gossip correctly, this would be Aiden Blackstone, his wife, Christina, and one of the younger brothers, Jacob. The utter weariness in their expressions spoke to the trials of the last week. Their brother Luke was currently in the hospital after being near the epicenter of the exploding bomb.

Suddenly another woman arrived through the break in the bar counter, pushing Sadie even farther back. The blonde beauty threw her arms around the one Sadie assumed was Jacob, holding nothing back. The surrounding people didn't seem surprised. The woman pressed light, quick kisses against his lips, then settled at his side. Her touch never wavered and never dropped. If Sadie remembered correctly from local gossip, Zach's sister, KC, was engaged to Jacob.

Zach studied them a moment, then asked, "How's Luke doing?"

"Much better," Jacob said. "They say he can come home tomorrow."

"No further damage to his legs?" KC asked.

Jacob shook his head. "None."

"Good," Zach added. "We don't need any more damn tragedies around here."

Everyone murmured their agreement.

"Anyway." Aiden stepped closer. "My wife is in firm need of sustenance that isn't hospital food, and I promised her some of your mama's fried chicken."

Zach grinned in a way that took Sadie's breath. "With a baby on the way, that woman should have anything she wants to have. She's doin' all the work, after all."

"Amen," Christina said, leaving the whole group laughing.

Sadie smiled, even though she knew it was a little sad around the edges. The group reminded her of her family. There were only three of them, but she, her mama and her sister had taken care of each other through a lifetime of heartache. They could often make each other laugh during the hardest times. And they never gave up hope that they would be together.

Zach stepped back to the kitchen to put in the order without so much as looking in her direction, intensifying Sadie's feeling of solitude in the midst of the crowd. She eyed the distance back to the table she'd come from, but the Blackstones simply took up too much space for her to squeak by without notice.

Then the silence around her registered and she glanced back to realize she'd become the center of attention. Four sets of eyes studied her. Her familiar technique of disappearing into the shadows where she wouldn't be noticed wasn't an option here, as she was boxed in by the wall on one side and the bar counter behind her.

Finally the woman she recognized as Zach's sister stepped closer. "Hi, there. I'm KC, Zach's sister. And you are?"

Sadie wasn't used to people offering her their hands, but she shook anyway. "Sadie Adams."

"Let me guess," KC said with a slight smile. "You must be Zach's new nemesis."

How had she known? "Um…"

"Oh, is this the woman from the mill?" Christina asked, interest lighting her eyes.

Suddenly Sadie felt as though someone had dialed up the spotlight.

"I believe she is," KC replied.

"How did you know?" Sadie asked.

"Honey, it's a small town." KC's smile was friendly, not condescending as Sadie had expected. "Trust me, everybody knows."

"I don't know," Aiden said with a frown.

Christina patted his chest. "I'll fill you in later, dear."

That didn't stop him from studying Sadie in a way that made her more reluctant than ever to stay. But KC picked up her now watered-down drink from the counter and dumped it before starting a fresh one. "Come on over and tell us about yourself," she invited.

Sadie hung on to that friendly smile, even though she knew more than anyone how deceiving it might be from a stranger. But she needed these people for her mission, so she forced her feet forward.

"What do you do, Sadie?" Christina asked.

"I'm a photographer." It wasn't the entire truth. She did take photographs. She just didn't do it for a living, as she'd led them all to believe.

"Oh, where's your camera?"

"Outside." She'd been afraid Zach would make a scene if she brought it in.

Christina didn't seem fazed. "Have you had anything published?"

"Yes, actually. A few pieces through Barnhill Press." The art press wasn't anything to sneeze at, so at least Sadie didn't feel like such a fraud.

Until another voice chimed in. "So you no longer describe yourself as domestic help?"

The people around her froze, unsure how to take Zach's comment. Sadie had no problem with being seen as domestic help. After all, she'd fallen into that category all of her life.

She'd tried to stick as close to the truth as possible. She'd only ever held two things back from Zach the first time around: her employer's true identity and her sister's situation.

Sadie raised her chin and spoke confidently. "Actually, my longtime employer recently passed away. I'm taking a bit of a break before looking for a new position."

"Good luck," Aiden said.

"Thank you." She took a deep breath for courage. "I have an idea I think might interest you."

Suddenly the trio on this side of the bar with her adopted that slightly uncomfortable look that rich people got when they know they were about to be asked for money. She'd seen it often enough back home. But that wasn't what she wanted...

"I wondered if I could have your permission to shoot a series of photographs about the rebuilding of the mill? I visited the town several years ago and became quite attached to it." If they only knew... "From what the people here have been telling me about your family and what you are doing to keep the town alive, well, it's incredible."

She smiled brightly at Christina, since the woman's calm features were easier to focus on. "If nothing else, I think it would make a wonderful memento for the people of the town."

Christina glanced back up at her husband. "Aiden, that sounds wonderful."

"I could talk to the publisher at Barnhill. I've worked with him on several projects...though this would be my first solo proposal," she added, feeling the need to be honest.

On the other side of the bar, she could feel a sense of frustrated resistance coming from Zach. He stared at her, though she refused to meet his gaze. Luckily, she'd already gotten a positive response or she had a feeling he would have blasted her before his employer, simply to keep her from getting close.

Though he still didn't know how close she planned to be...

KC must have sensed it, too, because she kept glancing sideways at her brother. But she didn't speak. Finally Aiden said, "That does sound good. I am a bit worried about safety issues—"

Before he or Zach could go further, she cut him off. "Not a problem. I've already seen the destruction at the mill, and I would definitely need someone to steer me in the safest direction. Someone local, with a lot of experience with the area who could introduce me to people who know the history, the ins and outs of the area. The people and places that make Black Hills so special…"

"That's a great idea," Christina enthused.

Jake and Aiden were nodding along with her. "Definitely," Aiden said. "Zach fits both those criteria and as head of security could keep us informed about your project, too. Would that be a problem?"

"Not for me," she assured him.

Only after speaking did she glance at her former lover, whose hard-won mask barely covered the resentment pushing to get out. Sadie wondered if anyone else could see it. Probably not, because they went on talking as if this were a done deal.

Only Zach kept quiet. Good thing he didn't know the whole story. Otherwise, she might have to worry about her safety.

But at least he would learn. She would get what she wanted…no matter what.

Four

"Just what the hell did you think you were doing?"

Sadie quickly suppressed her smile before turning to face Zach's rage. She and she alone knew the depths of despair she'd experienced since the last time she'd walked away from him. But she couldn't have realized she'd be thrilled to see him under any circumstances…including when he looked like he would choke her if he could.

"Who, me?"

Her innocent question only served to incense him even more. The show was quite spectacular, in fact. Zach's skin took on a ruddy color underneath, showcasing the extent of his anger. But a lifetime as help to people who only wanted things to go their way had taught Sadie to take her kicks where she could get them, even if she could only feel her amusement on the inside.

"You knew I didn't want to spend time with you. So why would you set this whole thing up?" he growled.

Ouch. That hurt, but she had known the way he felt before he even said it. "Look," she said, not afraid to push back. "You started this with your high and mighty attitude, not me."

"So this is all a game to you?" He waved a hand at the damaged building behind him. "This is not a game to these people. This place was their life."

"Yes, and I think it will mean a lot to them to have someone document its resurrection, don't you?"

She wasn't wrong in this. Knowing how much people got attached to places—like she had to Sheldon Hall, even though it would never be hers—gave her a glimpse of exactly how these townspeople felt. "Building positive memories will help shore up the community and keep people here. Isn't that what you want?"

She could see on his face that there wasn't a right answer. He did want that, but it meant spending time with her. Though the reality made her chest ache, she had a job to do just as much as he did. With just as much at stake.

Through clenched teeth Zach brushed her off. "I don't have time to mess with you right now. The fire marshal is here. Just go back to the B and B."

As he stalked across the parking lot, she couldn't help needling him a little more. "I can get some exteriors, though, right?" she called.

He might as well have flipped her the bird, considering the glare on his face. But he held his temper in a gentlemanly way, at least in the midst of the crowd of people he now walked through.

Sadie chuckled, simply because crying in front of everyone wasn't an option, either. She'd suspected that coming back here would be tough, but she could never have imagined the roller coaster of dealing with her own emotions while matching wits with Zach.

Ever comforted by her camera, Sadie set off around the perimeter, once more trying to capture the compound from angles that showcased both the tragedy but also the potential for rebuilding, because that was exactly what people needed to see.

Just a few minutes in, a bell sounded. Glancing around, Sadie saw numerous soot-covered men exit the site and make their way across the parking lot to a couple of huge tents that had been erected along the far edge near the fencing. Must be lunchtime.

After taking a few shots of the men, she edged away from the crowd. Her focus here was pictures, not food.

"Hey, there," a voice said from behind her a few minutes later.

Sadie sighed but finished up her shot before easing her camera down from her face. Had Zach sent another security guard to escort her away today? If so, he was going to have a hell of a fight on his hands.

Turning without any rush, she eyed the man behind her. There was no badge attached to his clothing, and he didn't look dirty like most of the men here. A buttoned-down shirt and Dockers weren't really appropriate attire for a disaster site. But at least he looked friendly.

"Hi," she said, her unease calming down a notch.

"Is that a Canon Mark III body?"

Warmth spread through her. A fellow photographer, maybe? "Yes, with a custom lens. You know it?"

"Ah, I admire from afar and spend my budget on paper and ink instead." The man grinned, looking young despite his thinning hair, and held out his hand. "I'm Lance Parker, editor of the local paper."

She met his hand for a firm shake. "Nice to meet you, Lance. I'm Sadie."

"You must be getting some good pictures, then."

Pulling the camera from around her neck, she clicked on the picture preview and turned the screen so they both could see.

Fifteen minutes of talking cameras and photo composition and lighting fed Sadie's artistic soul. None of her family were interested in photography. She had few friends because of all her responsibilities, but she had managed to join an artists' group near home that she tried to go to once a month. Sometimes it worked out, sometimes not. But she tried to get her fix in when she could.

"Would it be possible for me to use a couple of these in the newspaper?" he asked. "We'd compensate you, of course. These are wonderful and my two photographers are busy with the cleanup, which keeps them from snapping away right now."

Sadie barely had a chance to think before another voice cut in. "Hey, Lance. How's it going?"

She looked over the newspaper editor's shoulder to see Zach's sister, KC, approaching them. Lance smiled as she arrived.

"As good as can be expected, I think." He gestured to Sadie. "Just trying to convince Sadie here to share a few of her pictures with the community. They would be a great accompaniment to the recovery stories."

KC studied Sadie for a split second, but then her lashes swept down, shielding the expression in eyes so like Zach's. "That would be cool. So, Sadie, what do you think?"

That I don't like being put on the spot... "Yeah, I'll come by and we can look over them again. Tomorrow?"

"Great," KC said, as if she'd decided the subject was closed. "Now y'all want some lunch?"

Lance agreed enthusiastically, but Sadie shook her head. "I'm still full from the breakfast spread my landlady puts out, but I'd be happy to volunteer, if you'd like?"

KC's raised brow and hesitant "Sure" didn't make Sadie feel better. She knew it didn't really matter what KC thought of her, whether she approved. Sadie wouldn't be sticking around Black Hills long enough to make real friends…or sisters-in-law. Somehow that didn't stop her from wishing differently.

Although KC might be hesitant for completely different reasons. Had Zach told her about Sadie? How much did she really know?

Zach made his way back across the parking lot to the food tents KC and Christina had installed. He tried to keep an eye out for Sadie along the way, though he desperately wanted to curse himself for caring where she was in the first place. He could tell himself all he wanted to that it was about suppressing her plans, but deep down he was afraid there were far deeper reasons than that lame excuse.

He didn't see her until he was closer to the tents, and that fiery red hair came into view as she scurried behind the serving line. It wasn't entirely clear from this distance, but it looked almost as if she were in charge.

"Kind of amazing, isn't it?"

Zach glanced to the side to see his little sister approach, her arms filled with a box. He automatically reached for her burden, taking it on himself as he nodded his head in Sadie's direction. "What's going on here?"

KC didn't look at the other woman but continued to

watch her brother…making him very uneasy. "She volunteered to help after saying she wasn't hungry. I could tell she wasn't thrilled with the setup when she joined us, but she didn't say a word."

One side of KC's mouth lifted in a slight smile. "I wondered if she would, but she never did until I started asking for help. It took a few minutes to get her to open up. As soon as she realized she wouldn't offend me by making suggestions, she took the lead. We were whipped into shape in ten minutes and served hundreds in less than half an hour." KC shook her head. "She's good."

Very good. But Zach didn't want to think of that in front of his sister.

"She told me before that she made a living as domestic help, but never went into specifics," he mused as he watched Sadie navigate the chaos with the calm demeanor of a woman who had many pots on the fire but wasn't worried about losing one. He glanced at his sister, only to find her still studying him.

He was in trouble now.

"So you knew her before, as in before this trip to Black Hills?"

Why hadn't he just kept his mouth shut? "Hmm…"

But KC wasn't buying the noncomment. "Did you meet her while you were in the military?"

No, but those days right after he came home had been a blur of nightmares and worry over his mother, his family. He hadn't known how to tell them he was falling in love. After she disappeared without a trace, he'd been glad he kept Sadie to himself and not made her a thing—that thing he had to explain to friends and family, pretend not to miss, or realize hadn't been as real as he'd thought. He had happily done most of that without public scrutiny.

Now, though, he could talk about Sadie without having to get into all the ugliness of regret and pain. He'd never been a liar, but he kept it brief, strictly answering the question that was asked. "No, she's been to town before."

KC slapped her hands to her hips, making him wish he hadn't been gentlemanly enough to take the box. "She was here before, long enough for you to talk to her about her job, and you never mentioned her. Was she a customer? Or—"

"What's for lunch, my lovely?" Jacob's voice interrupted his fiancée's, much to Zach's eternal gratitude.

"Barbecue and fixin's," KC said, giving Jacob a big smile.

"What?" her fiancé's voice boomed over the lot. "Barbecued meat, a pretty lady and a cold beer? All I need is our son and it'll be heaven."

"Christina's got him at the manor," KC said, giving Jacob a quick kiss on the cheek. "Your mom started running a fever this morning, so she stayed home and offered to keep him, too."

Zach saw the flash of concern that crossed Jacob's expression, and knew that even the slightest bug could be very harmful for the Blackstones' mother, who had been in a coma for many years. But KC gave him a reassuring smile.

Jacob pulled her into his arms. "Well, how long is that gonna last? Forget the barbecue. Let's go home."

"Nope, sorry," she said, laughing as she swatted his chest.

Jacob buried his face in KC's neck. "Doomed" was all Zach heard before mumbling and giggling took over. He glanced away, grinning at the two lovebirds' antics. In the sea of chaos under the tent, Sadie stood oddly still. The look on her face, even from this distance, had a hint of sadness and longing before she blinked and it was gone. Actually, all emotion was gone, as if she were afraid for Zach to see too closely inside.

Funny, he felt the same way.

Finally Jacob and KC separated, walking to the food tent hand in hand. Zach fell in step beside them. They talked about the next step in their plan as they joined the dwindling line for food. Sadie certainly had stepped up the efficiency of the process, and now the parking lot was filled with hungry workers eating their fill.

"I'm so glad we could do this," KC said, surveying the scene.

Jacob kissed the top of her head. "Me, too. Whatever it takes to keep Black Hills alive, that's what we're gonna do."

They reached the steam table set up under the tent and chose their meal. Zach deposited the box in the serving area before taking his food tray. Sadie was at the other end in a cute apron with a pig on it, pouring drinks.

"Wow," KC said as she reached Sadie's table. "This was incredible. Thank you so much."

Sadie shrugged away the thanks. "It was no problem."

"No problem? I didn't think so." KC laughed. "Of course, I'm used to a well-ordered kitchen. Being outdoors and not knowing where everything is throws me off."

"Organization is key," Sadie said with a wink.

Jacob reached out to shake Sadie's hand. "Well, we are extremely grateful for your organizational skills."

Sadie shifted as if their praise made her uncomfortable. "I'm glad I could help," she said, handing him a large iced tea.

"Would you be free tomorrow to help some more?" Jacob asked.

Sadie blinked. "I'm sure I can," she said. "I'll be out here tomorrow to take more pictures anyway."

"Did you get any good shots today?" KC asked.

"Sure did."

Jacob looked over at Zach in a way that made him distinctly uneasy. He kept looking. Zach could see the wheels turning.

"Tomorrow," Jacob finally said, "we have a truck coming in with lots of supplies for the workers. Decent boots, heavy overalls, protective gloves and such."

Oh, no. *Jacob, please don't do this to me.*

Jacob didn't even glance in his direction. But his jaw twitched as if he were aware of Zach's dread...and amused by it.

"We need some help getting everything organized and out to the employees. I don't want them working cleanup without good-quality gear."

Zach looked at Sadie in enough time to see her eyes widen. "Isn't that costing a lot for a company that's not bringing in any money at the moment?"

Jacob nodded. "But we want them safe. Those that opted to stay on through the temporary closing and rebuilding are being paid wages to help with cleanup and reconstruction.

"We wanted to keep the work local, as much as possible," Jacob said, his tone firm. "We've got some donations, but everything else is at Blackstone expense. Ultimately, this is about the good of the town. The people who live here deserve to be able to stay."

KC chimed in. "Not be run from their homes by a crazy person."

"That's commendable," Sadie said.

"Not really," Jacob responded, giving her a puzzled look.

"Trust me." She met his look without wavering. "I've known some businessmen who couldn't care less about anything but their bottom line. They'd bring in the cheapest labor and not care who lost their livelihoods. Y'all are doing good here."

Zach could see Sadie mulling all this over, her brain working in overdrive even though she didn't ask any more questions. She simply picked at the puzzle, trying to unravel the complicated strands.

The fact that he could discern this made him uneasy. He didn't want to read Sadie's mind. Didn't want to feel her curiosity, her disbelief that the Blackstones were good people who cared about their workers. What had happened in her life to lead her to question that?

No, he didn't want to know.

"Sadie, if your organizing skills make this as easy as serving lunch, we'll be in business in no time. Zach will be here when the truck arrives in the morning around nine. He can make sure whatever you need is carried out."

Sure I will. Don't ask me what I want.

Then Zach wondered if his thoughts were showing on his face, because his sister was watching him—very closely.

Sadie, on the other hand, looked pretty pleased with herself. Considering how he'd treated her since she came back to town, he had to wonder why.

As his sister and Jacob moved on, Sadie smiled over at him. "Looks like it's you and me together—again."

Was that a statement…or a threat?

Five

"It's the truth, I tell ya."

Sadie couldn't help but grin at the man before her. Wearing the traditional farmer uniform of overalls, plaid shirt, ball cap and messy white hair, he was a perfect candidate for sitting on a bench in the town square. So were the other two grandfatherly types with him. But he was the talker.

"I think you're pulling my leg," Sadie insisted, knowing it would spur him on.

"No, I would never," he said with a sincere shake of his head. "But I betcha they're all in on it. The other cotton industries are pressuring the state to shut us down, because they want the business we've always had here. That's why all of this is happening."

She knew old men were prime candidates to become conspiracy theorists. They had too much time to sit around and think and talk and spin events into the way they wanted to see them. So she asked, "But Blackstone Mills has been here since the town started, hasn't it?"

"And still putting out quality product," one of the other men, Earl, said. "That's why they have to put us out of business."

Well, as much as she'd like to brush them off, the fact that a bomb had exploded here couldn't be denied. That was deliberate malice, so someone definitely had it in for Blackstone Mills. And the police weren't talking yet.

"I still don't understand why anyone would want to put you out of business," she said, hoping to get more gossip. "Wouldn't someone local have to be in on this? Have access to the plant?"

"Oh, they were," Mr. Farmer breathed.

"The other textile companies found someone local to do their dirty work, we're pretty sure," Earl said.

Farmer interrupted, "We heard about all kinds of things. Can't keep stuff like that secret. Equipment failure and missing shipments. But it was the cotton that was the kicker."

Now they were getting somewhere. Sadie forgot about the lines of men behind her, getting loaded up by fellow workers with their safety gear after she'd streamlined the process for them. Zach had introduced her to the lead volunteer then disappeared, which she was grateful for now, because she was pretty sure these old-timers wouldn't be speaking to her with him around.

Especially about the damaged cotton crop her landlady had mentioned.

"What about the cotton?" she asked, pretending ignorance.

"Oh, that Zachary Gatlin boy did it," Earl said, "though the police said he was innocent."

"We aren't so sure," Farmer said. "He's in thick with

those Blackstones, so..." He shrugged. "Why they'd want to damage their own business would be a mystery, but then again, there's a lot about all this that is."

Sadie nodded.

"But he sprayed the cotton, that's all we know. Either somebody loaded the poison in or he did it himself."

"Now he's heading up recovery efforts, so who knows."

"But poison the cotton, it did. Took a while, but they managed to get cotton in from elsewhere. Thank goodness, or the mill would have gone under by Christmas, for sure."

It was the same story she'd heard from her landlady. Something didn't add up, though. "Maybe somebody was trying to frame him?" she mused.

"Frame who?"

The voice from behind her had her stiffening. There was nothing like being caught red-handed talking about someone by the person in question. The men's wide eyes clued her in to their awareness of Zach's presence. Too bad she hadn't been watching them while she was over-thinking.

Quickly, she twisted around. "Zach, there you are. I was wondering what happened to you."

Under his breath, so only she could hear, he said, "Didn't sound like it."

Her cheeks flushed hot, but she didn't tuck her chin down the way she wanted to. *Don't show weakness.* Always her first line of defense against the world.

"Gentlemen," he said, glancing over her shoulder. "Glad to see you here. Thanks for supporting us." Then he clasped her elbow. "If you'll excuse us."

He pulled her away, quickly enough that she had to double her short steps to keep up. Looking back, she noticed the men talking and laughing. Goodness only knew what they thought he wanted with her, but whatever their assumption, they thought it was amusing.

Not breaking stride, Zach marched her around the side of the parking area to a more isolated spot before turning to face her. "What was that about?"

"What do you mean?" She had a feeling her innocent look wasn't going to work here.

She was right.

"What right do you have to talk about me, about my life, with the people of this town?"

"Well, technically the conversation didn't start out that way—"

"I don't care how it started." His voice rose enough to sting her ears. "Just that it stops. Now."

Unbidden, Sadie could feel her backbone stiffening and her expression becoming a blank mask. A lifetime in service had taught her how to deal with difficult people, usually men, and their expressions of displeasure. She instinctively took steps to protect herself, even if walking away from the situation wasn't an option. Which it usually wasn't.

Her voice was awfully formal when she spoke. "I'm sorry you feel that way, but I was simply asking about the mill and they offered information. I didn't dig into anything."

"I heard you asking questions."

She narrowed her eyes at him. If he thought she would just take this, he was mistaken. He didn't know her as well as he thought. "A question. You heard me ask a question about you, and that's after Earl brought you up." She cocked her head to the side. "But I do have another question."

"I'm not telling you anything about myself." His snarl said she didn't deserve it.

Which she didn't. "And thus my question. Why do you care if I ask?"

Zachary Gatlin hated being caught off guard. He'd spent his military career planning for the unexpected, but that didn't mean he liked it.

Luckily, Sadie didn't wait for an answer.

"Look," she said, "I have to ask questions. How else am I gonna know what to take pictures of? Who to take pictures of? Talking to people is part of that."

She cocked her jeans-clad hip, the hand she propped there drawing his eye more than he liked. "If that's a problem, I can do it on my own. After all, you are only supposed to escort me through the mill."

"No," he said through clenched teeth. Not just from his anger, either. Being only a foot away from her seemed to be causing his entire body to go haywire. "That's not what Jacob meant, and you know it."

"I know nothing of the sort." Her brows rose. He didn't remember her being so sassy before. This time she was pushing all his buttons. "I only know that the mill is dangerous right now and they want you with me when I go inside. That's the only sure thing."

"It's my job to make sure *everything* you go over is safe." They both knew what his emphasis meant, even if she wanted to pretend otherwise.

"Then I guess you'd better stick a little closer, don't you think?"

For a split second, that sassy pink mouth and raised brow made Zach drop his protective barriers. Without thought, he stepped in. Her back hit the wall behind her. His hand planted right above her shoulder. There was barely a hand's breadth between their chests. Their lips were even closer.

Zach's heart moved into double time. *Remain impassive.* But he couldn't when his entire body was straining to press in close and make contact in the most primitive way he knew how. *Touch.*

Their breath mingled. He allowed one point of contact. Only one, when he wanted so many more. He reached out with his other hand and curled it around her waist, soaking in the warmth of her body beneath the T-shirt she wore.

"Oh, I'm gonna stick pretty damn close, sweetheart," he said, relishing her eyes going wide with something akin to nerves. "I'll be keeping an eye on every move you make. Every word you speak. Every picture you take." No matter how creepy that might be.

He could be dedicated to his job, couldn't he? "No more snooping behind my back."

"Roger that," she whispered.

It was the barest brush of her lip against his that broke the hold she had over his body. That accidental contact shook him to his core—which was the last thing he wanted her to know. So he stepped back. Removed his hand. Controlled his breathing.

And met her gaze. He could have sworn she'd just gotten exactly what she wanted.

Which filled his mind with images of other times she'd gotten what she wanted, only they were much more intimate things, things he didn't want to remember when he was standing this close to her.

Then she threw him off guard again. "I'm sorry," she whispered.

Zach blinked, not switching gears fast enough. "What?"

"I'm sorry that you're angry with me."

He met her eyes, studying their green depths, not sure if he wanted to go back to the time when he'd known her before. But his body spoke before his mind could catch up. "But you're not sorry you left?"

Her expression flattened, her pale skin going almost white. The spare sprinkle of freckles on her cheeks stood out in contrast. "I didn't have a choice," she finally said.

"Zach?" someone called before he could push for more. He forced himself to pull back, to let his arm fall to his side, to clench his teeth together so he wouldn't ask why. Then he deliberately turned his head to the side, blocking her out.

Because he didn't need to know why. Knowing that she had walked away was more than enough.

Six

"Zach, are you ready?"

Sadie tore her gaze from Zach to look at Jacob Blackstone, who stood about five feet from them. To her embarrassment, she had to blink a moment before her gaze would focus on him. Instead she wanted nothing more than to turn back to Zach and press her lips to his. No matter who was looking.

So close.

But Zach wouldn't be there waiting. He strode toward his future brother-in-law, not looking back. "Yeah, I'm ready."

"Ready for what?" she asked.

"They've cleared us to take a preliminary tour inside before the workers go into the parts of the building that were damaged to start cleanup."

She glanced at Zach's retreating back. For someone who said he wasn't letting her out of his sight, he sure was moving away at a fast clip.

"Are you coming?" Jacob asked. Sadie found herself on the receiving end of his inquisitive look.

"Yes, if I may," she said. Apparently, Zach wasn't so far away he hadn't heard that, because his shoulders had straightened, hard.

Jacob led her back to the trailer and got some boots and coveralls in her size. Once she was dressed and had collected her camera, she approached the men again where they stood with two soot-covered figures with clipboards. She steeled herself as Zach turned toward her, but he held out a bright yellow hard hat. "This, too," he said simply.

Jacob introduced her to the fire inspectors, then they headed for the building entrance. To her surprise, a large group of workmen formed a crowded semicircle near the door. Jacob paused to shake a few hands and speak, but the still, respectful patience of the hundred or so people brought out an emotional response in Sadie.

She wasn't used to this. She had more experience with the spoiled variety of the human species. But the simple look on their faces told her this place meant something to them. When Jacob gave the word that it was time, they'd put their backs into rebuilding it—paycheck or no.

Stepping back, she got some wide-angle shots of the crowd, then the entrance. As she took her turn stepping through, her chest tightened. To be the first to see the destruction of this place felt significant. And this wasn't even the worst part of the damage. Her hold on her camera got a little tighter. Hopefully she'd be able to do her subject some justice.

The smell of smoke lingered in the air outside the building, but it hadn't prepared her for the thickness of it inside. It seemed to immediately dry out her throat and threaten to choke her. She found herself panting, trying to limit the air's access to her lungs.

The outer rooms were relatively intact except for their blackened walls, but as they traveled deeper, more damage began to appear. Bubbled paint, peeled portions of Sheetrock, black marks following trails that she assumed were electrical wires in the walls.

"Wow," said a masculine voice near her.

Sadie turned her head to see a big bear of a man staring down the hallway. The hard movement of his Adam's apple told her just how much seeing this affected him.

The rest of the group that had come in were just ahead, leaving Sadie and the man behind a bit. "What did you do here?" she asked.

There was no doubt he had worked here. Someone didn't view a building, especially an industrial building, with such emotion if there wasn't a personal tie.

He turned to her as if he hadn't realized she was there. He blinked rapidly. She knew the feeling well. Working in Sheldon Hall for the Beddingfield family, she'd learned early on all the tricks to hiding those telltale signs of emotion. Instead of pushing, she waited to see if he was interested in talking to her or wanted to be left alone.

Once under control, he offered a halfhearted smile. "Oh, I'm Bateman, the day shift foreman."

She snapped a few pictures of the group ahead of them, getting a long-range perspective, so the foreman wouldn't feel as if she was too focused on him. "So you must have worked here a long time to reach that position," she surmised.

"Since I was a young'un," he said, and this time his smile was more genuine. She smiled back, her heart softening even more.

He went on. "I was hired by the old Mr. Blackstone himself. I tell you, I about wet my pants that day."

"Intimidating?"

"Oh, yes," he said, moving forward once more. "He was a fierce one. I just happened to get lucky—or unlucky, as it were. The hiring manager was sick the day of my interview. But I must have passed muster, because he hired me on the spot. I was seventeen."

They picked their way down halls, pausing beside rooms with water and smoke damage. Sadie managed some more artistic photos of the damage, along with pictures of Bateman while he surveyed the areas. The deeper they journeyed into the building, the harder it became for Sadie to breathe, though she tried not to let it show. Her body felt hot, as if it could still feel the flames, even though she knew that was impossible.

The effects of the explosion became more evident as they proceeded. Sadie could tell they were coming closer to the heart of the plant. Closer to the connection to the admin building where the bomb had been placed. Here pieces of the ceiling were missing; what parts of the walls were left were completely charred and the smoke lay like a blanket over them.

Bateman paused just inside the entrance to a long, cavernous room. As Sadie paused next to him, she noticed the remnants of two-by-fours that had once formed wall dividers, the twisted metal remnants of filing cabinets against the far walls. This room had once been either offices or cubicles. At the far end of the room, the group of men ahead of them also paused. Sadie tried not to watch but couldn't miss Zach's proud bearing and confident interactions with those around him.

Her heart ached, even if she didn't want to acknowledge it. So she turned back to Bateman.

"Since seventeen? That is a long time."

Bateman's smile was tinged with something sad. "Yes, I've been here a long time. My sons work here. And last year my grandson came to work here, too."

"Your family is very important to you."

"Always." Again she saw that sheen of tears, though he tried to hide it by turning his face in the other direction. "If this place closes, what will happen to us? We've always been close. But they're already looking for jobs elsewhere."

Sadie rarely found herself in this position in her day job, but she'd spent more than her fair share of time in hospitals. Her natural compassion asserted itself. She couldn't help patting his arm, though she pretended not to see his tears. Grown men almost always preferred it that way.

"I don't think that will be necessary," she said, hoping her words would soothe him. "From the sounds of it, the Blackstones are gonna do everything they can to keep that from happening."

In her peripheral vision, she saw Bateman blink several times and nod. To give him more privacy, she glanced back at the other men—and found Zach's dark stare trained on her.

This time, she couldn't look away. She felt almost paralyzed by the intensity, as if by sheer will he could see deep inside her.

And for once, she wished she could show him.

Suddenly the connection broke as Zach glanced up and his eyes widened. "Watch out," he yelled.

Sadie quickly followed his example and looked at the ceiling. Her mind barely registered some kind of debris falling before she flung her hands out to push Bateman away.

It happened fast. She pushed. Bateman pulled. Pain slashed across her cheek. The camera shattered. They both went down, then Sadie saw stars across her field of vision before everything went blank.

"Really, I'm fine."

Zach watched as Sadie went a few rounds with the nurse in the temporary first aid center they had set up.

"No, you're not. That cut needs stitches," the nurse, Marty, said.

If anything, Sadie paled even more. "Just butterfly it."

"And mar that gorgeous face forever?" The young guy was aghast. And no, that slinky dark emotion wheedling into Zach was not jealousy—or any form of territorial assertion. "No, ma'am."

As others crowded the opening behind him, Zach turned to KC and Jacob, who both wore concerned expressions. "How is she?" KC whispered.

Zach answered at the same volume, for some reason not wanting Sadie to know they were talking about her. "Very unhappy in the face of treatment." An unusually strong panic had graced her features every time any mention was made of going to the hospital. She seemed to only want to go back to the B and B and pretend she was fine. Zach did not care for the curiosity leaking into his thoughts. "And she'll be even more unhappy when she realizes what happened to her camera."

There was a general chorus of winces before the nurse joined their little group. "She'll need some stitches for that cut on her face. The hard hat did its job. Still, I'd feel better if she wasn't gonna be alone tonight. Especially once she's got some pain meds in her."

There were a lot of logical solutions to this problem. Sadie could stay at Blackstone Manor with Aiden and

Christina. After all, Christina was a nurse. But she was pregnant and Ms. Blackstone, the brothers' mother, had been fighting some kind of infection lately.

KC—or hell, even Zach's mother—could take care of Sadie overnight.

So why did he hear himself saying, "I'll do it."

He ignored the myriad glances that swung his way. "She'll be more comfortable at the B and B with her own stuff," he said, offering a fairly reasonable excuse. "And I'm the only single person with no kids in this bunch."

Marty gave him a nod, as if this were the given option. "I'll get some instructions put together, but I imagine you know what warning signs to look for?"

He sure did. Zach's military background had trained him for this and a whole lot more. Unfortunately, he'd had to put that knowledge into practice a time or two. Times he'd prefer to not just forget but to completely obliterate from his memory.

Marty went back to his patient and the others talked quietly together in that intimate way couples had. Zach watched as Bateman lumbered in across the small space. He knelt by Sadie's chair, the movement oddly humble in a man his size.

Sadie smiled at the older man, then immediately winced. As they talked, Zach thought back to earlier, to Sadie's comforting hand on Bateman's arm, to her push to get him out of the direct path of the falling debris... All those things matched the Sadie he remembered from before she'd pulled her disappearing act.

The new Sadie had been more of a challenge, demanding, secretive almost—instead of just sweet. He didn't want to be intrigued, yet he was.

What had brought on those changes? Obviously there

was some of that sugary-sweet woman in there some-where—so where had the new spice come from?

Zach suddenly realized Sadie was staring at him, her big moss-green eyes uncertain and almost fearful. The nurse must have told her about tonight's sleeping arrangements. He didn't care if it was the coward's way out; he made a quick exit.

There was still work to do—and if it helped him avoid any questions, all the better.

But he couldn't avoid Sadie a couple of hours later as he drove her slightly dopey self back to the B and B. He'd gotten her key before they'd left the mill.

When they went inside, there was no nosy landlady in the lobby to ask too many questions. Sadie leaned into him on the stairs. He told himself it would be rude to make her climb them on her own in her current shaky state. If only he could just ignore the softness of her body as it pressed against his—in such an achingly familiar fit. The light caramel scent of her hair stirred an all-too-base hunger. He felt the echo of anticipation from another time when he had been leading her to bed.

No matter how many times he told himself it couldn't happen between them again, his urges were steadily drowning out the voice of reason.

"You don't have to do this," Sadie said in the same sexy drawl that featured in his memories of that one emotion-charged night five years ago.

"I take my job very seriously," he said as he unlocked her room and led her inside.

"I see that," she said, swaying slightly where she stood. Apparently Sadie couldn't handle pain meds very well. "You've always gone above and beyond."

Zach didn't deny it. That was a part of his nature he couldn't get rid of. Whether he was writing a grocery list, doing a job or taking care of his family, he was usually in whole hog.

A cute frown scrunched up Sadie's usually open features. "But I can take care of myself," she said. She shuffled toward the dresser. "After all, I've been doing it all my life."

He refrained from pointing out that she would have been driving impaired if he had let her go home alone, and watched her pull out pajamas. She shuffled to what he assumed was the bathroom and shut herself inside.

Right, he'd conveniently forgotten about the stubborn streak.

Dropping the overnight bag he kept stowed in his SUV, Zach strolled over and sank onto the couch to wait, banging his knee against the little coffee table in the process. The laptop before him sprang to life.

Four pictures filled the screen, all of him. These weren't the classic survey pictures he was used to seeing. Each one was artistically composed with strategic lighting and showed him absorbed in some task. Except for the one in the bottom right corner, in which he stared straight ahead with a sad look on his face.

The pictures had an indefinable quality portraying not just his emotion but the photographer's as well. Almost a wistful, yearning feel.

Looking at them, it hit him—Sadie had missed him after all.

The bathroom door opened. Somehow, Zach knew Sadie would not want him to see these pictures. With a flick of his wrist, he closed the laptop.

He looked away so he could avoid seeing the sway of her breasts beneath the short, fitted nightie she wore. Unlike the oversize T-shirts his sister had preferred as a teenager, Sadie was all girl when it came to pajamas and underwear.

Nope. Don't go there.

She plopped onto the bed then dropped back onto a mound of pillows. The minute her head made contact, she winced.

But her sleepy eyes met his defiantly. "See. I'm good."

Yes, you are. He smothered a smile. "Sure you are."

She ignored him, rolling onto her side. He could have been offended at her presenting her back, except he knew from experience that was the side she slept on.

He stood for a long time in the middle of the room, almost able to pinpoint to the second when she sank into sleep. His gaze traced the familiar S curve of her body he was desperate to curl around once more. He looked out the window at the darkening sky, then at the alarm screen on his phone that told him when he would need to wake her next.

And finally, the laptop.

He didn't have to open it to know what was inside. Those pictures were imprinted on his brain. Mixed with the yearning he'd seen on her face when they'd stood in the alley this morning, he knew deep inside that Sadie still wanted him, too.

Then he stripped down to his boxer briefs and climbed into bed beside Sadie. At some point, his body made up his mind for him. He might be a selfish bastard, but if this was his chance to have one more taste of the only woman who had tempted his heart, he wasn't going to turn it down.

Seven

Waking to the feel of strong arms and Zach's scent wasn't unusual for Sadie. He remained in her dreams no matter how many days they were apart. She let herself hover there between wakefulness and sleep, wishing the feel of him would never disappear.

Ever so slowly, the mist started to recede. "Zach," she whispered, her mind still not comprehending. "Zach, is that you?"

"Yes," he murmured. "I'm here."

"Please don't leave me."

"I didn't leave you. You left me."

"But I never really wanted to."

Only the sudden stiffening of the body beside hers awakened her enough to realize that he was real rather than a figment of her imagination. So warm and alive she could have wept in gratitude.

The confusion dissipated in a rush of fever as desire swept through her. She'd denied her need for too long.

His groan filled the air. The rough scratch of hair and smooth heat of skin graced her palms, telling her she had reached out to touch. To test whether the apparition of her dreams was indeed real.

And that's when reality returned in an unwelcome rush.

She shouldn't. She knew she shouldn't, that deep down it made what she was doing that much more despicable. Her betrayal then, and her betrayal now.

Her fingers curled, digging into the warm flesh as if to keep him with her just a moment longer. His quick catch of breath signaled a change in the air, a breach of a barrier that shouldn't be forgotten.

But it was too late.

Her mind cried out with joy as his body rolled against hers, sweeping over her to take control. He was the same Zach she remembered. His familiar scent and bulk enveloped her. Her need exploded deep inside. For this moment she would let go of the past, not worry about the future and do the one thing Sadie never did: enjoy the present.

For the first time in five years, she felt his lips against hers. Not the barely there brush from the mill, but a full meeting of lips that conveyed passion and want. Sadie's palms found the bare skin of his shoulders, tracing muscles bulked by years of true labor. For long moments his lips distracted her. It wasn't the tentative touch of new lovers, but the eager reunion, the rediscovery of each other.

Just as her hands traced sinewy muscle over his ribs, he dipped down. The heat radiating from him blanketed her, left her aching for more. She wanted freedom—freedom from her clothes, from her fear, from the secrets that stood between them.

The tips of his hair, much longer than the last time they were together, brushed her cheeks. It tickled, lightening her mood a little. She smiled against his lips. Her hands automatically burrowed into the silky strands, and she savored the thickness, the new weight that signaled his complete return to civilian life.

Her hands in his hair ramped up something for him, because his movements took on a frantic edge. A powerful purpose that plunged her into heaven.

He stripped her of her nightgown, then panties. His thighs settled between hers as he assumed possession. Then he traced her ribs with his palms, reminding her of the first time his hands had explored her body.

Time coalesced in a surreal effect, mixing this moment with a night five years ago when Zach had introduced her to an ecstasy she'd only ever dreamed of before. Now, as then, he touched every part of her as if committing her body to memory. Fingers kneading her muscles. Nails stimulating her skin. Palms controlling her hips.

From somewhere deep inside her a whimper erupted. His hands tightened at the sound, keeping her from lifting against him. The inability to move only ramped up her need. Her core melted in liquefied heat.

Suddenly his warmth receded as he crouched between her thighs. It took a moment of disoriented disappointment to realize he hadn't left her. Then he pressed his open mouth to her thigh. She tensed. Each sucking kiss brought him closer to the apex of her need, but never close enough. Her gasps filled the silence.

Just when she'd thought he would end her suffering, his mouth moved to her belly button, then out along her ribs. This time her breath caught, then she giggled at

his touch. He growled, his approval obvious as he rediscovered every spot that made her laugh, sigh and moan.

Finally he stretched out over her once more. He buried his hands in her hair. The long strands wound around
his fingers, and he took full advantage, tugging until her
chin lifted. Sadie wanted to weep as control and guilt
swept away from her. All she could do was enjoy.

His kiss against her neck was firm, demanding. This
time there was no stopping her hips from lifting, her
hands from clutching him to her. His mouth worked its
magic while his other hand guided his hardness to her.
The stretch right to the edge of fullness made her wince.
It had been so long.

Too long.

But her nails dug into the cheeks of his ass, pulling
him into her with devastating effect. Her entire body
exploded into tingles as he moved within her. It was exactly as she remembered, and so much more.

His body demanded her response. She gave him her
all. Hips clashing. Skin rubbing. Breath mingling. Until
the night erupted into a million points of light and emotion.

Cementing her to him...forever.

Zach's eyes opened when he heard the click of the
bathroom door the next morning...then the unmistakable turn of the lock.

In the military he'd trained himself to be instantly
alert upon awakening, but the habit wasn't always ben-
eficial in civilian life. For instance, at the moment, his
clear mind began to play last night over and over and
over again. Which wasn't what he wanted.

The feelings and memories urged him to get his
naked ass out of bed and into the shower with her. If

only he hadn't heard the telltale sound of the lock shutting him out.

So instead he covered his naked ass with a clean pair of jeans and headed downstairs for some coffee. At least he didn't run into the proprietress first thing—which was good for her. He wasn't in the mood to deal with Gladys before getting in a good shot of caffeine. The breakfast room was empty, though there were pans of fresh rolls and biscuits on the sideboard, and the dark smell of his favorite breakfast brew permeated the room.

The hot black coffee distracted him from what he would say to Sadie when she appeared, what he would do from this point onward.

Her agreement with the Blackstones meant he couldn't ignore her, couldn't get away. She hadn't been the clingy type—now or in the past. But he could honestly say this wasn't a situation he was used to being in with women.

His relationships since he'd been home from the air force had been few and far between. They weren't really relationships, per se. Life had been too full of obligations and change to indulge in something that required that level of commitment—and he'd never felt the urge for more than a good time.

Except with Sadie.

A flicker of movement in his peripheral vision had him looking to the doorway. Sadie straightened her gray sweater, smoothing it down over jeans-clad hips in the barest flicker of nerves. Then she continued into the room and joined him at his table. Her smile was artificial, but it highlighted the bow curve of her upper lip— the same lip that had felt so soft and hungry beneath his own the night before.

"Are you hungry?" Sadie asked quietly, tentatively

testing the waters. "Gladys's husband makes some incredible cinnamon rolls."

"I'm definitely not a man to turn down good food. My mama will testify to that," he said.

She waved him back as he started to rise, so he watched as she filled two plates with rolls and some fruit. Then she lifted a large metal lid and the smell of meat filled the air. She added a couple of slices of bacon to his plate. She'd remembered. He was an avid bacon lover.

Had she learned that so well in the week they'd danced around each other before giving in to their passion?

She laid the plate before him in silence, then fixed her own cup of coffee, doctored with sugar and a liberal dose of cream. This was a natural rhythm that he'd noticed from her before. Just like at the mill, where efficiency in a large-scale task seemed routine for her, so he'd also found her to take charge of these little, everyday domestic tasks, too. Not in an overbearing way, but with a calm efficiency that matched her approach to life in general—at least, as far as Zach could tell.

And probably a way to make herself more comfortable around here.

After she was seated, she drew a long sip from the blue-glazed pottery mug. He munched on bacon, but theirs wasn't a comfortable silence. He sensed Sadie wanted to say something, and wondered idly if he was facing the Dear John conversation he hadn't been subjected to the last time. Odd how the thought bothered him.

He would have preferred not to care one way or another.

"I didn't plan on that, you know," she said, her usual quiet, even tone belying the anxiety with which she stared at her food.

"I know." He noticed the slight puffiness along her upper cheekbone and the fresh bandage on her cheek.

She took another sip, her gaze still trained on her plate.

The least he could give her was honesty. "Neither did I. That wasn't why I brought you home."

Suddenly her gaze snapped up, and he found himself entranced by her brilliant green eyes. How could such a clear color hide so many secrets from him?

They both started as something heavy landed on the table. Zach had been so lost in their stilted conversation that he hadn't noticed the approach of Gladys. He glanced up, sure his expression portrayed just how much he appreciated her intrusion.

"Why, Sadie, you didn't mention you would have a visitor for...breakfast."

The overly long pause told Zach that Gladys was fishing. She must not have noticed him making his way downstairs earlier—surprising for a woman who seemed to know everything.

"Sorry, Gladys," Sadie said.

"Well, how lucky for me that it's Zachary Gatlin."

Zachary couldn't imagine a time when Gladys had ever been that happy to see him, except when she hoped to get a juicy bit of gossip. He looked up with an arched brow. This might be more interesting than he'd thought. "And why would that be?" Zach didn't believe in beating around the bush.

"Why, I get to be the first to congratulate you."

"On what, exactly?" There hadn't been a lot happening worthy of celebration lately.

"On being officially cleared for the cotton poisoning, of course."

She tapped the newspaper she'd dropped on the table with a well-manicured finger. The top headline read,

Founding Family Son Charged in Mill Bombing. Zach was still trying to put the pieces together when Sadie picked up the top section of the paper. Zach didn't need to read it. He already knew who was to blame. Which was a perk of being part of the inner Blackstone circle.

Sadie seemed to be devouring the text. Zach watched her for a moment, then glanced up at Gladys as she continued to stand next to the table.

"Isn't it great, Zach?" she asked with a gleam in her eye that said she couldn't wait to be on the phone the minute she had something to pass along. If he didn't give her something, she'd just make up something interesting. Of course, the fact that Zach was here, and had probably come down from Sadie's room, would be the first thing she'd offer.

"Yes, Gladys. It's very nice."

Even though I shouldn't need the validation of being proven innocent. His sister, his mother, Jacob and his new employers all believed in him, even when the evidence had been totally damning. Those were the people that mattered.

So he kept it simple.

As Gladys headed back to the kitchen with a disappointed look on her face, Zach turned to find Sadie's eyes on his. "Why blow her off like that?"

"Because she's looking for a scoop, something to share with the grapevine."

Sadie nodded. Her guarded expression held a hint of sadness, as if she understood his need to protect himself. But what he really wanted to know was what she hid behind the mask…and whether he would regret last night if he found out her true secrets.

Eight

"I'll finish getting ready."

At least, that's what Sadie told Zach to get a few minutes alone in her room. She needed to make a phone call before Zach took her anywhere this morning. Since her car was still at the mill, she didn't have any choice but to get a few things in order and hitch a ride into town.

Luckily, Zach hadn't pushed anything after their conversation at breakfast. She'd had the distinct impression he'd just as soon step out in the parking lot and get out of ready reach of Gladys. Not that she could blame him.

She was well acquainted with people who blamed first and asked questions later.

Sadie also loved the people who pretended she didn't exist, because it was easier than having to be polite.

Not that she was in a position to judge. As she picked up her phone, she was all too aware of that fact.

"I need a new camera," she said without preamble when Victor picked up.

He wasn't thrilled—not that she'd thought he would be. "What the heck does that have to do with me?" he asked.

Sadie explained how the camera had been shattered when she'd dropped it, then the falling debris had finished the job.

"My question stands."

"A photographer has a camera. A nice camera."

"Then I guess you should have held on to yours."

Why did she bother explaining anything to this guy? "According to our contract, you are responsible for all business expenses, including a camera. I could have considered it a regular expense, but it's not, so I'm actually giving you the courtesy of informing you that you need to pay for it." Sadie had covered every loophole she could think of in the deal with Victor. It was all completely spelled out in black and white. And he'd needed her, so he'd signed.

"So sue me."

"If you don't pay, I'll just have to wait for the insurance claim. They'll take care of it…eventually. But it will mean a delay—"

"Fine. What am I getting for my generosity?"

Nothing he was going to like…but Sadie kept that thought to herself. Better not to antagonize him any more than normal.

"Unfortunately, nothing at the moment. My biggest lead was blown away this morning." She explained how the newspaper article had laid out bombing suspect Mark Zabinski's connection to the local airfield and how his presence there would not have been questioned. This gave the police reason to look into his possible sabotage of the containers on Zach's plane. That meant Zach was innocent, and the crop poisoning couldn't be used to disinherit him. She'd have to find something else. Victor's curses rang in her ear even before she'd finished.

His voice rose in volume and ugliness with every word. "Then find something else. We're running out of time."

The sound of him slamming the phone down made her wince, but to her relief he disconnected the call. Letting her eyelids drift closed, she took a few moments to breathe. Her body and her emotions had been through a lot in the past few days. She was exhausted. Her head hurt. And she had to face the fact that she'd had sex with Zach, knowing good and well she would betray him before her time here was over.

Having to deal with Victor on top of all that was more than she could handle, as evidenced by the tremble in her fingers as she opened her laptop and accessed the internet. By the time she went downstairs to meet Zach outside, she knew exactly where she needed to go next.

"Would you mind if we went out to Callahan's before heading all the way out to the mill?"

Zach threw a glance her way but quickly returned his eyes to the road. "Sure. What do you need there?"

"Mr. Callahan can order a replacement for my camera. I'd prefer to get it done as soon as possible." Who knew what she might get involved in once she got to the mill? Plus, it was a long way from town. By the time she got there and got her car, it could be late afternoon.

If there was one thing Sadie wanted almost as much as Zach, it was her camera. Her fingers ached to curl around it once more. Only another shutterbug would understand the feeling, but it was there nonetheless.

"I was surprised when you dropped it," Zach said, his tone more than conversational somehow. "I knew before that your camera was your baby. This one was really nice."

She wasn't going to pretend she hadn't felt a twinge as it left her hands, because Zach already knew the truth in that. Still, she shrugged. "In the end, it's just a thing." And she knew all too well how little things meant in the long run. "Compared to a person...at least the camera can be replaced."

"Won't that be expensive?"

Goodness, yes. "That's what credit cards are for, I guess. The insurance will eventually pay me back."

Until then, Victor better have it covered.

"Why are we even having this conversation?" she asked, not backing down when Zach shot a glance her way. "Do you really view me as that heartless of a human being that I wouldn't value Mr. Bateman's safety over my camera?"

"No, but—"

"Wouldn't you drop whatever you were holding to push your sister out of the way?"

"Yes, but Bateman is a stranger."

"Who still has a family he cares about and who would miss him if something bad happened to him. You may not approve of all of my actions, Zach, but I still think I'm basically a decent human being."

"One who's grown a pretty decent backbone."

"I told you I was sorry. But I'm not gonna dissolve into sackcloth and ashes or let you whip me with the past. That isn't good for either of us."

She sucked in a breath, suddenly realizing the extent of her tirade. But she couldn't finish without saying, "It won't change it, either, much as I wish it could." Because in the end, honesty was important to her, so she would honor that where and when she could without harming her own family...

Zach didn't respond this time. Sadie's nerves tightened with every turn of the steering wheel, but she wasn't backing down on this.

It wasn't until they reached the little camera shop on one side of the town square that he finally spoke.

"You're right, Sadie. My apologies."

She'd have been happier if his tone hadn't been so formal, but in the end, it was for the best, wasn't it?

The store had a checkered awning that matched numerous others around the old-fashioned square, easily visible now that the leaves were mostly missing from the Bradford pear trees lining the streets. Sadie wondered what cute little Christmas traditions the town observed and whether those bare branches would be wrapped in holiday lights. She wished she could be here to see it, to walk along the sidewalks with Zach and soak in the atmosphere.

But her life was elsewhere. So were the people who were counting on her. She tried not to think about how quickly she might have to leave as she stepped through the door into a camera lover's paradise.

"Hello, my dear Sadie," Mr. Callahan said. "What an unexpected pleasure."

"For me, as well," she said with a smile, allowing the dapper Southern gentleman to press a gentle kiss to her cheek.

She caught a glimpse of Zach's surprised look as she pulled back. Why was he shocked? She'd made more friends than just him when she'd been here before.

"That is quite a large bandage you have there," Mr. Callahan remarked. "Did you, by chance, receive that yesterday?"

"Why, yes," Sadie said. "A cut, but it will heal. What I'm really worried about is my camera."

He nodded sagely, reminding her of a benevolent, skinny Santa. "Yes, I heard about that, too."

Well, this was a small town… "I see." After all, what should she say?

Zach wasn't having any difficulty coming up with words. "She was very brave, pushing Bateman out of the way of that falling debris."

For a moment, Sadie wondered why he was so open with Mr. Callahan when he'd practically refused to talk to Gladys at the B and B. But she knew it probably had to do with Mr. Callahan's integrity. He didn't need gossip as a source of entertainment.

"I'm glad you came to see me," he said. "Though there is no hope of repair?"

"Since the camera is sitting under a pile of loose plaster and two-by-fours, I doubt it," Zach answered.

Sadie winced as she remembered her last glimpse of the camera. "I was able to get almost all of my pictures off, since I download them to my laptop every night. But I'll bring in the digital card and see if you can get the ones from that day for me."

The gleam in the older man's eyes said he looked forward to the challenge. "It will be my pleasure."

"Until then, I need to order a new one."

Mr. Callahan moved over to a computer on the counter. "What kind?"

When she told him, he whistled. "You've stepped up in the world," he said.

"And now I'm in deep mourning." It was either brush it off or cry.

"Let's see if we can resurrect it," he said with a wink.

"The Blackstones would appreciate it," Zach said,

surprising Sadie. "She's using the camera to create a visual history of the mill's resurrection."

That had the older man's eyes widening. "Are you now? I can't wait to get a sneak peek at the digital card."

"I can bring my laptop down here later this week so you can see what I have so far. The building and people down there make fascinating subjects." Especially certain people. She'd have to make sure those photos were in a completely different folder.

"I imagine so," Mr. Callahan said, even as his fingers continued clicking on the keyboard. "I've always been interested in the juxtaposition of all that steel and metal with endless fields of cotton. From what I saw yesterday when I drove out there, the damage is quite picturesque."

He paused, staring into space for a moment. "Kind of interesting that James Blackstone's empire suffers ruin just over a year after his death."

"Was he the original owner?" Sadie asked.

"The original dictator," Zach scoffed.

Mr. Callahan agreed with a knowing look. "The original business was built several generations ago, and added to through the years, but it was James Blackstone who catapulted it into luxury quality linens."

"So he was a good businessman?" Sadie asked.

Zach was quick to answer. "Yes. And a miserable human being."

She studied his suddenly shuttered face. "That sounds like it comes from personal experience."

He simply shrugged and walked away, leaving her to wonder as he strolled around the length of the old-fashioned, quirky shop.

She glanced over at Mr. Callahan. He gave her a half smile. "I'm not big on telling other people's stories," he said, "but James was most definitely difficult. He ruled

Black Hills with an iron fist and had definite views on how things should be done." He, too, glanced over at Zach. "And he wasn't above using devious tactics to get what he wanted, either."

He finished putting Sadie's package together on the computer, checked it twice, then rang up a payment on her card that made her slightly nauseous. If Victor didn't come through with that money in her bank account by tomorrow, she was going to ruin him for sure.

He was used to throwing around that type of money, but Sadie definitely was not.

They headed back out to the car, Mr. Callahan's promise that the camera would be delivered in forty-eight hours drifting behind them.

Hopefully it wouldn't be a moment longer.

There weren't too many things that made Sadie impatient, but waiting on a camera was like a kid anticipating the bike they just knew they would find under the tree Christmas morning.

The silence in the car on the way to the mill wasn't helping her nerves. "So the Blackstone men I've met," she asked, "they're James Blackstone's grandsons?"

Zach nodded.

"You seem to know them well."

"Not really...at least, not until recently. Different circles and all that." The words were accompanied by a smirk, but at least he'd started talking.

"KC actually got involved with Jacob Blackstone first, months before I knew the family. Before that, I just knew *of* them. None of the grandsons lived here then. She met Jacob when he came home on a visit to his mother, and then she ended up pregnant with Carter."

The scowl darkening his features turned fierce. "That was my first up close and personal encounter with the patriarch of the family. He threatened my sister, scared her so badly she left town. I'll never forgive him for that."

Sadie recognized something in Zach's expression all too well. "Or yourself?"

He shot a quick glance her way before resolutely returning his eyes to the road. "She knew I wouldn't have held back. I've spent my life protecting my family. And I would have jeopardized my livelihood and my mother's bar to teach that son of a bitch a lesson." His knuckles whitened from his tight grip. "So she made a decision and left alone. She didn't come back until James was dead."

Zach took a deep breath, almost as if cleansing himself of the memories. "Jacob and KC were lucky. Their story ended in a happily-ever-after—but it never would have if James had had any say about it."

Zach's stiff shoulders and furrowed brow suggested that he was still angry. But it was obvious from seeing Jacob and KC together that they were very much in love. From the sounds of it, they'd overcome a lot to get there.

Sadie knew how Zach felt, though. It was his job to protect his little sister. He hadn't said it outright, but he must feel as though he'd let her down.

The question was, would he understand someone else needing to do the same for their family?

Almost a week later, Sadie stepped into Bella Italia with more trepidation than she'd ever experienced over a formal event. Mostly because she was usually at these things as the help, serving, blending in with the decor rather than standing out like a peacock in a brand-new dress.

She'd known exactly what she wanted to wear when KC had invited her to the Blackstones' party celebrating a new chapter for the mill. The bright blue dress had called to her from the moment she'd walked past the window on the square on the way to Callahan's. Sadie was used to admiring clothes she wasn't able to buy.

Not this time.

For once, she didn't blink at the price. She didn't even use the company card Victor had given her for regular expenses. Somehow that would taint the gift of being invited in the first place. This time she wanted to experience something on her own terms—even if it ended up being a fairy tale.

The sleeveless dress had a fitted bodice that hugged her generous curves and provided ample support. Her second favorite element, besides the color, was a mesh triangle cutout between her breasts, giving a shadowy glimpse of cleavage beneath. The flowy skirt was dressed in sparkles along the calf-length hemline, adding to her festive mood.

She'd indulged in a pair of sexy silver heels without once wondering how many other outfits they would match. Practicality had no place tonight. She wore a single piece of jewelry. The necklace had been a gift from her mother on her twenty-first birthday, the length perfect to nestle a teardrop opal encircled in silver wire in the indention at the base of her throat. A silver shawl completed her dream outfit.

She wasn't sure what had gotten into her, but tonight she would simply go with the flow. Especially since it meant more time with Zachary. A quick look over her shoulder let her watch her prince as he stepped in the door to the restaurant behind her. She'd seen him plenty at the mill in the past few days, but never alone. And there had been no repeat of the night at the B and B.

She wished he had come to get her because he wanted

to, not because Christina had asked him to, but the flutters in her stomach were the same, regardless. And the way his dark eyes widened when he saw her in this dress for the first time was very much appreciated.

Zach was a sight to behold himself. The fitted black suit and burgundy tie complemented his dark good looks, making her fingers itch for her camera to record tonight for posterity. She had a small one in her clutch—she was never without one—but wouldn't intrude on a personal gathering by breaking it out.

As Zach took her arm to lead her in, the look on his face was proud—at least, she liked to think so. Even though it didn't dim the wariness that would forever linger in his eyes when he looked at her, still, it made her happy.

This, at least, she could have.

"Well, somebody cleans up good," KC said, giving her brother the once-over before a quick hug.

Zach's gaze flicked to Sadie when she murmured, "I agree."

He wiggled his tie a little to adjust it. "You know I hate these things."

KC shook her head as if she were disappointed in his response. "What's not to enjoy? Great food, friends—even Mom's here." She looked between them, giving Sadie the distinct impression that she was sizing them up together. "Go introduce Sadie, why don't you?"

That definitely started the butterflies in Sadie's stomach. When she'd been here five years ago, she hadn't met any of Zachary's family, though she'd heard a lot about them.

Luckily she had time to compose herself before doing the family thing. She and Zach couldn't get more than a few feet across the floor without someone stopping them to chat. The Blackstones had spared no expense in renting out the entire restaurant for this impressive soiree, and they'd invited all of the upper management from the mill and their families, as well as Zach and KC's family, the mayor and some city officials.

To her surprise, she was almost as much in demand as Zach. The people at the mill and in town had been beyond friendly, and it was no different with tonight's crowd. Sadie felt more at home here than she ever had in Dallas, where she'd lived her entire life. Mostly because the people of Black Hills actually saw her. The real her...or as close to the real her as she could risk showing them.

Suddenly a man with an authoritative bearing appeared at Zach's side, reaching to shake his hand. "I told you this would eventually be cleared up," he said.

"You didn't say it would take this long," Zach answered with a knowing look.

"This is true," the man said with a laugh.

"Sadie," Zach said, pulling her into reach of the conversation, "this is Officer Stephens, my arresting officer."

"What?"

To her consternation, both men chuckled. "Sorry, ma'am," Officer Stephens said. "A little joke. I didn't actually arrest him... I just brought him in for questioning." His wink set her at ease.

"And question me he did," Zach said.

"Just doing my job. But you did good, buddy. Real good."

Zach shook his head. "In the end, it wasn't even me who caught him. It was Luke."

"But you kept pushing," he said, patting Zach's back in that casual way comrades have. "The truth always comes out, my friend."

Sadie forced herself not to shift in her three-inch heels as she heard the words.

"How is Luke?" the officer asked.

"Good." Zach nodded. "He's home, but he opted to stay with Ms. Blackstone tonight. He's had enough of the spotlight for a while."

The officer laughed, shaking his head. "I bet he has."

The men chatted for a minute more before Officer Stephens moved along. Then Sadie turned to Zach. "Luke is the brother who was there when the mill exploded, right?" She'd heard the name all over town, but never met the man himself.

"Yes, Jacob's twin."

As they approached the table where Jacob was solicitously getting KC settled, Sadie studied him. "After seeing the damage, I can't imagine how scary that must have been."

Zach nodded. "They were able to dig him out, along with Mark Zabinski, who set the bomb. They were both injured, though Mark ended up in worse shape than Luke. A wall came down, pinning his legs to the floor."

Sadie winced. "Ouch."

"Ouch, indeed," Zach said as they reached the table.

Not long after everyone was seated and introduced, Aiden and Christina Blackstone also made their way to the table.

"How's Mom?" Sadie heard Jacob ask after giving Christina a quick hug.

"About the same," she replied.

For a moment, Sadie was struck by the silent communication between the Blackstones. Each gaze was tinged with sadness, with a knowledge no one wanted to admit about their beloved mother. But the words weren't spoken aloud. Her own shared glances with her mother were the same. Sadie's heart ached for what the Blackstones were going through; she was going through it with her sister's illness.

From her understanding, Lily Blackstone had been comatose for many years, but in good health…until recently. A series of infections had raised concern for the matriarch. And for Christina, Sadie realized as Aiden pulled his wife close for a moment, resting his palm against her pregnant belly. Sadie was sure the added worry of being Lily's primary nurse did not help in any way.

"What? No camera?" KC asked, distracting Sadie from her sad thoughts.

Sadie lifted her clutch. "In here. I'm rarely without one. Mr. Callahan let me borrow one of his smaller digital cameras, but I didn't want to intrude on a personal gathering. Sometimes people have a hard time enjoying themselves when a camera is in the room."

"What a lovely consideration," Zach's mom said.

"Yes," KC added, "we appreciate the thought, but please feel free. We don't want people to see Black Hills as simply a pile of burning metal and soot." She waved her hand around the room. "Life is a mixture of good and bad, not just the bad. Parties have their place, too."

Sadie signaled her agreement with a smile, but she couldn't help but wonder why everything good in her own life had always led to heartache.

The rich, decadent Italian food only served to make the atmosphere even merrier. Laughter and the scent of tomato sauce mingled in the air. After eating, Sadie excused herself to take a few photographs but seemed to keep Zach in her peripheral vision no matter where she ended up.

He stayed close to his mother, making sure she had

everything she needed, though she was far from frail. The family talked easily and continuously, leaving the impression of a perfectly formed group of people that life had brought together. Sadie knew, probably more than most, that it wasn't perfect, though. Zach's father had been a selfish man, leaving Zach's mother with a legacy of heartache and a child to raise alone. The fact that KC's father did the same years later made it that much sadder. And she knew about the Blackstone brothers' sadness over their mother and the danger they had personally faced during the mill's destruction.

But it looked postcard perfect. As did the darkly handsome man in their midst. The man who so easily cared for his family—and possessed the strength and the means to do it.

Unlike Sadie.

Suddenly feeling as if someone had dropped a bag of bricks on her chest, Sadie hurried outside. For long moments she couldn't breathe, couldn't think beyond the need for the cool, fresh air. Ever so slowly, her lungs loosened, letting the air inside, until she no longer felt that her body had seized up. Without thought she drew her phone from her pocket. A quick swipe and she was calling her own mother, almost desperate for the reassurance that she still had some semblance of a family to go home to.

Only no one answered.

There could be a lot of reasons for that. Her mother was in the other room, or tending to Amber. Still, tears welled beneath Sadie's eyelids. She missed her mother so much. And her sister, who was often too weak to talk for more than a few minutes on the phone.

Careful steps took her to the window. She looked in at the party, which was still in full swing. Raising the camera, Sadie took a few shots of the people inside, framed by the decorative greenery on the window casing. She hoped to capture the essence of revelry, especially the family who had so generously offered this opportunity.

But she was on the outside looking in.

And just as Sadie started to feel sorry for herself, Zach turned to face her. His gaze unerringly found her, holding her immobilized with a simple look. A look that laid his soul open, telling her he could be trusted. That a man so beloved by those around him didn't have any dark secrets to hide.

No. The secrets were all hers.

Nine

The minute he'd seen her through the window, he'd known he had to go to her.

Zach wanted to hold her, touch her as he had too few times. But now that he was here, he found himself hesitating. Her beauty in the half darkness, illuminated by the twinkling lights surrounding the window, took his breath away.

She didn't look at him, remaining in profile. "Your family is beautiful," she said.

So are you.

But the yearning in her voice kept him quiet. Somehow he knew, though he could easily seduce her, that this wasn't the time.

"You've built a good life here," she went on. "Are you happy?"

"For the most part," he conceded. Though even surrounded by family and friends he was often lonely, aching. His nature made him a protector, yet he yearned for someone to share the burden with him. "Are you?" he asked, curious.

Sadie had talked very little about her life away from him. Oh, they'd discussed books, music, photography and many other things. But looking back, he realized how little of herself she'd actually given him. As if she were afraid to do so.

"Not often."

In the dim glow he could see her eyes widen; she was surprised by her own response. Why? It was certainly honest. Was she surprised because she'd told him the truth?

And that would be the crux of his wariness when it came to Sadie's return. The more he was with her, the more he was convinced she was holding back, keeping things from him. That wasn't what he wanted. That was why he hadn't gone back to the bed-and-breakfast with her again, even though he wanted more than just one night with her.

So he asked, "What about your family?"

Her hesitation sparked impatience deep inside. "You do have a family, don't you, Sadie?" He took a step closer. "Or are you alone in the world?"

The thought brought sadness for her, tempered by the knowledge that he could have kept her from being alone…if she had let him.

"Tell me, Sadie." *Something. Anything.*

Then she turned to face him, and his impatience melted away. Tears stood in her eyes like small puddles left from a wintry rain. "I miss my mom," she whispered.

Those gorgeous green eyes slid closed, cutting him off from the aching vulnerability. When they opened again, her gaze was still glassy, but more controlled.

"Where is she?" he asked.

"Dallas." A small smile graced her lips. "I'm not a complete vagabond."

She went quiet once more, a long silence that made him wonder if she would speak again. Just when he gave up hope, she said, "Your mom reminds me of her—hardworking, concerned over her children, never giving up hope." Her deep breath cracked his heart. "I wish I could take care of my mom the way you take care of yours."

"I'm sure she knows that, Sadie." He glanced through the window, seeing people in various groups having a good time. Then he looked at Sadie once more, here on the outside. She wasn't a loner, by any means. He'd seen the way she got along with people, could draw out their stories and make them feel comfortable with her. But yes, she did still keep a part of herself distant.

Just as she did with him.

"If she needs you, why are you here?"

For a moment, he thought she wouldn't answer. Finally she shook her head. "It's the only way I know to help her now."

She didn't elaborate on the cryptic words, so Zach asked, "Your father?"

Sadie shook her head once more. "I don't remember him. He left when I was little. We're a lot alike in that, you and I."

Zach stiffened, bracing himself with one hand against the wall. "How did you know that?" He never talked about his father, preferring not to give attention to someone so utterly lacking in human decency. "You've been snooping around again?"

Her eyes widened, appearing almost scared in the twinkling light. "I wasn't snooping about that. I promise." Her brows drew together. "I can't help it if people like to talk."

"About me?"

"Well, I like talking about you, so why not?" Her lashes lowered over her expressive eyes, as if she knew she'd revealed too much. Suddenly she shivered, drawing the sparkly shawl closer around her shoulders. "Goodness, I didn't realize how cold it had gotten. We should go back inside."

Not yet. As she tried to pass him, Zach reached out. His arms encircled her, his body warming hers in the only way he could in public. Then he leaned down and kissed away the chill.

When he finally pulled back, he felt rather than saw her grin. "Zachary Gatlin, are you coming on to me?" she asked.

That's what they needed—a little light, a return to the celebration inside. "I don't know—are you willing to risk another interrogation by Miss Gladys?"

He felt her breath catch beneath his palms on her back. "Oh," she whispered. "I think it might be worth it."

As they walked back inside, Zach let his arm remain around her shoulders. Anticipation built, bubbling beneath his skin, only to fizzle out as they rejoined their table. The Blackstone brothers were quietly gathering coats, readying everyone to leave.

"Luke called," Aiden said, turning dark eyes Zach's way. "Mother's temperature has spiked again, but something else is going on. He's concerned. We need to skip out, but I don't want to ruin everyone's evening. Can you take over from here?"

Luckily the mingling of the crowd and the dancing in the back room distracted most everyone from the family's departure. As Zach started making final arrangements, he noticed Sadie falling into organization mode—directing the restaurant staff, taking care of last-minute requests from guests, coordinating cab rides for those who needed them.

Then Zach was left with a final conundrum: the Blackstones' butler and chauffeur, Nolen, had taken them all to Blackstone Manor, where KC and Jacob had a suite with all the baby stuff they needed. That left Zach's mother without a ride home—and her house was in the opposite direction of Sadie's B and B...by quite a distance. While he pondered, Sadie appeared at the table. "It was a pleasure to meet you, Ms. Gatlin," she said, her voice smooth and in control.

Which simply reminded him of just what drove her out of control...

"And you as well, young lady," his mother said. "You handled this party like someone in the know."

"Cleanup is an art form," Sadie said with a slight smile and dismissive wave of her hand. "Just not one normally appreciated by others."

Her words left him to wonder just who she was always cleaning up after.

"Let me just get Mother home, then I'll come by—"

"Nonsense," Sadie said, her eyes overly bright. "The last thing I want to be is trouble. I booked a cab for myself." She patted his arm. He tried not to notice how her touch lingered for a few seconds longer than normal, because it reminded him of an opportunity missed.

"Y'all have a nice night," she said.

Uncomfortable would be more like it.

Sadie told herself she'd come to Lola's because four days was way too long to go without seeing the object of her investigation. Also, a woman had to eat, right?

The impulse had nothing to do with her body's

mourning over the lost opportunity or lack of a Zach fix. Not at all. Even though she knew it would have been wrong to accept, she couldn't help but think of his invitation the night of the party with longing. She wished she hadn't given him—and her—the least complicated way out, when her heart had wanted nothing more than to take him home.

The last week had been a busy one for him. The Blackstone brothers had been less hands-on at the mill, splitting their time between there and home with their dying mother. At least that's what gossip around town said: Lily Blackstone's precarious health was finally failing.

The woman's tragic story—of being comatose for many years after a car accident followed by a stroke—left Sadie weepy. She tried not to think about it. Her own sister's terminal illness made the story hit too close to home.

The situation had left Zach with a lot of administrative work on his hands, along with directing his own business. She'd watched at a distance, waiting for the moment when he'd invite her back into the inner circle… but he never did. She told herself he was tired, overworked, but a panic had started deep inside. Yes, she needed to get close to him. She seemed to have found all the superficial evidence about Zach's character she was going to get from the town. Family history, rumors and accusations—none of it would disqualify him from his inheritance. She needed to dig into the parts of his life that no one else could see. In order to find something truly damning, she'd have to find it out from Zach himself.

But the truth was, as wrong as she knew it to be, she wanted that time with him. His attention. His intensity focused on her...for just the few minutes she had left with him.

She'd guessed that he'd be here tonight. He couldn't be spending a lot of time with his family during the day, and family meant a lot to him. That much she'd learned about Zachary Gatlin. So even though he didn't have to work at Lola's, she figured he would be here in some capacity to check on his mother and sister.

The restaurant was full, but not as packed as the last time she'd been here. The scents of grilled meat and some kind of spicy barbecue sauce had her mouth watering in anticipation. She waved to a few friends she'd made as she crossed the floor to nab a small two-top along the wall near the bar, hoping the position would help her see and be seen by one very specific person.

Her disappointment mounted as a waitress took her order and served her food. She'd shared a smile with Ms. Gatlin, Zach's mother, as she busied herself behind the bar. But as dinner wore on, there was no sign of Zach, or even his sister, KC.

As Sadie finished up, the arrival of three women distracted her. They claimed the table directly in Sadie's line of sight near the dance floor. As she looked closer, she noticed that only two of the girls were young, probably early twenties. The other was significantly older. They settled in the chairs and ordered from the waitress.

As soon as she headed back to the kitchen, the older woman smiled at the other two. "You girls head onto the dance floor. It will be a while before the food is here."

They each kissed one of the woman's cheeks, then walked toward the dance floor with eager steps. She smiled after them but didn't look sad to be left behind in the least.

Without warning, her gaze swept over the room before coming to rest on Sadie. They shared a smile.

"Hello, my dear," she said, their tables close enough together that she didn't have to yell, though her voice had certainly not been weakened by age. "Are you dining alone tonight?"

Sadie nodded. "Yes. Just finishing up, actually." She wiped her lips with her napkin, hoping she'd removed any stray barbecue sauce. "Lola's has some of the best food I've found in town."

The woman patted the empty chair next to her. "Indeed they do, which is the excuse I give my granddaughters for bringing me here," she said with a knowing smile. "Join me for a moment. Are you visiting Black Hills?"

"Yes," she confirmed, sliding into the chair. "Thank you, Ms...."

"Saben, dear."

"Ms. Saben. I'm a photographer, working on documenting the rebuilding of the mill."

"Ah, yes. I heard about that. Very exciting."

It certainly had been, but probably not in the way Ms. Saben meant.

"The town—and the Blackstones in particular— have had a very exciting year," she went on. "What with young Aiden coming home and marrying Miss Lily's nurse. Christina is such a lovely young lady."

Ms. Saben smiled at the waitress as she served the drinks. Sadie asked for a refill on her tea and got one. "You doing okay, Miss Saben?" the waitress asked.

"Sure am. Glad to be back in for a bit."

As the waitress went on about her way, Ms. Saben explained, "I've been coming up here for a long time. Ms. Gatlin and I are old friends. But we each have very busy lives." She took a sip of what Sadie had overheard to be a rum and Coke. Ms. Saben tipped the drink in salute. "My granddaughters say it's bad for me to drink, so I've gotta sneak in a little tipple when I can. Otherwise I'd be left watching them down margaritas while I'm drinking water."

Her sass had Sadie laughing out loud.

"Especially now," Ms. Saben went on with a small smile. "I'm just fully recovered from pneumonia. Off all my medicines and pronounced one hundred percent by my doctor. If I had to stay in that house one more second, I'd have gone stir-crazy. So I offered to come out here with the girls.

"They get a fun night out from watching me," she went on. "And I'm not afraid to get out on the dance floor myself in a bit."

"I'll bet you know a thing or two about dancing," Sadie said, inspired by the older woman's daring.

"Honey, you've gotta dance while you still can. Besides, I'd rather break a hip that way than push a walker at the old folks' home."

"Amen," Sadie said with a salute of her tea.

The same muscular server who had delivered Sadie's food earlier came bearing Ms. Saben's potato skin appetizer. Sadie suppressed a grin when the older woman said, "It's a vegetable, right?"

"You got that right, Ms. Saben," the man said before ambling back to the kitchen area.

"I'm so glad Zach was able to hire some decent men to work around here, now that he and KC have so much going on in their lives," Ms. Saben said. "But life does go on, especially new babies." She eyed Sadie. "You have any babies at home?"

"Not yet," Sadie said. Babies were far in her future,

if ever. Right now, she had her mom and sister to take care of.

"Well, that little Carter is a joy, and KC deserves her happiness."

"I heard James Blackstone tried to keep KC and Jacob apart..." Sadie prompted, sensing the woman enjoyed telling her stories.

"Indeed he did. And KC had every intention of telling Jacob about the baby, but she was fearful—for herself and her family. James threatened their livelihood, you know."

"No, I didn't."

"Oh, yes. He owned the land Lola's is built on. Luckily, Jacob and Aiden have deeded it over to KC's mother. You know, so she could feel secure."

Sadie murmured her approval.

"Jacob Blackstone is a good guy. Not like his grandfather. None of the boys are, but there's a lot of men who are none too happy about having the responsibility of a child sprung on them. A lot who would walk away. Ignore it. Not Jacob. And soon there will be a wedding to celebrate, once the, well, sadness is done."

For Lily. They would definitely need some celebration after losing a woman so important to all of them.

As if she were a hunting dog, Sadie suddenly caught the deep timbre of a man's voice and knew immediately that Zach had arrived. Her eyes searched restlessly until she spotted him coming out from the kitchen area, where she knew there was a back entrance.

Apparently Ms. Saben didn't miss her interest. "So that's the way it lies, huh?"

Sadie swung guilty eyes in the older woman's direction. "What?"

"Oh, honey, don't be embarrassed."

Too late. The dreaded heat had bathed Sadie's cheeks already.

"There's not a woman your age who hasn't pined over that one…and a few not your age, too." Ms. Saben giggled like a schoolgirl. "Talk about another good man. One who's had a hard life, but powered through. Nothing like his daddy, either."

And just like that, the seed was planted. There was a theme in both their families' lives—unwanted children. Did Zach have any kids out there he'd neglected? The heart that had yearned for him for five years said he was too responsible for that, too protective. But people were crazy sometimes. Did he have an ex hovering on the fringes, waiting to pounce or holding a child as leverage?

One glance at Ms. Saben told Sadie she had an inkling of the direction of her thoughts, so she might as well be honest. "Does he date a lot?"

Admiration shone in the older woman's gaze. "Honest answer? No. I haven't seen or heard of him dating more than three or four women—why, since he got home from the air force, I guess." She studied Zach as he greeted his mother behind the bar.

So did Sadie. The strong, protective stance drew her, as did the hug he gave his much smaller mother. Her heart instantly melted.

"Maybe that's why…" Ms. Saben mused.

Sadie turned her way. "What?"

Ms. Saben's gaze met hers. "He loves his mama."

Sadie nodded. "And his sister."

Approval lightened the older woman's gaze. "Men who know how to take care of women don't normally play around, because they know how it affects the woman being played with."

Like a ton of bricks, the knowledge hit Sadie. Zach

hadn't been playing with her—he wasn't that type of man and didn't have that kind of reputation. And she'd ruined it by walking away…even if she'd done it to protect him.

She couldn't face him with that knowledge so fresh in her heart. Not tonight. Maybe not ever.

Ten

Sadie had been to several impressive mansions throughout her lifetime. Her boss's home was essentially a villa at the end of a lane full of overblown palatial residences that offered every amenity imaginable, including an entire apartment for her in the refurbished barn whose rent came out of Sadie's salary.

But Blackstone Manor gave the impression of a family home despite its grandeur, starting with the red-rimmed eyes of a very fragile-looking butler. "Good afternoon, madam," he said solemnly, prompting an urge to hug him close and comfort him with hot tea.

Neither of which Sadie did, because this wasn't her home or her rodeo. But her natural sympathy, coupled with the fact that she genuinely liked the Blackstones, made it hard to remain objective.

Lily Blackstone had lingered into January. The family had been able to celebrate Christmas at home, and the

announcement of another brother's engagement, without
the black cloud of death intruding. That had come with
the frigid winds and gray skies of deep winter.

Sadie had been around Black Hills long enough now
to give her a tempting feeling of belonging. Some days
she wished she could live forever in this sleepy friendly
town, with its good, its bad and its quirks.

And except for a brief flight home one weekend to
visit her mom, she had.

She and Zach continued to participate in a dance of
sorts, a waltz that separated them and brought them close
again, but not nearly close enough. Sadie began to recognize that she was procrastinating. She didn't want to
have to make a decision, didn't want to figure out what
she'd do back home if she didn't get the money to bail
her sister out.

At least she was being paid for her current job, even
if it meant phone calls from a yelling, screaming Victor
almost every night.

Today, she wouldn't think about that. She wouldn't
give him the satisfaction of knowing how much he upset
her, and she would hold on to the knowledge that his private investigator hadn't had any more luck digging up
dirt on Zach than she had.

She greeted Mr. Callahan, Ms. Saben and the Batemans as she made her way across the front parlor. Finally she was beginning to feel welcome. How would
she ever live without this when she returned to Texas?

Christina and KC remained at the back of the parlor near the fireplace while many townspeople mingled
throughout the room.

"Hello, Sadie," KC said, pulling Sadie into a hug.
"We were hoping to get to see you."

"I'm so sorry," Sadie said, feeling the inadequacy of having no true way to comfort them.

"Thank you," Christina replied, ever gracious. "I'm glad you could come by."

Sadie glanced around. "This place is incredible."

KC grinned. "I felt the same way when I first stepped inside. I bet your photographer's senses are at full attention."

"Definitely."

The sound of a large group of people in the foyer had them all turning their heads in that direction. Several couples who had all arrived at the same time made their way to the Blackstone brothers first.

"Looks like we're about to have our hands full," Christina said, patting Sadie's arm. "We'll see you more in a little while, but please feel free to explore."

"And Zach is around here somewhere, too," KC added, her smile looking a little sly to Sadie.

KC hadn't made any secret of her approval as the two women had gotten to know each other more, and had hinted a time or two that she didn't understand why Sadie and Zach didn't at least go on one date. Obviously Zach had not filled his sister in on their history. Sadie wasn't going to do it for him.

It was simply another dark mark on the friendships she was creating here. She told herself she need never see these people again after she betrayed one of their own, which only reinforced the notion that she didn't want to cut them out of her life.

Dangerous thinking.

Sadie wandered around the room, studying the architecture and antiques while she conversed with more of the townspeople. Several of the men she'd gotten to know at the mill introduced her to their families. The

Batemans led her across the breezeway into a glorious dining room that had a full spread of food laid out.

They met up with another couple and were distracted talking, so Sadie wandered to the front of the room to look out the window. A man in a dark suit stood to one side of the front windows. He reminded her of other men she'd just passed in the breezeway and front parlor. They were so still they almost faded into the woodwork.

Security.

Then Sadie saw another man approach. She took in the dark tanned skin and close-cropped hair for the first time since she'd returned. He wore a dark suit and tie, along with dark sunglasses to protect his eyes from the winter glare. He paused beside the first man, the angle of his pose allowing her to see the wire for a communication device running up to his ear.

The entire time Sadie had been back in Black Hills, the impact of Zach's new position hadn't really become a reality to her. He'd been directing cleanup and safety crews at the mill. There were other days when she didn't see him at all, and she knew he had taken over an old, established house not far from the town square as his new business headquarters, but she'd never really asked what actually running a security firm entailed.

It made sense that a family who had been targeted for over a year and a half would want this time of grief to be peaceful and safe. They knew the most prominent people in the county, not to mention in the region, and all of the brothers had contacts elsewhere. A lot of people were going to be in and out of this house over the next week.

As he glanced up at the window, it hit home that it was Zach's job to ensure all ran smoothly and safely. Ever the protector. Ever the hero—without all the glory.

Looking at him only brought home just how opposite

they were in this situation. He was here to protect those around him. She was here to betray the one they trusted.

Turning, Sadie took her shame with her as she walked away. Surveying the people mingling and eating in the room, she noticed a small woman at one end of the sideboard picking up a half-empty tray and moving toward a door at the end of the room. Sadie hurried her steps to reach the door just as the woman did.

With a smile Sadie held it open so the woman could slip through unhindered. Sadie herself had performed the maneuver many times, but a helping hand had always been appreciated…and rarely offered.

"Thank you so much, sweetheart," the woman said.

Sadie followed her into a large kitchen filled with the scents of baking. "No problem," she replied, feeling her body relax almost instantly into an environment that held some familiarity for her. Being behind the scenes was much more her forte. "Is there anything I can do to help?"

Stacks of prepared foods in boxes lined several feet of counters. Coolers ran the length of the wall beneath the windows. A glimpse into an open pantry showed shelves lined with dishes and glasses. "Are you doing all of this yourself?" Sadie asked.

"Bless your heart for asking," the woman said, wiping her now empty hands on her apron before extending one toward Sadie. "I'm Marie, the Blackstones' cook and housekeeper." She glanced around at the organized chaos. "And while they know I can work miracles, no, they didn't leave me to do this alone. But the girls who are helping me have taken a quick break."

She shrugged her tiny shoulders, making her Kiss the Cook apron dance. "I thought we would have a bit of a lull, but I was obviously wrong. Normally Nolen would help, but he's got his hands full, too. But those girls have been on their feet all day—they deserve to at least eat lunch sitting down."

"And you don't?" Sadie asked, but she knew exactly how this went. When an event was in full swing, you simply performed the most urgent task, then the next, and the next, until everyone was satisfied. But this event would go on for a few days, which could get grueling.

Reaching for an apron hanging nearby, Sadie draped it over her dark gray dress. "Just point me in the right direction."

They chatted seamlessly for a good twenty minutes as they prepared and replaced platters. Sadie brushed aside Marie's protests as she loaded the dishwasher. It needed doing, so she did it.

Until a six-foot-two hunk of dark charisma walked through the doorway. Sadie couldn't help it—her every motion stopped, including her breath. Not too long, but long enough for Marie to notice.

Long enough to earn her a knowing grin from the older woman.

"So you're still here," Zach said.

If she hadn't been glancing in his direction, Sadie wouldn't have known he was speaking to her. She straightened. "Where else would I be?"

"When you disappeared, I assumed you went home without at least saying hi."

Her heartbeat resumed, a little faster this time. For a moment, she'd thought he meant here as in Black Hills, not here as in Blackstone Manor. "No, I'm just trying to lend a hand."

His dark gaze slid over to Marie. "She's good at that, isn't she?"

"Most definitely."

He approached the older woman and folded her carefully into his arms, as if she were too fragile to be in charge of an army's worth of food. "I'm sorry, Marie."

Tears prickled behind Sadie's eyes as the older woman seemed to melt into him. She'd given Sadie, and probably everyone else, the impression that she was coping just fine, thank you very much. But one hug and the facade shattered. She didn't cry, but the pain showed on her aging face nonetheless.

"I'd been with her since she was a baby," Marie said.

"I know," Zach murmured, so tender Sadie had to look away.

"The car accident was hard," Marie went on. "But she was still here, still with us. Then the stroke…she's really been gone since then, but it wasn't real, you know."

The words struck Sadie's heart unexpectedly. There were times when her sister got so sick that she disappeared into unconsciousness for days. One time the doctors had to put her in a medically induced coma. But she always came back…there was always hope. Lily Blackstone had had none.

A rustle of fabric drew Sadie's gaze once more. Marie had straightened and was smoothing down her apron. "I wish she could have been here to see all the boys come home." She smiled at Zach, though it was a little shaky around the edges. "Your sister. Carter. This new young'un on the way. She would have loved all of it."

Life. It had been all around Lily, but she'd been unaware. Amber was the same, in certain ways. Her life was a series of doctor visits, debilitating treatments, recuperating and quiet nights at home with her mom and sister.

How much longer before she had no life at all? The

weight of the thought sat on Sadie's chest, constricting her breath.

"Yes, she would have," Zach said. "She created a beautiful family."

"A legacy," Marie agreed.

And Amber would have none.

Suddenly the walls wavered. Sadie knew if she didn't get out of there, she was going to embarrass herself by either weeping copiously or passing out. Neither option made her very happy.

Her throat was too constricted to speak, to excuse herself. She lurched for the back door, stumbled through a closed-in porch, then burst into the weak sunshine. Not sure why, she kept moving forward, as if the motion would somehow jump-start her body into behaving again. But suddenly she was halted by a set of heavy hands on her shoulders.

Her body was pulled upright, then back against a solid, muscular chest. The warmth soothed her, making her aware that she was out in the cool January air with no coat over her dress. Just an apron. The thought made her want to laugh, but her lungs were strained.

Zach leaned in close, burying his face against her neck. His heat surrounded her. "Just breathe, baby," he murmured against her ear.

Zach felt Sadie's body unlock as if he'd turned the key. Breathing deep, she rose up on her toes. Then she collapsed back against him.

Leaving him feeling like he'd won the lottery.

He sensed her beginning to relax. The feel of her ribs expanding beneath his palms. The loosening of her muscles against his chest. The sigh that finally graced his ears.

He waited for her to sag as the tension drained from her, but Sadie was too strong for that. Instead her knees locked. She didn't pull away, but she wasn't relying solely on him for her stability, either.

That was the essence of the woman he'd come to know.

And she was kind, compassionate, hardworking. Today, he was determined to learn something new.

Stepping back was a hardship, but he substituted holding her hand for the embrace. A poor substitute, his body said. He led her to a bench near this end of the sloping back lawn. During the summer, irises bloomed plentifully here, but the now-barren leaves didn't detract from the richness of the view.

He took a quick inventory of her. Breath steady. Eyes closed. Pulse slowing beneath his palm. He waited a few minutes more before pushing.

"Tell me what that was about."

"A panic attack," she said simply. "I've had a few over the years, but they're so rare that I never feel quite prepared for them."

Her deep breath drew his gaze down to the fullness of her chest, even though he knew that's not where his focus should be right now.

"Marie's words...they just brought up some bad memories for me."

"Did you lose someone you love?"

She shook her head, but it wasn't really an answer—more the movement of someone trying to deny reality. "Not yet...but I will."

He waited, trying to wrap his mind around her words. Was it her mother? That was the only relative she'd ever mentioned.

"I have a sister...a baby sister."

Zach felt his world tilt slightly, then right itself.

"She was diagnosed when she was a teenager. The cancer is terminal at this point." A sad smile tilted the corners of her lips. "She's a trouper—it's been six years since her diagnosis. They said she would only live two."

Zach could read between the lines. "But she won't be able to fight it forever?"

Sadie shook her head, her lips pressed tight for control. Fortunately, he could read all her emotions in those expressive eyes.

"No," she finally conceded. "She's fought long and hard, but her resolve is weakening. As is ours—mine and my mother's. We take the best care of her we can, but there's only so much we can do."

"And that's heartbreaking."

"My poor mother—she's handled the majority of Amber's care, but it's too much. We had to place her in a type of halfway house. Not hospice…yet." Sadie looked away, but Zach could still see her neck working as she swallowed.

As he'd done with Marie, he reached out to comfort her. Only this wasn't Marie. He reacted in a completely different manner that shook him deep inside. But he didn't let go.

"I was still young myself, but about a year into her treatment I took over my mother's position as housekeeper for our former employer so she could stay home with Amber full-time. This trip is the longest I've been away from them, ever."

In her voice, Zach heard an echo of his own struggles with responsibility. The burden of doing whatever you had to in order to care for someone you love, regardless of where you wanted your own life to go. It was a heavy weight, one he hated to think of on Sadie's slim shoulders. But it came with its own rewards.

He was sure she knew that by now also.

"Why did you leave now, Sadie?"

She went still beneath his touch, and for a moment he worried that his question had seemed judgmental. But Zach was the last one to judge. He'd left his entire family behind for the military because that's what he'd needed to do to provide a better life for them.

"The trip—it was a legacy, of sorts, from our former employer," she said. "The chance to travel outside our little world. My mom wouldn't hear of me giving it up—neither of them would."

He knew he shouldn't ask, but he couldn't stop himself. "So you could go anywhere, and you chose to come here."

She quickly glanced at him out of the corner of her eye, which told him she realized the significance of the question. "Zach, this is the only place I wanted to be." She wiped shaky fingers over her cheeks. "I'm sorry. This is just a little too close," she whispered.

For a moment, he thought she meant him. But now she clutched his arms, her body leaning into his. Then he understood. Marie had been talking about life, the life Lily should have had.

The life Amber should have had.

"I know it is," he said. "And that's okay."

With a jerk her gaze swung up to meet his. He could read the conflict in her eyes. The woman she'd shown him was strong, independent, but soft with others. Now she needed to take care of herself.

"It's okay, Sadie. Feeling that way doesn't make you weak. It makes you human."

That's when the tears appeared, just like the night

she'd told him she missed her mother. They pooled like shiny puddles in her eyes, reflecting that incredible green color. He knew then, no matter what he really wanted, he would never be able to get over Sadie.

Whether she stayed or not.

Eleven

When her phone rang, Sadie was surprised to see Zach's name lighting up the small screen. But her hesitation lasted only a second before she answered.

"Pack a weekend bag and meet me downstairs."

She opened her mouth to reply, but the line went dead. Was he already downstairs? Should she go question him? Why was she even thinking about this?

Letting go of her worrisome thoughts, she packed her travel toiletries and enough clothes for two days into an oversize purse in record time. The sound of her feet on the stairs as she descended ramped up her heartbeat.

It had only been a day and a half since she'd seen him, but it seemed like forever. She'd chosen not to attend Lily Blackstone's funeral today, figuring she'd simply be lost in the throng of people who would be there. But Zach had surely braved the crowds for the family who had done so much for him.

When he'd last said goodbye at Blackstone Manor, he'd told her he would be in touch, but not when. That made sense, considering his position as head of security for the family. She definitely hadn't expected to speak with him tonight after what had undoubtedly been a long day.

Shouldn't he be home relaxing? Sleeping?

Yet there he stood in the foyer of the B and B, looking a little tired around the edges, but fresh in a pair of jeans and a T-shirt. She wished she could run her fingers through his hair or savor the sexiness of his gaze as he did a little inspecting of his own.

But he didn't linger. He quickly took her bag and led her out to a low, dark sports car. Still without an explanation, he seated her in the front, then stowed her bag in the trunk. Her first clue as to his intentions was his quick lean across the seat after he climbed behind the steering wheel. His lips on hers were hot and hard, telling her without words of the need he barely held in check.

Her anticipation exploded into full-blown excitement.

Good thing he wasn't dangerous, because she had no recollection of where they drove. Her entire focus was on the smallest of things: his hands on the steering wheel, the barest hint of music on the radio—too low for her to tell what it was—the shaking in her core that had nothing to do with fear and everything to do with Zach.

It wasn't until he pulled the car into an almost empty lot and parked that reality hit. She realized she needed to know. "Zach," she stalled, before he could open his door.

"Yes?"

His low voice only sent further shivers up her spine. "I'm guessing we're not going out to dinner?" She tried to keep her tone light, but Zach plunged straight into the deep end.

He leaned closer, invading her comfort zone. "We both know what's happening, Sadie. I think it's time to stop beating around the bush, don't you?"

"Um…"

"Don't pretend this isn't what you want." If his words didn't convince her, the way his lips traced her jaw definitely did.

But for once, she needed honesty between them. "I won't." Heaven knew she couldn't. "But how can it be what you want?" She swallowed hard but forced herself to finish. "After I left?"

"You were trying to do the right thing, weren't you?"

He would never know it, but she had. Her attempt to protect him from the callous, self-centered man who had been his father might not be the right thing in his mind, but it had been in hers. "Yes."

"That's the most important thing to me, Sadie."

She instantly cooled as he got out of the car and walked around to her side. If she hadn't known she would ultimately lose Zach, those words had spelled it out loud and clear. But she didn't have time to contemplate. Zach opened her door. His hand folded over hers, and he eased her out onto her feet. "I want you," he said, no longer holding back. "You have responsibilities away from here. I totally understand that."

He lifted her chin with his other hand, positioning her lips exactly right for his kiss. "If I only have you for this weekend, so be it."

Her defenses and resistance fell with his words, and she had a feeling she'd never be able to rebuild either again. Instead she took a deep breath and nodded. "Okay." Her voice wasn't too shaky, at least.

As he locked up the car, she glanced around. Parts of Black Hills had become fairly familiar to her by now, but she had absolutely no idea where she was at the moment. Zach grabbed their bags, then her hand and led her across the asphalt to a large metal building.

They were spending the weekend in a manufacturing plant? It certainly didn't have the romantic feel she would expect, but then, Zach was a guy. The dark night kept her from reading the sign farther down the wall. It wasn't until they passed through the double doors that Sadie got a clue.

They'd arrived at the small municipal airport. The too bright, fluorescent-lit space wasn't big enough for commercial traffic—mostly crop dusters and shuttle planes. Which also explained why it was mostly deserted at this time of the evening.

Zach dumped their bags near a grouping of chairs and waved her into a seat. "I'll just get everything set up."

Sure he would. She remembered him talking about loving every minute of learning to fly in the military, and he'd done some crop dusting in town until the notorious cotton killings last year.

"Zach, would you mind telling me what we're doing?"

He paused a few feet away, his expression filled with an almost childlike excitement. "Do you like surprises?"

A frown started between her brows. "I haven't had any good ones in my life."

"Well, let's try this one and see."

Zach felt like he'd spent the entire two-hour flight grinning—and he wasn't a grin type of guy. He preferred a smirk or a glare. But the reaction to Sadie's every gasp and sigh was unstoppable.

Despite her initial shock, it was clear she'd enjoyed the view, no matter their altitude. Zach's new private plane, no matter that it was small, made the trip pure pleasure. It was the first thing he'd bought for himself since he'd hit the big time. Add on the anticipation of being with Sadie, and yeah, he grinned.

He was giving himself a gift, and hopefully giving her one, too. He'd told her the truth: the past was the past. He didn't need a crystal ball to guess the future was uncertain. But for this weekend, they would have all they wanted of each other.

No more interruptions.

He took the plane down and handled the technicalities at the airport with ease but not nearly enough speed for his liking. It took way too long to get everything loaded into the Jeep he kept at the airport and get started on the road.

"We'll be at our destination in about twenty minutes," he said.

At least, he hoped so. He hadn't checked the weather forecast the way he normally did before his trips, and a light snow had started to fall as they ascended the mountain.

"Where are we going?" she asked.

"My favorite place in the world."

She didn't question him further but grinned herself. Then she turned her gaze back out the window to the darkened landscape. "Well, I already know it's beautiful," she said in a hushed voice.

As did he. The real estate agent was the most trusted in Black Hills, a woman Zach had known most of his adult life. He'd laid out his specifications, and in a week she had an even dozen options from a trusted network of agents all over the South. This one had stood out from the rest at first glance. He'd made the purchase without hesitation—and without familial consent. Heck, his family didn't even know the specifics about this place. And they'd never actually been here.

He came to the cabin regularly. Always alone. It was the one place he could let down his guard, let go of the ever-present responsibility and truly relax. He'd never wanted anyone else's personality to imprint on the place...until now.

Maybe he should have planned this a little more, but Zach knew all about trusting his instincts. The impulse was true. At least when Sadie was gone, he'd be able to come here and remember her.

Even he had to admit that the cabin looked charming as they arrived. The light, fluffy snow had started to accumulate on the nooks and crannies of the log house and roof. He parked out in front instead of pulling in close. The cabin wasn't large, though it did have two bedrooms and two baths. The second story held only the master bedroom, bath and sitting area.

Not big, but it had all the amenities he'd wanted. A wide wraparound porch perfect for relaxing. A balcony with a hot tub, accessible from the master suite. An environmentally friendly exterior finish. And the whole thing was surrounded on three sides by a forest dense with cedar and pine.

"Wow, Zach. This is gorgeous."

He helped Sadie out of the Jeep and grabbed both of their bags before leading her up the stairs to the porch. Her red hair glinted with snowflakes, tempting him to keep her outside to admire her beauty. But his body protested any further delay.

The security system and locks were a minute's work for him. Then they were stepping through the door into the slightly cool interior. Dropping the bags, he made a beeline for the opposite wall and adjusted the thermostat.

"I keep it cooler in here when I'm away—just high enough to keep everything from freezing—but it will warm up soon."

She nodded, her eyes twinkling with excitement as she surveyed the interior. "I'm serious, Zach. This has to be your best-kept secret. I love it."

Arms tucked around her to combat the chill, she wandered through the downstairs area. But her words held him still. Because the cabin was a secret of sorts. He never talked about it with anyone; he'd never even described it or shown his family any pictures, even though they knew of its existence.

Because deep down, he felt guilty for taking this time, this space for himself.

The admission stunned him. Guilt was a weakness he couldn't afford and didn't have the time to wallow in.

Suddenly Sadie stood before him, her appearance shaking him from his daze. "You're right," he told her, "it is my secret. You're the only person I've ever brought here."

Her green eyes widened. He could almost see the impact as his confession hit her. Then she narrowed her gaze on him. "Why, Zach?" she asked, soft-spoken but demanding in her own way. "Why wouldn't you want people to know about this part of your life?"

"They wouldn't understand why I want to be here… need to be here." The explanation burned in his throat.

Sadie reached out to him, offering comfort instead of the passion he'd planned on when he'd first walked through the door. "I understand. Sometimes life is overwhelming, and you need to recharge—somewhere away from all the things you feel like you have to take care of."

She stepped in close, the arm around his waist making him wish there was nothing between his skin and hers. "You've worked incredibly hard, Zach. You deserve this sanctuary for yourself."

"Sometimes it doesn't feel like it."

"Why?"

He shook his head. "If it wasn't for the Blackstone brothers, I'd probably be rotting in jail from that crop dusting incident. To have everyone patting my back... it just feels false."

Sadie wasn't buying it. "You've worked at the mill a long time, right? Long before you were head of security for the Blackstones."

Zach nodded.

"You've known most of those people all of your life, right?"

"Yes."

"I saw you with them, Zach," she said, squeezing him a little tighter. "I've watched you interact with them since that first trip out there. They respect you. Your direction and judgment."

Her gaze remained clear and direct, pulling him in.

"That doesn't come from Blackstone backing. You have to earn that. Which you did with your integrity and hard work. They know you because you've proven yourself time and again. And that's why they won't judge you for indulging in some of what we girls call me time every so often."

Her assessment left him speechless and in desperate need of a few minutes to himself. As if she completely understood, she graced him with a sweet smile and continued on her exploration.

Leaving him and his emotions behind.

Twelve

Eager for something to do, Zach carried the bags up the stairs to the master suite. Simply furnished in beige suede with accents reminiscent of the nearby woods, the atmosphere was soothing without being feminine. He dropped the bags, wondering where he would put Sadie's stuff.

With a self-deprecating shake of his head, he conceded that he hadn't thought through his plans for this visit very well. He could put her bag downstairs, but he wasn't about to give even a ghost of an impression that he wanted her that far away. Upstairs, he had a few drawers built into the closet, filled with his own clothes.

Maybe they'd stay busy enough that clothes wouldn't be necessary.

They definitely weren't necessary for what he had in mind. He glanced from the bed to the French doors leading to the balcony and hot tub. For the first time, Zach planned to explore every fantasy he could with a woman. Until now, he'd always held back. The intensity of his nature kept him cautious.

But tonight he was cutting the caution tape and diving in headfirst.

As he heard her footsteps on the stairs, a tremble started in his hands. Not hard enough to be seen, just subtle enough to be felt. He clenched his fists, unwilling to give in to the need to pounce the minute she strolled through the doorway.

But when she came in, she didn't look around, didn't inspect her surroundings with the curiosity she had downstairs. Instead her gaze rested solely on him.

Just as she had downstairs, she reached for him. Only this time, her touch wasn't intended for comfort. She moved in close. The faint scent of sugar drifted over him as her hands traveled across his chest to grasp the edges of his open flannel shirt. Slowly she pulled down, just hard enough for him to feel the weight. Then she let go and slipped her hands inside. The same feeling of need came over him, multiplied by a hundred.

But he refused to take the reins…just yet.

The light scrape of her nails against his ribs through the undershirt tested his resolve. His eyelids slid closed. A few deep breaths might help…

She pressed her mouth against the underside of his jaw.

…maybe not.

His heart raced as she nibbled and licked her way to his neck, then down along the sensitive skin of his throat. He growled a warning.

And heard her giggle.

With a quick move, he lifted her by her arms and tossed her lightly onto the bed behind them. A high-pitched squeal signaled her surprise. He stood his ground at the mattress's edge, staring down at her with the knowledge that the game was now his. He was in control. He would make the next move.

For both their pleasure.

"Strip."

The command sounded loud in the room, firm in its intent. Her eyes widened, and he didn't miss the catch in her breath. Slowly, as if to tease him, she crawled to her knees, then straightened. Her fingers traced up her sweater to the trio of buttons right below her breasts. He could almost feel the seconds tick out as she released each one with agonizing delays.

If she only knew just where that teasing would lead.

Next came the long-sleeved T-shirt beneath. How could a woman make pulling a shirt over her head so incredibly sensual? As she reached for the button of her jeans, the tremble in his hands became a reality.

The zipper traveled down ever so slowly. Just when he wondered how she would complete the move, she rolled confidently down onto her back. Holding his gaze with her own, she braced her knees and lifted her hips into his line of sight. She worked the heavy material down over her hips, then paused with her palms flat against her thighs.

Now it was his turn.

His patience at an end, he grasped the material and pulled. The jeans came off in one easy move. Sadie lost her balance as her feet were swept off the bed and fell back with a little bounce. The lamp on the bedside table left no shadows to hide her body. Zach was free to savor every inch with his gaze as much as his touch.

He took advantage as he systematically stripped his own clothes away. As he crawled onto the bed, a new feeling took hold of him. He didn't recognize it at first.

When he did, he probably should have been ashamed. After all, this was the age when women weren't owned by men. But deep inside, the urge to brand her as his was undeniable. To cover her body with his own and take her until no other man would dare touch what was Zach's alone.

Primitive. Forceful. Necessary.

He could concede that this relationship wasn't forever as long as he wanted to...but his body would never believe it.

Straddling her stomach and arms, he bent low over her upper body. Just as she had earlier, he pressed kisses along her lower jaw. Only his were openmouthed and hard, drawing moans from deep within her throat. He moved lower, sucking at the base of her neck where the delicate indentation between her collarbones begged for his attention.

She squirmed, but he wasn't giving her the chance to distract him with her touch. As he traveled out to the delicate structure of her shoulder, he swept the strap of her bra aside. Then he stripped the bra itself down to reveal pale, trembling mounds of succulent flesh. Pressing them together with his palms, Zach admired their strawberries-and-cream color before lowering his head to drive her wild.

Because he remembered everything that made Sadie moan, sigh and cry out. And he used that knowledge to his full advantage.

As much as he wanted to hold out, to extend their loving to the brink of insanity, the throbbing pulse between his thighs insisted otherwise. He made quick work of her undergarments, then took immense satisfaction in lifting her legs and wrapping them around his waist.

She needed no prompting but immediately pulled him

in tight. He barely had enough reach to snag a condom from the bedside table and cover himself. Then he slid home.

This time, there was no controlling his rhythm, no holding back. Their bodies strained in time with each other. Her cries filled the air. The feel of her fingernails on his back sent a sharp zing down his spine.

Almost over. Not yet. *Not yet.*

He buried his face at her throat, absorbing the vibration of her hoarse cries with his mouth. Her body tightened around him, a long, slow squeeze that pulled him in and sucked him dry.

It was many moments before Zach could open his eyes to the glare of the lamp beside them, even more before he could ease away from the tangle of their limbs. He made them both comfortable, then plunged the room into darkness.

A dim glow from outside permeated the French doors. Not the light of the moon, but maybe its shadowy reflection off the ever deepening snow on the deck. He lay on his side watching it, Sadie pulled close and secure against his chest. As he listened to the deepening of her breath, he had the same feeling he'd had on the nights before a few missions gone wrong. The sense that he'd made a mistake, missed something that was going to come back to bite him in the ass.

But he was too happy to care. If Sadie was a mistake, she was by far the best mistake he'd ever made.

"But I didn't bring a swimsuit."

The amused, calculating look in Zach's eyes told her he didn't care. Not in the least. "Well, I have one, but I promise not to use it."

Oh, she was in trouble. But she tried to protest anyway. "It's cold out there." The idea of the hot tub in the snow sounded romantic, but she'd have to actually go outside naked to accomplish it.

"So…"

As Zach tracked her around the bedroom, Sadie tried to think of another motive for staying inside. Normally, dawn was something she only saw for photo shoots. But this seemed to be her punishment for trying to ease out of bed and find a robe to cover her naked body. Now she attempted to both avoid Zach and keep the robe, which proved useless as he pounced.

Her squeal echoed in the room when he swept her into his arms and stalked for the French doors. The first blast of cold air on her bare bottom made her gasp.

Yep, exactly what she had wanted to avoid.

The Neanderthal carrying her didn't appear fazed. "Zach," she said. "I'm naked."

"And all the more beautiful for it."

Thankfully Zach had prepared the tub while she'd been in the bathroom. The cover was already off and steam rose in smoky tendrils from the water. After a few steps, he tilted her until her toes met the blessed warmth. Inch by inch he eased her in until the water covered her like a blanket. Then he slid his sleekly muscled limbs in behind her.

The water bubbled against her skin, reawakening the sensual needs that simmered below the surface whenever Zach was anywhere close. Zach's strong hands kneaded her shoulders, further weakening her resistance.

"See," he murmured. "This is worth the walk, right? Or rather, the ride?"

"Totally," she mumbled back. "And I'll believe that until the minute I have to get out and walk back into the house."

Zach laughed, the sound echoing around them. "Then I better make the interim worthwhile, huh?"

You always do.

But she didn't let herself say the words out loud. She let her body speak them instead.

It wasn't long before Zach's hands moved from working their heavenly magic on her shoulders back up into the wildly tangled locks of her hair. He alternated hands, squeezing and pulling one at a time, just enough to release the tension from her scalp.

Sadie thought she might melt into eternal bliss.

Every touch, every word spoken became a treasure to hide in her heart. The only gift she might ever be able to give herself, because once she had to leave him, nothing else would ever compare to these memories.

Suddenly his hand in her hair was guiding her. A nearby seat hidden in the bubbles became a shelf for her to brace against. The vista before her swirled with dancing snow swept up from the forest floor, and the saturated pinks and blues of sunrise reflected off sparkling icicles.

She felt Zach's warm skin against her back, forming a shield between her and the cool air. Not that she noticed. Her mind was too focused on the moment when he made them one, bringing their bodies together in a connection as glorious as the beauty around them.

He moved inside her, all around her. The water splashed and bubbled in an accompaniment to their harsh breath. His fingers continued their ballet of tightening and letting go, building her anticipation.

"You're so beautiful, Sadie," he murmured with his mouth against her shoulder, only adding to the myriad sensations.

How could she ever let go of such perfection?

In response to the thought, her body clamped down, desperate to hold him within her for as long as she could. She arched her back, trying to take him deeper. To make him as much a part of her as she could.

He moved in and out, every drag and pull intensifying her response. The low rumble of his voice added to the tingles, coaxing her into submission, commanding her response. Finally, just as the sun peeked over the horizon, her orgasm rolled through her, forcing Zach to catch his breath. He held still, buried in her inch by glorious inch.

Her mind exploded along with her body, screaming the knowledge of her love for this man. So loud, she had to bite down on her tongue to hold the words inside. Instead tears fell, mingling with the steam surrounding them.

Zach groaned, thrusting a few last times before he slowed down with a sigh. He pressed firm kisses along her shoulder as his arms surrounding her trembled ever so slightly. He murmured tender, soothing words against her skin.

Something inside Sadie died at the thought that she couldn't have him forever. But as her eyes drifted closed, she did her best to imprint every second to memory.

Then again, how could she ever forget any of these incredible moments? She only hoped she never did.

There was a lot to be learned about another person when you spent several days in a row alone together, just as Sadie did during their time snowed in at the cabin. Sharing the same bed brought a whole wealth of knowledge.

And not just about sex.

For instance, Zach was a side sleeper. He cuddled in

close every night, but her position didn't seem to matter. She could face out spoon style, or snuggle her cheek against his chest. Either way, he almost never moved more than the barest shift. He wasn't a tosser and turner, which made sleeping with him a bit like having access to her own human pillow that supported her body and didn't self-adjust after she'd made herself comfortable.

It might have sounded uptight, but Sadie had learned after many interrupted nights' sleep with her sister that she could only be awakened so many times before her brain started to short-circuit. Sleep was, quite frankly, important to her.

Tonight, their third here, started the same as both the other nights. Sadie drifted off to sleep wondering how many more nights she would have like this. Would they be going home tomorrow? Were the roads safe up here? She hadn't had more than the briefest of glimpses out at the road and wasn't sure that she wanted one.

Frankly, she didn't want their time together to end.

An adulthood spent in a sickroom had given her the unfortunate ability to instantly wake up at the slightest noise or movement. Only Zach's movements weren't slight.

First he flopped onto his back so that his side bumped against her back. She rolled over to face him then snuggled up to a pillow instead. He was probably trying to get comfortable. Then he jerked again, mumbling something under his breath.

A little odd for the man who usually slept like a rock for six hours a night. Reaching out, she laid her palm against his bare chest. His skin was hot, with a light sheen of sweat.

A few seconds later, he jolted again. Then again, and again. It took her a few minutes to realize that the man she thought couldn't be shaken was having a nightmare. Seconds later he rolled over, this time throwing out an arm that caught her unawares as it struck against her side.

Her gasp sounded loud in the room. Suddenly, Zach sat straight up, his body at attention. Sadie froze, too, not sure whether or not it was safe to reach out again. Who knew what Zach was reacting to—and she had a feeling he wasn't entirely awake.

So she held still, counting the spaces between his breaths, waiting for him to gain consciousness. As he did, the feel of the room changed. His muscles loosened one by one. Then the sound of a ragged breath met her ears, interrupted by a hard swallow.

When he turned to her, she couldn't see his expression in the gloom, but she could hear the emotion in his voice. "Sadie? Sadie, are you okay?"

Now she sat up, automatically reaching out a hand to rest against his biceps. "I'm okay, Zach."

She barely made out the shadow of him shaking his head. "I think—I think I hit you." His ragged breathing continued. "I'm damn sorry, Sadie."

"I'm perfectly fine," she assured him. "It was more like a bump. I was just in the way, Zach. No harm done."

"I still shouldn't have…"

That's when she realized there was a slight tremble beneath her palm. Not a full-blown reaction. Something she suspected he was using all his might to control. But it was there, all the same.

"That must have been a doozy of a nightmare," she said.

Even Sadie, who kept a lot to herself, would have wanted to talk something like that out. If for no other reason than to rid herself of the haunting images that could linger after a very intense nightmare.

Apparently Zach didn't, because he was silent. Which was fine. It wasn't for her to decide what Zach wanted to share. But that didn't stop her protective instincts from surging to the front.

Being protected, being taken care of, was as foreign to Zach as it was to Sadie. She wasn't going to let that hold her back.

Curling her fingers around his elbow, she pulled him in her direction. He resisted at first, but she wasn't giving up. As he twisted toward her, she reached for his other arm, then used them to guide him down against her. She lay back against her pillow, positioning him along her side.

"It's okay, Zach," she repeated softly.

Her heart leaped as he buried his face against her neck, but she held still. It took time. Soon his skin was flush against hers, his breath puffing gently along her collarbone and his arm heavy across her waist. There were no more signs of the shakes, but she sensed a struggle for balance. One she couldn't influence, but she could provide a safe haven until he found it.

She embraced his shoulders, securing him to her. Then she closed her eyes and measured her breaths. Soon his breathing matched hers, his rhythm evening out. Only then could she truly relax deep down inside, no longer worried that the nightmare would win.

He might not sleep well, but at least his body could rest.

But sleeping didn't seem to be what he had in mind. Just as she began drifting toward slumber, his leg shifted over hers, sliding between her thighs. Languidly his hand explored what flesh it could find.

And she was more than happy to welcome his touch. She kept waiting for him to speed up, to channel the adrenaline from his dream into a headlong rush for oblivion. Instead, he seemed to lose himself in pleasuring her, drawing out every caress to gift her with the ultimate in sensation.

Sadie found herself drowning in the unexpected sensuality that lasted longer than she could have dreamed possible, until every inch of her body was imprinted with the memory of Zach on a cellular level that meant he would be with her forever.

She still wasn't sure if a forever without him was something she could survive.

Thirteen

Zach let Sadie sleep.

It was the least he could do after waking her up last night. The thought that he could have hurt her during his dream hung like a chain around his neck.

Something he wasn't proud of.

But he'd survive. He'd learned long ago that he could do this. He would do this. Healing just took time.

As did other things.

He remembered staring down at Sadie's back as he made love to her in the hot tub. The flex and pull of her muscles fascinated him, because they represented the strength and character of a woman who worked hard and provided for others when she could. A woman he loved.

If he'd had any doubts before now, they'd been obliterated last night. But emotions were much easier to face and acknowledge in the dark of night. Now he was about to face her across the breakfast table, and he had some explaining to do…

Which always went down better with food. His mama had taught him that.

He was in the middle of cooking up waffles, scrambled eggs and bacon from the supplies his caretaker had brought in when Sadie made her way into the kitchen. The sexy tumble of her hair made him think of all the things he'd done to her during the night. His body's elation muted the slight panic over his plan for this morning.

Her gaze followed him as he moved, but she didn't ask any questions. He could go with it and not bring up the nightmare he'd suffered for the first time in a year or more, keeping his secrets to himself. He hadn't even fully shared the experience that caused the nightmares with his family.

But he saw that as the dipwad way of handling this. He wasn't going to take the easy way out—that wasn't the kind of man he was.

"Are you trying to butter me up?" she asked, peering over his shoulder. "Because waffles are definitely the way to go."

He'd noticed her love of both waffles and pancakes whenever Gladys served them at the B and B. So he might have been working with a little insider knowledge.

"Do I need to?" he asked, glancing at her over his shoulder as he plated the food.

Sadie didn't look away or back down. Her gaze held his. "Absolutely not."

Good to know. He hadn't hurt her when he was thrashing around last night. She'd told the truth—she was fine. Now he would do the same.

He let her dig in first, lifting forkfuls of buttery,

syrupy goodness to her lips before he got down to the dirty details.

"A lot happens in the years you serve your country," he started. "Some of it is good—very good. Like the men and women you serve with. They become like a second family."

He chewed thoughtfully on a piece of bacon. Sadie had slowed her own bites, as if her initial hunger had been eased somewhat.

"Some of it is bad—very bad."

"I'm sure." Her soothing voice coated his nerves like a balm. It was the very thing that had drawn him to her five years ago, that voice.

"One particular day was beyond bad." He blinked, questioning for a moment whether he could actually do this. With a deep breath, he forced himself to continue. "I thought we were all gonna die. My platoon. My brothers." Without warning his throat tightened, closing off his voice, his breath. The memory of that day could still tear him up even now. "But a friend, my best friend, actually, saved us all by throwing himself over an IED."

Unable to handle whatever sympathy he might see in her face, he stared down at his plate. "He died instantly."

Abstractly, he noticed the tight grip his fingers now had on his fork and forced them to loosen one by one. This mere exercise in concentration helped get him back on track.

"The nightmare is always the same," he said. "I go back through the entire day, but I'm only observing it. I can't stop anything from happening. I see all of the things I missed, everything I could have done to stop it."

He clenched and unclenched his fists. "I yell at myself until I'm hoarse, but it does no good. I watch helplessly, unable to prevent his death like I should."

Her gentle voice intervened. "Why should you?"

"It's my job," he said, handing over the rote answer, the least complicated one.

"You're right," she answered. "You are responsible."

That had him looking up, misery snaking through his heart. But she reached out to cover his hand with her own. "Because you've made yourself responsible. But your friend would not want you to spend your life beating yourself up.

"Just like my sister doesn't want me to stay home—" she pulled back from him "—to stop living, just for her. Their wishes don't ease the sense of obligation or guilt, but ultimately, they want us to live, even though they can't."

Sadie dropped her fork onto her plate. He thought about her sister and how hard it must have been for her to encourage Sadie to leave her. He thought about his own mother and the many times she'd told him to go out and have fun.

Yet the only way he could do that was at an isolated cabin in the woods, because everywhere else he went there were things to do and people to take care of.

"Is that why you left the military?" Sadie asked.

Zach sat for long moments, unable to answer. The turmoil and confusion of that time complicated his thoughts. He finally said, "No. I really did want to come home to take care of my family. I hadn't planned to re-up for another tour. After the inquiry, I didn't have the heart for another go-round anyway."

He glanced over at Sadie, surprised to find her eyes had widened as she stared at him. But her expression quickly melted into a compassion he hadn't even known he was hoping for.

"Your family needs you," she said, then waved her

hand through the air. "You need this. There's nothing wrong with it."

Taking the few short steps around the table, Zach knelt next to Sadie's chair and buried his face in her lap. His eyes were squeezed tight. He stayed there for a few minutes, taking comfort from her wisdom and willingness to share.

His grip tightened for a moment, unwilling to let go, and for the first time in over five years, he started to believe.

Sadie knew what she had to do the minute she got back to Black Hills, but still put it off for a few days. Every phone call from her mom increased her procrastination instead of spurring her to finish this farce. Every angry email, text and phone call from Victor increased her guilt.

The excuses were growing slim.

It hadn't helped that she'd been completely out of contact for four days. Rather than risk a call while she was with Zach, she'd simply shut her phone down, turning it on only to call her mother each night. She'd sent her pictures of the gorgeous scenery covered in snow, including some she took when they went hiking in the dense woods.

Those four days seemed like a space and time outside harsh reality. Now she had glorious memories of Zach to hold on to for years to come—years that were sure to be even lonelier and colder than the last five.

But she had to check one more thing about Zach. This was the last avenue open to her. If nothing came of it, she'd already determined that she wasn't going to lie just for the money. No matter how scared that left her.

She would call the lawyer, bypassing Victor completely, and tell him she would give an affidavit testifying to what Victor had hired her to do, all the avenues she'd explored and that Zach was squeaky-clean and eligible for his father's inheritance.

Then she'd walk away once more. At least if she disappeared she wouldn't have to see Zach's face when he realized who she really was, why she was really here.

It was the coward's way out—but her reserves of strength were leaking out with the speed of an hourglass. So she was looking into the only option left: Zach's military service.

The chance that she might have to use something so personal—his very intimate confession—against him...

Well, the thought made her sick to her stomach.

She'd done a preliminary search on her laptop, just to see if there was anything out there. Gaining access to military records wasn't an option, but if the incident was big enough, it might have been reported by local media outlets in the US, especially in the deceased's hometown.

Quite a few hits had shown up, but she didn't dare read them when Zachary could walk in at any moment. Lately he spent more time with her at the B and B than he did at home—though he never offered to take her to his place.

They spent so much time together, the landlady had casually mentioned charging her for a second person. Sadie had adopted a deadpan expression and said, "Sure"—which had left Gladys a little startled.

Now Sadie glanced around the local library, wondering exactly how to use the computer system. She figured doing this anonymously on a public computer was the safest way to go. If she signed in as a guest, no one would be able to trace it back to her.

Finding the bank of computers near the back of the

building, she was grateful to see they were mostly un-occupied. She signed in at the desk, using her sister's name on the form. Then she chose the last computer on the end of the row, figuring there would be less chance of people reading over her shoulder.

Logging on, she retraced her internet search on this computer in a safe browser. Odds were, it was a useless precaution. After all, who would think to look at her browser history here? But just in case...

The first link happened to be to the website for the local Black Hills paper. Following it brought her to the electronic archives for the paper, but it needed a log-in for access. Deciding to come back to that, she tried a few more links.

The local paper for a small town in Pennsylvania wasn't password protected. Sadie was able to learn the name of Zach's friend who died, read the basics of his death and see pictures of him, his fellow soldiers and his grief-stricken family.

Sad. Very sad.

As if that wasn't heartbreaking enough, there were excerpts from Zach's speech at his friend's memorial service, held after the soldiers made their final trip home. But it was a random sentence, late in the article, that told her she had to search further. As commanding officer, Zach had faced an inquiry into his friend's death. No results were mentioned there, or in any other articles she read.

Frustrated, Sadie dropped back against her chair with a short sigh. What should she do now?

"Are you finding everything you need, ma'am?"

No. Sadie looked up into the face of a young woman who had a library volunteer tag on her shirt. No one had bothered her here in the corner, and Sadie had been grateful for the privacy. But maybe this young woman would know…

"Does the library have access to the local newspaper's archives?"

The woman smiled. "We have the oldest editions on microfiche, but we have a subscription to the modern edition that's available online."

Well, wasn't that handy. Sadie might have been happy if this wasn't such an awful thing to be doing.

The young lady got her logged in and showed her how to search the archives.

"So I can just put in a date range, like this?" Sadie asked, typing in the dates for the two months after the incident.

"Yes," the volunteer answered. "When you do that, it comes up in this neat preview version." The screen filled with rows of little preview boxes, each with a thumbnail picture inside and a date directly below it.

"Cool," Sadie said, scanning the pictures.

"You're the photographer lady, right?"

Startled, Sadie looked up at the girl. Cautiously, she nodded, but the other woman didn't seem to notice her sudden reticence. What if she started blabbing about Sadie's search?

"I thought so," the young woman went on. "I saw you at the mill one day when I was there to take my dad some medicine while he was working on the cleanup. I heard some of the workmen talking about you." She reached across to take control of the mouse so she could choose one selection pretty close to the middle. "You might find this interesting, since I heard you were spending a lot of time with Zach Gatlin."

Sure enough, the preview had a photo of half of Zach's face on one side, something that Sadie hadn't had time to scan down to see yet. When the woman clicked, the front page of the paper loaded, including a story with the headline Hometown Hero Returns After Tragic Ending to Tour.

Sadie sat frozen, unwilling to believe the woman had picked out the very story she needed to read.

"It was the talk of the town, even before he came home," she went on. "He was lucky to even be alive. I just happened to be in Lola's when KC brought him home from the airport. I'll never forget his mama's face."

Having met Zach's mom and seen how much she loved her son, Sadie could very much imagine.

The young lady looked up as another employee appeared on the other side of the computer terminals and said, "Sweetie, Miss Jane needs a bit of a hand with story time, if you don't mind."

"Sure," the volunteer said with an eager smile, then turned to Sadie. "Hope that helps. If you need anything else, just flag one of us down." Sadie was grateful for her eagerness to help, but she needed to be alone...now.

"Will do." But Sadie sincerely hoped this was her last avenue of investigation.

It wasn't until the women walked away that Sadie read through the story. It looked as though Zach's involvement had indeed been questioned. But right below the picture of him and his sister embracing at the airport, it stated that he'd been found not guilty of any wrongdoing.

Sadie searched through nearly a month's worth of articles until she finally found the most in-depth account she could have gotten. It was obvious from the cautious tone of the article that the author didn't yet know the outcome of the inquiry.

According to the author's source, there were accusations of inadequate planning and reconnaissance, which could have meant anything, since the military was unlikely to release every detail that was being questioned. Zach was being held responsible in his friend's death, since he was the highest-ranking member of the team and had given the orders during the mission.

After reading all the way through, then one more time for good measure, Sadie cleared her browser history and closed the window. She leaned back, then looked up at the ceiling, as if the answer to her question could be found there. Even without her bias toward Zach, Sadie could tell this was just an instance of wrong place, wrong time. Zach had gotten off without even a reprimand, as far as she could tell.

But that didn't stop him from searching for what he could have done differently to save his friend. The nightmares were his mind's way of playing out his questions and his guilt. They were lessening with time, but would probably never go away.

That was punishment enough.

Now Sadie knew the truth. Her own search was over—her own guilt just beginning.

Fourteen

Sadie was once more wearing her fancy blue dress from the Blackstones' party, hoping those who had seen it before would understand she was from out of town and hadn't traveled with a steamer trunk full of formal gowns.

Her heart pounded as she waited for Zach, nausea welling up inside her. He'd paused to talk with the country club valet, whom he knew from working at the mill. If she could just stand here and watch him forever, she'd be so happy.

But deep down, she knew she had to end this tonight. Somehow she would find the courage to tell him the truth. He deserved to know how to claim his inheritance, and she'd decided he should hear it from her.

But first, just one more night together. One last memory.

Finally he headed her way, his dark good looks set off by the black suit and tie. She savored the way his gaze traced her body. No other man would make her feel as wanted as Zach did. She knew that beyond a doubt.

They joined the Blackstones at their table. Sadie realized she must be getting used to attending these events with Zach, because that feeling of unreality she usually experienced had disappeared. Too bad this wouldn't last. As soon as she returned to Dallas, she'd be extra busy looking for a new position. Hopefully in the same social circles her former boss had enjoyed, so she could continue to keep their heads above water as best she could.

Victor had continued to pay her regular salary, in addition to all of her travel expenses, as if she were on a regular business trip, instead of seeking to ruin a man's reputation. But when she came back empty-handed, all of that income would end.

She had some contacts within those social circles, so that might help. But her foremost concern was that her sister needed to remain close to the hospital and doctors who currently treated her. Sadie would hate to be separated from her family, but without the bonus from Victor, for finding dirt to disqualify Zach from his inheritance, finding work would be essential.

Wherever she could find it.

Christina sat opposite Sadie. The tired cast to her face prompted Sadie's concern. The poor thing must be exhausted after handling her mother-in-law's death, plus her own grief and her pregnancy, too. "How are you, Christina?" Sadie asked quietly, not wanting to draw undue attention.

The other woman's smile seemed bittersweet. "I'm managing. Just trying to focus on what's right in front of us, you know?"

Sadie didn't, but she could imagine, so she nodded.

Before she could respond further, Aiden rose from

his chair to look over the table. Everyone's attention turned to him. He appeared comfortable in his role as head of the family. His normally tough gaze as he took in those around him seemed to soften and glow. "Thank you for being here tonight. We wanted our family and closest friends here to celebrate the joy that is coming to our family—our newest baby, who will be joining us soon, along with the return of our brother Luke and his engagement to one of Black Hills's own treasures, Avery Prescott."

Quiet applause and smiles erupted. Sadie glanced down the length of the table, noting the people she recognized. Luke Blackstone and his fiancée were new to her, along with an older couple someone had mentioned were a doctor and his wife, friends of both the Blackstones and Prescotts, and mentors of Avery Prescott. Zach and Bateman and his family were there from the mill. She was impressed to see both Nolen and Marie present, along with a younger woman Marie had introduced to Sadie as her niece, Nicole. There was a mix of ages, stations in life and connections, but Sadie had found that the Blackstones embraced others based on their presence in their lives, not what they were capable of doing for them.

The viewpoint was refreshing for Sadie. She only hoped she could find future employers who were as real as the people she'd come to know here.

As they were served their meals, Sadie felt Zach's hand circle around her own. She turned to find him watching her with the fire and need she so desperately wanted to see in his eyes.

"You look beautiful tonight, Sadie," he said. "I love you in this dress."

Her throat closed for a moment. Hearing those first

three words on his lips meant the world to her, even if he didn't mean them the way she wished. "I love you in that suit," she finally whispered. "Very dashing."

"Dashing, huh? Debonair, too?"

Oh, that grin was dangerous. "Most definitely."

"Well, I promise to be a gentleman." He leaned forward to brush a kiss high on her cheekbone, right in front of her ear. Then he whispered, "For now."

The shiver that worked its way down her spine caused her to squeeze the hand still holding hers. How much longer could she hold him to her?

They were interrupted by the arrival of their food. Sadie leaned back as her soup was placed before her, followed by a plate of oysters for their end of the table to share. As she glanced over the half shells coated in some kind of breading and cheese mixture, her stomach turned over again.

She sucked in a breath through pursed lips, then slowly released it. *Nope, not helping.* "Excuse me a moment," she murmured to Zach.

Luckily she'd seen where the restroom was on their way inside. Her stomach had calmed again before she reached the door, but she went inside anyway. Running cool water over her wrists helped also. Lord, she needed to get her nerves under control. Life was never easy, but why ruin her last night with Zach by anticipating the earthquake that she knew was coming?

Did she even believe what she was telling herself right now?

The door opened behind her. Christina and KC stepped inside. Both women flocked to her with concern in their expressions.

"Are you okay?" Christina asked, patting her back gently.

She nodded as KC asked the same. "Yes, I've just been feeling a little off somehow."

"Zach was worried when you left so quickly. I told him we would check, though you were probably fine."

"Sorry. Didn't mean to scare anyone."

"Well, I only have to make about fifty trips a night to the bathroom right now," Christina said with a laugh as she headed for a stall. "So I'd be here soon enough anyway. If it had been any earlier in my pregnancy, those oysters would have turned me green. I wouldn't have even made it back here." She flashed a grossed-out face over her shoulder before shutting the door.

"Oh, me, too," KC said from beside Sadie as she patted over her hair. "Of course, any kind of seafood got to me. It wasn't so much the look of it as the smell. Yuck." She grinned. "I was so glad when that stage went away, because I love me some shrimp."

Sadie felt her stomach twist again as her mind conjured up the image of shrimp scampi, usually one of her favorites. She breathed carefully, glancing at the mirror to make sure her queasiness didn't show on her face. No need to cause more concern.

KC opened her little clutch purse and proceeded to touch up her already perfect makeup. Christina returned and washed her hands. "It's not completely gone for me," she was saying. "The nausea isn't nearly as bad as it was in the first trimester, of course, but some things will still set it off sometimes. And the exhaustion. Oh, boy."

"I know what you mean," KC agreed. "You have more than just the pregnancy to make you tired, but I sure remember trying to wait tables with swollen feet and that bone-tired feeling weighing me down. That was rough."

As the women talked around her, Sadie stared into the mirror. She could actually see the blood drain from her already pale skin. Her light dusting of freckles stood out in stark contrast, as did the glossy pink of her lips. Nausea. She'd put it down to nerves. Exhaustion. She'd simply pushed it aside as too many late nights with Zach.

Her gaze dropped to her chest, as she suddenly remembered the recent tenderness of her breasts. She'd chalked it up to hormones, but this would be about the third week they'd been unusually sensitive.

That wasn't normal.

"Are you coming, Sadie?"

She glanced up, realizing the others were readying to leave. "Oh, I'll just, you know." She nodded toward the stalls. "Then I'll be right out."

They smiled, sure they'd done their duty, then headed back out to their dinner. Sadie couldn't have felt less like eating.

As the sound of their chatter faded, she closed herself in a stall, leaning heavily against the inside of the door. Her mind raced, frantically counting out the days she'd been in Black Hills, the number of days since she'd first seen Zach again. Finally, the number of days since they'd made love that first time.

Please. Could she please just stop thinking? Stop remembering? But it was no use. She didn't have experience with pregnancy herself and had never been around anyone who was having a baby. Her time with Christina was as close as she'd gotten.

Which wasn't much. But based on how off she'd felt the last few weeks—something she'd chalked up to guilt, nerves and grief—Sadie was afraid she'd added one very large complication to her already tangled situation.

Heaven help her.

* * *

Zach lengthened his stride, hoping to make it through the foyer before Gladys heard the door close behind him. He didn't have long before he had to be at the office. KC was helping him get their newest team member settled in town. They were signing the paperwork on his new apartment before she brought him by the office for the first time.

Zach needed to be there.

But he was worried about Sadie. She'd gone home early from the dinner the night before, afraid she'd come down with a stomach bug. She'd even insisted on taking a cab home, expressing concern about interrupting the event and also about infecting him.

He'd let her go, only after she'd promised to text when she got back to the B and B. There were still things they didn't know about each other—for all he knew, she was the type who wanted to be left alone when she was sick. Like him.

She'd texted him when she got back and had even mentioned that she'd stopped at the pharmacy for some meds to help calm her stomach. He hadn't heard from her since.

A quick peek to assure himself that she was okay would be enough for now.

But later, they needed to have a talk. Zach was perfectly happy to let her be, as long as she touched base every so often to let him know she was okay. Preferably from the other end of the room, rather than the other end of town.

Otherwise, those dang protective instincts kicked in, and he worried something had happened—

Zach paused outside Sadie's door, hand raised to knock. The contrast between what he wanted with Sadie and what he had with her hit him hard. He'd proceeded on tiptoes, not demanding too much too soon, not asking for what he truly needed, afraid that if he pushed too hard, she would leave again.

Maybe he'd been overcautious. They were practically living together, and yet he'd let her go home sick without him the night before. He stood outside her door right now, waiting to knock, because he didn't want to intrude. How ridiculously careful all of this was.

With a frown, Zach tried the doorknob. It clicked, then opened. He walked inside. It was that easy.

Glancing around, he was alarmed to see the bed empty, blankets half hanging off the side, as if they had trailed after the person trying to leave them behind. No Sadie in sight. He heard the shower running.

Okay. She was steady enough to want to shower. Good deal. He'd just wait until she got out. After making sure she didn't need anything, he'd head over to the office for a while, then come back. He crossed to the bed to straighten up the covers. A tissue box and mound of crumpled, used tissues covered the nightstand.

Odd, she'd said her stomach hurt, not that she had a cold.

Once more he looked around, this time hunting for the small trash can he knew to be around here somewhere. He finally located it under the low table in the sitting area. It was already filled with tissues. That explained one thing, at least. As he stood there wondering if he should risk calling Gladys for a new trash bag, Sadie's phone lit up.

An incoming text message.

He didn't recognize the name Victor Beddingfield, but the preview of the message on the screen below the name made Zach do a double take.

Hell no, I don't care what happens to Zach Gatlin, as long as he doesn't show up here wanting...

Wanting what? And why was this stranger texting about him?

The mere use of his name gave Zach the right to pick up that phone, in his opinion. And right now, his was the only opinion that mattered. He swiped his thumb over the screen. Zach only wished he could honestly say he didn't know Sadie's combination to unlock the screen. Unfortunately, it was a connect-the-dots picture that he'd watched her swipe in many times. The order of the combination played out in his mind's eye with ease.

He didn't even hesitate.

As a soldier, Zach knew that doing ugly things was sometimes necessary to get the job done. Right now, breaking into Sadie's phone was one of those necessary things. Regardless of how other people would see it.

A violation of her privacy? Sure. Overstepping his boundaries? Definitely. A decision he'd regret in time? Absolutely not.

Zach would rather know the truth than live in a fantasy world. The phone blinked its notice that Sadie had a text message at the bottom. He clicked on it and saw the truth in full color.

At the top of the screen, there was a text from Sadie in a white bubble: I will call soon.

Then a blue bubble from Beddingfield: If you don't call me within the hour, this is gonna get really ugly. I want this over. Do you hear me?

Followed by Sadie's response: Don't you care at all what happens to Zach? I'm trying very hard to do the right thing.

Hell no, I don't care what happens to Zach Gatlin, as long as he doesn't show up here wanting our father's money. You said you would dig up the dirt and I want it now. If you have to lie to disqualify him, that's what you'll do. I make the rules here. You simply obey me.

Deep in Zach's chest, coldness bloomed, then spread. Questions whirled in his brain. First and foremost: Who was this person? And what did he mean by "our father"? Was Victor Sadie's brother, talking about the two of them when he said "our"? But they had different last names.

Or was he Zach's brother?

Zach didn't know his father, so half or stepbrothers were definitely a possibility. Though the fact that his father would want to have other children when he couldn't be bothered to care for the one he already had was hard to take.

The second line of thought was the more painful one. He didn't even want to think about it. Didn't want to form the words that would rip apart the foundation he'd thought he was standing on for the last two months. But as the water shut off in the bathroom, he knew the detonation was coming.

The phone was still in his hand. He didn't bother to put it down, didn't bother to move. By the time Sadie came through the door, he'd even stopped breathing. That cold, cold part of him wanted to thaw, wanted to go to her.

Her long auburn hair was piled in a messy bun atop her head. She looked tired, her features slightly drawn. Her naked body was wrapped in one of the fluffy towels he'd often used to dry her. When she saw him, her eyes widened, but then she produced a small smile.

"Zach, you startled me," she said. "I didn't know you were coming."

Before he could speak, the phone in his hand rang. Her gaze flicked down to it, alarm invading her expression when she saw it in his hand. It played through an entire ringtone, then went silent. Zach's fingers tightened. Almost immediately the ringing started again.

Zach reached out, offering the phone to her. "Beddingfield wants an answer to his question," he said. "Don't you think you should take his call?"

Fifteen

The fact that she could take the phone from Zach's hand and switch it to mute actually amazed Sadie. Her body shook so hard she wouldn't have thought the move was even possible.

But she did it. Because she had to—because she deserved whatever Zach was about to dish out.

But she'd rather not do it in just a towel.

Turning away, she dropped the phone on the bed and reached for her robe. She hadn't even gotten it over her shoulders before Zach's questions started. She was actually surprised he'd waited at all.

"Who is Victor Beddingfield? Your brother? Your lover? Your what? Employer?"

Sadie's stomach turned, this time from more than just the pregnancy she'd confirmed after a stop at the drugstore last night. She couldn't think of that now. Luckily, she hadn't eaten, so there wasn't anything to come up.

"Tell me now, Sadie."

She absorbed the blow of the staccato words as she tied the robe's belt around her waist. Then she faced Zach, attempting to keep her expression blank.

"Victor is my current—temporary—employer."

As if her calm answer infuriated him, Zach spoke next through gritted teeth. "And what the hell does he have to do with me?"

She slowly drew in a breath before answering. "He's your half brother."

Should she say more? This was one reason why she'd put off this moment—there were no guidelines telling her how much or how little information she should give to the man that she'd lied to for two months...no, five years.

"That doesn't tell me what he wants with me." Zach's harsh expression didn't give her any clues or guidance as to how to proceed.

Okay, here goes... "Your father recently passed away." She paused to give him a moment to absorb that, but his expression only grew harder. "There is a rather, um, large inheritance."

"Then this Beddingfield should take it and leave me alone. My father never wanted anything to do with me. Why would I want his money now?"

That wasn't technically true, but Sadie wasn't going to explain that his father had sent her before. At least, not now.

"It isn't that easy," she said instead. "Victor can't inherit your father's estate because it has been willed to you."

Zach frowned, but didn't say anything.

"On one condition."

Then his gaze flipped to her phone on the bed before returning to her face. "The dirt?"

Reluctantly, she nodded. "You've been selected to receive the bulk of your father's estate, provided you haven't been immoral or corrupt in any way. There can be no arrests, convictions, scandals or incidents showing distinct lack of character in your—" she had to swallow "—history. Your father wanted to reward you for being a better man than he was."

"That's ridiculous."

Sadie shrugged. "Mr. Beddingfield played by his own set of rules."

"So you're, what, here to spy on me?"

Leave it to Zach to get to the heart of the matter.

"Wait. Were you here to spy on me before, too?"

Straight to the heart. "Yes." Why prevaricate? He was going to hate her anyway. She might as well cut the ties cleanly, even if the frost encasing her heart was starting to bite. "Your father sent me the first time." She could go into details later, if necessary. "Victor sent me this time—"

"To find out the truth? Or to make up some plausible lies?"

"Victor doesn't really care either way."

"He made that clear."

"But I can assure you, I'll be telling your father's lawyer the truth."

She couldn't stop herself from flinching as Zach stalked to her. He seemed to grow larger and more menacing as rage lit his features. "You know nothing about the truth. You've lied to me from the beginning, haven't you?"

"Not about the things that matter."

Rage mutated into disgust. "I doubt you have any idea what matters to me. None at all."

Oh, but she did. He valued family, loyalty, honesty, compassion, helping hands and going the extra mile. He was everything Victor wasn't. With each thing she'd learned about Zach, Sadie had known she fought a losing battle for his heart.

Because the core of her mission was the opposite of everything he held dear.

Only she couldn't turn away from these few weeks of pure bliss. That had been selfish on her part—indecisive, too. But she couldn't change it—not her choices, nor what had pushed her into those choices.

But she wasn't making excuses or asking forgiveness. She didn't deserve it.

"I'm sorry, Zach." It was as far as she could let herself go. Anything more and she'd fall to her knees right here, begging for the one thing he would never give her now: his love.

She expected him to let loose that rage on her. To rant or throw things or scream. His father would have. His half brother certainly would have.

Zach did none of that.

Instead he turned and stalked to the door. He was probably done with her. But despite her resolutions, she found she couldn't keep one thing inside. The one thing he deserved to know.

"But I do have one last thing to say, Zach. And I mean it with everything in me. That you are a good man."

He paused before the door but didn't turn around, didn't grant her one last glimpse of a face carved in stone. Instead he said, "Pardon me if that offers very little consolation."

She was sure it didn't.

* * *

Somehow, some way, Zach managed to get through what he absolutely had to that afternoon without exploding, and then he ditched the rest of his appointments. His car ate up the miles to the airport. His only thought was of running, fast and far, but where—he didn't know.

The cabin wasn't an option right now. The memories were too fresh, would be too painful. Only now did he regret taking Sadie there, because even a complete makeover would never erase her presence in what had once been his sanctuary.

Anger had him pressing on the gas that much harder. He was anxious for speed even though it wouldn't really help anything. That's when his phone dinged to signal an incoming text.

Sadie. He knew it before he even looked. His instinct was to hurl the phone out the window, but that would be giving in too easily, so he forced himself to pull over and read the text instead.

I've gone home. The room at the B&B is paid thru end of week. Left some of ur things on table and some important papers for you. I'm so sorry. S

Zach let his eyes slide closed. He didn't want to see the screen, didn't want to read about how sorry she was. If she'd been sorry, she never would have lied to him. Hell, she never would have come here. Why would she do something so incredibly dishonest?

No, he didn't want to know. Motive didn't matter, because he refused to feel sorry for someone who would go to so much trouble to integrate herself into his life, his bed, just to find out if he was a bad person.

And who was his dad to judge? That man had never

done anything good in his entire life. He'd abandoned Zach's mother when he was little, simply vanished, never paying a lick of child support or sending so much as a single birthday present or Christmas gift. They'd been okay. They'd made it without the old SOB. But that seemed to make the terms of his will even more ironic.

There had to be more to the story than what Sadie had told him.

Some important papers for you.

Dammit. He spun the car into a U-turn and headed back into town. No matter what he told himself, he really did want to know what was going on.

He flashed a strained smile at Gladys when she glanced out at him from the dining area as he made his way through, but didn't speak. Neither did she. Did she realize Sadie was gone? Or had Sadie simply left without saying anything so Zach would have a chance to come by and collect his stuff without Gladys's interference? He didn't know what to think anymore.

He let himself into the room, noticing Sadie's absence at once. The low table no longer held her laptop, just a pile of odds and ends. Her robe wasn't thrown over the high back of the winged chair near the dresser. Her extra fluffy blanket no longer graced her side of the queen-size bed.

But her vanilla-caramel scent still lingered in the air. Tantalizing, but also a reminder of how deceptive that sweetness truly was.

Zach dropped onto the couch in front of his stuff. A T-shirt he'd left here. A toiletry bag with an extra toothbrush and deodorant and things for his overnight stays. His black leather belt. He wished now that there hadn't been so many nights, that she hadn't made it so easy.

Next to the pile was a manila envelope. Zach stared

for a long time before he made himself reach out and open it. The quality of the fax wasn't the best, but it was still readable. The time stamp along the top showed she'd had this sent not long after their talk this afternoon.

The letterhead was from a lawyer's office in Dallas. The text below explained that this lawyer was in the process of executing Zach's father's last will and testament. Based on his father's unusual requests, adequate time had been given to search every avenue necessary. If Zach had any questions, he was welcome to call them for explanations.

Should he wish to refuse his inheritance, there were instructions on how to do that and what that would mean for him in terms of future claims. The exact sum wasn't mentioned, but Zach was guessing it was significant for a lawyer to have been hired to set up something this elaborate.

The lawyer seemed like a man who knew what he was doing. Zach planned to reserve judgment until he had experience with the guy himself.

The envelope also contained what looked like legal papers that Zach would look over in more depth later. There was a photograph of a man Zach assumed to be his father. It was blurred with age. But Zach wasn't that interested in the picture; he'd put his father out of his mind long ago. After all, his father hadn't been willing to think about Zach or his mother when he'd left them. Zach had been four at the time.

There was a professional bio. From what Zach read, his father had hit oil when he'd traveled to Texas a couple of years after abandoning them. Of course, he hadn't looked back to the family he'd left behind. Zach's mother had worked her fingers to the bone to provide for him, and later KC. She'd deserved better than that.

As if she'd known he would be curious, Sadie had printed an article about his father's stroke and how it had affected his company. Apparently he was well-known in the Dallas area. Zach scanned it and moved on to the next piece. It was another photo, this one of a younger man with distinct features matching his father's. This one was labeled Victor Beddingfield.

Zach couldn't help it—he studied the picture for any resemblance to his half brother. There were a few. Zach certainly hoped he didn't share the petulant expression and self-indulgent softness that didn't sit well on an adult male.

All in all, the envelope contained straightforward information that Zach could take or leave. It all depended on his plans. He put the papers back. He could find out pretty much everything he needed to know about the players in this game at his office, now that he knew where to start.

This time, he wasn't about to hesitate to dig hard and deep.

Standing, he loaded his arms with everything that belonged to him. He had no intention of leaving anything of himself in this place. As he moved toward the door, he remembered another time, the first time, when he'd faced the same choice. He'd had the chance to exit and never look back, but the lure of Sadie had been too strong.

He glanced toward the bed. The same one that had tempted him that first night here. Memories of nights wrapped around Sadie under those covers made him ache with a mixture of desire, sadness and anger. He wasn't sure if he'd ever get over that. Maybe one day he would. Maybe one day he wouldn't think of her at all, and he could live the rest of his life without thinking her name or remembering her face.

Maybe one day.

As he turned toward the door, a glimpse of something that didn't belong flashed in his periphery. Something neglected on the floor between the antique nightstand and the bed. Zach should leave it. After all, the odds of it being his were slim.

Still, his feet carried him forward, and he cursed himself the entire way for caring that she might have left something of herself behind.

He shifted his load into one arm then bent low and patted around for whatever it was. Finally his fingers brushed against something hard. Long and rounded, it fit easily in his hand as he picked it up.

Zach glanced down as he stood, then totally wished he hadn't.

His mind flashed back to another day. One when he found his sister crying all alone at the bar, late at night after everyone had left. In her hand was an identical white plastic stick with a plastic cap on the end. There were two solid pink lines in the little window in the middle. He dropped onto the bed, and wondered if this day could get any worse.

Sixteen

Sadie quietly let herself into her apartment early the next morning, her body beyond tired. Sitting at the airport on standby was hellish on a good day. Yesterday had been almost unbearable.

She set down her luggage and made her way down the hall into the living area. Maybe she could catch a few winks before her mother woke up to get ready to go to the treatment center to see her sister. How in the world Sadie would explain to either of them what had happened was beyond her at the moment.

Zach hadn't been the only person she'd lied to. Despite their desperate need, Sadie had known her mother and sister would have never condoned her cooperation with Victor's diabolical plan to disqualify Zach from his inheritance. So she'd told them the same story: that their former employer had gifted her with the trip of her dreams to explore her photography.

Now she had to find a way to tell them the truth.

As she came into the spacious room, she saw her mother sleeping on the overstuffed couch. Sadie frowned, worried for a moment that something had happened. Or maybe her mother had fallen asleep waiting for her to arrive. But a soft sound drew her gaze in the other direction, where she found her sister propped in the recliner Sadie kept angled toward the line of windows along the front of the room.

But her sister wasn't watching the early-morning sun as it lit up the rolling lawns of the Beddingfield estate. Instead her gaze met Sadie's. Tears stung Sadie's nose and eyes as her sister gifted her with a weak smile of welcome.

Quickly crossing the room, she bent over and carefully pulled Amber close. She still had an IV attached to keep her from dehydrating. But otherwise she was awake, and the staff must have thought her well enough to come home for a while.

Bending down, she met her sister's eyes, green like her own, and whispered, "When did you get here?"

Amber grinned, though she didn't lift her head from where it rested on the chair. "Just yesterday. We were gonna Skype you last night, but when you called to say you were coming home we decided to surprise you."

"Well, I definitely am."

Her sister's thin hair had been cropped close, leaving a pale auburn halo of curls that highlighted the too-prominent cheekbones in her pale face. Sadie brushed her fingers over the softness. "How are you, kiddo?"

"My white blood count is closer to normal, for now. Electrolytes are good. And I tolerated this latest round of treatments better than they expected, so I got to come home a few days early."

"That's great."

"She's getting stronger," their mother said. Sadie glanced over at her; she hadn't moved but had opened her eyes to watch her daughters. "The doctors are quite pleased."

"I bet."

Any improvement in Amber's condition was considered wonderful at this stage. Their goal now was to halt the deterioration from the disease and keep her as pain-free as possible, without the disorientation and fatigue that could come from the wrong drug combinations.

"I'm so glad you're home," Amber said, reaching out to squeeze Sadie's hand.

The chill from her sister's skin always startled Sadie. She reached up with her other hand, creating a little sandwich pocket in an effort to warm the cold fingers with her own. It never seemed to help, but Amber told her it felt good, so Sadie had formed the habit over time.

"And just why are you home?" her mother asked.

Her tone said she knew something was up. Not that Sadie was very good at hiding things. Or maybe she was too good, since she'd been able to deceive Zach for so long. "It was time," she said simply.

It was more than time to cut the ties. Maybe Zach seeing that text was for the best, even though her breaking heart didn't think so. If it had been up to her, she inevitably would have delayed. And then where would she be?

She pressed her sister's hand a little more tightly. "You rest a bit. I'll fix you some tea," she said.

"That would be good." But Amber didn't close her eyes. Instead she turned back to gaze out the window. She'd often told Sadie that she slept enough at the treatment center, pumped up on pain meds and other drugs.

When she was home, she wanted to experience life, even if it was only through the window of their apartment.

Trying hard not to let a new wave of tears overwhelm her, Sadie retraced her steps down the hall to the kitchen. As expected, Sadie's mother joined her.

"For someone who has just been on the trip of their dreams, you do not look like you had a very restful time," her mother said quietly.

Sadie appreciated her mother's attempt to keep Amber from hearing her.

"That's because I lied," she said, figuring the straight-forward approach was probably best.

There was no shock from her mother, only an understanding nod. "I see."

Why did life have to be so hard? "I did a very bad thing, Mom."

"I'm sure you did."

Sadie glanced over in surprise, spilling a bit of water over the edge of the electric kettle. "What? Why would you think that?"

"Sadie," she said with a sad shake of her head, "when was Mr. Beddingfield ever involved in anything good? Yes, he might have changed his perspective somewhat on his deathbed, but that man never did something only from goodness. There was always an ulterior motive."

Ulterior motive indeed. "Mr. Beddingfield didn't send me on this trip. Victor did."

Her mother's eyes widened. "Yes, I can see why you didn't share that with me. There is nothing benevolent in that man. I was surprised to even come home to find our stuff still here yesterday. I couldn't figure out why he hasn't made us leave the estate yet."

"It was part of our agreement," Sadie confessed.

Then she went on to tell her mother the how and why

of her trip back to Black Hills, South Carolina. About halfway through she looked away, unable to bear what was sure to be her mother's disappointment in her. She managed to keep the tears at bay until she mentioned the baby she was now sure she carried.

The silence of several minutes was only broken by the release of steam from the kettle. Sadie couldn't bring herself to steep her sister's tea. Instead she remained with her arms braced against the counter, praying that the pain in her heart would ease enough to let her breathe again.

"So this man, Zach, will we be seeing him again?" her mother asked.

Sadie nodded. "I'll have to tell him about the baby, but it was so new, I just…couldn't." A deep breath braced her for her latest decision. "I will contact him soon enough, but I want to be established in a new job, a new place to live. I just couldn't bear to give him the impression that I told him about the baby to get some of his money."

"But Sadie, how will we afford—"

"I don't know. We just will. Somehow." But she knew beyond a doubt she couldn't face asking Zach for money. She wasn't even sure she would be able to take it if he offered. So much of this whole situation had been motivated by her struggles to simply keep their heads above water.

But other people would only see it as greed.

"We will figure something out," she assured her mother with a false smile. "I'll start looking for another job today. One thing—the only good thing—Mr. Beddingfield did was to safeguard me against any attempt Victor made to discredit me. I have a certified reference from him, with his lawyer's signature as witness. That will at least give me a place to start."

Some of the strain on her mother's face eased. "Yes, it will help. I could look for something—"

"Absolutely not." They'd had this discussion time and again. "Amber needs you with her. We both know that. I'll fix this, somehow."

Even if the solution was a complete and total mystery to her right now.

Zach took a seat in the substantial waiting area at the offices of Beddingfield's lawyer, Timberlake. Apparently, Beddingfield Senior had been a big man in town, and he'd paid for the best in everything. Including lawyers.

Zach couldn't bring himself to think of the man as his father. He'd contributed DNA, but that was about it.

Except now, after his death, he was about to gift Zach with a fortune that still boggled his mind, according to his phone conversations with the lawyer. Beddingfield hadn't just hit it big in the oil business after coming to Texas, he'd then diversified, which had protected his assets from market fluctuations and downturns. Zach would be in a tax bracket far removed from the one he'd moved into after opening his own business. The thought was so far outside reality that he'd stopped trying to comprehend it.

But in terms of the man who'd sired him—it was a case of too little, too late.

Zach had chosen to make an impromptu trip to Dallas before telling his family all that had transpired. He preferred to have all the facts at hand first.

Besides, his sister had become increasingly curious about Sadie, not buying Zach's excuse that she'd returned home for a family emergency. Of course, after his investigation into her history, that excuse might not have been as far from reality as he'd thought when he made it up.

Sadie had told the truth about some things. This time around, Zach hadn't held back, using all the resources at his disposal when it came to investigating her. She'd used her real name. According to her tax records, she'd indeed been an employee of Beddingfield Senior for several years. And her mother had held the same position for the same employer until the year Sadie took over. Her mother had no employment records since then.

The few things Zach had been able to find out about Sadie's younger sister's illness had confirmed what he knew: she'd been ill a very long time and her prognosis was terminal.

The most eye-opening portion of his investigation had been his inquiries into Sadie's finances. That's when he'd started to feel dirty. She didn't have the usual expenses of a woman her age. No apartment or housing loan. No car loan, either. Two maxed-out credit cards that hadn't had any activity recorded in two years, other than payments. And astronomical debts to several medical institutions in the Dallas area.

Sadie was apparently financially responsible for all of her sister's medical bills.

As much as Zach didn't condone lying and dishonesty, factoring Beddingfield's huge fortune into Sadie's crippling financial situation didn't add up to a woman spying on him on a whim. He wanted more information before he confronted her about the little bombshell he'd discovered at the B and B after she left.

Feeling restless, as thoughts about Sadie often made him, Zach stood up. He prowled around the empty area for several minutes before coming to a stop in front of a long bank of windows overlooking busy traffic on the streets below. Coming to the office at the end of the day, he'd known he would wait for an extended period of time. Probably until after Timberlake's last client left.

But he'd see Zach—the man about to take the place of his, and his firm's, biggest client.

Zach heard a rumble down the hallway, the sound of a raised voice behind a closed door. He glanced over at the receptionist, who looked uneasily toward the glass wall behind her. When she noticed him watching, she flashed a strained smile and pretended to get back to work.

The rumble increased, and Zach realized other voices had joined the fray. One of the lawyers must have a very unhappy client. Just as a door in the back hallway opened, the receptionist's phone rang. She answered with a clipped, "Yes, sir." Then she immediately hung up and redialed. "We need assistance on floor four near the conference room, please," she said in a slightly raised voice.

The commotion in the hallway got louder. Zach wasn't sure what was happening but decided to offer his assistance regardless until security could arrive. Just as he reached the receptionist's desk, a man's voice rang out.

"I will get you for this. You will never work in this city again, you hear me! Not only will you not see a dime from me, but I'll see to it that you'll never find a way to support that dying brat, either."

The sound of men's voices protesting and the shuffling of dress shoes carried through to the reception area. One was louder than the rest. "Mr. Beddingfield, stop right now. There's nothing to be gained by this behavior."

"There's nothing to be gained by me being a Goody Two-shoes, either. This bitch just cut me off from my inheritance. She's gonna pay."

The elevator dinged as the doors opened, heralding

the arrival of two security guards. But the raucous group in the hallway now appeared around the corner, plainly visible through the glass wall behind the receptionist.

Zach saw Sadie jump backward just as a male hand grabbed for her. A sharp cry rang out. The men around her dropped their polite facades. Yelling commenced as they tried to force Victor Beddingfield back. The security guards waded into the fray, quickly subduing the man Zach now knew was his half brother. He watched as they cuffed the tall man, whose blond good looks made him Zach's polar opposite.

As did his spoiled attitude.

A stocky, gray-haired man guided Sadie back with an arm around her shoulders. For the first time in a month he glimpsed her wealth of auburn hair and full features through the wavy glass. He couldn't make out her expression with precision, except to tell that her lips were pulled into a frown. By the time he looked back at Victor, the security guards were leading him back down the hallway.

A few low words were exchanged with the other two gentlemen, then one broke away and followed the guards. After a few minutes, the gray-haired man led Sadie around the opposite side of the glass wall and over to the elevator bank.

They never even glanced in Zach's direction.

"Thank you again, Ms. Adams, for coming in to give your deposition. I'm very, very sorry for the commotion. I have no idea how Mr. Beddingfield found out you would be here today."

Sadie shook her head, but Zach could see that her hand remained clasped over the front of her throat. Her arms were pressed close against her torso. "No, it's not your fault. I just hope I've done what I can to make sure y'all know the truth about Zachary Gatlin."

An electric pulse set Zach on edge as he heard his name on her lips. He knew it shouldn't affect him—or rather, he shouldn't let it affect him. But he was a man who'd been in love, after all.

He stood quietly as the two finished their conversation. The lawyer, whom Zach now knew to be Timberlake, delivered her carefully into the elevator, as if worried about any lasting effects from the confrontation. Only as she faced the reception area once more did she glance beyond where the lawyer stood.

Her eyes widened in surprise just as the doors slid closed.

Seventeen

"Will she?"

"Pardon me?" The lawyer's confused look confirmed Zach had spoken out loud, even though he hadn't intended to.

"Will Sadie be able to support her sister? Or will Beddingfield be able to keep her from getting work?"

The confusion cleared. "Oh, no. He won't be able to poison future employers against her—I drafted your father's reference letter for Ms. Adams myself. Plus, she has a good reputation with the people who have visited his home over the years. She'll be fine, professionally."

Zach sensed something more. "But?"

"I'm afraid I don't know of a job in her field that will pay enough to take care of the medical bills."

Zach knew about that all too well.

Timberlake leaned forward, his expression earnest. After their conversations over the phone, Zach had found him to be someone he felt pretty comfortable with. The man's motives seemed straightforward.

"I wouldn't normally say this," he started, "but I know you've met Sadie personally. The deposition she gave is proof of that."

"Was it now?"

"The contents will be made public in court, but yes, she was very clear about your values, your family and the respect you have from your business associates. She explained in detail her efforts and inability to find any complaints against you or any criminal activity."

Zach hadn't realized that she would be so thorough in her report.

The lawyer went on. "I wonder if you know what a gift that is?"

Zach raised his brows in question.

"She didn't have to do that. She could easily have lied. If she had, she'd have been set for life."

What? "I don't understand."

"She confided to me, when she first came in, that Victor Beddingfield had offered her a quarter of the inheritance if she could find anything that would disqualify you. That money would have more than paid for her sister's treatments. Sadie would never have had to work again."

That was the truth. From everything he'd seen, a quarter of the inheritance, even after exorbitant estate taxes, would still be a fortune. A fortune Sadie desperately needed.

"But she never spoke against me?"

Timberlake shook his head. "Not a word." His gaze met Zach's directly. "Look, I'm not telling you this because I expect anything. I'm going to connect Sadie with some organizations that might be able to help her with her sister's treatments from here on out. But once you have that debt, it often can't be wiped away...at least not in any way that Sadie would accept."

The lawyer smiled sadly. "I could tell from the way she spoke that Sadie is not neutral in your case." He raised his hands. "I don't know what happened, and I don't care. But I think she should at least get credit for trying to do the right thing—in the end."

Could he do the same? Zach wasn't sure. He wanted to, and Lord knew he and Sadie had one more major hurdle to cross before their future was decided. He would never be able to leave the mother of his child behind completely. And he wasn't enough of an asshole to cut her out of their lives, even if that had been his first instinct.

Everyone made bad decisions when they were angry.

"There's something else," the lawyer said. The curiosity in his eyes making Zach just a little nervous.

"Yes?"

"Sadie has asked me to contact a family named Blackstone, and see that the pictures she took in Black Hills were copyrighted to them to do with as they wish."

Holy hell.

"She also provided the name of a publisher who was interested in the story."

Why? Zach thought back to that pregnancy test and tried to imagine how she must have felt when she took it. She could have been elated...could have imagined all of her problems were fixed with the luck of the draw. After all, one DNA test and he would be legally liable for at least child support. With the inheritance he had coming, she could probably have jockeyed for a lot more than that. But if that were so, why would she have subjected herself to Beddingfield and having to give her deposition alone? Given up the rights to pictures that he knew meant more to her than the money?

One phone call to Zach could have put her on top of the world instead of the bottom rung. One call she'd refused to make to save herself from a lot of worry and fears.

But was this proof enough that he could trust her?

A quick change into clean clothes had helped Sadie feel more in control after her ugly experience with Victor at the lawyer's office. But she also felt an increased need to get them packed and out of the apartment over Mr. Beddingfield's renovated horse barn.

A need that rose exponentially after realizing Zach was now in town.

She could have gone back into the office, could have asked what he'd seen and heard and tried to defend herself against any ugly things Victor might tell him about her. But what was the point?

Zach already had enough ammunition to blast her out of his life. Anything more would just be overkill.

Still, she needed to get her family moved. The probate of the will would be moving forward, and hopefully one of the interviews she'd had over the last week would pan out for a new job. She'd found a medical halfway house that would let her mother and sister stay temporarily while Sadie arranged for a new place. All the apartments on the cheap end had been scary, but with her credit, something small in a bad neighborhood was the best she could do.

If her luck turned around, her new position would also offer living accommodations, or at least a supplement toward her rent. Fingers crossed on that one.

She moved down the hall to her sister's bedroom,

stepping into the circle of cardboard boxes and packing tape and scissors she'd left there earlier. She'd splurged by hiring a mover, simply because her mother was completely unable to lift anything. Moving furniture alone wasn't an option, but Sadie wanted to pack all of the keepsakes and items with sentimental value herself.

The sun had completely disappeared by the time a knock sounded on the apartment door. She must have lost track of time, moving from her sister's bedroom to her own. The five full boxes now standing in the hallway attested to her progress.

The knock sounded again as she crossed the kitchen into the hallway. "I'm coming," she hollered, wondering if it was one of the staff from the big house.

Even though she wasn't technically employed anymore, they still showed up to ask her questions about various things. With that in mind, she flung the door open without thinking...and came face-to-face with Zachary Gatlin.

Panicked, she turned on her heel and strode back to the kitchen. Her quick steps took her all the way to the other side of the kitchen island. Only when she was facing the door with something solid between them did she feel a little more secure.

And slightly stupid for her reaction.

As he came through the door, words started to tumble out of her mouth. "Zach, I want to assure you we are in the process of moving. I've gotten everything arranged and we will be out—"

"Shush."

Sadie felt her eyes bug out a little at his harsh tone, though she wasn't sure why. It was nothing more than what she'd expected. "I just didn't want you to think—" she spotted his glare, but couldn't seem to stop "—we were…taking…advantage…now that you own the estate."

"Well, it's a little early in the process, but I will be looking into the estate and how it is run pretty soon." Zach spoke a little more mildly this time. "Still, I don't believe I said anything about you leaving."

"I just assumed…"

His raised brow told her exactly what he thought of that.

Maybe he was right. She should just shush. Everything she said right now was coming out wrong.

"Do you know why I'm here, Sadie?"

"Apparently it's not to throw me out of what is now your apartment."

He simply stared. "Sarcasm isn't pretty."

No, but it was her go-to option in this bizarre situation that she was completely unprepared for. Unless she chose honesty—and that was a scary thought. "No, Zach. I really don't know why you would want to see me."

He took a step closer to the island. "No reason at all?"

Sure—if he knew about the baby. But he didn't, and she wasn't ready to tell him yet. She would later, after everything was settled. "After what I did to you, Zach? No."

"The lawyer told me about your deposition."

Shock shot through her. That was the last thing on her mind. "Oh. I thought it would be kept private until the hearing."

Zach shrugged. "Does it really matter when I learn what's in it?"

"I guess not," she murmured, though she wished he hadn't learned about it while she was here. She could have done without a face-to-face discussion.

"And about the photos. Why, Sadie?"

Then his tone caught her attention.

She simply couldn't meet his gaze. "It's not right for me to keep them, not after…"

"You lied to me, Sadie."

"Yes, yes, I did," she said, dropping her gaze to the countertop. "I'm sorry, but I did lie to you." What more could she say?

"Why?"

This was exactly what she didn't want. She shook her head. "Zach, excuses won't change it."

"Try me."

She straightened her shoulders but still couldn't force herself to look at him. "The first time, I didn't know you."

"But then you did."

Why torture herself by admitting the truth? Why torture him? But with him standing so close, yet so far out of her reach, her need prodded her. He deserved the truth—the whole thing. "I did know you," she said, though her voice was so weak as to be almost nonexistent. "And it scared me so badly, all I knew to do was run."

"Five years, Sadie." The pure anguish in his voice twisted her heart. One look confirmed the same emotion in his expression. "Why didn't you come back to me?"

His cry echoed inside her, forcing her reality into words. "Why would a man like you want a woman with all my problems?" She grasped the edge of the counter until her knuckles turned white and her fingers went numb. "I'm sure the lawyer must have told you—the real me is nothing like that Sadie."

"She's not?" His voice softened. "Are you sure?"

"Yes." *Most definitely.*

He moved closer until he was flush with the other

side of the counter. They were as close as they could be in this space. "I'm not sure, Sadie. Because the woman I knew was compassionate and interested in people. Organized and hardworking. Artistic and able to see the beauty in the world, even in the midst of destruction."

Tears welled up, forcing her to squeeze her eyes closed.

"Isn't that the same as what you do here? Take on a hard job at a young age so your mother can stay home with your sister? Care about the people you meet in your job every day? Worry about your mother being tired, even though you're the one on your feet for twelve hours? Teach your sister to appreciate the world around her, even though she's dying? Sounds like the same Sadie to me."

She couldn't stop the tears. They dribbled down her cheeks without her permission.

"But she's also prideful."

Her lashes automatically lifted, her gaze connecting with his. "What?"

"Sadie only wants to be the caregiver, not the receiver."

So? "Doesn't everyone?"

"No." Zach's dark eyes offered compassion, but he didn't back down. "Lots of people want their dirty jobs done for them. They ignore the hard parts of life. You power through them."

"That's a problem?" she asked.

"Only when it makes you blind to other people's desire to help care for you." He leaned forward over the island between them. "It took me five long years to become vulnerable to you, Sadie. Don't you think I deserved the same?"

She took a step back, needing space, needing to

breathe. "But me being vulnerable, opening up to you would have placed an obligation on you. A demand, even if it was unspoken, for you to take care of me and my problems."

"It's never an obligation when you love someone."

That took her breath away. "I've never had someone love me that way," she murmured.

"Haven't you?"

That dark gaze wouldn't let her look away, wouldn't let her pretend to not see the truth. "Yes."

Silence stood between them for long minutes, almost as if the world held its breath, waiting to see what came next. Sadie wasn't sure what it was.

Finally Zach spoke. "I want you to do something for me, okay?"

She nodded, not trusting herself to speak.

"When you're ready, truly ready, for me to love you that way...you let me know. Okay?"

A tremble started deep inside. What he asked seemed like almost too much.

"Okay?"

She could barely get the word out. "Yes."

"Goodbye, Sadie."

Her whole body screamed in protest, but she kept her lips sealed as he walked away. She could hear his footsteps down the hallway, then the click as he opened the door.

"Wait. Zach," she called, then forced her timid feet to follow him. She paused a few feet away from where he waited by the front door. "I—I know I disappointed you." She swallowed at the lump trying to form in her throat. "But there's something you need to know. You can't leave without knowing...two things, actually."

He nodded, but didn't encourage her by word or any further gesture.

"One is… I love you. I'll always be glad that I experienced loving you, even though I screwed it up so badly."

His expression didn't change, and she died a little inside. But this had to be done.

"And two?" he asked.

She almost couldn't say it, almost told him to leave, but that was as selfish as every choice she'd made up until now. "Two is—I'm pregnant."

"I know."

"I don't want you to feel obligated—wait, what?"

Now she detected a touch of amusement in his voice. "I already know."

And from his softening expression, she knew he accepted it. "How?" she breathed.

Very gently, he closed the door. "You dropped the test. I found it when I went to get my things."

Sadie groaned, collapsing with her back to the wall. "Oh, goodness. I was putting it back in the box to bring home with me. I knew if I threw it away there—"

"Miss Gladys would have found it and the whole town would know, not just me?"

"Right." She opened her eyes to find him right in front of her. "I was trying to figure out how to tell you without making you feel…"

"Obligated?"

She nodded. "And I knew I couldn't do that with you looking at me, touching me. So I thought it was better to wait." She offered a halfhearted smile. "After what happened between KC and Jake, I couldn't keep your child from you. I wouldn't do that, Zach."

"I know that now."

"You do? How?"

"You just showed me. Thank you for trusting me with the truth, Sadie."

"So you aren't angry?"

He shook his head, stepping in until they stood body to body. "I'm not angry. We have a lot of things to work out, and I think we will both have to learn to let someone else take care of us, instead of always being the strong one." He brushed his lips gently over hers, leaving her weepy and boneless.

"We can make all of this work," he said, "but I think it's gonna take the two of us."

"You don't mind?"

"Never have."

That's when she started to weep in earnest. And Zach stood right there with her, supporting her through the storm.

"I love you, Sadie," he said when she finally quieted.

"Oh, Zach, I love you, too."

For long minutes neither of them spoke. They simply held each other and let their bodies confirm what they had known all along.

"Just promise me one thing," Sadie finally murmured.

"What's that?"

"That you will never do anything for me or my family that you don't feel completely comfortable doing," she insisted.

"The same here," he said.

After she nodded, he added, "And never walk away without letting me know where you're going."

"It's a deal."

* * * * *

LET'S TALK
Romance

For exclusive extracts, competitions
and special offers, find us online:

f facebook.com/millsandboon

🐦 @MillsandBoon

📷 @MillsandBoonUK

Get in touch on 01413 063232

For all the latest titles coming soon, visit
millsandboon.co.uk/nextmonth

MILLS & BOON
A ROMANCE FOR EVERY READER

FREE delivery direct to your door

EXCLUSIVE offers every month

SAVE up to 25% on pre-paid subscriptions

SUBSCRIBE AND SAVE

millsandboon.co.uk/Subscribe

WANT EVEN MORE
ROMANCE?
SUBSCRIBE AND SAVE TODAY!

'Mills & Boon books, the perfect way to escape for an hour or so.'

MISS W. DYER

'Excellent service, promptly delivered an very good subscription choices.'

MISS A. PEARSON

'You get fantastic special offers and the chance to get books before they hit the shops.'

MRS V. HALL

Visit millsandboon.co.uk/Subscribe and save on brand new books.

JOIN THE
MILLS & BOON
BOOKCLUB

* **FREE** delivery direct to your door

* **EXCLUSIVE** offers every month

* **EXCITING** rewards programme

50% OFF
YOUR FIRST
PARCEL

Join today at
Millsandboon.co.uk/Bookclub

MILLS & BOON

THE HEART OF ROMANCE

A ROMANCE FOR EVERY READER

MODERN
Prepare to be swept off your feet by sophisticated, sexy and seductive heroes, in some of the world's most glamourous and rom locations, where power and passion collide.

HISTORICAL
Escape with historical heroes from time gone by. Whether your pass for wicked Regency Rakes, muscled Vikings or rugged Highlanders the romance of the past.

MEDICAL
Set your pulse racing with dedicated, delectable doctors in the high sure world of medicine, where emotions run high and passion, com love are the best medicine.

True Love
Celebrate true love with tender stories of heartfelt romance, from rush of falling in love to the joy a new baby can bring, and a focus emotional heart of a relationship.

Desire
Indulge in secrets and scandal, intense drama and plenty of sizzling action with powerful and passionate heroes who have it all: wealth, good looks…everything but the right woman.

HEROES
Experience all the excitement of a gripping thriller, with an intense mance at its heart. Resourceful, true-to-life women and strong, fear face danger and desire - a killer combination!

To see which titles are coming soon, please visit

millsandboon.co.uk/nextmonth

JOIN US ON SOCIAL MEDIA!

Stay up to date with our latest releases, author
news and gossip, special offers and discounts, and
all the behind-the-scenes action
from Mills & Boon...

 millsandboon

 millsandboonuk

 millsandboon

might just be true love...

GET YOUR ROMANCE FIX!

MILLS & BOON
— *blog* —

Get the latest romance news, exclusive author interviews, story extracts and much more!

blog.millsandboon.co.uk

MILLS & BOON

MODERN

Power and Passion

Prepare to be swept off your feet by sophisticated, sexy and seductive heroes, in some of the world's most glamourous and romantic locations, where power and passion collide.

◄ Modern stories published every month, find them all at:

millsandboon.co.uk/Modern

MILLS & BOON

Desire

Indulge in secrets and scandal, intense drama and plenty of sizzling hot action with powerful and passionate heroes who have it all: wealth, status, good looks…everything but the right woman.

Four Desire stories published every month, find them all at:

millsandboon.co.uk

MILLS & BOON
True Love
Romance from the Heart

Celebrate true love with tender stories of heartfelt romance, from the rush of falling in love to the joy a new baby can bring, and a focus on the emotional heart of a relationship.

our True Love stories published every month, find them all at:

millsandboon.co.uk/TrueLove

CS